Ratcatcher held his tongue. He could feel rope sliding across his chest, wrists and ankles, and then it was gone. Slowly, gingerly, he sat up. "Thank you," he said, not trusting himself to say more. Something about the healer's prattling and incessant good cheer got on his nerves, but for now, she was the sum total of the protection he had from the outside world, and he needed to learn more before he decided on a course of action.

"Think nothing of it. Now, as for your eyes, well, that's the bad news. Something got at them. I was hoping you could tell me what it was."

"My eyes? Again?" The words slipped out before Ratcatcher could think, and he instantly regretted them. His hands went to the bandages on his face and tore them free. "What happened?"

"No! Leave the bandages be!" The healer tried to stop him, and reflexively he slapped her aside. She fell, heavily, against the cloth side of the wagon even as he stripped the bloody cloth away.

"What's going on in here?" A man's voice called out suspiciously. Ratcatcher jerked his head to the right, toward the source of the sound. A faint shape was there, dark gray against the black.

"Nothing, nothing at all," he could hear Clever Tiger say. "I just slipped while removing his bandages, Ragged Fox. He was a little surprised by the news I had for him, that's all. Everything is fine." Her voice was surprisingly soothing.

"Well, all right," the man she'd called Ragged Fox said. "Call me if you need anything."

"Of course," the healer replied, and turned back to Ratcatcher. "Don't make me lie for you again," she hissed. "Ragged Fox is very protective, and if he thought you'd hurt me, you'd have a whole new set of injuries to deal with."

Copyright © 2002 by Paradox Interactive AB
ISBN 978-1-63789-220-6
Beloved of the Dead is a product of Paradox Interactive AB.
White Wolf is a subsidiary of Paradox Interactive.
First Printing 2002
Crossroad Press Edition published in Agreement with Paradox Interactive
Cover art by Ghislain Barbe
Crossroad Press Trade Edition

BELOVED OF THE DEAD

Trilogy of the Second Age Book 2

By Richard Dansky

Chapter One

The dead man sat up from the stone slab upon which he had been laid out, and groped for something sharp, which he might then plunge into his right eye.

It was perhaps an hour after sundown when he rose, and even the youngest apprentices and most dedicated artisans in the city of Sijan had long since departed to their cheerless homes. The embalming chamber in which the man's corpse rested was a busy one, and a half-dozen other bodies in various states of preparation for entombment lay upon slabs all around him. His body had been the last brought in during the day, and apart from a preliminary examination by a journeyman embalmer, it had escaped the attention of Sijan's finest. Even the usual incantation to prevent an evil spirit from entering into the cadaver had been forgotten in the rush, as apprentices dashed this way and that to deliver canopic jars, bone saws and fragrant herbs to their demanding masters.

And so, once the last of the oil lamps had been extinguished and the great doors to the chamber had been closed and barred, the dead man sat up. Faint light seeped under the doorway, just enough for him to see by. Slowly, he turned and took in his surroundings, his right hand still twitching frantically.

"This," he said slowly, "is not where I expected to be." Slowly, he raised his right hand before his eyes, while gripping his right wrist with his left hand, lest it somehow find a way to act of its own accord. The hand was small and fine-boned, the fingers stained with ink and the skin a deep shade of tan. It bore none of the calluses that would attest to time spent at swordplay or hard manual labor, and the nails were neatly tended and trim.

"This," said the dead man, "is not my hand." His gaze traveled down his body, which was slender and mostly hairless, and entirely naked. He could see no sign of violence, though his lips tingled and a dull ache told him that something unpleasant was burbling away in his stomach.

"Poison," he said, and slid off the slab onto the stone floor. The room was kept chilled for the sake of the bodies, to prevent decay, and with mild disinterest the dead man saw gooseflesh form on his bare arms. Shaking his head, he shambled forward, his movements becoming smoother and surer with each step. Before him was another slab, chest-high and unoccupied, and he stopped to lean against it. Old, dark stains marked the stone surface, and a series of knives, saws, scalpels and other tools of the embalmer's trade were laid out neatly at the far end.

"This body was poisoned." The revelation surprised him, and he frowned. "This body. Not mine. Where am I?" Memories flitted in and out of his mind's eye—images of fire and pain, of a man in priest's robes he somehow understood to be his enemy, of a dark chamber in a high tower that he knew had once been his home, of a man clad in black whom he both loved and hated. "My…prince?" he said, startled. "That seems right, somehow." Weakly, he shuffled around the side of the slab and down its length to where the tools rested. With fumbling fingers he picked up a half-dozen, discarding each in turn. Finally, he found what he was looking for—a long, slender spike of metal that gleamed in the dim light.

"Ahhh." With infinite care, he held up the pin and gazed upon it. "This looks familiar. Not poison. *This*. This killed me." Again, the memories came—a duel fought atop some great machine, fire and smoke and howling rage, and a tiny, delicate woman with eyes full of murder.

Eyes… there was something about eyes he did not want to remember. With a shrug, he closed his fist around the spike of steel and stepped forward, past the silent rows. None of the other corpses stirred; no ghosts marked his passing. One of the lamps gave out a small spark, causing his shadow to rise monstrously across the far wall for a brief instant. He grinned, humorlessly, and watched himself shrink back into darkness.

"That's death, you see," he mumbled. "Rise up for a moment, labor until you rot, and then wait for the next spark of hate to send you up again. No rest, though. They lied about that." He passed the last row of slabs and found himself before the doors to the chamber. They were made from massive slabs of mahogany, a deep red that gleamed unwholesomely in the flickering light. Demonic faces had been carved into the surface of the heavy wood, set there to guard against foul spirits or the unquiet dead. He traced their lines, his fingers gliding over a tusk here, a leering grin there. As expected, they didn't move.

"Not much good, are you?" he inquired of them with surprising gentleness. "An evil spirit walked right by you, if that's what I am. I'd... assume so. It doesn't matter, really." Once again, he addressed the carved faces, frozen forever in expressions of warning and horror. "And now, my good demons, I have to walk past you again. You'll pardon me, I am certain."

He placed his left hand on the door and shoved lightly. It didn't budge. "Eh?" Curiously, he pushed harder. A faint creak from the other side told him what he needed to know.

"Barred. Blast." He took a step back and looked at the metal spike he still clutched tightly in his right fist.

"Why am I carrying this?" he asked the silent room, and paused a few seconds for the possibility of an answer. None was forthcoming. "Why in Creation am I carrying *this*?" It shone silently in his fist, its smooth symmetry somehow mocking him. "*Why*?"

A low growl filled the room, and to his mild surprise he discovered it was coming from his own throat. He could feel anger begin to boil up with him, and gleefully he let it carry him along. Why *not* rage now? Who would dare tell a dead man otherwise? With an incoherent shout of fury, he slammed his fist against the door. There was a sound like the ringing of a silver bell, and the spike slid into the wood. Screaming, he pulled it loose and hammered the door again, and then again. Each time the spike sank in deeper, tearing his hand as it went. The sluggish blood made his hand slippery, but he tightened his grip and brought the metal down harder.

Harder...

He saw the spike, now. Saw it in the tiny woman's fist. Heard her voice, its perfect, clipped diction. "I am going to kill you," she said, trembling with fury as she raised her fist. "You've destroyed my life's work, and for that, I will have your life. I do not care if the prince then has mine. It would please me, Ratcatcher, if you begged for mercy."

He did not remember begging, and he clung to the hope that he had not done so. He did not remember defending himself, either, though a vague recollection of pain told him that he had no longer been capable of doing so.

And he remembered seeing the spike clenched in that tiny hand as she plunged it into his eye. There was a single, sharp memory of searing agony exploding against the light, and then nothing.

Nothing at all.

"I know my name," he said, softly, astonished. His hands dropped to his sides, finally empty. The metal spike still quivered in the wood of the door. Outside, he could hear the rushing footsteps of curious guards. He ignored them. "I know my name."

He looked up, and his face bore a smile. It was a smile no sane man could ever wear, the smile of a man who has gazed upon hell and deemed himself not satisfied with one lifetime's worth of sinning.

Outside, the scraping of heavy wood on wood told him that someone was lifting the bar from the door. Soon, cautiously, the guards and embalmers of this place would be opening those doors and looking inside. They'd be looking for some minor disturbance; a rat, perhaps. Instead, they'd find him.

"My name is Ratcatcher," he whispered, clenching his bloody fist. "And I am waiting for you."

Chapter Two

It was the serpents that finally convinced Eliezer Wren to move.

Alone in the dark, he lay where he had fallen. For some reason he had expected to find stairs on the other side of the door in the Prince of Shadows' dungeon, and he remembered feeling horribly disappointed as he plummeted backwards into space. Then he had fallen, fallen some more, and kept on falling until he no longer had any sense of how long it had been since he had launched himself into the darkness.

The end, when it came, arrived suddenly. One instant he was plummeting down, marveling at the utter lack of wind and light, and in the next something rose up out of the dark and struck him like a hammer. There was a bright explosion of pain, and then everything went dark once again, for a very long time.

When Wren awoke, pain was waiting for him. If he lay still, he could feel smooth, cool stone beneath him, as if he lay on a polished slab intended for some unholy god's forgotten altar. Hardly an unreasonable hypothesis, actually. Any movement, however, brought pain so intense that he saw pinwheels of white light. The slightest twitch of a finger brought killing agony. And so he decided not to move, and he lay on the cold stone in the dark, waiting for death.

He should have died, he thought muzzily. The fall should have killed him, should have shattered every bone in his body and rammed the splinters through every vital organ he possessed. He'd seen what happened to men who fell from great heights; he'd even been responsible for more than a few of those falls. The results of those instances had made a tremendous impression upon him, instilling in him a strong resolution never to fall from any height greater than his knees, and even then only onto a soft cushion or a softer woman.

This, however, was something utterly different. And so Wren lay as still as he could, hoping against hope that his bones would knit and his wounds heal, because in this place there was precious little else to hope for. After a while, the realization struck him that he was neither hungry nor thirsty, and had not been since before he'd tumbled into the dark. This alarmed him at first, then oddly soothed him. After all, he was in no position to find food or water. The stone he lay upon, he noticed, always remained cool, but not cold. There was no wind where he lay, not even the faintest whisper of a breeze. Alarmed, he risked agony to bring his hand to his chest to see if he still breathed. The answer was that he did, but with the disquieting sense that doing so was more out of habit than necessity.

The total absence of light and wind, however, was more than made up for by an omnipresence of sounds. Wren could hear them constantly, a symphony of screams, howls of challenge and other, less identifiable noises. Sometimes he could hear the din of clashing arms, or the crisp sounds of killing magic, and at those moments he feared lest he be found by one of the warring parties. At others, he heard the crack of whips, and was thankful that he could not move, lest he give himself away by doing so.

And always, he heard the serpents.

They were all around him, he was certain. He could hear them slithering on the cold stone, sometimes to his left and sometimes to his right. At times he'd swear he was surrounded, then there were moments when he was seized by the fear that there was but one monstrous snake all around him. The sounds of scales on stone and flickering tongues never abandoned him completely, however. They became his lullaby and his gentle call to wakefulness, and each time he opened his eyes onto blackness he marveled that the serpents had not devoured him.

What Wren was not prepared for, however, was when they began to speak. At first all he heard were whispers, half-formed phrases that made no sense. Slowly, though, the phrases knitted themselves together into sentences, and the sentences into a litany of blasphemies. The serpents spoke of hungry ghosts, of cities erected by things that walked like men but wore the skins of snakes, of the proper sacrifices to make to each of the ruling entities of the Labyrinth and how to summon baleful spirits in the world above.

Wren listened. Unable to flee, he listened. For a time he tried shouting above the din of the serpents' whisperings, but soon his voice faded to nothingness, and the snakes continued. And so he listened, and in listening, learned many things he did not wish to know. He learned things that ghosts had whispered in the dark about the missing Empress, and war-poems that the last of the Lunar Exalted had chanted as they went into battle. He learned nineteen ways to make poison from a dead man's bones, and six from the eyes, and five from the fingernails, and discovered the magical properties that can be obtained if one makes powder from a corpse's soles and palms.

Most of all, though, he learned about the dead gods. The serpents whispered to him of from whence they had come and of their ultimate destiny. They sang songs of praise, softly, so as not to wake those gods as they slumbered. And they told him of the rites by which one foreswore the Unconquered Sun and swore fealty to the lords of endless night.

And this is what finally gave Wren the strength to stand. Crying out with the effort, he forced himself to sit up. Around him, he could hear the snakes closing in and he struggled to his knees. Somewhere, a fierce howl echoed hollowly, followed closely by another.

Come to the dark. Forsake the Sun as He has forsaken you. The whispers came ever closer. Ignoring them, he gave a bellow of agony and wrenched one foot forward. His ribs ached and his breath rasped in his throat, but he was kneeling.

One of the snakes slithered across his calf, and he froze. Its touch was cold, like metal, and he could feel each scale as it brushed against his skin.

Stay in the dark. You know the rituals of endless night. Share in them.

Pain shot up his arm as he reached down to steady himself, and he gritted his teeth. "I'm afraid... I must... decline... your kind offer," he gasped, and struggled to rise.

Once, when he had been in an odd mood, Wren's patron, the priest Chejop Kejak, had shown him some of the less savory areas beneath the Palace Sublime. The tour included oubliettes, storehouses, and most disturbingly, the chambers where enemies of the Immaculate Order were put to the question. At the time, Wren remembered feeling quite sorry for the poor bastards in irons, and praying fervently that he'd never find himself in their position. One prisoner in particular had impressed him with the awfulness of her situation; the interrogator had in his hand a wand of bottled lightning, and every so often he would brush it lightly against the soles of her feet. The released energies were visible as they climbed along her flesh, twitching and dancing along even as they left trails of scorched meat behind them. She'd screamed once, and then pain had robbed her of the ability to do even that much.

As he struggled to stand, Wren finally felt he understood what she had endured. He could feel the agony scribe itself along his legs and arms. His fingers shook uncontrollably, and a gray haze descended across his vision.

Whimpering as he had not done since he was a child, Eliezer Wren stood.

Follow us to the Master. He waits for you.

Blinded by tears, he shook his head. "He'll be waiting awhile, you know."

He knows, was the last thing he heard the serpents say, and then they were gone.

Wren rested, alone in the dark, for as long as he dared. A ways off in a direction he randomly decided was north, he could suddenly hear something weeping great racking sobs of gut-wrenching grief.

"It's as good a thought as any other down here," he said to himself, and hobbled off in that direction. Behind him, a pair of monstrous snakes glided forward in the dark, infinitely patient and always watching.

Chapter Three

Barefoot and bleeding, Yushuv ran. A miserly trickle of moonlight spilled down on him through the forest canopy, providing just enough patches of brightness to render the rest of his path pitch black. Branches slapped against his face and bare chest like the hands of a starving hag, leaving angry red welts when they didn't tear his skin. Stones and brambles tore at his feet, but he dared not stumble. Pursuit was coming, and coming quickly. If he were caught, there'd be hell to pay.

Ahead of him, the forest was eerily silent. The usual night noises—insects, birds, even the fall of acorns to the forest floor—were absent, as if the entire wood were holding its breath. Only the slow rush of distant water over rocks broke the silence, promising water somewhere downslope and perhaps a chance to lose his pursuer. He could hear the footsteps on occasion, far enough away to give him hope but close and constant enough to inspire fear. Each time he heard the clatter behind him, he was struck by the sudden fear that he was being heard as well. He'd abandoned his sandals for that very reason, to move more quietly through the brush and dead leaves, but every so often the slap of his bare foot on bare earth rang out, and Yushuv knew he'd just set the hunter back on his track.

The path the boy had chosen led him over a low ridge and then parallel to its crest, in the hopes that stone and earth would hide him from view as he ran. Animals had made the path but had abandoned it some time ago, judging from the density of the undergrowth that barred his way. Brambles caught in his black hair, longer now than it had been when he'd fled his village six months ago, and the scars he'd acquired in his travels shone pale across his tan skin in the intermittent moonlight.

A sudden crashing sound in the brush behind him made

him break stride and glance over his shoulder. It was a mistake. A protruding root caught his foot, tripping him and sending him tumbling off the path, into the brush. The skin along the top of his foot tore as he fell, and he could feel the hot blood begin to flow. Thorns pierced his palms and fingers as he put out his hands to stop his fall, catching himself after a brief tumble. Branches snapped under him when he pulled himself into a crouch and looked around for the path. In the dim light, it was nowhere to be seen. Even the vegetation he'd crushed in his descent had sprung back, as if by magic. He stared uphill for a moment. The path surely lay in that direction, but so did pursuit, and heading up *toward* the dark figure hunting him struck Yushuv as an exceedingly bad idea. That left three choices: Forward and parallel to the path through the brush, or down toward the water, or silently back along the line of the path in hopes that the hunter would pass him by.

Frowning, he held himself perfectly still. The sound of his pursuer crashing along the path was louder now, branches snapping under the man's weight. Yushuv nodded to himself once, then began scuttling downhill and to his right, angling down towards the water while reversing his direction. He moved slowly, keeping low and bending back branches with his bare hands lest they snap underfoot and give him away. The sound of the water was louder now, the growth overhead thicker.

Above him, on the rough path, the hunter blundered onwards. Confident in his pursuit, he made no effort to hide his presence, and Yushuv found himself wondering if the man was deliberately making as much racket as he could, in order to panic him. *Not this time*, he told himself, and hunkered down lower as he slid to his right. More branches slid by, and he found himself moving more and more rapidly. He could almost feel where the next patch of bare ground would be, which stone wouldn't set off a clatter of pebbles and which one would.

The sudden sensation of soft, cold mud between his toes made Yushuv gasp involuntarily, and he nearly slipped and fell again. Blinking, he realized he'd had his eyes closed for the last several minutes while he slipped down toward the stream. He'd *felt* the hill, let it tell him where to place his feet. "It worked," he said to himself softly, in a voice filled with amazement. He felt himself smiling, then put another foot down in the cool mud and followed the sound of water to the creek.

◈

Cool water washed the mud off his feet, and eased the sting of the myriad cuts that marked them. Yushuv sat on the bank of a low creek, resting with the water lapping around his ankles. Small fish brushed against him, then flickered away in an instant and left him to himself.

I'll just rest here a minute, Yushuv had thought when he found the creek. The position of the moon through the trees told him he'd been running for over three hours, and he was bone-weary. He'd tried counting how many places he'd been cut during his flight, but they seemed countless, and he worried that infection and illness would catch him before anyone or anything else could.

So he'd rested, and carefully washed out each of his wounds. The foot that the root had caught was worst of all, and he winced just to look at it. All of the skin had been torn off the top of it, leaving a hideous mélange of scabs, dirt, leaves and oozing blood. With a frown, he'd washed it off, gritting his teeth as the sting of it hit him. A few small pebbles had gotten themselves lodged in the wound somehow, and digging them out was sheer agony. It took almost a half an hour to clean the wound to his satisfaction, but now it was clean, wrapped in several broad leaves bound with bits of vine, and resting in the cool water.

He'd heard no sounds of pursuit for some time, and that worried him. He'd only half-expected the trick of doubling back to work, and he didn't think he'd been that silent going down the hill. Then there was the question of the blood from his cuts. No doubt it had left a trail, and Yushuv sincerely doubted that the night would hide the scent of fresh blood from his pursuer. After all, it never had before.

Then again, he'd never before felt the land underneath him the way he had tonight, and the creek was more than noisy enough to hide him. Perhaps he'd managed to evade pursuit after all.

A fish tickled his ankle, and impatiently he kicked to drive it away. *No sense taking chances,* he thought. *Another minute, then into the water and upstream, and he'll never find me.* The fish brushed against him again, and with a certain indignation, Yushuv leaned back and hauled both feet out of the water.

"Stupid fish," he muttered softly. He shook his feet once, then again, to flick the excess water off, then put his hands on the bank in preparation for hoisting himself up.

Strong hands the color of a storm-washed sky reached up out of the water and seized his ankles before he had the chance to move.

"Hey!" he shouted, and then he was dragged off the bank into the shallow water. The hold on his legs was incredibly strong, the pressure so great it was painful. Yushuv twisted in its grip, his hands scrabbling behind him on the stones of the creek bottom. Again and again he seized a stone in hopes of hanging on, only to have it torn out of the creek bottom, or to have his grip broken by the relentless strength of his captor. "What do you want?" he tried to say, but water filled his mouth and nose, and suddenly he was choking.

It's dragging me to deeper water, Yushuv realized. *Somewhere downstream there's a pool, and it's going to drown me there.* The sudden revelation made him struggle even harder, but to no avail. The creekbed had gotten less rocky as the water got deeper, and his fingers now carved long furrows in the sand. Panicking, he kicked harder, but the hands held firm.

"Help!" Yushuv's head broke water, and he grabbed the opportunity to call out. Then he was submerged again, and the sound of rushing water drowned out everything else.

A quick jolt of pain caused Yushuv to suck in a mouthful of water, and he began choking and coughing. He'd struck a stone, he saw, and for an instant, at least, his grip on it was holding. Filled with sudden, desperate hope, he reached out with his right hand and held on with all his strength.

The tug at his ankles slackened for a second and then redoubled. Yushuv screamed into the water, churning it to foam with his struggles. *This must be what being on the rack is like*, he thought dimly, as the pain tore at his shoulders, at his knees, at his fingertips. *I can't let go. Can't let go or I'll die.*

A sound like a waterfall rang in Yushuv's ears, and he realized that the creature that had him was roaring with its effort. Encouraged, Yushuv clung tighter, closing his eyes and willing all his strength into his bruised and torn fingertips.

Then, with an eddy of dirty waters, the rock pulled loose from the creek bed. Accompanied by a deep, hollow sound, it came free in Yushuv's hands, and a swirl of mud and sand blinded him when it did so. Desperate, he turned and twisted as best he could, his hands still on the traitorous stone. It was perhaps twice the size of his head, heavy and slick, but it was the only weapon he had. With fading strength, he raised it up into the air, preparing to hurl it in the rough direction of whatever clutched him. He could feel his feet being drawn down into a deep pool and knew that the rest of him would follow shortly. It would kill him there, hold him under until he drowned, unless he forced it to let him go. And that wouldn't happen unless he acted quickly. With the last of his strength, he hurled the stone forward.

He missed. The stone hit the water with an unimposing thunk, and sank. Yushuv had enough time for half of a string of particularly foul curses before the water filled his mouth. He closed his eyes and prepared to die.

"Enough."

The voice was deep and commanding, and Yushuv had last heard it telling him that he had better run.

Instantly, the pressure on his ankles vanished. He scrabbled backwards and sat halfway up, the water swirling around his elbows. "Dace?" he asked, weakly.

Dace sat on a rock at the side of the deep pool Yushuv was half-submerged in. He wore no armor, only a brown tunic and leggings, and he looked deeply unhappy. His usually handsome face was twisted into a scowl, and Yushuv could see the man's massive fists clenching and unclenching reflexively. This, he decided, was not a good sign.

"Hello, Yushuv," Dace said, his tone flat. "What exactly are you doing in that pool?"

"What do you think I was doing?" Yushuv felt his face growing red. He backed up a bit more and got his feet under him, allowing him to settle in a wary crouch lest the thing that had attacked him came back. "Drowning, I guess. Or at least I was until you came along."

Dace sighed. "Drowning. And why was that?"

"Something in the water attacked me!"

"Oh, really?" Dace's face was a mask of genial surprise. "Imagine that. Something attacked you."

"Don't laugh at me, Dace." Yushuv stood up, feeling a hot rush of embarrassment and on its heels, anger. "I tripped on the path and fell partway down the hill. When I recovered, I decided I'd try to reverse field while heading downhill toward the water, so the sound of the creek would cover me."

Dace nodded. "And a very clever idea it was, too, though the blood trail hindered its effectiveness somewhat. You need to be more careful. Why did you trip?"

Yushuv shrugged. "I heard you coming and got distracted."

A single eyebrow rose on Dace's weathered face. "I thought I'd taught you better than *that*."

"I know, I know." Disgusted with himself, Yushuv kicked at the creek bed, to no observable effect. "It was stupid, and the root caught my foot. So I fell, and wound up halfway down the hill. I kept going downhill, then, until I reached the creek." He paused, his face touched by wonder. "And I think I felt the hill. At least, I just… somehow knew where I should go next."

Nodding, Dace said nothing. Yushuv barely noticed, his hands cutting the air as he continued his tale.

"Anyway, I found the creek and didn't hear you, so I decided that I needed to clean out the cuts I'd gotten while running. The next thing I knew, something grabbed me by the ankles and pulled me into the water. I tried to hold on to something—anything, really—but it was just too strong, and my head kept on going underwater. I really thought I was going to die until you showed up."

Dace shook his head. "So you were nearly drowned by something swimming around in the water of the very stream you've been standing in while you were telling me all about what you did in the woods tonight. Have you ever thought that it might still be there? Waiting? Ready to strike again?"

Yushuv spread his hands, his expression quizzical. "But you're here now, aren't you?" His voice was plaintive.

Stroking his beard with his left hand, Dace spat very carefully off to the side of the pool. "That I am. But I'm not alone. Say hello to Yushuv, would you, Shooth?"

Even as Yushuv realized the Dace was looking not at him, but up over his shoulder, a heavy hand descended on the top of his head. The sheer power of the blow forced him to his knees. "Hello, boy-child," said a slow, deep voice behind him. "You're a brave one."

"Dace, help!" Yushuv squeaked. Terror struck him again. He could feel his lungs filling up with water, could imagine being dragged down into the pool while Dace watched. He struggled against the pressure the hand on his head exerted, but it inevitably forced him down. There was nothing he could do. "Please," he pleaded once more. "Help me!"

"Wherefore?" Dace scratched his bald pate, then looked concernedly at his fingernails. "I don't think you need help, except with your manners."

"What?" Yushuv shrieked. "My manners? He's trying to drown me!" A low, burbling sound filled Yushuv's ears, and he realized that the thing holding him captive was laughing. He looked up as best he could against the relentless weight of the thing's hand, and Dace was laughing, too. "What?" he asked, incredulous. "What's so funny?" He looked around in a panic as trickles of water ran down his scalp, and realized that he'd been forced to his knees, but no further. The water, however, was very cold.

"Ahem." Dace reined in his chuckles for a moment, and looked sternly down at Yushuv. "Shooth has introduced himself. Why don't you do the same?"

"The... same?"

"Yes. Introduce yourself to him. After all, he went to the inconvenience of waiting all night for you to fall into his clutches, on my behalf, of course. He's the part of tonight's exercise I didn't tell you about."

Yushuv gaped, as the on his head eased slightly. "But he's... how did he know?"

"He knew because he is a spirit of some power, and because he and I have known each other a very long time, ever since he was chased here by some idiot priests from the Immaculate Order. Because we have known each other for so long, he and I occasionally do each other favors. I told him that I'd be chasing you through this part of the forest tonight, and that I'd appreciate some assistance in teaching you a useful lesson. He, being a sensible spirit, agreed, and told me he'd put a good fright into you to help prove my point." Suddenly, all traces of joviality were gone from the older man's face. "Now, what did you do when Shooth found you?"

"Nothing, really. No, I kicked him away the first time. Then I tried to get out of the water, and that's when he grabbed me." Yushuv frowned. "But I didn't know he was, well, what he is. I thought he was some fish."

"That was the first thing you did wrong. Well, besides not paying attention to where you were going." Sighing, he slipped down from his perch and began pacing back and forth along the water's edge. "Yushuv, Creation is filled with a host of absolute marvels. It's also bursting at the seams with a thousand different beasts, spirits, monsters and servants of various dark powers who have one thing on their mind: showing you what the insides of their guts look like. And to aid in this, most of them work very hard to make themselves look like all sorts of innocuous things. I've seen serpents that look like flowers, armed with venom that would boil your blood in an instant. I've seen beasts that resemble nothing more than a blanket of dry leaves, but step on them and they'd flay the skin from your bones in seconds. And I've seen things lurking in the waters of the world that you wouldn't even see coming before they tore you to bloody chunks. All you'd feel is a slight tickle, like a fish brushing up against you, as they made sure you were actually worth the effort it would take them to chew." He grimaced. "Good thing we weren't along the coastline, or you'd be feeding those fish by now. Be alert, boy. It's the only thing that will save you. I won't always be able to come running. Hells, I won't always want to. One day—and it will be sooner, not later—you'll be on your own. And when that day comes, you *will* face something unexpected, and you *will* have to do more than just splash around and throw some rocks if you want to survive."

Yushuv nodded, his gaze locked on the creek bottom. "I understand, Dace. May I get out of the water now? It's cold."

"After you introduce yourself to Shooth. Formally. Then we'll get you dried off and take you back to the camp, and we can go over in fuller detail everything you did wrong." He looked up through the trees at the sky. "Not much time until morning. You made me work for it, Yushuv. You're improving. Not much, but you're improving."

"Thank you, Dace." Yushuv turned, slowly, even as Dace began the slow process of hiking back up the ridge. "I do have one question, though."

Dace paused and looked back over his shoulder. "Yes?"

"How do you introduce yourself to a large water spirit who has its hand on your head?"

Dace laughed. "Carefully," he said, and walked off.

Chapter Four

"Disappointed."

That had been the word Chejop Kejak had used to describe his opinion of Holok's performance on the mainland, and it stung. Sitting on a hard wooden bench near a pier in Port Calin, Holok looked out over the sea in the direction of the Blessed Isle and, with great deliberation, spat. The wad of saliva landed on the stones of the harbor wall, inches from the ten-foot drop to the greenish waters below, and Holok mentally shrugged at yet another failure.

It was early morning, and the wind off the water had yet to change. Quick gusts tugged at his robes and beard, while out over the sea the gulls whirled slowly, looking for garbage or fish. He leaned forward, resting his chin on his powerful hands, and pondered what Kejak had told him.

"Disappointed." He said it out loud, and found it still distasteful to hear. The very word was an insult, making it seem as if Holok were some sort of postulant, charged with a minor task that he'd somehow managed to bungle. Instead, he'd been handed a crisis neatly bound up in an enigma, with no time to prepare and a surly lot of Wyld Huntsmen to shepherd across half the Scavenger Lands, all in search of one small boy. The fact that he'd found the child at all, Holok reflected, was something of a miracle and proof of the heavens' favor. The interlude with an emissary of the Abyss at the ruined temple? Nothing more than a diversion. The boy had been the real prize.

And when cornered, he'd proved to be something else as well. Such a young boy, so newly Exalted, should not be privy to that much power. He should not be so deadly with bow and knife, not against trained Huntsmen. And, injured and alone, he should most certainly not be able to stand toe to toe with

Holok, a veteran of a dozen centuries' diligent study and bone-cracking violence.

"He had help," Holok said to the morning air, and fished in his pouch for the stale crust of bread he'd stashed there. Most of it was intact when he drew it forth, though the pouch itself was now littered with crumbs. With great care, he tore the crust into a half-dozen chunks of equal size, and began tossing them at the water. The gulls clamored and whined as they dove for the tidbits, and Holok watched them vanish behind the harbor wall.

The boy had had help. That much was clear. The questions that remained, however, were dangerously vague. Who had helped him? Why? And how much? How much power did the boy already possess on his own, and how much training had he received? All of these were vital questions, ones that demanded quick answers and relentless follow-up.

Yet Kejak had waved his hand airily and told Holok he'd gotten some "new information" that supposedly made the situation "much more interesting." He'd snorted at that; how much more interesting could this blood-spattered mess of a situation get?

Kejak had noticed, and had not been amused. Holok, for his part, knew what that meant: he was in trouble. More specifically and more immediately, it meant that he was on a bench in Port Calin with a fistful of jade and no clear direction. He had no horse, no weapon, and for the moment at least, no ambition to be anywhere but on that bench. Kejak had charged him with a pair of tasks that struck him as mutually contradictory: find the boy and find out what had happened to the mysterious Eliezer Wren. "I dreamed of him. Twice. That's never good. Two's an unlucky number for dreams," Kejak had said. "Find him. Find both of them."

Find him. Find both of them. It was a joke, a punishment for his failure that had been prettied up with a bronze-plated chance at redemption. Find both of them? On foot, with no idea where to start or what finding them might entail? Dumped in this city with no assistance, no subordinates and no direction? To entertain even the smallest hope of success was foolish.

Then again, Holok was well aware that he'd been a fool on more than one occasion lately, and that at this point, he had little left to lose.

He'd considered simply walking away. That, perhaps, had been what Kejak intended, for him to vanish into the Scavenger Lands, never to be seen again—or to be re-activated by Kejak at a suitable time. Ultimately, he'd decided against doing so, in large part because he felt in his bones that his defection would have pleased Kejak to no end. At this particular moment, he felt like doing Kejak no favors.

That left two options: carry out his assignment poorly, or carry out his assignment well. That, of course, was no choice at all. He was too intrigued by the mysteries the boy represented to approach the matter in slapdash fashion. Furthermore, he was a tidy man, and he hated doing a job halfway. If it were worth any of his time, it was worth enough of it to do the job right. And that, he mentally added, also counted the times when the job included walking halfway across Creation.

Besides, if that weren't enough, there was also the small question of precisely how great a threat to Creation itself the boy was. It was Holok's strong feeling that loose ends like that ought to not be left untied.

Yawning, Holok stood. He had no choice, really, but to pursue this, and to pursue it in his own way. He hadn't been officially barred from seeking help from the Immaculates, but the implication had been clear enough: do this yourself, or do it not at all.

What it all meant, he decided as he picked his way back along the docks to where a broad, paved avenue led into the heart of the city, was that Kejak was playing a game. This was nothing new. He'd known Kejak most of his very long life, and the man had been constantly involved in a double fistful of schemes the entire time. Surely the old leopard hadn't bothered changing his spots now, not after fifteen centuries and more of intrigue for its own sake. That meant that this ludicrous assignment was part of whatever Kejak was up to, and would, ultimately make sense. Either that, or Kejak had finally gone mad, and in that case being as far away from the Isle as possible was an even better idea.

A merchant hailed Holok and, a trifle lasciviously, importuned the priest to try her sticky buns. They were hot out of the oven, she swore, and for such a distinguished priest, very cheap. He ignored her, but the harshness of her voice cut across his ruminations and made him pay more attention to where he was going, rather than simply letting his feet guide him where they willed.

All around him, the city was waking up. Shutters across store windows came clattering down as merchants prepared for the coming day. Pushcarts and wagons jostled for space in the street with the ever-increasing pedestrian throng. The fishermen had long since gone out to sea, but there were plenty of sailors, stumbling out of brothels or searching for a morning meal as they awaited work on one of the ships constantly leaving this place. The distant crack of a whip told him that somewhere, a cargo ship was unloading, and soon oxen-drawn wagons would be straining their way up this very street, headed for warehouses scattered across the city. Beggars took up stations, haughty in their pride of place on street corners they'd squatted on for decades. Street urchins ran laughing through the crowd, no doubt taking a purse or two with them as well. A steady tromping sound told him that an imperial patrol was headed this way, nailed boots ringing loud upon the cobblestones.

In other words, it was another normal day in Port Calin, and for the first time in a very long time, Holok realized that it was altogether wonderful. Never mind that he'd never know any of these people, or that he'd dislike the vast majority of them if he did. The city was alive, thousands of lives woven together in an intricate, fragile pattern. In its own way, it was wondrously, vigorously alive.

This, ultimately, was why he hunted Anathema, those souls whom the skies had corrupted with power and madness. Something in them changed when they were Exalted by the haughty sun; something human in them died. Sooner or later, the people around them ceased to be people and became objects, or worse, obstacles. An Anathema would look at this scene and see only potential threats, potential slaves and potential victims.

A small child with a soot-smeared face bumped into him,

and reflexively he reached for his purse. Instead, as expected, he grasped a thin wrist attached to both a dirty hand and a dirty child. He looked down into the child's face, and saw eyes full of fear.

"Don't you know it's bad luck to steal from a priest?" he said, softly, not releasing his grip on the girl's wrist. "It might get you into trouble."

She stared at him for an instant, surprised. "Don't bother turning me in to the city guards," she said, her dark hair falling over her face. "They'll just beat me and let me go." She made an effort to tug her wrist free, but Holok's grip did not loosen.

"Will they now? It's a good thing, then, I had no intention of giving you to the guards." He looked at her again, and was struck by the dichotomy between how young she was—eight or nine at the most—and how old and weary her voice sounded. Her tunic was reasonably intact, but dirty and made from rough cloth. Strips of cloth tied to her feet served for shoes. They'd serve her poorly in winter, Holok thought.

"Then what are you going to do with me?" The question held no fear, only resignation. The thickening crowd swirled around them, oblivious.

"I am..." he started to answer, then found he had no idea. Just letting her go seemed the best solution, but a sudden inspiration struck him instead, and he grinned. "I am going to buy you a sticky bun," he said. "And then you and I are going to talk about running away from home."

Chapter Five

Three horsemen came up over the rise on the edge of the shadowland, a long cloud of dust rising up behind them. A pair of heavily laden pack ponies followed on ropes, plodding methodically along with stolid indifference to the terrain. Scrub plants lined the poorly defined trail, clinging to life more out of habit than anything else. The land itself was a series of gentle hills and long, dry valleys, all continuously swept by dry winds from the south. Gray dust rode that wind, caking their clothes and gear until they looked like pieces of the land come to life, stalking its borders like vengeful ghosts.

In truth, they were hunters, not ghosts. Wickedly curved swords dangled at their sides, and short bows hung, easily accessible, on their packs. A closer look at their baggage revealed the tools of their cruel trade: weighted nets with thorns twisted into the mesh, bolos adorned with spikes, long pikes with broad crosspieces.

They wore no helms, only broad-brimmed hats weighed down by long use. Dark cloaks protected them from the wind; leather gauntlets covered their hands well up past the wrist. They gripped worn reins loosely, trusting their mounts to know the way, for they'd taken this route many times before.

They were hunters, after all, hunters of men, and this arid wasteland was their preserve. They labored in this shadowland but not for it, preying on refugees and stragglers, the weak ones who could be found along this border with the Underworld. They paid tribute to the agents of the deathknight who ruled this place, surrendering a percentage of the loot they took out in the wastes, and told themselves it was good business.

Occasionally, though, they found victims who had no money worth stealing and no items worth looting. Too weak to be sold as slaves, too beaten down to be worth a sliver of jade to the Fair Folk, they were useless for anything except practice.

Reining in, the lead rider held up his hand. Behind him, the other two halted obediently. "Heesh, what do you see?" the leader snarled, his voice muffled by the scarf wrapped tight around his mouth and nose. He pointed to the west. "There, on that hillside."

Wordlessly, the second rider in the procession reached into the pouch at his waist. From it he pulled a small brass tube, much-scored by wind and sand, and banged it against the heel of his hand. In response, it telescoped out into the shape of a spyglass, and the rider put it to his eye with all due speed.

"I don't like taking it out in this wind. The crystal scratches," the man called Heesh grumbled. "Where do you want me to look, Traal?"

"There, idiot," the leader said, with some irritation. "The third hill up from the dead tree that looks like it's bowing. There."

Heesh's spyglass followed Traal's directions, the man nodding as he did so. "Nothing... nothing there... noth—wait. Near the crest of the hill. Yes. One person, in black. Seated. No baggage. Dressed like a woman. Old woman, I'd say. Yes. One old woman, that's all." He put the spyglass down and carefully tucked it away again. "What do you want to do about it, Traal? You think she's worth our time?"

"Anything out here is worth our time," the man called Traal replied, and dug his heels into his horse's flanks. With a resigned whinny, it cantered forward into the wind. Heesh turned to his other companion, who met his eyes and then shrugged. Then they, too, were riding forward into the dust.

✦

The woman looked up at the sound of hooves approaching. Shielding her eyes from the wind, she peered out into the clouds of dust sweeping over the plain. Dim shapes moved at the edge of her sight, and once again, she cursed the ravages of age that dulled her faculties.

The fact that she was scarcely more than three decades old, as one measured such things, and that the years that had marked her features had been bestowed upon her by processes both unnatural and cruel was of secondary importance. To the eyes of others, she was old, and she feared that in her bones she felt old as well.

"Three of them," she said, dismissively after a long moment. "I shall wait here, and provide them with the opportunity to be courteous." Settling back down into a lotus position, she smoothed her long black skirts and adjusted the veil she wore as protection against the wind. Her hands she folded demurely in her lap. All that could be seen of her face was her eyes, which were dark, and the skin around them, which showed the evidence of many years' passing.

From where she sat, she could see the riders spreading out as they cantered toward her. Two fanned out to the left and the right, presumably to intimidate her, as the leader rode straight for her position. She shook her head ever so slightly, and continued watching. One of the riders' mounts stumbled briefly, and she could hear a string of curses faintly over the wind. She smiled at that, and hoped they'd hurry.

It had been weeks since she'd seen anything amusing, ever since she'd left the Prince of Shadows' palace in search of she knew not what. The prince himself had been surprisingly kind in the wake of the destruction of her orrery, which meant that she could no longer serve him as astrologer. He'd manufactured work for her, discussed the possibility of rebuilding the device, and generally been far more pleasant than he'd had any right to be. This was all the more surprising, considering that in the heat of the moment, she'd provided an extremely painful demise for the prince's servant, Ratcatcher. But the prince had returned from chasing his escaped prisoner and viewed the destruction that Wren and Ratcatcher had wrought, he'd simply glanced at the corpse on the floor, nodded, and expressed his condolences for the smoldering wreck of the orrery before strolling out.

But weeks of busywork had turned to months, and the task of reconstructing the orrery seemed hopeless. Eventually, she had petitioned the prince for the opportunity to leave his service temporarily, to seek something else until she could serve him properly once again.

"You'll be back, you know," he'd said languidly, stretched out on his throne. "This, I foresee for you." Then he had waved her off, and the door to the throne room had shut behind her.

He'd set out rich supplies for her journey, jade and wine and rich food. He'd given her a horse as well, a coal-black gelding she'd expressed admiration for once or twice. But in the end, she'd chosen to take only what she could carry, and to walk, rather than ride. It had seemed somehow appropriate.

The Prince of Shadows, for his part, had been much impressed with this show of humility, and had praised her to the other members of his household. She had been much embarrassed by this effusive show, and had begged him not to say such things. Solemnly, he'd acquiesced and done her the singular honor of bowing his head to her ever so slightly before leaving her in the courtyard, alone.

For this, Unforgiven Blossom was profoundly grateful. She was quite certain, after all, that the prince would have given her a much different send-off if he'd known that tucked into a secret pocket in her robes was the orichalcum dagger he'd taken from the monk Eliezer Wren. She had no idea why she'd taken it from the hidden chamber where the prince had sealed it, other than a sudden urge to do so, and she was quite certain she'd regret doing so later. But initially, at least, no harm had come to her. She had stridden out from the gates of the prince's citadel with it securely in her robes, and none had been the wiser.

The idea of finding Ratcatcher had come to her much later, when she was well on her way. She'd been cursed with occasional visions since she was a child. This was what had led her to the prince's service, initially, though the visions had long since faded. But she'd awakened one night with the image of Ratcatcher's face in her mind, and his voice swearing vengeance in her ears. This, she decided, was a sign. While interpretations of such things were fuzzy, she suspected she knew what this one meant: it would seem that Ratcatcher had, in his own clumsy fashion, returned from the dead. If she did not find him, she suspected, he'd find her.

And so she'd changed her path, and headed north toward Sijan, where they remembered many secrets the dead should never have shared. There, she would find the path to Ratcatcher.

If she dealt with these three imbeciles first.

She looked up, and was gratified to see that the lead rider was almost to where she sat. His horse looked distinctly unhappy with the weight it bore as it wended its way up the slope, and the man astride it looked no happier. The other two men followed, twenty paces behind and ten to either side, and behind them was the pair of pack ponies, being led on ropes. With grim satisfaction, she watched the leader finally reach the spot where she sat, and rein in his horse. He seemed the energetic type, a brute who ruled by force rather than charisma or skill. His followers, no doubt, were easily cowed and more easily roused to brutality. They'd certainly have unpleasant ideas as to what to do to a single old woman alone in the wasteland. They'd certainly have no comprehension of whom they were dealing with.

She ran her fingers through her hair, once, and mentally chided herself for her nervousness. "Patience, little flower," she told herself, and waited for the lead rider to speak.

✦

"Who are you?" Traal asked roughly. He stared down into the old woman's face and was surprised to see no fear. Instead, he saw a calm acceptance, one that he found deeply unnerving. To cover his nervousness, he moved his hand to his sword hilt. The woman's eyes followed his hand, and as her hand rose to her face to undo her veil, he could see that ever so slightly, she was smiling.

"You," she said in carefully modulated tones that spoke of a wealthy upbringing, "are rude. You should dismount before addressing a lady of superior rank, and if you were from one of the more civilized cities, you would know to prostrate yourself and touch your forehead to the ground three times before speaking to me. However, considering the circumstances, I will ignore your lapse this time. Now, dismount."

Traal caught himself swinging a leg over his saddle, and shook his head angrily. Behind him, the other two laughed. Traal reddened, and drew his sword from its leather scabbard. "I bow to no woman," he said a trifle more loudly than necessary, and glared back at his companions. They stifled their snickers, and reached for their swords as well.

"Now," he said, turning back with a look of satisfaction on his face, "I asked you a question. What is your name, old woman, and what are you doing out here?"

"That's two questions," she replied patiently, and stood. She was tiny, perhaps five feet tall, and she moved slowly, as befitted one of her years. "You'd only asked the one previously. Now, what is your name?"

Traal bristled and brought his sword down in front of her eyes. The blade was notched and pitted, showing signs of much unpleasant use. "I don't think you understand your situation, *milady*. You have no guards out here. No help. It's just me and my men, and the dust." To accentuate his point, Heesh and his other companion dismounted, landing in the dust with a pair of heavy thuds. "For the last time, what is your name?"

She did not answer immediately. Instead, she took a step forward and put her hand on the muzzle of Traal's horse. Uncharacteristically, it whickered and bobbed its head up and down. The woman nodded her approval, then looked left and right, taking in the two men with swords striding cockily toward her.

"Ah," she said. "It's to be like that." She reached up to her brow and smoothed back her hood. It fell to her shoulders, showing iron-gray hair bound up tightly in a bun by two metal pins. "My name, if you must know, is Unforgiven Blossom, and I am here because I wish to be. I carry treasure beyond your comprehension, and I have no intention of giving it to you. Is there anything else you desire knowledge of before you force me to kill you and your companions?" She dropped into a fighting stance, an impossibly small figure against the background of the scrublands.

Traal threw back his head and laughed. "You've been out here too long, Madame Blossom. The sun's cooked your wits."

He waved his sword in the air, the dim sun flashing off the blade. "Heesh, Stonos, did you hear that? This ancient thing is going to kill us!"

Blossom looked away from Traal and met Heesh's eyes. "You don't have to die, you know," she said softly. "Detach your fate from his."

Heesh took a step back, awkwardly. He brought his sword out in front of him, gripping it with both hands. "You're a witch, aren't you?" he breathed. "Traal, we can't kill a witch. She'll curse us if we do."

"She's no witch," Traal replied. "She's an old fool. Now pretend you know her business, and kill her!" He brought his sword down in a vicious slash, bellowing with rage as he did so.

Blossom dropped into a squat, and the sword passed through empty air. Then, with the disappointment of a bored instructor, she reached up and caught Traal's sword arm at the wrist. "You overextend," she said with clinical detachment, and tugged.

Overbalanced, Traal toppled out of his saddle. He landed on the hard-packed earth in a tangle of arms and legs, his weapon clattering away from his awkwardly bent wrist. Stonos rushed forward and stabbed expertly, at her midsection, but she was already spinning away behind Traal's horse. Stonos stepped over his fallen leader to try another stab underneath the horse's belly, but she spun first left and then right, and his sword whistled past her harmlessly.

"Mind the horse," Blossom called, then vaulted up and over the animal, landing behind Stonos. He turned, his mouth open in an O of amazement, and she punched him precisely, once each in the belly, groin and throat, ending the sequence with an open-palm strike against his nose. With an unpleasant crunch, he dropped to the ground, and a spatter of bright blood fell with him.

Heesh's sword whistled past her ear, and Unforgiven Blossom whirled. A series of short, sharp slashes drove her back against the horse's flank, and every time she feinted left or right the hunter's blade flicked out and forced her to the center.

"You're not going anywhere, old woman," he stated levelly,

his sword tip tracing small circles in front of her throat. "I don't know how you did that to my friends, but here's where it ends. I'm going to kill you, and the scorpions are going to have your eyes."

"You're too much of a poet to be doing this," she replied, her eyes darting back and forth. "It is not too late for you, you know."

"Shut up, witch," he growled. "It's too late for you."

Without taking his eyes from her, he called back to Traal. "Are you all right?" A moan was the only answer he got, and it seemed to galvanize him. "Now you die, witch," he hissed, and drove the sword forward.

Blossom let her legs collapse underneath her, and the point of the sword passed over her as she dropped to the ground . It plunged into the horse's flank and the animal screamed in pain. Bucking, it wrenched the sword from Heesh's grip, flinging him backwards as it did so. With a cry, he staggered back and reached for the broad-bladed knife he kept at his belt, but before he could reach it, Unforgiven Blossom was on him. Holding the index and middle fingers of her left hand tightly together, she drove them into his eye. An explosion of wet jelly burst forth, followed by dark blood, and he fell to the ground in slow, jerky stages. His hands scrabbled at the earth until she neatly crushed each one beneath the heels of her sandals. "A waste, really," was all she said, and walked over to where Traal's horse had collapsed.

It was on the ground perhaps twenty paces distant, a stream of blood soaking the soil around it. Heesh's sword was still in its side, and with each labored breath the horse took, it quivered alarmingly. Bloody foam flecked its nostrils, and its eyes were mad.

"You poor thing," she said, voice full of concern, and knelt down to cradle its head. "The pain will end soon, I promise. Just hush. Hush." With each word her voice became quieter, and with her left hand she stroked its sweaty mane. With her right, she reached back to the pins that held her hair in place, and drew one out. Several locks of her gray hair tumbled down to frame the right side of her face. She looked at it for a moment, as if to reassure herself that it would serve, then addressed herself to the horse once more.

"This will end your pain," she crooned. "Just a little sting and it will all be over." Even as she spoke, she lined the pin up with the horse's throat, and with practiced ease, slid it in. The horse shuddered once and was still.

"Choose better masters in your next life," Unforgiven Blossom said, and waited a minute to pull the pin from the beast's neck. A single bead of blood, red against the horse's dusty coat, welled up as she did so. "You've earned your rest."

A sudden kick caught her in the side and sent her sprawling, the pin flying out of her hand. She tried to scramble to her feet, but Traal closed in, landing another blow against her ribs. It knocked the wind from her, and she tumbled down the slope.

"Stupid bitch," Traal boomed as he stomped downhill after her. "You killed my horse."

"Your friend killed your horse," she replied as she eased herself to her feet. "I put it out of its misery."

"Hah." His left hand held a dagger with an ugly array of barbs on its edge, though his right arm dangled uselessly at his side. "Keep lying. Your lies will escort you to hell, you know."

"I've been to hell," she replied. "You don't frighten me. And you are lying to yourself."

"Oh am I?" He made an experimental slash with the dagger, and Unforgiven Blossom sidestepped, awkwardly. "I don't think I'm lying when I say I'll kill you. What did you do to my horse, anyway?" He thrust, and the blade tore her garment as it nearly caught her side. "Witchcraft?" he asked, and circled to the right. Unforgiven Blossom backed away, limping slightly. "Magic? Or just plain butchery?" He feinted left and then thrust right, and she nearly impaled herself neatly. "Running out of tricks?" Traal smiled, his teeth bloody. "Good." He took a wild swing and again she backed away. "What do you have left, old woman? Anything up your sleeve now?" Another swing brought another dodge, but this time Traal was ready. Even as Unforgiven Blossom dodged his dagger, he lowered his shoulder and charged into her. She went over backwards, and he landed on top of her. Quickly he planted his knees on her shoulders, pinning her. She attempted to roll first left and then right, but his weight was too much.

"You're going nowhere, little flower." Traal's breath stank of rotten meat and rotting teeth. He leered down at her, dagger held high. "You've cost me two bad men and one good horse, witch. And since you have no baggage and I doubt you've any money, I'll have to find another way to make you pay." He spat down into her face. She blinked, once. "Hands behind your head, now, or I'll have to cut you sooner than I'd like." Slowly, she obeyed.

"Good, good. You know, you might have been pretty once. Too bad you're good for nothing but practice now."

She squirmed away from him, and he laughed. "Don't try to get away. It'll just make the cuts sloppy."

In a whisper, she said "Wait."

"Wait? Why?"

" I do have one thing that might be of interest to you," she said, revulsion tainting her voice.

"Oh?" Traal sat back, his dagger at the ready. "What is it?"

"Poison," she replied, and flung the last pin from her hair upward. Traal's mouth opened in surprise, and the metal shard flew up and pierced the back of his throat.

"You..." was all he gurgled, and then he toppled, slowly, into the dust.

Unforgiven Blossom waited a moment, and then stood up. With slow deliberation, she brushed the dust from her robes, and frowned at the gash Traal's dagger had left in them. "Idiots," she said succinctly, and retrieved her weapon from between Traal's blue-tinged lips. Carefully, she bound up her hair, and then turned her attention to finding the pin she'd dropped when Traal struck her. It took several minutes to find, and by the time she'd located it, both of the remaining horses had wandered off. The pack ponies, however, stood obediently in place, oblivious to the carnage that had just taken place.

With pursed lips, she considered them for a moment, then looked at the bodies of the men on the ground. They had swords, and presumably other items of value. No doubt they had coin pouches somewhere in their garments, and weapons that could be sold for a profit. But the notion of rummaging around these particular corpses was unappealing. It was not that she had an aversion to the dead—on the contrary, she quite preferred their company—but Traal and his companions were a thoroughly unpleasant memory, and she wanted nothing of their stink on her as she walked out of the shadowland.

Finding the dead man she was looking for would be difficult enough, she reasoned, without having three more trailing her. These three might rise, but she'd give them as little to track her by as she could. A cold scent and their innate stupidity would keep them off her trail, even if by some miracle the Deathlords sent them back.

With a tiny shrug, she made her decision. A whistle brought the ponies to her at a trot, one stepping over Heesh as it did so. Unforgiven Blossom looked at them approvingly, then drew her hood over her head and her veil across her face. Taking the ponies' halters, she started walking north, in the direction of the shadowland's border and, with luck, towards the man she sought.

And with real luck, she'd thought, he would not yet have started moving again.

Chapter Six

The weeping sound Wren had heard had come from deep within a pit, one that he almost fell into in the dark. Only the fortuitous tumble of some stones into the chasm kept him from treading right off the edge into the unseen depths below. Shuddering, he halted, and felt empty air under the toes of his right foot.

You can learn the ways of the Labyrinth. The darkness will be as bright as day to your eyes.

It was the damned snakes again. They'd followed him since he started walking, whispering suggestions and what they no doubt thought were seductive offers almost constantly. The effect had been almost precisely opposite of what they'd intended. Instead of intrigued or convinced, he'd first become bored, and then annoyed, until finally he'd reached enraged. At this point, if they offered him a way out and Ratcatcher's head on a plate, gratis, he would have spat in their scaly faces.

Irritated beyond comprehension, he turned carefully and faced them. As always, they stopped just out of the range of what little sight he could muster, but he could hear their scales gliding back and forth against the stone in the dark. "Would you please just shut up?" he asked wearily. Normally when dealing with spirits or other unnatural entities Wren was the soul of civility, but these were neither normal circumstances nor normal spirits.

You do not wish us to be silent, one of them said after a short pause. *There are things here you are not ready to hear.* Another wail arose from the pit, punctuating the statement.

"Perhaps, but most of them have been spoken by you." Wren spat on the ground, and ran his hand over his head in frustration. His hair was starting to grow back, and the short bristles scratched against his palm. "What do you want from me?"

We want nothing. The one we serve wants much. You are important, oh Chosen of the Sun.

The answer took Wren aback. He was not used to straight answers from spirits. Normally their replies to direct questions were similes wrapped in riddles seemingly composed by drunken poets. But the serpents who had tormented him for unknown hours were baldly admitting their role—and their knowledge of what he had become. It was astonishing.

And it also gave him a weapon, though perhaps not one his escorts would expect.

"Oh, really," he said, injecting his voice with as much boredom as he dared. One foot traced a half-circle on the rough stone—at least he thought it was stone—near the edge of the pit. "Important. How important?"

Important enough that we shall tend you. You should feel honored. The answer came with what Wren swore was a trickle of annoyance, and he permitted himself a grim smile. They would tend him. That meant that it was their charge to keep him alive so that he could eventually be brought to their master, whoever that might be. And this master clearly had uses for him, uses linked to that gift which he had been forced to accept in the Prince of Shadows' dungeon. No doubt they had been instructed to keep him safe from all of the Underworld's myriad perils, regardless of the cost.

He, however, was under no such obligation.

"Tend me? Fascinating," he said, and pivoted. Before the snakes could move, he deliberately stepped off the edge and into the pit.

The crescendo of wails emanating from the depths he'd just flung himself into rose to a deafening shriek, even as the serpents let out a monstrous hiss of shock. Then, suddenly, Wren felt a sharp pain tear at his left wrist as one of the serpents struck at him with its fangs. So sudden and deep was the bite that Wren could feel his flesh tear as his descent abruptly halted, and he dangled, like a ham in a smokehouse, over the depths of the pit.

Fool! Whichever serpent was speaking was enraged. *Another instant and you would have been beyond rescuing! You would have fallen to your death, and the thin paste of your bones devoured by the nameless things that dwell within the pit.*

The former Immaculate priest chose to say nothing, content to dangle for the moment. He could feel the blood trickling down his arm from the punctures the snake's fangs had made, and for a panicked moment he thought about poison. The serpents were not supposed to kill him, but few of the snakes he'd ever run across had struck him as particularly farsighted. "You can lecture me better on the edge of the pit," he called up. "Especially when one of your mouths isn't full."

Wren heard a disappointed hiss, and felt himself rising. Within seconds, he felt a thick coil wrapping itself around his waist, its scales large and pleasantly cool against his skin. Then it squeezed, and suddenly the sensation was not quite so pleasant.

"Too… tight" he gasped, and was rewarded with an ophidian chuckle.

We do not wish you to fall again. We must make certain of such things.

"Very… kind… of you." Wren's chest felt like it was on fire, the breath being forced from his lungs. A red haze rimmed his vision, and he knew this was not because the lighting here had suddenly improved. Did the serpents mean to crush the life out of him, and then drag him, unconscious, to their master? He hoped not, for if they did, there was precious little he could do about it.

Then, abruptly, he was on the stony ground, his hand free and the coil slithering free from his midsection. He wheezed for a moment, then coughed, then sat up.

Do not attempt that again, he was warned, and he laughed.

"Do not attempt that again, or what? You'll let me fall? I don't think so. I think your master would disapprove of that." He lurched to his feet, clenching his fist and holding his bleeding hand against his belly. "All you can do is threaten, and maybe bully. Oh, and you can rough me up a bit, no doubt, but frankly, you're amateurs. Ratcatcher did twice the work you two have in half the time, and he only had one head." *Had,* he thought to himself, and he briefly wondered precisely what Unforgiven Blossom had done to him as payment for the destruction of her orrery. A mental image rose before him unbidden, and he shuddered and dismissed it. He had no time for other men's horrors now.

The scrape of scale on stone was faster now, the serpents gliding back and forth agitatedly but not speaking. Wren smiled. Even snakes, he decided, have their pride.

"As a matter of fact," he continued, "I'll make a little wager with you. I'll bet my life—or whatever this existence is—that you still have to rescue me, no matter what I do. Even if I do this again." He turned toward where his best guess told him the pit was, and made as if to stride forward once again.

No! With a cry of desperation, the serpents flung themselves forward. Even as they did so, Wren leapt straight up. Desperation and perhaps something else lent his feet wings—suddenly there was a dim light in the chamber, and with shock Wren realized that the source of the light was him.

He could see both of them now, and gasped at what he saw. Their bodies were thick and black, easily a foot across and twenty feet long. Each bore two heads on long sinuous necks, and they were maned like horses and horned like bulls. To call these things serpents was to do a disservice to things that crawl in the dust, Wren realized. These were monsters.

Even as he realized this, Wren began his fall back to the ground. The first serpent had misjudged its position, he saw, and had flung itself past where he had been standing, into the pit. Already, it was plummeting, and its companion was striking to save it in the same way it had presumably once saved Wren. There was the unpleasant sound of fangs sinking into flesh, and then a cry like steam escaping from a punctured kettle, and the second serpent had caught its companion with both its maws. It hung there for a moment, the bulk of its body on the edge of the pit as it fought desperately for balance, the weight of its twin threatening to topple it.

As he fell, Wren assumed the Striking Falcon stance, one knee drawn up nearly to his chin, the other leg straight. Thin wisps of light tore around him as he fell, and his foot struck the serpent's spine with a resounding crack.

He landed badly, rolling to his feet as best he could even as the serpent thrashed in agony. It had shrieked when he had struck, both its cavernous maws opening in a spasm of pain, and in that instant the first serpent had fallen into the pit with a wordless cry. Enraged, it tried to turn back upon itself to strike at him, but it was too far over the edge to do so, and with titanic slowness it toppled down, into the dark. One head snapped at him as it fell, barely missing, but then with a rush of air it was gone, and all that was left was a fading pair of howls.

Testing his foot gingerly, Wren decided it was sore but not broken. He waited for a minute at the edge of the pit, watching the light that had surrounded him fade, and wondering when the two serpents would hit bottom. A moment later his patience was rewarded, as first one thump and then another announced his escorts' untimely and presumed demise.

As he limped off, Wren noted that the incessant cries from the pit to which he'd consigned the serpents had ceased. Instead, dimly but unmistakably, he could hear the sound of flesh being torn, and a low, greedy chewing. Any moans or pleas for mercy that also emanated from the depths of the chasm were, he told himself, doubtless figments of his imagination. He gave thanks to the Unconquered Sun that whatever light had shone from him had not illuminated the bottom of that pit. Whatever dwelt down there, he was quite certain he did not want to know what it was.

Off in the distance, he saw a light. It was faint, and it was pale, but it was light. His foot aching, he headed toward it. After all, whatever light he'd produced in this place was gone.

Chapter Seven

Yushuv took a deep breath filled with the scent of cooking meat and decided that all things considered, there were far worse places to be. There was venison roasting on a spit over the fire, and strong red wine in a skin that hung at Dace's side and a stew of plants that Yushuv had found in the forest earlier in the day. Above him, the moon sailed in a cloudless sky, surrounded by a double fistful of bright stars.

"See that, boy?" Dace sat sprawled out on a finely woven reed mat. The wineskin next to the man was half-empty, and he had gone so far as to remove his armor. It sat in a neat pile near the rocks that marked the edge of the circular clearing that held their camp, though his long, heavy blade was, as always, within arm's reach.

Now, however, he wasn't holding a sword. Instead he pointed up, to a spot in the sky occupied by a particularly bright star. "That, Yushuv, is Jupiter. Mistress of Secrets. She and her four sisters roam the heavens and help keep the world in some kind of working order. They're not as powerful as the Unconquered Sun or Luna, mind you, but they're nothing to be trifled with." He sniffed, then sat up abruptly. "Hey now! Don't stop turning supper just because your eyes are somewhere else! Keep your mind on your tasks, boy. Haven't I taught you anything?'

Belatedly, Yushuv jerked his gaze back from the heavens to the hunk of deer on the spit. A single breath was enough to tell him that the bottom of the meat was in fact burning, and he hurriedly restarted the cranking process lest more of it be scorched. "Sorry, Dace."

The older man made a lazy wave, and took a long pull from the wineskin. "Not to worry. There's plenty for both of us. I'm more concerned about your focus than our supper." He stretched and his stomach rumbled, loudly. "Just tell me it's almost done."

Yushuv nodded. "You can get the stew now, if you want. The pot's on the flat rock in the fire pit, and the bowls are stacked next to it. You'll want to wipe the dirt off the ladle first, though."

Dace stood. "Excellent. I think I can handle that." He ambled over to the fire, the light playing off his skin. The ladle rested atop a pile of stones next to a stack of wooden bowls, and he reached down to scoop both it and one of the bowls up. With a "Hmm," he examined the ladle and then judiciously knocked it against the rock twice, then used it dexterously to flip the lid off the pot of stew. The savory scent of vegetables wafted up, and he took a deep, contented breath before ladling healthy portions of stew into a pair of bowls. As he did so, Dace looked over at Yushuv, whose face was knotted in concentration on his task. Dace's expression softened a fraction, and he turned his head so he wouldn't meet Yushuv's eyes. "You're really coming along well. Don't let what happened this morning bother you. You're learning fast."

"Am I?" Yushuv refused to turn, instead keeping his gaze focused on the ground. "It seems like I can't do anything right. I fail every lesson, and most of them nearly kill me one way or another. If that priest came back today, I'd try to do nine different things and fail at all of them, and he'd kill me."

"If that priest came back," said Dace, dropping to his haunches, "we'd both run. Do you understand me, boy? He's positively dripping with power, and I still have no idea how you survived your duel with him. By all rights he should have sliced you thin and then strolled down the road and roasted me for dessert. I don't know how you caught his attention, but it was a black day for you when you did. But the best thing you can do is prepare for the day you see him again, and not waste your time worrying about the impossible. Am I understood?"

"You're right." Yushuv took the knife from his belt and carved a long slice of meat off the haunch of venison, then neatly dropped it into Dace's stew. "How many other students have you had, and what happened to them?"

"Here's another lesson, Yushuv," Dace said, as he set the

boy's bowl down and turned away with his own. "Never ask questions you don't want answers to. Now eat your supper, and then go back to your lessons when you're done."

❖

"Dace?"

"Yes?" Dace looked over at where Yushuv was sprawled out on the ground, an empty bowl beside him. The boy had gotten one of his sleeping furs from his tent, a wolf pelt from one of the child's own kills. He was good with a bow, Dace noted to himself, better than good, though he always seemed worried about how many arrows he had left. He was progressing in other areas as well—everything from juggling the potent energies of Essence, to long-distance running, to cooking a meal.

Dace was pushing him hard, but only because of the message the bird-spirit had brought him from the Lilith woman. She was a cold one, frightening and disdainful, but she'd sent him word that he *needed* to protect and train this boy, and to do so quickly. There had been no other details, and when he'd asked for them, the bird had laughed—it had actually *laughed* at him—and then flown off.

So now he was stuck with the boy, whom he was training desperately for he knew not what. And since he didn't know what he was training Yushuv for, that meant training him in a little bit of everything, because you never knew when the ability to hunt up roots and tubers might be as important to survival as the ability to put an arrow in a squirrel's left eye from fifty yards. What was certain, though, was that Yushuv had an incredible and unconscious knack for manipulating Essence, the very lifeblood of Creation, and that he'd been doing so since the mark of the Unconquered Sun had first flared into life on his forehead. Dace was sure there was a story there, but Yushuv was extremely close-mouthed about his past, and every time Dace tried to pry the lid off that box, the boy simply withdrew into himself.

Frustrating. That's what it was. Dace grunted, and absently

scratched the back of his neck. He was used to training soldiers, not boys, and especially not sullen, stubborn boys who fought him every step of the way.

"What happens next?" The boy rolled over onto his back and looked up at the stars. "Why are you doing all this for me? Or do you make a habit of rescuing orphans and strays?" Unconsciously, Yushuv reached out to touch the bow that lay nearby, reassuring himself it was still there. Dace had seen him do that several times a day for months now, and worried a little over what it implied.

"I'm doing this because you're special, though you knew that." Dace set down his own bowl, now empty, and belched explosively. "Ahh. Good stew."

"Dace," Yushuv said warningly. "Don't try to change the subject. Why?"

"Fine." The older man shrugged, and leaned forward on his haunches. "You've got a mark on your forehead, Yushuv, same as mine. Well, not quite the same; yours shines a little brighter. That means you've been given power by the Unconquered Sun, and specifically in his aspect as the lightbringer at dawn. That's how I understand the theology, and it means that whatever life you used to have," the boy flinched at that, visibly, "is over.

"More specifically, it means that priests and their tame dogs in the Wyld Hunt are going to try to kill you, because of what you are. They're extremely sincere about this sort of thing and they've got centuries of practice at it, which means that when the come for you, they're going to come hard. And unless you're trained, ready and lucky, you're going to end up dead.

"The second thing is that, like it or not, you're in the service of the Unconquered Sun now. What that means for you is uncertain—different things are asked of each one of us, and sometimes we're just left alone to find our own way—but it means your life isn't your own any more. You can try to walk away—everyone does, at least once—but either your destiny will call you back, or the world's going to look unkindly on you. Too unkindly, as a matter of fact, for you to survive on your own. Of course, you could always take the third route and swear yourself to the Abyss, though I don't think you'd like the cost of that very much. They take things from you, boy, when you do that. Things like a piece of your soul."

"No," Yushuv interrupted, wrapping his arms tightly around his chest. "I've met one of those. I don't want to be like that. I never want to be like that."

"You have?" There was no response. Dace shook his head, waited a moment, and continued. "I'm sorry to hear that. Deathknights are monsters at the best of times, and for a boy..." He let his voice trail off thoughtfully.

Yushuv sat up. "I stopped being a boy, I think, when *he* came to my village." He shuddered. "I don't know what I am, but I'm not a boy any more."

Dace carefully said nothing for a moment, and then handed Yushuv the wineskin. The boy took it solemnly squirted some of the rich, dark wine into his mouth, and then promptly choked and spat it back out all over himself. Dace roared with laughter, and after a minute, Yushuv laughed, too.

Eventually, Dace found his voice again. "Damn, Yushuv, now I know which part of your lessons I'm neglecting. Tomorrow, boy, we start on wine!" And that set them off into gales of laughter again, which rose up into the night alongside the smoke from their campfire.

THOK

It was the sound of an arrow burying itself in the ground between Yushuv and Dace. Laughter died in their throats as they reacted, Dace sidling toward his armor while Yushuv reached for his bow and rolled toward his quiver. Another arrow suddenly sprouted in the soil between the boy and his destination, and he stopped. The shaft was an oily, iridescent black, and the fletching seemed to grow right out it. Yushuv tried to roll the other way, and in response, three more shafts appeared. One landed neatly between Dace's knees as he crouched, while the other two bracketed Yushuv within inches of his skin.

"Are you all right?" Dace froze, turning his head slowly. He knew very well what the arrows meant and that meant refraining from calling upon his own not-inconsiderable powers. It was his deep suspicion that the second the cloak of light around him flared into existence, he'd be turned into a pincushion. And no matter how much the Unconquered Sun favored a man, a passel of arrows in his throat and gut would still end his days without any fuss.

Particularly, Dace thought, *with these archers.*

Slowly, Yushuv pulled himself to his knees and then to his feet. No more arrows flew. "Dace?" he called. "Are they gone?"

"Don't move," Dace responded. "They're toying with us."

Another arrow lanced out of the woods and landed between two of Dace's splayed fingers on the ground.

"Damnation!" He pulled his hand back as if it had been scalded, and another arrow, this from directly across the clearing, landed where it had been. "Yushuv!"

The boy had dropped his bow, Dace now saw, and had struggled to his feet with his hands in the air. "If you're going to kill us, kill us," he could hear Yushuv saying. "If you're not going to, leave us alone."

Dace held his breath. Yushuv, for his part, took a step forward and spread his arms wide. "Here I am," he said. "Do what you have to."

There was silence for a moment, and then a single note from a huntsman's horn rang out. It was sharp and high, and cut the air like a blow from an ax. It promised terror and relentless pursuit, and a sharp knife to the throat at the end of the chase. It carried with it fear and arrogance, and it shamed the beasts of the forest to whispers even as it died away.

As the blast from the huntsman's horn faded, a rustle like the north wind through fall leaves whispered through the grove. The crack of a single branch, stepped on by a careless tread, announced itself and was swallowed by the night, and then there was nothing.

Minutes later, Yushuv finally dared to turn and face his mentor. "Are they gone?" he asked.

Dace summoned a nod. "They're gone for now. They'll be back, though, and soon. This was just to frighten us."

"It looks like they've succeeded," replied Yushuv innocently, which earned him a sharp look.

"Boy, if you're not afraid, you're a fool. Do you know what

that was?"

"No, but whoever they are, they seem willing to listen," Yushuv said helpfully.

"That's fool talk, boy. They," Dace said grimly as he started buckling on his armor, "are the Fair Folk. I've seen their arrows before. And they seem to want you dead, later if not sooner. Douse the fire and pack up your goods. We're leaving tonight."

Chapter Eight

"Is the chamber empty?"

Pelesh the Exchequer cringed, and did his best to unobtrusively shuffle toward the throne room doors, away from the Prince of Shadows' anger. The prince himself slouched on his throne, eyes dark with fury. He wore all of his armor save his helm, which rested at his feet with his mace, and small gouts of scarlet flame danced around the chamber in time with his words.

"Yes, my prince," the elderly man said, and bowed his head for the deathblow he expected to follow instantly. When it didn't, he looked up, and found himself staring into the prince's eyes.

"Details, Pelesh," the prince said softly. "I would very much like some details. Now."

Pelesh swallowed, hard. He was not used to moments like these. Normally, he stayed in his tower and simply sent reports to the prince—how much money had been spent, how much had come in, the balance of trade with the living lands nearby, and so forth. The numbers had nearly always been good, and even when they hadn't been, the prince had most often dealt with him through other servants. It was rare for him to be called on the carpet like this, but these were not normal times. Ratcatcher was dead, if not gone, and Unforgiven Blossom was gone but not yet dead. The prince, furious in the wake of the Wren incident, had decimated the staff to vent his anger and sent most of the other deathknights and servants of note out on various errands of diplomacy or mayhem.

That left Pelesh alone in the citadel with the prince and the ghosts, and he found himself nervously wondering whose company he preferred. "I..." he started, then licked his dry lips. "My prince, on your orders, I unsealed the chamber in the dungeon where you had placed the dagger for safekeeping. The stone upon which it had been placed was still present, as was the cushion upon which the dagger had rested. The lock to the chamber appeared to be unmarred, and only you, I, and Unforgiven Blossom even knew of its existence. However, the dagger itself was missing, and in its place rested this." He drew forth from a pouch at his belt a clumsy iron replica of the missing blade. "She no doubt left it behind when she took the real one, though I know not why." Pelesh paused briefly, then added, "There were footprints in the dust on the floor. Small ones." Hastily, he bowed, and kept his head down.

"Ah." The prince nodded once, then turned and took a pair of steps toward his throne. "And you are quite sure that the protections and defenses placed on the cell were sufficient to keep out any of my other servants who might have gotten dangerous ideas."

"Quite sure, my prince," Pelesh squeaked. "I swear it on my life."

"I already own your life, Pelesh. Swear on something that still has worth." A sudden thought struck the prince and he whirled, his brow furrowed with concern. "Could Wren have returned? Might this be his doing?"

"No, my liege." Pelesh dared to lift his head, and saw what might almost be worry on the prince's face. "The door to the Underworld has been triple-barred, and guards placed before it against the unlikely eventuality of Wren's return. Nothing's passed that way since Wren fell."

"Good." The prince half-turned and waved a dismissive gesture in Pelesh's general direction. "So you're quite certain it was Unforgiven Blossom? Fine. Go back to your numbers, Pelesh. I have other servants who will deal with this. She'll be found, and your deduction will be put to the test. And if it turns out that my astrologer has betrayed my trust, well, then I shall have to demonstrate my disappointment upon her tired flesh." The prince took another step toward his throne, then narrowed his eyes. "You are dismissed, Pelesh. Or did you not hear me?"

"Of course, my prince," the little man stammered, and nearly ran out of the throne room. Behind him, the massive doors swung shut silently, leaving the prince alone. Faintly, the sound of rain on the citadel's roof could be heard, and thunder grumbled softly in the distance. Exhausted, the prince flung himself upon his throne, the cushions and furs draped across it only partially dampening the clang of armor on stone.

"Finally," he said to the air. In response, a hum of fluttering wings filled the chamber, and a fog of bats descended from the shadows near the room's ceiling. They swooped and chittered throughout the chamber, filling the air around the prince. He held out his arms and they came to him, the cloud collapsing inward on itself until it seemed as if a solid wall of black hovered around him.

"Did you hear that, my children?" he asked, palms upraised. "Did you hear what you must do? Find where my wandering flower has run to and watch her. Tell me where she goes and whom she sees. A beautiful blossom cannot hide in this barren land. Go!"

He brought his hands together over his head, and a clap of thunder shook the citadel to its very foundations as he did so. The bats spiraled upward, shrill voices swearing fealty to the prince in their secret tongue, until they once again reached the shadows of the room's ceiling, where they vanished. The prince stared up after them, and when the last had merged with the darkness, he smiled.

And when he was quite certain he was alone, he began to laugh.

Chapter Nine

Ratcatcher held his breath until the thunder of heavy-soled boots on stone thundered past, then realized that doing so was wasted effort. Dead men didn't breathe, after all. He shook his head infinitesimally and relaxed, then edged forward from his hiding place in a tiny chamber between two massive carved pillars, in order to see if the corridor was clear.

It was. The guards he'd just heard going past were headed in the rough direction of the embalming chamber he'd vacated a few short minutes previously, or more accurately for the carnage he'd left in and around it. No doubt the entire city was in an uproar now, and he'd best move quickly if he wanted to escape before more drastic measures were levied against him.

◆

The first guards Ratcatcher saw in Sijan broke down the doors to the room he awakened in, and were remarkably unsurprised to find a cadaver standing in front of them. He counted four pikes and two torches in the hands of the pale, black-clad guards opposing him, and no looks of terror from beneath their black hoods.

Ratcatcher supposed that revenants of all stripes were more common in Sijan than they might be in other places; after all, the city dealt more with the dead than with the living. Of the thousands of corpses brought to Sijan by wagon, horse and barge each year, surely at least one or two decided that cerements and evisceration for the sake of well-stocked canopic jars was not for them. On the other hand, that meant that the city guards of Sijan were used to dealing with walking dead, nemissaries and the like, and this gave them a certain advantage over a freshly-returned dead man who was still figuring out precisely how his new body worked.

"You're probably confused," the man at the front of the herd of pikemen said, the ornate stitching on the shoulder of his hooded black tunic indicating that he was most likely the leader of the squad. "It's all right," he continued in soothing tones. "You'll just want to stand there and relax until we can get a necromancer down here to send you where you belong. In the meantime, just be calm. There's nothing to worry about." Behind him the other pikemen stood resolutely, while the two warders with torches—one of them a woman, Ratcatcher now saw—flanked him to the left and the right.

He growled low in his throat, and saw the pikemen take an involuntary half-step back. "Easy," the leader said, the tip of his weapon bobbing a bit lower. "You'll be resting again soon enough."

"I have had," Ratcatcher said thickly, "quite enough rest for the moment." He stepped forward, hands raised, and a palisade of pikes met him.

"He's aware," the captain said to his men, who murmured in response. "Remember, we're just supposed to hold him here until the necromancer can arrive." He looked from side to side calmly, as if this were nothing more than a drill for his troops. One of the torchbearers edged closer, until Ratcatcher drove her back with a hiss. Ratcatcher's unseemly grin punctuated her retreat.

He looked back and forth, counting his opponents. Six. Four in front, two to the flanks. That meant no one behind. Idiots. They were no doubt expecting him to be docile—the captain's words had confirmed as much. He could hear distant footsteps along the corridor, though. That was undoubtedly the sound of help for these incompetents, and with them possibly the aforementioned necromancer. And though he felt strong, stronger than he had any right to in this poison-addled body, he had no idea what a fully trained and professional sorcerer would be able to do to him.

After a moment's deliberation, Ratcatcher decided that he

had no interest in finding out. With a hideous shriek, he let his eyes roll up in his head, and fell over backwards. His head hit the stone of the floor with a soft thunk, and he lay still.

"Sir? He just collapsed." It was the other torchbearer, the man. He edged closer, his brand held out before him. "Maybe we don't need the necromancer."

"In a case like this, you always need the necromancer." The captain's voice was firm, and the reproach in it was unmistakable. "Either he's actually gone back to wherever he's supposed to be, in which case the necromancer will confirm it, or it's a trick and the necromancer will put an end to it. In either case, we follow the usual procedure for such things. Now take a step back."

"But, captain," the man said, leaning closer, "He's not moving. My cousin Resplendent Chrysanthemum had one like this. The corpse just fell over, never moved again. It was like magic."

And at that precise moment, Ratcatcher's new right hand shot up like an arrow, catching the incautious warder by the throat. The man's cry was cut off by an awful crunch as Ratcatcher's fingers crushed his windpipe. An instant later, the dead man grabbed the guard by the wrist and hurled him forward. His torch fell to the floor as he flew through the air. The other torchbearer tried to dodge, but couldn't take more than a step before the still-twitching corpse of her companion caught her in the side. She went down, her torch skittering across the floor for an instant before it went out.

"Pin him!" the captain shouted as the room plunged into darkness. Ratcatcher drew his knees up, then gave a mighty shove against the floor. He was rewarded by a sudden burst of speed backwards and a shower of sparks as metal pikeheads scraped across the floor where he'd been. The footsteps in the corridor were faster now, and even from flat on his back Ratcatcher could see the flickering lights that meant more torches. The darkness was his ally; he had to use it fast. Frowning, he rolled left and crouched behind an embalming table.

"Spread out and stick him like a butterfly on a rich woman's hat," the captain bellowed, and stepped forward. With each step his pike came down, hard, on the floor. "He can't hide for long. Keep your formation and don't do anything stupid. We'll have light in here in a minute." A chorus of responses echoed around the chamber, and, pleased with his troops' discipline, the captain took another step forward.

That was his mistake. As the captain's pike struck stone, Ratcatcher reached out and, with a contemptuous grunt, shoved it back at the man, hard. It struck him in the chest, knocking him backwards. With a surprised shout, he fell to the floor. Even as the captain was falling, Ratcatcher rose up, pike in hand. With one swift motion he reversed it, then plunged it deep into the man's chest. The captain shuddered once, blood pouring from his mouth, and was still. The pike remained, quivering in his chest.

"There!" A pike came whizzing out of the dark, and Ratcatcher ducked, allowing it to vanish into the darkness. He grinned as he did so; another idiot had just disarmed himself. "That's not a spear, you fool!" called an another voice even as the weapon clattered to the floor. "Head for the door!"

Pounding footsteps told Ratcatcher the man obeyed. A hand around the man's throat told the unfortunate guardsman that Ratcatcher had gotten there first. A short, sharp crack cut the silence, and then the man dropped to the floor. Flexing his fingers, Ratcatcher glided back into the dark to wait for more prey.

The scraping of boot on stone alerted him to movement to his left, and he stopped. There it was again—faint footsteps and even fainter breathing. The light in the corridor was strong now, but the joy of the kill was upon him. He wanted to finish this pack of fools. Another two steps and he rose up behind the guardsman, whose halting, measured steps betrayed a quaking fear.

"Captain?" he called out, his voice trembling. "Bronze Sparrow? Aejus? Are you out there?"

"Not any more," Ratcatcher hissed in his ear as he snapped the man's neck with savage glee. The guardsman toppled slowly, turning as best he could to gaze on his killer, and then sank to the floor.

"One left," Ratcatcher said aloud, and stooped to retrieve the fallen guard's pike.

With a sudden, shuddering crunch, the last guard's pike came down through Ratcatcher's back, just to the left of his spine, and punched through his rib cage. Gagging in shock, Ratcatcher dropped the pike he'd scooped up and instead clasped his fingers around the metal point protruding from his chest. Staggering, he straightened and turned as best he could. The pain was surprising, something he thought he was long past. He could taste blood—his new body's blood, cold and congealed—on his lips, and could actually feel the shaft of the pike grinding against bone. It was not a pleasant sensation.

"That should stop you long enough," the guard said with some satisfaction, her arms folded across her chest. It disturbed Ratcatcher slightly that what he could see of her was tinged with rot and disease. Her flesh looked soft and sunken, the fabric of her uniform increasingly threadbare with every second he gazed at her. *She looks dead and rotted already*, he thought. *This is life in the eyes of the Abyss.* "Try skulking around in the dark with four feet of pine through your gut," she added.

"A... terrible... idea," he agreed, gasping, and reached behind him with his left hand. The wood of the pike's shaft was slick with blood, but he gripped it firmly and tottered forward. Confident she'd dealt with the unliving menace, the guard stood her ground.

"It... hurts," he continued, limping a bit more than was perhaps strictly necessary. He stretched out his free arm and moaned, piteously. "I'm getting cold."

"Serves you right, you murdering bastard," she replied, and nodded primly. Ratcatcher took another step, and then another, almost falling to his knees. The guard smiled like a righteous god gazing down upon a blasphemer's misfortune, and shook her head. "You'll be much warmer when we throw your body on the pyres."

"Yours first," Ratcatcher muttered, and swept her into a loveless embrace. His bloody lips caught her scream even as he held her to him, and then he thrust forward with the pike. He could feel it slide through his body and into hers with a rasp, and then the blood on his tongue was warm and fresh as she died.

"A dead man doesn't care about a piece of wood in him, you know," he said to the corpse sagging off the pike shaft that ran him through. "You may find that out more fully soon."

He wiped his hands on her tunic and, ignoring the pain her weight on the pikestaff caused him, snapped the heavy wood in two. The cadaver, still spurting blood, fell to the floor, and he gingerly drew the remainder of the pike's handle from his back. After a moment's reflection, he dropped it on the floor near his latest victim. It rolled to a stop against her shoulder, and Ratcatcher looked down on it.

"Dead men lie, too," he said, and licked her blood off his lips.

✦

The troop that followed had, inexplicably, not contained a necromancer either, though the captain had cursed both loud and long about this fact. He'd also complained about the incompetence of the first captain into the room, and commanded his troops competently. Torches were lit around the door, a defensive hedge of pikes and axes set up, and a runner dispatched for more help and the quote-unquote sheep-humping, pox-ridden weasel of a necromancer, whose assistance was clearly needed immediately. He could smell the blood in the air, this one could, and he'd let it be known he had no intention of seeing any more shed.

That had been his thought, anyway, until, at Ratcatcher's amused command, the very shadows had crept out from under the tables and smothered the torches. Under cover of darkness, a rain of dissecting knives and bone saws fell upon his men. They went down, howling, under the onslaught, and a scalpel with a blade of black glass took him in the eye, last of all. He'd barely hit the floor before the figure of his killer strode past, careful not to step in the pooling gore for fear of leaving tracks.

Ratcatcher had no idea how he'd called the shadows to douse the torches. He'd simply wished it devoutly, and as if in answer to his prayer, the shadows came. He'd seen the not-dead in the prince's service do similar things on occasion, and found himself curious as to how many of their powers he was now heir to. A good many, he'd found himself hoping as he gazed down the corridor looking for a hiding place.

The hall was long, marred by many cross-corridors and supported by rows of towering stone columns. The echoing toll of alarm bells spurred Ratcatcher to move quickly. He'd been to Sijan once before, to defile the corpse of an enemy of his prince, and those memories had led him when his conscious mind could not. He'd turned down a narrow corridor, slipping from shadow to shadow, then had slunk through a servants' entrance and down an access corridor paneled in rotting wood and peeling black lacquer. This brought him to yet another portion of the vast necropolis, where the scent of incense hung heavy on the air, mixed with the stench of burned human flesh. There he'd hidden himself behind yet another of the omnipresent pillars—for a people so concerned with interment, they built an unholy number of things reaching into the heavens—and now waited to regain his strength and a sense of what he should do next.

He was garbed now in the black hooded tunic and leggings of one of the men he'd killed. A snapped neck had ensured no unsightly tears or bloodstains. The man's boots were on his feet, and the ragged hole in his chest had long since stopped bleeding. A sneaking suspicion struck him that it never would heal, though, and that this body was going to prove less durable than the one he'd originally been given. He'd seen others of this sort over the years, and they went through bodies like a fat man went through roasted chickens.

That, however, was an issue for after his escape from Sijan. He had more pressing concerns at the moment. There were doubtless hundreds of soldiers looking for him, in addition to sorcerers, necromancers, whatever Immaculate priests were in the area, and the inevitable handful of Dragon-Blooded present to make sure that their great-great-great-grandfather was properly reduced to greasy ash. Looking both left and right, he stepped out from his place of concealment and strode, purposefully, toward where vague memories told him the docks could be found.

Chapter Ten

The rats were nearly all gone now, and the survivors had grown clever at fleeing her presence. The spiders she'd devoured as well, though their numbers had always been small. Piles of small, cracked bones and spatters of dried blood marked her trail through the ossuary maze, a crazed, meandering path that spoke of no plan save her insatiable hunger.

Twice, Shamblemerry had approached the stairs that led up to the temple where she'd fought the Sidereal priest, and twice she'd fled in fear before her foot touched the first step. He'd toyed with her, she realized. All of her bravado, all of her strength, had been nothing. He'd let her exhaust herself, like a clever child performing for a stern tutor, and then unveiled his own power as casually as if he were performing a morning's exercises.

He'd left her for dead, then, and that had given her time to drag herself down into the catacombs, where she could wait, and heal, and plan revenge. But every time she thought of facing the priest again, her guts turned to water and her blood turned to ice. She'd known pain at his hands the likes of which she'd never imagined, and the memory of it haunted her brief hours of sleep.

Part of her was well aware that her fear was foolish. She knew that he could not possibly still be waiting for her at the top of the stairs, but that still did not allay her fear. It had been weeks, if not months, since their duel, and surely he had more pressing things to do than to stand guard against her possible return. But that didn't keep the small voice of panic from whispering *He's waiting* in her ear every time she thought about a new ascent. No, she decided, it was far better to wait down here in the dark.

And what if he comes looking for you? the voice of panic had asked, and for that she had no answer.

◆

There was a crack in the ceiling of Chejop Kejak's sky chamber, and he found it moderately worrisome. The line was barely visible, a hairline-thin vein of white that cut across the carefully painted blue-black sky so delicately that at first he'd doubted that it was truly there.

A second, closer look (levitation was, he decided, one of the most practical of his arts) revealed the blemish, and inspired in him a minor tingling of dread. He'd resolved to have the damage repaired immediately, of course, and within minutes temple artisan-monks were at work with brushes of a single hair's thickness, restoring unity to the beautifully rendered image of the night sky. It took them several hours, for Kejak demanded no less than perfection, and only when he was satisfied did the craftsmen make obeisance and leave. Satisfied, the man who had created the Immaculate Order folded himself onto a cushion and sank into meditation.

When he opened his eyes, the crack was back. His shout of rage could be heard seven chambers away.

He'd since made several attempts to have it repaired, each more drastic than the last, and all had failed. He'd set priests to watching the ceiling, but inevitably they fell asleep or were called away by emergencies (two suspicious fires had spontaneously flared to life in the chamber itself, one blossoming from the very bolster that Kejak had used for meditation) or otherwise took their eyes from the ceiling just long enough, and then suddenly the crack was there anew.

Worse, it was growing. At first it had been perhaps a handspan in length, no more. Now it stretched for over a yard, and its rate of growth was accelerating. After his initial fury had subsided, Kejak had assigned a team of astrologers to study the patterns of stars the fissure divided, and tasked them with discovering what it meant. Thus far their efforts had yielded nothing, but they assured him that soon, very soon, they would have results.

They had better, Kejak thought to himself as he stood in the chamber's center and gazed upwards. He'd dismissed the monks for the moment, and relished the solitude. *This had been a place of power and serenity once. What had happened to it?*

Involuntarily, his mind drifted to Holok, and he wondered how his old friend—no, not friend; his duties and responsibilities meant that no man could truly be his friend. How his old acquaintance and ally was faring. Holok had not taken Kejak's decision well, which was the main reason Kejak had decided to handle the situation in precisely that manner. Holok was stolid, reliable and stern, but he always did his best work when his back was against the wall. The fewer resources he was given, the more he relied on his own considerable talents, and the more determined he was to succeed.

That, in the end, was why Kejak had sent him out into the wild charged with the impossible. He didn't actually expect Holok to bring in the boy. He did, however, expect something. Holok always brought back *something* at times like this.

A flicker of motion caught his eye, and Kejak looked up. A tiny fleck of blue-black paint was drifting down from the ceiling, visible only because it had crossed in front of one of the many hanging globes representing the planetary Five Maidens and other celestial spheres.

Frowning, he licked the tip of his finger and extended it. The paint fleck wafted right to it, and stuck there. He held it up before his eyes and examined it. It was paint, nothing more—made from the finest and rarest pigments, yes, but still just paint. The mystery was infuriating.

"And the sky is indeed falling," Kejak said, and left his chamber to find the artisans once again.

✦

The Prince of Shadows was not amused, not in the slightest. The evening's marionette show had singularly failed to distract him from his concerns, and even the screams of the untalented puppeteer provided him with no diversion. It was, he decided, a singularly unpleasant evening.

"Take three fingers and let him go," he directed. "Oh, and have Pelesh pay him. The full amount. Otherwise it will be impossible to get other entertainers to journey here, much less competent ones."

His torturer looked up, dead eyes wide and questioning beneath her hood, and paused in the application of a glowing coal to the puppeteer's left foot. The young man had been stripped naked save for a loincloth and strapped to a granite slab with many leather thongs. In an attempt to raise her master's spirits, the torturer had been tracing lines of poetry the prince had composed on the offending puppet master's body. The combination of the torturer's poor handwriting and the prince's tendencies for long couplets had, however, rendered this less pleasing in execution than it had been in concept, and now the prince was bored.

With a wordless grunt, the torturer put down both the book of poetry she'd been quoting from and the long tongs holding the hot coal, and reached for a rack holding a palisade of knives and saws. Her hand paused over the many options available, and she looked questioningly at her prince.

"Oh, a sharp one, I suppose," he said in response to her unasked question. "He wasn't that bad. And have his equipment loaded back onto his wagon."

Dumbly, the torturer nodded and selected a scalpel with a thin blade of obsidian. She hefted it once, tested its edge against her dead flesh, and then went to work again.

The screams followed the prince as he left the chamber, still bored. His feet took him, as they often did, down the corridor past his throne room, and into the chamber that had once been his astrologer's. The doors here still sagged on their broken hinges, and the shattered wreck of the orrery still dotted the floor. He'd ordered that it remain thus as a reminder to himself not to be overconfident, but he suspected that it had helped encourage Unforgiven Blossom to leave. He'd discussed resurrecting the device with her, but refused to let her bury the pieces of this one, and it had no doubt rankled her.

He'd had word of her travels, of course. The spies he'd sent forth reported back to him, those that did not fall prey to birds or hunters or other servants of darkness who guarded their secrets jealously. She was well, and that was enough for the moment; soon enough she'd rejoin his service and return to him what she had stolen, though precisely why he'd allowed her to take it in the first place still bothered him. It had been a dream, he remembered, but a dream of *what*?

Other news had been more slender. Of the boy there was no sign, though the Fair Folk tribes to the northeast were gathering for some unknown reason. That was an interesting development, but he was wary of sending his creatures too close to such things. The Fair Folk had ways of capturing his servants and turning them to their own ends. Once they'd sent him a week of stolen nightmares through the eyes of one of his flying spies. "A rich gift to a noble ally," read the card he'd received the day the nightmares started, and the disdain of the Fair Folk who'd written it was apparent.

A faint scent of cooked meat, overlaid with hot pitch, drifted past, and the prince noted with some pleasure that the torturer had decided to cauterize and seal the wounds on the puppeteer's hands. It would prevent him from dying of gangrene before he and his wagon reached civilization, and that, after all, was the point.

Something bumped against his foot. Surprised, the prince looked down. It was a mirrored sphere, the one that had once represented Mercury, Maiden of Journeys in Unforgiven Blossom's orrery. He had vague memories of it being destroyed, but apparently he was mistaken, for here it was, in one piece. He nudged it gently away. It rolled for a moment, then came right back to stop against his foot.

"Odd," the prince noted, and stepped around it. The floors in his citadel were all flat, he was quite certain. Stonemasons who fear for more than just their lives do good work. There was no way the floor could be angled so sharply that the ball would simply roll back, and besides, none of the other surviving planets or moons were rolling on their own.

Carefully, he stepped around to the other side of the ball, and gave it firmer kick in the opposite direction. Again it rolled a few feet, and again it came back.

"Even odder," he said, and bowed to the inevitable. Stooping, he lifted the sphere and stared into the reflective surface, equally curious and irritated. For a moment it showed him only his face, distorted, but then the scene shifted. He saw Unforgiven Blossom, and a bearded man's face that he did not recognize, and finally the gnawed and tattered carcass of a dead rat.

"Oh. Him." The prince dropped the sphere with disdain. It crashed into fragments at his feet, and he exited the room and continued down the corridor.

Several hours later, amongst the fragments, something moved.

Chapter Eleven

"Dace, would you please tell me what's going on before my feet fall off?" Yushuv adjusted his pack, grunted, and hurried to keep up. Ahead of him on the path, Dace strode forward like an automaton, his long legs carrying him over the ground with surprising speed, despite the weight of the pack he carried. In his left hand was a sturdy redwood staff he'd hewn himself; in his right a short but wicked-looking hooked sword. Yushuv, for his part, carried his father's bow, strung and with an arrow nocked. He'd rigged the quiver to sit to the side of his pack, so that he could still reach his arrows easily, but this meant that every fourth stride or so his elbow hit the bottom of the quiver. It was an annoyance, and if it resulted in any arrows being spilled, it would be more than that.

Without turning, Dace called back, "What's going on is that you're learning a valuable lesson in the fine art of tactical retreat. The Fair Folk could have turned you and I into pincushions back there before we'd known they were there." He slowed a bit as the path they followed—the same one he'd pursued Yushuv along so recently—began zigzagging its way up a wooded hillside. "So we are leaving as fast as we can and headed for a rendezvous with someone else who's taken a protective interest in you, in the slim hope that it's the site they want and not us."

"What if it's not the site?"

Dace stopped and stared at Yushuv levelly. "Then treasure your dreams tonight, boy, because they're the last ones you'll ever have."

Duly chastened, Yushuv picked up his pace. "Are they pacing us, then? Can they pick us off along the trail?"

"Damnation, boy, you're full of questions. Yes, they can pick us off along the trail, though I don't think that's their game. The

Fair Folk aren't into just killing their enemies, not in the same way people are. They're after dreams, Yushuv, dreams and things like them. So they'd rather push us and harry us, make us jump at shadows and go half-mad with fear. They'll come for us only when we're ready to drop, exhausted from chasing phantoms. It'll make the dreams taste better, or so I'm told."

"What happens if we don't frighten?" Yushuv stopped for a second. He'd heard a rustling in the woods off to the right, but when he turned to see if there was anything there, all he could see was dark greenery and darker night. Impatiently, Dace caught his elbow and yanked him forward again.

"Then they'll get bored and kill us after all."

✦

They'd split off from the main trail some hours earlier, after a quick meal of jerky and water, and had been heading roughly southwest on what could only be described as an animal track that even animals preferred to shun. Dace struggled visibly to resist the temptation to hack his way through the obstinate vegetation, and on one occasion it had taken a pointed reminder from Yushuv that they were trying to leave as few signs of their passage as possible to prevent him from doing so. Thick spider webs with sticky, greasy strands often barred their way, and Dace cautioned Yushuv not to disturb their inhabitants: fist-sized spiders with green and gold markings and fangs that would make a serpent envious. After his first near-miss with one of the creatures, Yushuv needed no further encouragement to leave them be.

"Dace, I'm getting tired," he called out. The first light of dawn was steadily forcing its way through the forest canopy, and with it came an unholy cacophony of shrieks, whistles, calls and howls from the forest's usual residents.

"No, you're not." Dace plodded on, grimly determined. "Remember what I taught you about using your Essence to sustain yourself? This is a perfect time to practice. Feel it inside you. Use that energy. It will restore you better than a night's sleep. Just don't take too much, or you'll want to sprint for an hour and then collapse. I'm not carrying you, in case you were wondering."

Yushuv nodded. "I'll try." Without slackening his pace, he shut his eyes, trusting his other senses to guide him. He could feel the warm store of energy inside him. It always felt like it was hovering in his gut, though Dace said that it was kept in the liver, or perhaps in the heart. But none of that mattered now. What did matter was that he could feel the swirling currents of power that now belonged to him. In his mind's eye, he could see each shimmering mote of energy dancing gracefully on its own, intricately ordered path. He could sense the threads binding them together, threads that were somehow of his own crafting. Gently, he reached out with his mind and plucked one of those shining ephemerae and drew it forth. Even as he did so, he could feel its power pouring into his body as a whole, a surge of gentle warmth that banished pain from his joints and weariness from his muscles. Even the dull headache that had plagued him for hours vanished, and he was filled with a sudden wild exuberance. He *could* run all night, he knew now, and he could run all day as well. And with day coming up and a light pack on his back, why not put himself to the test? Surely the Fair Folk wouldn't be able to keep up with that! Surely—

Eyes still closed, he walked straight into Dace's back. With a grunt, he opened his eyes and took a half-step backwards. "Wha—"

"Shhh." Dace held up his left hand in a silencing gesture. "Get your bow ready, and turn to cover my back."

"Of course," With practiced ease, Yushuv spun on his heel, an arrow already nocked. His eyes scanned the dim expanse of the forest floor. "There's nothing here."

"There will be in a minute." Dace gently laid down his walking stick and re-sheathed the short blade he'd been carrying, only to take his daiklave in hand. It hummed, palpably. "Do you remember that when we first took this trail, you commented that it seemed completely deserted?"

"Yes. Why?"

Dace pointed with the daiklave to an opening in the path ahead. "That's why. We've found some wolf spiders."

Yushuv stole a peek over his shoulder and around Dace's side. The path ahead broadened considerably, opening up to a small clearing half the size of the one that had formerly housed their camp. Every entrance to the clearing, however, was bound with thick, ropy strands of silk the color of an old man's rotten teeth. Beyond that he could see black shapes the size of large dogs scurrying back and forth, chittering with excitement.

A sudden sound in the bushes made Yushuv turn, but it was only a squirrel. He glared at it, and it scampered out of sight. Nervous now, he scanned the woods again, then began looking up in the trees. Surely spiders that large couldn't climb, but the thought of having something like that drop out of the canopy onto his back made his skin crawl. Better safe than sorry, he decided, and began wildly looking from side to side and up and down. After a minute, a sudden thought struck him. "Dace?"

"Yes?"

"Do wolf spiders like to eat Fair Folk?"

Despite himself, the older man laughed. "You know, I don't think that question has ever been satisfactorily answered, though right now I'd love to know. I do know that wolf spiders like to eat anything else that moves, but at least they're not poisonous. Not so far as anyone's reported, anyway. The pack we've got in front of us is big enough to be dangerous, but not overwhelming. We could probably charge right in and take them."

"I don't like the sound of that 'probably,' Dace. Why don't we just go around?"

"Because wolf spiders aren't stupid. There are web traps all over the forest near the clearing. Try to go around and you'll step in something sticky that won't let your foot go until a week after you're dead."

"That doesn't sound so good either," Yushuv observed. "So if we can't go in and we can't go around, what can we do?" He pondered for a moment. "Set the web on fire?"

Dace nodded. "That's good tactical thinking. However, the web's between us and where we want to go. If we torch it, we stand a good chance of having the flame get out of hand, and chase us right back into the Fair Folk's arms."

"But the forest is green! It won't burn."

"Are you willing to bet your life on that?"

Yushuv shook his head. "No. And I don't want to step into one of those web traps you talked about with a wall of flame behind me."

"Good, good. So what else can we do?" Dace had once again become the teacher, the peril they faced nothing more an exercise. Yushuv banished his fear and thought furiously. Nothing the wolf spiders could do to him, he decided, would be as dangerous as disappointing Dace now.

After a moment, he said, "We make them come out."

"And how do we do that?" Dace's voice held just a trace of satisfaction, which Yushuv knew meant more than effusive praise from most men.

"We get them mad. Let me get past you." Dace sidestepped, and Yushuv stepped around him. He shrugged out of his pack, which he placed on the path in front of him, adjusted his quiver, and knelt down so that the bulk of the pack gave him some cover.

"Excellent thinking," rumbled Dace, who laid down his pack as well. "Now what?"

"Now I get them mad. How many should I shoot?"

"As many as you can. That's basic tactics, boy. If you've got range and the enemy doesn't, then you kill him at range. If he's got range and you don't, you get in close. Now, you've got range with that bow of yours. Put it to work."

In response, Yushuv took an instant to clutch at the fetish of bone and sinew hanging around his neck, and then looked up and drew. He sighted along the arrow at the first murky shape he could see moving beyond the curtain of webs, waited a moment and then, whispering a prayer, released.

With a thrum, the arrow leapt forward and pierced the spider's swollen abdomen. Green ichor fountained out from the spot where the shaft buried itself, and the nerve-wracking chittering was split by a high-pitched whine of pain. Before the spiders could react, Yushuv had already drawn another arrow and loosed it, and then a third. One took the largest spider through one of its great, glowing eyes; the other impaled a beast at the base of its head. It collapsed with a hiss, while around it the clamor of angry wolf spiders rose to a terrifying din.

"Good, boy, good," Dace whispered, stealing a glance over his shoulder. "Use the power in you."

And indeed, Yushuv could feel those swirling motes of energy flowing through his arms and into his bow. He nocked, sighted, drew and shot, again and again without pause. He was an automaton, the perfect mechanical archer, and all enemies in his sight died. Some took shelter behind the corpses of their comrades, but his arrows arched high and found them. Others fled, but not as fast as an arrow could fly. Down they tumbled, and Yushuv felt neither pity nor joy. He could feel the bow in his hands, feel the grain of its wood as if it were his own flesh, and his arrows were the servants he sent out into the world to do his terrible bidding.

Suddenly, roughly, a hand on his shoulder broke his concentration. His shot went wide into the trees, and he stumbled roughly to his right. "They're charging, boy! Get behind me!"

Yushuv stood stock-still in momentary disorientation, and with a roar Dace leapt past him. A shove in passing sent Yushuv sprawling to safety, and he desperately tried to keep his remaining arrows from tumbling out of his quiver.

The surviving wolf spiders were indeed charging, boiling up the path at where Dace now stood. His daiklave held high, he put one foot atop the piled packs and bellowed a challenge.

The wolf spiders took it. The first leapt at his throat even as the second hurled itself at the tempting target of his foot. Laughing, Dace stepped back and kicked the packs forward, catching the second spider in mid-leap and throwing it back. His daiklave came out in a broad, flat arc that intersected the wolf spider's leap, slicing through its front legs and shearing off half of its head. It spun to the left and crashed into the bushes, ruined head gushing ichor and legs thrashing wildly.

A third wolf spider had been holding back, but when Dace's sword decapitated its packmate, it charged. Dace's blade came down too slowly to catch it, and once inside his guard it pounced, hurling itself against his chest. The weight of the wolf spider bore him down, and with terrible eagerness it surged forward to sink its fangs into his throat. With a desperate push,

Dace shoved an armored forearm into the thing's maw instead, and he could feel the metal give under the relentless pressure of its bite. Releasing his grip on the daiklave with his other hand, he curled his fingers into a fist and began relentlessly smashing the wolf spider's eyes. With each blow the beast shuddered and redoubled its efforts, but Dace was relentless. Wet, cold jelly showered his face with every strike, but with cold precision he finished his task, then brought his fist down on top of the wolf spider's savaged head. It let go of his greave with a squeal, and backed away frantically.

That proved to be a fatal mistake. Rearing up, Dace reached out for his daiklave, swinging it in a wild arc and impaling the wounded spider in the center of the path. It kicked once, piteously, and died.

Shaking his hand in attempt to cleanse it of excessive vitreous humor, Dace looked around for more opponents and found none. He did, however, see Yushuv sitting in the path next to a dead wolf spider, his dagger buried neatly in the center of its head. The boy looked up. "I thought you were having too much fun to interfere."

Dace shook his head. "That'll teach me to try to impress my student. Are they all dead?"

Yushuv nodded. "Dead or fled. Though we made quite a racket. I'm sure that if the Fair Folk had lost our trail, they've found it again."

"No doubt. Let's move on before scavengers arrive. In this forest, they tend not to be picky about whether their prey is still moving or not."

Yushuv pulled his dagger out of the spider's head and carefully wiped it on the animal's thick, coarse fur. "Let me get my arrows back. I have a feeling I'm going to need them."

"Of course." Dace stooped to take up his pack again—it wasn't too badly spotted with spider ichor, he noted to his satisfaction—and examined his dented greave. That had been entirely too close. He had been showing off for Yushuv and it had nearly cost him. That was a very bad lesson to teach. Grimly, he resolved to be more focused in the future. More than his pride depended on it.

Chapter Twelve

"I don't do priests, not even for sticky buns."

The girl gazed at Holok over the rim of her teacup, the look in her eyes unreadable. She'd looked to be no more than seven years old in the street; here she looked perhaps nine, but in either case there was a coldness in her eyes that he found disturbing in a child.

"That's not why I brought you here." Holok resisted the urge to shudder. He knew of those in the Empire—and even a few of his peers—who indulged in such things, but the thought never held the slightest appeal for him. He'd been born on a farm, fourteen centuries ago, and in some ways he was still a farmer's son at heart.

They were seated in a bustling teahouse near the docks, their table located outside under a brightly colored awning. Both Holok and his companion sat on benches, a teapot and thick clay cups on the table before them. The girl clutched a sticky bun possessively, and Holok found himself idly wondering if she'd ever get her fingers and tunic clean again.

"Oh?" She gave him a look that was one part curiosity, two parts defiance. "Don't tell me this is a new temple charity."

Despite himself, Holok chuckled, and took a sip of tea. It warmed him, and he found himself fighting the irrational urge to wipe the honey from the girl's chin. "It's not. I just want to ask you some questions."

"Really? Why not just ask another priest? You monks are supposed to have all the answers, after all." She slurped her tea, noisily, and wiped her mouth with the back of her arm.

"Because none of them are seven."

"Eight."

"Pardon?"

"I'm eight," she repeated firmly. "Seven was a long time ago."

"Ah." For some reason, Holok didn't know how to respond to that. "And your name is?" he said lamely, floundering for a way to recapture the rudder of the conversation.

"Leeshu."

"Leeshu. That's a pretty name." He smiled gamely, took another sip of tea, and wondered what the hell he was trying to do here.

"It means 'muskrat.' It's not pretty at all. Can I have another sticky bun?" She took a final, ferocious bite of the one Holok had bought her from the street vendor and gazed at him with a very serious expression. Her hair was short and spiky, and her dark eyes were huge for her face. She wore the typical garb of a street ragamuffin; the cast-off tunic of someone much larger, belted at the waist with clothesline. Strips of cloth served as makeshift sandals.

He sighed and rested his elbows on the table. "We might be able to do that, if you're willing to answer a few questions." She started to speak and he held up a hand in warning. "No, no, it's not about the Immaculate philosophy, and it's probably not about anything you could imagine a priest asking about. But it is very important." He paused. "A boy's life is at stake."

And that, he thought, was true enough, in its own way.

"Huh." Leeshu lifted the teacup and drank, leaving honey-sticky prints on it when she set it down. "Why are you asking me about a boy?"

"Well," Holok replied, "he ran away from home, too, and I need to find him."

She blinked at him. "Is that it?"

Holok's brow furrowed in surprise. "Why, yes."

"Wow. You priests are dumber than I thought."

"I beg your pardon?"

For the moment, the girl ignored him. Daintily, she sucked on her fingers to get the honey off, then wiped her hands on her tunic. When she was finished she looked up at him, and there was pity in her eyes. "Everyone runs away from home for a different reason. Asking me why I did isn't going to help you find him. I don't think he would have run away for the reasons I did, anyway." Her gaze was old again, and Holok found himself briefly thankful that she hadn't told him why she left home. He'd killed thousands of men in his lifetime, and yet he still felt his blood run cold at the thought of horrors that could drive a child onto the streets so young.

"I'm sorry," he found himself saying. "I shouldn't have bothered you. I'll buy you that other sticky bun, though. I owe you that much." He reached into his purse and found a slender piece of jade. Too much for a sticky bun, far too much, but perhaps she could take the rest and find some shelter with it. He laid it on the table.

She pushed it back at him. "I haven't earned that yet. You'll want to try the slavers."

"The slavers?" Dimly, Holok was aware that his part in this conversation consisted of buying treats, asking simple questions and looking foolish. Oddly enough, he didn't mind.

Leeshu nodded. "The Guild. They buy children they find on the street and sell them to the Fair Folk. Then they buy what's left back." She reached out and grabbed the jade sliver. "Now, I've earned that. He's probably dead in an alley or something somewhere, but if he's alive the best chance is that the slavers have him." She looked thoughtful for a moment. "They won't treat him badly until they sell him. But once they do..." Her voice trailed off to nothing. "You'd better hurry," she added after a moment's reflection.

"I suppose I'd best," Holok agreed. "Thank you."

"You already thanked me," she said. "You paid me." Then, clutching the jade tightly, she slid down from the bench and ran off into the crowd. Within seconds, she'd vanished.

Holok watched her go, sipped his now-cold tea, and gloomily debated pouring himself another cup. The Guild had no love for Immaculate priests. Truth be told, they had no love for anything save money, and the scraps of jade in his purse wouldn't buy him an hour with a dockside whore, let alone a valuable slave whom the Fair Folk would no doubt pay a pretty penny for.

"That's an unworthy thought for a priest," he said to himself, and hid a chuckle under a cough. Still, it was a practical one. If he was going to chase the boy in this fashion—never mind the fact that he was quite certain that no Guildmaster alive could hold this boy against his will—then he'd have to find some money. He'd also have to figure out how to attach himself to a Guild caravan without either getting his throat slit or wreaking havoc on innumerable Guildsmen who allowed their dislike of Immaculates to get the better of their common sense.

Holok yawned and stretched. He was well aware of the real reason for the antipathy between Guild and Order. It went back to people like him. Just as he, Kejak and their fellows had been crafting the Immaculate Order for centuries, so too had others had their equally ancient and dirty hands deep in the fabric of the Guild. There was no love lost between these factions and their rivalry was played out between itinerant monks and teamsters who had no idea why they despised one another. They just knew that they did, and that was enough to keep the blood flowing. It was a point of some pride to the elders of the Bronze faction that the Immaculate monks usually came out on top in these little brawls, and they basked like proud parents in the glow of each tiny victory.

Pouring himself another cup of tea, he debated his options. There really was no good reason to go hunting the Guild. The odds of them having the boy were, after all, slim. On the other hand, he had few other leads. Traveling to where he'd been stabbed by the young Anathema would do no good; it had been weeks since they'd fought. No doubt the boy was gone and the trail was destroyed, and he had little desire to go trudging back into that swamp for no reason. Beyond that, he had no idea at all where his quarry had gone, and as a result one direction was as good as another, really.

So that, perhaps, was why he had decided that Leeshu's— he wondered if her name really did mean 'muskrat,' and if so, why anyone would do that to a child—suggestion was worth following. Guidance, he knew, came from mysterious sources. Perhaps the Maidens were working through a slip of a girl to direct him this time.

"Or perhaps I'm just looking for trouble," he said aloud, and signaled to the young woman who bustled about the shop, refilling teapots and taking money. She scurried over with gratifying speed.

"Can I get you more tea, revered one?" she said, and inclined her head at just the right angle to show proper deference to a monk. She was short, with red hair tied back in a scarf, and she wore gray. A wax tablet was in her left hand and a stylus in her right, and she smiled when she spoke. Holok found it charming, and instantly wondered what she was really up to.

"More tea is unnecessary, though I thank you. I do have a question that you might be able to answer for me, though. Two, now that I think on it."

"Of course, revered one." She tucked the pad and stylus back up her sleeve and nodded. "What can I help you with?"

"You'd make a remarkably good acolyte, you know." Holok gave her his most paternal smile, then shook his head and got back to business. "Ahem. In any case, I do have a pair of questions. I've only newly arrived, you see, and am still a bit... disoriented."

"That would be the tea, sir," the young woman said primly. "It sometimes has that effect on... older men."

Not ones as old as I, Holok thought. He forced a chuckle and shook his head. "No, no. I mean I need to find something, and was hoping you could help me." He jingled his purse in what would have been a significant manner, had there been much jade in it.

"Revered one!"

"No, no, no! Is everyone intent on misunderstanding me today? Listen, child, I have two very simple questions for you. The first is simple: What route do the Guild caravans take out of town? You don't even have to tell me. Just point. It's probably safer that way."

"East," she stammered. "They go east. No point to going along the water, they say."

"Good, good." Holok's voice was soothing. "Now, for my other question." He dropped his voice conspiratorially. "Can you tell a poor bored priest where he might find a place where men gamble on dice?"

Chapter Thirteen

Sijan's docks were less heavily guarded than Ratcatcher had anticipated, which gave him hope for the first time since he had risen from the dead. Rows of black barges bobbed gently at their moorings, their gangplanks drawn up on deck and their crews scanning the waterfront anxiously. But there were only a handful of soldiers here, patrolling the length of the stone quay with nervous footsteps. They had halberds and hand-axes, the better to hack apart unliving flesh should it materialize in front of them, and they traveled in groups of three. Long gaps separated the patrols, which were frequently interrupted by catcalls from the decks of the barges.

The docks themselves were impressive, in a somber sort of way. The entire waterfront was constructed from massive blocks of obsidian. Inlaid in the black stone were incantations, symbols and wards against the restless dead, the better to reassure the spirit world and the living that this was an area where the dead kept to their place. It was an open secret that Sijan dealt in necromancy, and that a great many of the dead who came into the city left it under their own power. The difference was that in most cases, the various flavors of walking dead who were reborn here had either paid for the privilege (and so were treated as honored guests) or were brought back from the grave under tightly controlled conditions, and were thus immediately clapped into servitude before they could cause any trouble. Most of that sort was too dull to cause much trouble in any case, and could easily be dealt with even by guards as idiotic as the ones he'd been afflicted with. A few prods with a halberd, and that sort moved sulkily right along. As for the other sort, they were rarely inclined to cause much of a fuss. This was due in large part to the fact that their resurrections were also overseen by necromancers who could at least theoretically enforce good behavior by ripping their freshly raised souls right back out of their bodies at the first signs of intransigence. Sijan's morticians and lords of dead magic were well prepared to handle any situation dealing with their clients, living, dead or somewhere-in-between. It was the accidents that caused them problems, and he, Ratcatcher, was an accident on a scale that this city had never seen.

All of this passed through Ratcatcher's mind in a fevered instant, as he calculated his chances for escape. He stood in the shadowed entrance of one of the many embalming houses that lined the dockside. Under normal circumstances, the spot where he crouched would be busy with wagons bringing in fresh corpses, bustling morticians with their apprentices and weeping family members. Tonight, however, the city of the dead was in a panic. The gates had been shut, and all traffic by land or river had been ordered to wait where it stood until the rogue dead man had been brought to heel. Patrols of guards and sorcerers scoured the city's heart, intent on making sure that they had the appropriate number of walking dead within the city limits. Even from where he stood, Ratcatcher could hear the shouts, slamming doors and occasional screams as the search continued. Soon, he knew, they'd decide that the city proper was clear and start looking elsewhere, and then he would be in trouble.

Again, he looked out at the river, whose waters seemed a dirty, greasy gray to his tainted eyes. There were fifty yards of open stone between him and the barges. If he crossed that without incident, there was still no way to get onto a ship, and even on a ship there was no guarantee of safety. Besides, Ratcatcher was quite certain the city fathers of Sijan would be happy to drop a torch and a few barrels of pitch onto any barge he found his way onto, just to make sure that he was dealt with permanently. He did still have his guard's uniform, but it was torn and soaked in blood, and any prolonged interaction would quickly expose him as a fraud.

"Hoy!"

The shout came from a rather stout woman on the nearest

of the barges, whose ornate robes led Ratcatcher to believe she was the ship's captain. The patrol nearest her vessel broke off their pattern to walk to the quayside opposite her ship. "Yes?" one of the guardsman inquired pleasantly, his tone as bored as could be.

"When do I get to push off? I don't have anything to offload. You've gotten all the stiffs from my ship's hold that you're going to." Her voice was loud and brassy, and Ratcatcher could see the lead guardsman wince.

"You'll be allowed to leave as soon as the current situation is dealt with. That should be soon."

"Soon my ass. I've got a half-dozen pickups downstream that aren't getting any fresher, and I'll be damned if I have to wash corpse-sludge out of the cabins again. Either you get me permission to cast off, or I'll just cut the hawsers and deal with it when I get back." Around her, the crew leapt to the tasks of departure, while the guards hemmed, hawed and stammered. Finally, one muttered, "The hell with it," and cast off the ropes. Slowly, accompanied by outraged shouts from the crews of the other vessels, the barge caught the current and slowly moved out toward the center of the river.

And in that instant, Ratcatcher saw his opportunity. Casually, he walked out from cover toward the point on the dock closest to the now-departed barge.

"Hey there!" It was the recently humiliated captain of the patrol, looking to save face. "Where are you going?"

Ratcatcher turned but did not stop walking. "I was told to come out here to get some air," he said, hoping the lie would buy him enough time to get to the water's edge. The clatter of boots on stone told him that he might have seriously miscalculated.

"Where's the rest of your patrol?" The voice was closer now, and Ratcatcher could hear the suspicion in it. "Halt, and let me have a look at you."

"I think we'd both regret that," Ratcatcher replied lightly, and broke into a sprint.

"He's headed for the river! Stop him!" The captain urged his men forward, but it was too late. Ratcatcher reached the dockside a good ten steps before his nearest pursuer did. He could hear cheers from the barge out in the stream; presumably they were enjoying the guards' embarrassment and hadn't realized why they were chasing him.

He looked back over his shoulder at the panicked looks on the faces of the guards and laughed. Then, arms spread wide, he turned to face his pursuers. "Come get me!"

The lead guard, a tall woman with a figure like a badly sawed plank, took the challenge and lunged forward with a shout. Her halberd caught Ratcatcher square in the sternum, despite his attempts to catch it and soften the blow. With a shriek—an overly long shriek, one observer later said—he toppled backwards into the river, still clutching at his chest and disappeared under the dark waters. Amidst hoots and catcalls from the barges, the guards gathered around the spot where Ratcatcher had gone in, several of them making tentative stabbing gestures toward the surface of the river. A hurried conference later, the senior captain scurried off to make his report to his superiors as to how the fugitive had been spotted with at the riverside and dealt with by the heroic efforts of his troops. They'd cornered the villain, fought valiantly, and dispatched him into the river below.

As he passed under an archway commemorating the seven stages of ritual desiccation, the captain, who bore the unfortunate name of Shimmering Snake, decided against embellishing his story to include the fact that he'd struck the decisive blow. The fact that his soldiers had done so was enough. The threat was dealt with, and at least some of the associated glory would come to rest on his shoulders. That would be enough. After all, he told himself, his men had taken care of whatever that thing was. They'd knocked it into the river, and it hadn't come back up.

And that, as far as he was concerned, was that.

◆

Out in the river's main current, Ratcatcher drifted a full fathom below the surface of the water, occasionally propelling himself forward with a series of lazy kicks. With no need to breathe, he could take his time implementing the next stage in his rough plan, namely, to find the barge and attach himself to its underside, allowing the vessel to carry him downriver. This, he reasoned, would allow him to get somewhere more pleasant than Sijan with a minimum of interruptions, and would grant him sufficient time to think about where to go next.

He'd been sent back for a reason, he knew that. Nemissaries always were, though often the reason in question was a nothing more than a formless urge to wreak havoc. While the thought of simply cutting a swath of destruction across Creation appealed to him, it simply didn't feel right. He'd certainly enjoyed educating the guards in the embalming chamber, but surely murder wasn't his real reason for returning, or he would have felt more of a compulsion to wade into the guards on the dockside. As it was, he'd simply caught the shaft of the halberd as it snaked toward him, and let it push him back rather than pierce his flesh. The guards had seen what they'd wanted to see and with luck, they'd decided that their problem was now dealt with. That would eliminate any pursuit from Sijan and allow him to make a fresh start once he arrived at his destination.

A shadow loomed over him and Ratcatcher quickly realized he'd managed to catch up with the barge already. A couple of kicks bought him enough of a change in depth to allow him to get both hands on the barge's hull, and, to his satisfaction, he saw that enough shellfish had made the vessel their home to allow him a decent handhold. Securing his grip took only an instant, and then he relaxed. The barge would decide where he was going, and until it got there, he could close his eyes, rest, and pretend he was truly dead.

Chapter Fourteen

It was Dace who found the burrow lok's lair, naturally, by walking on it. One moment he was expounding on the ancient wars against the Fair Folk at the time of the Contagion, back before the dawn of the Scarlet Empire, and the next he was plummeting down from the night-dark forest into an even darker cavern. He landed with a grunt and rolled to his feet.

"Dace!" Yushuv called down from the edge of the pit, voice filled with concern. "Are you all right?"

"Yes," he replied warily, unsheathing his daiklave. "That's subject to change, though, depending on what lives here."

"What kind of animal digs a hole like this?" The boy had already perched on the pit's rim, arrow nocked and trained on the darkness ahead of Dace.

"If I'm lucky, one that's long gone. If not, a burrow lok."

"A burrow lok?" Yushuv sounded confused. "What's that?"

A snuffling roar gave the boy his answer, as a wall of fur, fangs and claws exploded out of the darkness at Dace. Its strikes clanged off the metal of his blade, which seemed to be everywhere at once.

With a shout, Yushuv loosed his arrow, which struck the beast just behind its left foreleg. It half-turned on itself in pain, and Yushuv could see dimly its badger-like muzzle and long yellow fangs. Unnerved, he took a step back and reached for another arrow.

With a battle cry of his own, Dace slashed back and forth across the creature's belly, cutting through matted fur and thick fat. Blood gushed forth, and a golden light blazed forth from Dace's brow as he reached within himself for the power he'd so often urged Yushuv to use. "No hesitation, no mercy," he grunted to himself, and drove forward.

At the first blaze of light from the mark on Dace's brow, the burrow lok squealed with pain. It reared up, trying simultaneously to shield its eyes and run away. Blindly, it struck out with one clawed paw, but Dace easily sidestepped the blow and thrust up and in, his sword taking the creature in the center of its chest. He let go of the blade then and stepped back to watch the beast in its final agonies.

Clawing at the massive length of metal that pierced it, the burrow lok retreated two steps and then fell. It opened its mouth in shock and pain, and a rivulet of blood spilled out instead of any sound. Still thrashing madly, it hurled itself one step further and then collapsed, its massive bulk crashing to the ground and then laying still.

Wordlessly, Dace retrieved his daiklave and wiped it clean on the burrow lok's back. He stared at the corpse, the light from his brow—his anima, he'd heard it called—fading with his battle rage. Now the burrow lok was just a poor dead beast, all its fury gone so that nothing remained but blood, fur and bone awaiting the attention of the forest's innumerable scavengers.

"Are you all right?" Dace heard Yushuv calling, and ignored him for the moment. The tunnel the beast had carved continued well down into the dark, and it gave him a sudden idea. Burrow loks, it had been theorized by some brave and foolhardy naturalists whose works he had read, dug not one burrow, but rather intricate networks of tunnels, with many pits near the surface for trapping prey. If that were the case, then it might make very good sense for he and Yushuv to travel via this route, rather than through the forest. The rendezvous with Lilith was still days and leagues off, and an alternate path free from overgrowth and the hazards of the forest might make that journey shorter.

At best, it would shake off the Fair Folk's pursuit. Over the last few days, he'd seen signs deliberately left by the hunters to let him know they were there, and they were growing both more frequent and less subtle. While he hadn't wanted to alarm Yushuv, he'd known that the Fair Folk's patience seemed to be wearing thin, and the forest simply gave them too much of an advantage. If he could lose them in the tunnels, so much the better; if he had to fight them, better that it be done in an enclosed space where their superior numbers wouldn't matter quite so much.

"I'm fine," Dace finally called back up to the surface. "But I want you to find a way down here. "

"Are you *sure* you're all right?" The boy's voice was full of concern. "Do burrow loks have poison?"

"Yes and no, in that order. Now get down here. We're going to be taking a route that the elves should find fairly inhospitable."

"What if the burrow lok had a mate?" Yushuv was already clambering down, though, his efforts showering Dace with loose dirt.

"Then we make our condolences and kill it, too. Would you hurry?"

"It's dark in there," Yushuv pointed out as he leapt, lightly, from the chamber wall.

"And we serve the Unconquered Sun," Dace replied with a dignity he did not quite feel. "Light will be provided for. Trust me."

❖

Four days had elapsed between the fight with the wolf spiders and the encounter with the burrow lok, during which time Yushuv had become increasingly aware of how closely they were being followed. He'd long since learned to distinguish between the noises made by forest creatures and the deliberate rustlings that the Fair Folk made to remind him of their presence. He'd seen them, too, them or their creations. At times impossibly beautiful faces would rise up out of the greenery for an instant and then vanish; at others, flashes of light or twisted, tortured marks on trees and plants would give evidence of some hideous magic. He'd not known what they were until he'd prodded Dace into telling him stories of the Fair Folk, and heard how they were born of the formless chaos outside all Creation. While those who'd chosen to dwell within Creation's borders had bound themselves to shapes, Dace had said, they still served chaos, and could call upon its powers when they chose. Matter would melt and reshape itself under their touch, and so the whorled branches and stone blossoms Yushuv saw gave a clear sign that that the Fair Folk had passed this way. Order and form were blasphemy to them, Dace had said, and they worked toward the day when all of Creation could once again be dissolved in the boiling sea of chaos. Until then, however, they dwelt within Creation's boundaries, often trading with wary humans in artifacts and slaves, and keeping their depredations mild lest the measures which had been used against them once be called down again.

Dace, Yushuv decided, knew far more than anyone who wasn't a priest had a right to. That, however, didn't keep him from trying to soak up the man's knowledge like a cloth sopped up spilled wine.

He wasn't sure that dropping down into the burrow lok's tunnel had been the best idea, but then again, staying in the forest hadn't seemed like a good idea, either. And so they'd gone down into the dark, a faint gleam from the marks on their respective brows illuminating the way and hopefully serving notice to any other dwellers in the darkness that they'd do well to step aside.

The tunnel itself was lined with hard-packed dirt, and sloped gently down from the pit-trap Dace had fallen into. Dace had been right, it seemed; cross-tunnels intersected it at regular intervals, their openings yawning off into the depths. The older man had chosen their path seemingly at random, though Yushuv noticed that more often than not, he selected the tunnel with the floor least likely to take prints. After a few hours, they'd stopped for a cheerless meal in the dark, and Dace had indicated that they'd keep moving until they found another chamber close to the surface.

"We keep going down," Yushuv had said.

"I know," had been Dace's reply, and that effectively ended the conversation.

Now they stood at a junction of massive tunnels, one going straight on and the other curving away to the left. Dace shifted from foot to foot as he assessed the options, and frowned.

"Which do you think, boy?" he asked.

Yushuv sniffed. There seemed to be a faint breeze coming from the tunnel to the left. "There's fresh air down there," he offered noncommittally.

"I know," Dace admitted, frowning. "We're far below where we should be getting breezes, though."

"Maybe it slopes up?"

Dace nodded. "There is that possibility. Shall we?"

Trying not to sound too eager, Yushuv simply replied, "Yes," and waited for Dace to take the lead.

The tunnel did indeed slope up, which Yushuv noted with satisfaction. It also held a regular shape, and after they'd traversed several hundred yards, Dace stopped. Behind him, Yushuv halted as well.

"Did you hear that?" Dace asked, suspicion in his voice.

"Hear what?"

"That." Dace lifted his boot and stepped down solidly. The click of nailed heel on stone was unmistakable. Before Yushuv could respond, Dace was crouched down and brushing away at the dirt with his hand. Within seconds, he'd revealed a square, smooth stone, set into the tunnel floor. A little more work revealed more, set together so tightly that Yushuv couldn't wedge his dagger blade between two of them.

"A road," he said, wonderingly.

"A road indeed," Dace replied. "And where there are roads, there are usually road-builders. Be on your guard."

Yushuv nodded, and once again Dace took point. The road continued to slope ever so gently upward, and now the features of the cavern resolved themselves into recognizable shapes. Pillars supporting the tunnel's roof, carved with strange, serpentine motifs, emerged from the darkness, and the dirt covering of the paving stones grew thinner and thinner until it was hardly there at all. Mosaics now lined the passage, intricate patterns in whorls, circles and coils that had been inlaid with the same cunning as the road itself. All, however, were done entirely in shades of gray, a condition that Yushuv at first blamed on the poor quality of the light. But when Dace called a rest and he went to examine the work, the evidence stood there in stark relief: all gray, no color.

"Who could have built this, Dace?" he asked. "And why?"

"Who, I have no idea," the man replied as he shook a pebble from his boot. "Why, well, presumably to get from one place to another. If I had to guess, I'd say that whoever made this is long gone, and the burrow loks stumbled onto it as they were tunneling back and forth. I don't think that a society of intelligent burrow loks made this place and then devolved into barbarism, if that's what you're asking."

Yushuv smiled at that, and turned away from the mosaic. "The breeze is getting stronger," he said. "I'm going to go up a little ways to see where it's coming from."

"Not too far," Dace warned. "We don't know what's up there."

"No, we don't," Yushuv agreed, and half-sprinted off.

Dace rolled his eyes and returned his attention to the detailed process of extracting the pebble from his boot. Somehow it had gotten wedged in quite thoroughly, and had done a remarkable job of rubbing his big toe raw. Dace had been a soldier all his life, and he could deal with almost any hardship in the field, but when a man's own boots turned on him, he felt a sense of betrayal that reached right down to the bottom of his soul.

"Dace?" The voice came from up ahead, out of sight.

"Yushuv?" He leapt to his feet, still holding the boot. "What's wrong?"

"Nothing's wrong," Yushuv's voice echoed back. "I just think you need to see this. Now."

"Coming," Dace replied, and glared balefully at his boot before turning it upside down one last time. A small brown stone rattled out and plinked itself against the stone floor of the tunnel. "Perhaps it's a good sign after all," Dace told the dank air, and then attacked the serious problem of once more lacing up his boot.

❖

Yushuv had been right, Dace thought as he gazed out at the vista before him. This was something worth seeing, and then some.

They stood underneath an archway carved from gray stone, and looked out on the ruins of what once been a city to rival any on the Blessed Isle. It sat in a titanic crater, its spires crumbling and buildings ruined. No motion disturbed its avenues; no birds flew here or beasts roamed the streets. There was only gray stone and green vines devouring it.

Once the initial rush of awe wore off some, Dace noted that the city had been laid out in an intricate spiral pattern. Roads circled inward from the city's edge, intersected by smaller avenues that radiated out from the massive courtyard at the city's center. Dominating the skyline was a massive step-pyramid, its sides unmarred by even the boldest vines, which echoed the city architect's fascination with circles.

"Where are we, Dace?" Yushuv asked quietly.

"I honestly have no idea," he replied, and frowned. He'd visited the lost city of Rathess once, on a trip he would rather forget, and this place made Rathess look like a collection of mud huts on a flood plain. Frowning, he tried to estimate how far it was to the city center. The archway they stood beneath was halfway up the crater's side, and the road they'd followed lead straight down to the city proper. Small outbuildings, which Dace guessed had once been guard outposts, dotted the city's perimeter, which was also bounded by a cyclopean wall. The wall, Dace saw, had been breached in a dozen places with what looked to his eye like some sort of unholy fire; in places the stone looked as if it had melted and flowed out of the nameless invaders' way.

"Should we go forward?" Yushuv clearly wanted to. The boy was positively quivering with eagerness to explore. Dace suspected he'd kept him underground too long.

"I suppose," was his laconic reply. "Hopefully, there'll be another way out of this crater on the opposite side. Just be careful. The Sun alone knows what sort of condition those roads are in. All that we need is for a flagstone to flip over and dump you in a makeshift oubliette."

"You weigh more than I do," Yushuv pointed out, and then ran on ahead.

Dace watched him go, and then cautiously began picking

his way down the slope. Caution, it seemed, was one lesson that had not yet sunk in.

❖

He caught up to Yushuv at the first guardhouse, where the boy stood, pensive. "I don't like this," he said. "Look."

Dace looked. The guardhouse door had long since rotted away, but Dace could see from the doorframe that it must have been nine feet tall. The rough comforts inside, which consisted of a stone bench and what looked to be a bathing basin, were similarly scaled, which gave a disturbing impression of how tall the city's builders had been.

"You know, I don't blame you. Hmm. Come with me." Dace turned his back on the guardhouse and, leaving the road, made for one of the breaches in the city's massive wall.

"What are you looking for?"

"Evidence," Dace replied curtly, and then broke into a trot. Yushuv had no choice but to follow.

It took them five minutes at a near-run to reach the wall, and then another five to find a place where the walls had been breached. Yushuv stood, awed, at the scale of the city's defenses. The walls that had seemed so frail from their perch on the crater rim proved to be twenty feet thick and forty tall. Nor was there a single seam or chisel mark anywhere on their surface, though Yushuv looked long and hard for hints as to their construction.

Dace, for his part, examined the breach itself. It was almost fifty feet wide, and the stone did indeed appear to have been melted out of the way. Massive splashes of stone and what could only have been cooled puddles marked the area around the gap, and Dace could see faint, worn footprints in the stone in places.

The prints themselves were puzzling. All were massive, but no two sets were alike. Some showed three toes, some four, and some five. Some were round, others elongated like a human foot. In places there were furrows like a tail had been dragged through, though those furrows were easily a foot across.

And all of this over molten stone, Dace reminded himself. *No wonder there's no sign of life. Whatever did this would have been capable of killing everything here.*

Abruptly, he made a decision. "Come on, Yushuv. I want to be through this city as quickly as possible."

"I agree," Yushuv called back, clambering toward him over a pile of gray slag. "This place smells funny, too."

Dace took an experimental sniff. The faint whiff of rotten eggs greeted him. "It's strongest where the steam comes out of the ground," Yushuv added as he arrived. "There are four or five places like that around here. The steam's yellowish, and smells awful."

"Fascinating." Dace frowned. "Let's go in through here," he said, pointing to the breach in the walls. "I want to see what the invaders went after, and maybe get a look at that pyramid before we leave. A great deal of this bothers me."

"Me, too," Yushuv nodded. "But I don't know why."

"'Why' is because you're starting to develop a sense of self-preservation, Yushuv. Now, let's walk."

Yushuv nodded, then bent down to pick up a hardened blob of stone. With an embarrassed shrug, he tucked it into his belt pouch. "Might as well take something to prove this place exists," he said, and walked on.

They passed through the gap in the wall, and entered the city proper. From within the city's defenses they could see cunningly hewn staircases reaching up to the wall's crest, which defenders had presumably ascended, only to be overwhelmed by the magics brought to bear against them. Oddly enough, there were no skeletons to be found, which to Dace's mind, was not comforting at all. If the war had been a war of conquest, it would have made sense to dispose of the bodies of the casualties. But this had been a war of sack and slaughter, it seemed. In that case, why bury the dead?

They passed through what appeared to be a residential quarter, the buildings five and six stories tall and marked by massive gates and windows. No doors hung anywhere on these hinges, and delicate stonework, smashed in places, showed hints of the beauty that must once have been. Vines and creepers tugged at stone blocks everywhere, making the first footholds in what must have been a centuries-long assault on the ruins' construction. But even under the verdant greenery, the outline of simple gardens could be seen, and massive trees bloomed in what once might have been carefully tended rows along the avenues.

A few minutes' walk brought them into a neighborhood consisting of long, low buildings, where the streets were wider and the walls thicker. The sulfur smell was strong here, and the two travelers found themselves hurrying to escape the stench. The smell faded after a few blocks, even as the architecture devoted itself to a series of high, narrow towers belted by spiral walkways. Most had crumbled to greater or lesser extent, and massive blocks of stone occasionally blocked the way. Yushuv and Dace picked their way through these carefully, and continued onwards. Ahead, the monumental pyramid beckoned, and from this distance they could see a feature that had escaped them before. What appeared to be massive stone chains seemed to bind the pyramid at all four compass points.

"Strange." Dace wasn't feeling talkative, but the sight of an imprisoned building was enough to rouse him from his suspicions. "Never seen that before."

"I think the pyramid's bigger than my home village was," Yushuv breathed. "And that includes the temple."

"The temple?" Dace looked over at his pupil. Most of what Dace knew about Yushuv's history had come second-hand, during one of Lilith's infrequent visits. The woman claimed to have been told the pertinent details by spirits, and clearly had passed on to Dace only what she felt it important that he know. That, in Dace's opinion, wasn't nearly enough, but he was in no position to compel Lilith to do anything that she didn't want to do.

Yushuv shrugged. "We had a temple. A big one. Everyone in it is dead now. So's the rest of the village. The man from the catacombs killed them, after he caught me." The set of the boy's shoulders told Dace he wasn't going to get any more, and so he quickly changed the subject.

"Have you noticed there aren't any statues here?"

The boy nodded. "Or paintings, or frescoes, or mosaics. No pictures. Just swirls and curlicues. I wonder why."

"I don't know," Dace admitted. "Just another mystery of this place, I suppose. Not that what's here isn't lovely."

"It seems pretty enough," Yushuv agreed. "I suppose they must have been rich, too. Otherwise, why come all the way out here with an army?"

Dace nodded. "No easy way to supply it, no other targets anywhere near—they must have been fabulously wealthy. Unless..." His voice trailed off to silence.

"Unless what?" Yushuv prodded.

"Unless they were simply in the way." Dace stopped and pointed. "There."

Yushuv looked. There, before them, was a tumbled block of stone that had most likely once crowned one of the city's proud towers. Now, it was a fragmentary reminder of past glories, a broken wreck waiting for wind and water to do their work.

And on its side was a single handprint.

The hand that made the mark was human-shaped, at least roughly. It had four fingers and a thumb, all in the right places and with the right number of joints. But few human hands had ever been that long or that slender, and no human hand could ever have sunk an inch into the stone to leave its mark.

"Dace?"

"Fair Folk," the older man said dully. "This city fell during the Contagion, when the Fair Folk armies tore through the veil at the corners of the world and converged on the Blessed Isle. No wonder they could burn through the walls, and their war beasts were so strange."

"I'm not sure I understand, Dace."

He turned to Yushuv and grabbed the boy by the shoulders. "Yushuv, what happened here is very simple. It's not that this was a war of conquest, or a war of revenge. This city was destroyed for one simple reason: *It was in the way.*"

"You know what that means, then," Yushuv said quietly.

"What does that mean? Can you imagine the sheer power arrayed against this place? It wouldn't have mattered who lived here, or what. They didn't stand a chance."

"It means," Yushuv said quietly, "that the Fair Folk know exactly where this place is."

They stared at each other for a moment, and then, Dace grabbing Yushuv's hand like a father guiding his son, they ran.

Chapter Fifteen

The glow Wren had seen turned out to be cast by a row of thighbones, hammered into sconces and burning like candles. They lined the wall of the chamber he stumbled into out of the dark and gave it a warm, almost friendly glow. This, more than anything, brought Wren up short. He looked around and was unaccountably dismayed by what he saw.

The room itself was nothing spectacular. Rough-hewn gray stone made up the walls and floor, though the ceiling was obscured by a heavy gray mist that stank of rotting meat. The torches, such as they were, lined only the wall to the east, while the one on the west was unadorned. At the north and south ends of the chamber were massive openings into darkness, which the pitiful light from the bone torches did little to penetrate. Far off in the darkness, he could hear a confused jumble of sounds—laughter, crying, flames, the crack of a whip—but here there was absolutely nothing. There was no sign of life, no reason for the torches to be lit, no sign what the gaping doorways led to—nothing. The chamber simply *was*, existing for its own dark pleasure, and that was enough.

And with that realization, Wren finally understood where he was. This was the Labyrinth. These were the halls where the Malfeans, the demonic gods of death, slumbered restlessly, and where the spirits of the dead—and worse—waged eternal war upon one another for reasons no mortal could comprehend.

The living, it was popularly believed, were not welcome here.

Wren looked back at the rough archway he'd just passed through. Beyond it was the vast emptiness he'd fallen into, and Dragons alone know what sort of monstrosity lurking in the dark, and somewhere beyond that, a door back to the sunlit lands. There had been stairs leading up to it, he remembered; he'd struck them twice during his fall. Mayhap he could find them again, and once again find the door.

"A door which by now has no doubt been barred, nailed shut, and sealed behind brick, and beyond which wait Ratcatcher and his prince," he said aloud, his voice echoing hollowly. A gust of wind followed his words, blowing out a pair of the bone torches and sending shadows dancing across the walls.

Frowning, he wrestled one of the remaining torches from its sconce, raising it high to avoid its acrid smoke. "Hmm. You wouldn't think you'd find a breeze down here. Well, hopefully that's the worst surprise I'll face. Forward it is."

"*Forward,*" whispered a voice in the darkness, beyond the doorway that Wren now faced. He stopped, freezing in his tracks. The voice had most definitely not been his own. It had been sexless, a whispered suggestion that considerably dampened his enthusiasm for advancing. For a moment he wondered if the serpents that had escorted him had somehow escaped the pit, but this voice was different, and, thankfully, less insistent. Breathing shallowly so as not to make any noise, he waited.

Silence greeted him, broken only by the crackle and hiss of the burning bones against the wall. The quiet beyond the tiny chamber was absolute, the stillness perfect.

"Damnation," he said, sensibly, after a half-hour's wait, and then pressed forward into the dark.

❖

The bone torch, Wren noticed, had a peculiar set of advantages and disadvantages. In its favor, it never seemed to burn down, and Wren was fairly confident that it would last as long as he sojourned through the Labyrinth. On the other hand, the light it gave was fitful and dim, and seemed to ebb and flow according to unseen tides that Wren simply did not understand. Sometimes it would flare into dazzling prominence as he walked through a narrow corridor, causing all manner of small, scuttling thing to squeal and pain and dash for their dark hiding places. At other times it dimmed to something barely brighter than an ember, and Wren could sense vast, looming entities in the encroaching shadows, watching him hungrily.

He'd left the chamber and headed north, picking his way along the broken stone that made up the majority of the passages he'd traversed thus far. Occasionally he'd seen manacles or grates in the walls he passed, but there was nothing to indicate whether these had been forged or simply extruded out of the very stuff of the great maze itself. Ominous brown stains indicated that some had been used, though, and recently.

The sound of stone scraping on stone behind him made Wren turn, torch held high in his left hand. The corridor was empty. With an audible sigh, he lowered the torch and reversed himself again. "This place is starting to get to me. I'm surprised it's taken so long."

"Why? How long have you been here."

The voice came from above, even as long fingers attached to a long hand at the end of a long arm came down and pinched out the flame of Wren's torch. Stumbling backwards in the dark, he swung it wildly until he felt cold stone at his back. "Who are you? Show yourself!"

There was no answer for a minute, only the leathery sound of something heavy dropping to the floor on bare feet. Slow footsteps followed, and then a quiet reply. "If I meant you harm, I wouldn't have spoken." The voice was quite close now, a raspy whisper that spoke of long years of disuse. For a second, Wren thought he could feel cool breath on his face, but dismissed that as paranoid fantasy. Here, of all places, he was unlikely to feel a living man's breath.

Instead, he swung the now-extinguished torch in front of him, back and forth at chest level. As he expected, he struck nothing. "Forgive me for doubting your intentions. I've little reason to expect hospitality here."

"Why?" Now the voice came from hard by his right ear. "Because you're a living man?"

"That could be it," Wren agreed, and jabbed a quick elbow toward the point the voice seemed to originate from. A quick chuckle and the impact of his arm against the stone wall told him that he'd missed again. "Damn. Ow. Do you blame me?"

"Not in the slightest." Again came the footfalls, circling first left then right. "Still, I must assure you that I mean you no harm. You have my apologies for putting out your torch, incidentally. It's simply... better... if you don't see me."

"Better that I be blind? Down here? Forgive me for disagreeing." Nevertheless, Wren lowered the torch. He'd learned blind fighting from Kejak himself, and had his skills honed by the finest teachers in the Order. If it came to a fight, he was reasonably certain that he could give a good account of himself to his unseen opponent. And if fighting was pointless, well then, he was no worse off blind than he might have been otherwise. His real worry was continuing on in the dark, assuming he survived this meeting. He'd already passed several pitfalls and oubliettes on his journey, and the thought of simply stepping into one of them in the dark filled him with a leaden sense of dread.

"You may disagree all you wish, but that will not change matters. *Your* wishes mean naught here." Did the voice sound further away? Wren hoped so, and then edged right. "And I would not go much further that way if I were you."

"Oh?" Wren stopped. "Why not?"

Instead of a reply, Wren heard the solid plink of a pebble striking stone. There was silence for an instant, and then a grinding, gnashing sound. Wren felt, rather than saw, a fine cloud of dust waft past him, and stayed very still.

"Even the stone can be hungry here. It tends to pick up the habits of the things that dwell in it for a long time."

Wren hazarded a guess. "And something near here has an appetite?"

"Something near here *is* appetite. It is a good thing I found you, or you'd have walked right into its maw. Well, one of them, anyway."

Shaking his head, Wren sat down on the floor. "Would you do me the great and good favor of speaking plainly for a few minutes? Tell me who—or what, if you prefer—you are, why you were following me, what I nearly walked into—oh, and if it's not too much of a bother, where the nearest exit is."

Again came the low laugh, from closer to the floor this

time, and Wren surmised that his invisible companion had sat down as well. "The last answer I'll give you first: the door to the prince's cellars."

"Marvelous. How about the second closest? Perhaps a place to get a flint and tinder as well?"

"Does the absence of light bother you so much?"

"Only when it's dark," the priest said, dourly. "May I please have at least one or two answers? Just to make the conversation more interesting, of course."

There was a pause, and Wren got the sense, somehow, of a tired shrug. "If you insist. My name is Idli, and I am a guide. I dwell here but owe my allegiance to none of the Deathlords, and can be persuaded to lead travelers for a fair price. You stand on the borders of the domain of she who is sometimes called The Mistress of Hungers, and she is aware of you. Another dozen steps and you would have been lost. Even dallying here is hardly safe; she may yet decide that you are a big enough prize to risk an incursion into the prince's little warrens."

"Ah." Wren felt oddly dissatisfied with the answers. They seemed truthful enough, but hearing them gave him the sense of looking at a half-completed puzzle. The outline was easy to discern, but so were the gaps. "So out of the goodness of your heart—assuming you have one—you chose to follow me and rescue me from my own folly?"

"Don't act the fool, priest." For the first time, there was an undercurrent of something besides amusement in the unseen thing's voice. "You're valuable, for one thing. For another, I don't like the beasts out there who are bidding for your head. And for a third, I expect you'll pay better to protect your skin than they'll pay to flay it off you."

Wren felt himself nodding. "Good points, all. So let's suppose I do want to use your services. What would you charge to get me safely back to the lands of the living, and how do I know I can trust you?"

There was a sound of stones shifting, and a nervous cough. "It's not a matter of want any more. Without me, you're dead. My price is small, though. A finger."

"A finger?" Wren felt the hackles on the back of his neck

stand up. "What do you mean by that?"

"Exactly what it sounds like. I get you to one of the places where the wall between worlds is thin—no guarantee of what you find on the other side, mind you—and I take one of your fingers. Your knucklebones will have power someday, once they've been suitably polished. Hmm. You could do with some polish yourself."

"What do you mean?"

"You ask that a lot. Find some answers for yourself, Chosen of the Sun. You'll find it'll make negotiations easier. In the meantime, however, you need me. And you don't need all of your fingers. I've got no incentive to trap you, drown you, or sell you out, because if I do so the knucklebones won't be half so powerful. They have to be freely given, you see." There was a growing impatience to the voice, and behind it, Wren could hear distant slithering in the dark. "Make up your mind, priest. There's not much time before *She* comes calling."

Wren gazed down at his hands, or at least at where he felt his hands were. A finger? Which one would he give up? His hands had always been clever. He'd had a knack for undoing locks and knots from an early age, for pleasing a woman (*Not that one was allowed such things in the Order*, he thought) or taking things apart. How would it feel to be missing a finger? Would the others become more clumsy? Would they retain his old skill?

And if he died here, in the dark, would any of it matter?

With a shudder, he stood. "You have a bargain, Idli. Lead me to the light, and I'll give you a finger—though I choose which one."

"Of course." There was a hint of dry triumph in Idli's voice. "And I'll take it as painlessly as I can. We should be on our way. Now."

Wren nodded. "I agree. Lead on."

"No. Lead *up*." And strong hands seized Wren, and pulled him off his feet, up into the dark.

The tunnel Wren found himself in was small and cramped, barely tall enough for him to crouch. The walls were uncomfortably warm, and crumbled ever so slightly under his touch. Ahead, all was darkness, though he thought he could glimpse a roughly man-shaped shadow scrabbling against the darker shadows of the tunnel itself. Behind and below, the sound of a rushing torrent rose up, filling the narrow corridor with echoes.

"Idli?" he called out, tentatively.

"Yes?" The voice came from ahead. Wren felt a small rush of relief.

"What's that river I'm hearing?"

In the darkness, he could see the shadow shaking its head. "Not *what*. Who."

Comprehension dawned. "That sound is...?"

"It is Her, yes. She must want you very badly. I may have undercharged. We are safe here, though, as long as we keep moving. Come along." The sounds of scrabbling renewed and redoubled, and Wren hastened after him.

Eventually, they emerged into a chamber with smooth curving walls. "This feels like glass," said Wren to no one in particular, and he was unsurprised when Idli responded "It is." Echoes of both of their voices rang back and forth for several seconds, then faded to silence. Short, sharp flashes of blue and yellow light skittered across the room's walls, blinding in intensity and brief in duration.

"What is this place?" Wren asked, awed. If he slit his eyes and looked away from the flashes, he could almost see what Idli looked like....

"A place where many passages meet," the guide replied distractedly. "From here, I can feel how the tunnels have shifted themselves, and find us a safe path. They will speak to me, if I am allowed to listen to them." The last was said with pointed annoyance, and abashedly, Wren bit his lip. There were other questions he wanted to ask, but now was not the time.

Instead, he wandered over to one of the walls. The slope of the floor told him that the chamber was roughly spherical, and as his eyes adjusted to the sudden, tiny bolts of lightning, he could see greater darknesses here and there, places where tunnels emptied themselves into this hall. Curious, he placed his hand on the smooth glass of the wall, and watched a series of blue sparks dance around it. Grinning for no reason he could understand, he drew back his hand and gently flicked the surface of the glass. The entire room rang like a bell.

"Would you please stop that?" Idli's voice was rife with annoyance. "You've just spread word of our presence here through a thousand corridors. There are things hunting you that can hear you lick your lips from a dozen leagues away. Please don't give them any more help than necessary."

"I'm... sorry." Wren felt oddly crestfallen, as if disappointing Idli was suddenly something to avoid. To cover his embarrassment, he turned back to the wall and once again placed his hand against it. Again, the sparks danced around it, but this time, he didn't pull away. Instead, he felt the sharp stings as they brushed against his hand, and then a curious tingling as they began moving up his arm. "Idli?" he said, worried.

"Not now."

"Are you sure?" The sparks had snaked past his elbow, leaving trails of light along his skin. A faint glow radiated from him, cold light on the cold glass.

"Perfectly sure," came the irritated reply.

The glow had reached his shoulder, and when Wren pulled his hand away from the wall, he could see a small ball of dancing lightning in his palm. Yellow mixed with the blue now, and occasional flashes of red appeared as well. "If you're certain," he said, and turned.

The light now covered half of Wren's body, scurrying across his face and down his torso. The glow around him was stronger now, reflecting his image again and again in the glass of the chamber walls. A soft, crackling hum filled the room, buzzing in counterpoint to the still-echoing chime from before. The light filled his eyes, and he gazed on Idli for the first time.

The guide's figure was half turned, a hand over his eyes to

shield himself from the light. He was naked, his skin the color of old bark on a long-dead tree. The best that could be said of his shape was that it was roughly human, though its limbs were too long and its fingers too many. Those many fingers now covered Idli's face, hiding it from the light.

"What have you done?" he moaned. "You can't see me!"

"I think I *can* see you, Idli," he replied, and strode forward. "Let's have a look at you."

Idli made no move to run, but instead huddled on the floor, whining softly. "Too bright, too bright," he whimpered. "This is not a place for light."

"It is now," Wren said pitilessly, and pulled Idli's hands away from his face.

Part of Wren's mind told him that he was foolish for doing this. After all, Idli had effortlessly hoisted him from the floor earlier, and no doubt could tear him limb from limb if he really felt like it. But with the coming of the light Idli was suddenly a different creature, and Wren felt compelled to take advantage of it. There were too many questions the guide hadn't answered, too many things Wren had been told to take on faith. Proof, however, did a lovely job of reinforcing faith; they'd taught him that at the temple, and now seemed an excellent time to put that teaching into practice. Then he saw Idli's face, and realized that sometimes faith is enough.

Idli's visage was a horror. It might have been human, or something like human, once, but that had been before fire, disease and rot had worked their will on it. His oddly elongated skull shone forth from beneath the blotched skin in places; in others, both skin and meat were gone. One good eye of shocking blue lolled in an eye socket; the other was filled with a mix of writhing grubs and gangrene. Long strips of skin hung down in tatters from his scalp, much of which was a mass of burned flesh and scars. Incongruously, his mouth was perfect, with full lips and even teeth. His one eye met Wren's, and he smiled, bitterly.

"Are you happy now?" he asked, softly. "Have you seen enough?"

"Dragons..." Wren took a step back.

Idli shook his head. "No, not dragons. There are older and

crueler powers in the world than they. Now, please. Remove the light."

"I... I can't." Wren looked helplessly at his hands, both of which were illuminated now. "I don't know how."

"Please," said Idli. "I can't bear the light." Even as Wren watched, bits of flesh flaked off Idli's face, wafting to the floor.

"How?" Wren asked, frantic. "I don't know how!"

Idli moaned, softly. "You know how. Use your will. Draw the light into yourself."

"I'll try." Wren closed his eyes and thought about the light. He imagined it burrowing beneath his skin, pulling away from the darkness. He saw it dwelling within him, a constant burning core that even the Labyrinth couldn't extinguish. He could feel the sparks sliding into him, tracing paths of fire along his nerves, could hear Idli's whimpering echoing off the glass. *This is yours by right*, he heard a distant voice not his own whisper. *Bend it to your will.* There was a moment of transcendent pain in his chest, a rising flame that threatened to consume him, and then nothing.

Then, suddenly, it was over. He opened his eyes, blinking at the all-consuming dark.

"Idli?"

"Here." The voice came from the floor some feet away. It was weak and pained, but it was unmistakably Idli.

"Did I...?"

"You did." There was a hacking cough. "Just in time, I might add. I thank you."

"I'm sorry I—"

"No need. You did," and Wren could hear the bitter smile, "what you thought you had to." There was another cough, and the sound of a body sliding along the glass. "We should start moving again. What you did here will not be ignored."

"Can you travel?"

"I shall have to, won't I? Otherwise I'll never get your finger. Help me up, if you're still willing to touch me."

Without speaking, Wren extended his hand. Idli's leathery palm clasped his, cool and dry. There was a brief sense of weight as the guide pulled himself upright, and then his hand was free.

It itched, ever so slightly, but he resisted the urge to scratch or rub it against the glass. Somehow, he knew, Idli would know, and right now for whatever reason he very much did not want to disappoint Idli.

"So where do we go now?" he managed after a moment's silence. "Out?"

"Down," Idli replied. "Sometimes down is the only way to go up." He shuffled forward, his bare feet slapping on the stone. "But please, I beg of you one thing."

"What's that?"

"Hide your light," Idli said, and started walking.

Chapter Sixteen

After seven days on, or rather *in* the River of Tears, Ratcatcher was waterlogged, wounded and murderously bored. He'd spent the first two days of the trip doing his best to avoid being scraped off on the muddy bottoms of the salt marshes the barge had traveled through, water so shallow that he would have simply walked alongside the craft if he hadn't feared being seen above the waterline.

The turn into the River of Tears itself had brought some relief, but not much of one. Much to his sorrow, Ratcatcher quickly learned that the channel was full of fish with a taste for carrion, all of which regarded him as a particularly delectable morsel. The next week was a constant, running battle between Ratcatcher and innumerable piscine enemies, all intent on snatching a mouthful of his unliving flesh. The experience was akin to being swarmed by particularly aggressive biting flies, for no sooner had Ratcatcher shooed away one inquisitive fish than a half-dozen more appeared, and shooing them away often rendered his perch on the barge's hull a precarious one. Now that the ship was in faster waters he had no wish to lose his grip. When he'd hit the water in Sijan, Ratcatcher had learned to his shock that his new body didn't float, and if he were somehow to tumble free of the barge he'd run the risk of sinking into the riverbed's mire.

In practical terms, that meant that he continuously clung to the mussels that lined the bottom of the barge with what could earnestly be called a death grip, despite the fact that this rendered him vulnerable to the occasional nip from a fish cleverer, faster or simply more truculent than its fellows. Unfortunately, each bite of this sort also put more thin trails of Ratcatcher's blood in the water, and that meant that more fish came swarming around in search of a meal.

By itself this would have been bad enough, but the incessant swatting at swarms of sticklebacks and the like was the only thing to occupy his time, and by nature Ratcatcher had never been a patient man. The combination of the barge's relentless crawl and the impenetrably murky water left him with the same unappealing vista for days at a time, broken only by occasional river snags and the incessant fishy flurry. It did, however, leave him plenty of time to brood on his situation, and ponder his next move.

Returning to the Prince of Shadows was out of the question, he'd decided early on. He'd not been particularly high in the prince's estimation even before the fiasco with Wren, and recent events—at least he assumed they were recent, as he'd had no chance to examine a calendar or chat about the time while in Sijan—were unlikely to improve that. After all, the prince had allowed Unforgiven Blossom to put her accursed needle in his eye, thus setting up his current predicament. No, he'd not be welcome at the prince's citadel, nor did he have any wish to return there for a good while. Perhaps after he'd accomplished some great task, something that he could lay at the prince's feet which would force him to recognize Ratcatcher's worth....

But after ruling out the prince's citadel as a destination early on, Ratcatcher had been unable to come up with a suitable alternative. Seek revenge upon Unforgiven Blossom? She was no doubt in the bosom of the prince's protection, rebuilding her seven-times-damned orrery and muttering about how the stars had told her to commit murder.

Hunt down Wren, again? He was gone, somewhere in the depths of the prince's dungeons and no doubt a pile of cracked and gnawed bones in the bargain. He'd even heard the priest's name whispered in the Underworld while he'd sojourned there, and devoutly hoped that the discussion had been one in which the efficiency of new and exciting torments was being weighed.

The best alternative, he'd decided, was to hunt down the boy that the prince had shown so much interest in. A child couldn't possibly cause him as much trouble as the priest had, and just to make certain there were no unfortunate escape attempts, he'd be certain to shatter both of the child's ankles. It was hard to run, Ratcatcher reflected, when you couldn't stand.

The longer the trip lasted, though, the more he brooded on the sheer impossibility of the task he'd set himself. Saying that he was going to find the boy was all well and good, but so was saying he was going to burst from the river waters and fly to the Imperial City by flapping his arms. The search was liable to be long and frustrating, and Ratcatcher had little tolerance for frustration. Still, he knew the boy was important. And when one was important to the grand scheme of things, Creation itself had a way of warping its fabric around you, to bring you to the place you needed to be at the time you needed to be there. There'd be signs of the child's presence. He'd already disrupted the auguries and disturbed the spirit world; no doubt as he progressed along whatever path destiny had laid out for him the boy would leave more and grander traces of his passing. All Ratcatcher had to do was look for them.

All of this cogitation, however, had filled perhaps a day and a half, after which Ratcatcher was left with nothing to do. By the ninth day, he'd finished plotting his thousandth vengeance fantasy against Unforgiven Blossom and imagining his thousandth triumphant homecoming to the court of his prince and grown exceedingly bored with both scenarios. Furthermore, he'd been forced to admit to himself that if the boy was leaving traces of his presence, the last place they would be visible was the underside of a barge full of corpses on the River of Tears. It was time to move on, especially while there was still enough left of him to move.

And so when the barge tied up for the night, Ratcatcher released his grip on it, leaving shreds of pale flesh caught between the sharp mussel shells. He'd dropped to the bottom and gingerly walked through the soft mud to the riverbank, which fortunately sloped gently away from the water. There were fires on deck for the benefit of the two watchmen, one keeping an eye on the river and the other observing the shore. The custom was ancient and pointless, Ratcatcher knew; no one bothered the black barges. Even the Deathlords and their minions knew better than to anger the Lords of Sijan, whose labors had won them many friends in the Underworld. Still, there were always desperate and uneducated fools willing to try their luck on any vessel that came down the river, and it was against this eventuality that the watch was kept.

The reasoning behind the sentries' presence did not concern Ratcatcher nearly as much as the mere fact of their existence, however. He doubted he'd be pursued even if he were spotted, but some clever Sijanese might connect his descent into the river with the misshapen thing lumbering out of the water later, and even belated pursuit from the necromancers would be an unpleasant thing. A distraction was needed, and he crouched low in the water while he studied the barge for possibilities.

The vessel itself was broad, and sat low in the water. It was black, of course, lacquered to a reptilian sheen. A series of austere cabins marked the deck, and gilt lettering at the stern proclaimed the ship to be named *The Rudder Steered by the Icy Hand*. Personally, Ratcatcher felt the barge's name was a bit much, and he suspected it had been bestowed by some functionary who'd never been more than a day's ride from the city gates. There were railings all along the deck, and shutters above the waterline where rowers' oars could be extended in an emergency. Normally the barges were poled upriver by their sweating crews, but of late the Sijanese had gone in for innovation, and ships like this were the result.

It was, Ratcatcher decided, one of the most singularly ugly vessels he'd ever seen, an opinion not at all improved by the week or so he'd spent staring at its belly. He'd be happy to leave it behind, and as soon as possible.

A fish took a nip out of his left leg, and Ratcatcher swatted at it in annoyance. This caused a small splash, which in turn caused a small commotion on deck. Even as Ratcatcher sank below the water to hide, he could hear the sentries arguing over what might be out there, which gave him an idea.

He waited a few minutes, until he was sure that the sentries were bored of staring at a dark spot on a dark river on a dark night, and then he cautiously poked his head above the water. A hail of arrows failed to meet his re-emergence, and he smiled grimly. Live men made poor sentries. They were too busy trying to stave off their own boredom to keep an effective watch, and that made them vulnerable.

Slowly, Ratcatcher brought his hands out of the water. They were torn, he saw, tattered by the sharp edges of the shells he'd held fast to and ripped by the unsleeping attentions of the river's inhabitants. Where it wasn't shredded, the flesh of his fingers and palms was bloated and white, soft to the touch and stinking unpleasantly of rot.

This, he decided, would do.

Biting his lip against the knowledge of what he was about to inflict on himself, Ratcatcher circled his right hand around his left wrist and gripped it, tight. His fingers sank into his gnawed flesh, which oozed river water and thin blood, and he began to pull.

It came away from the bone like well-stewed meat. Softly, gently, the flesh of his fingers slid off under the pressure of his other hand, leaving him with a fistful of sodden scraps and a left hand that was nothing more than a dangling patchwork of bones and ligaments. He flexed it, once, experimentally, and was astonished to see that it still obeyed his commands. The ragged edge of torn skin and meat at his wrist stank sweetly of rot, but for the moment, at least, this body was still his to command.

"Time to feed the kings of the river," Ratcatcher said to himself, then hurled the handful of scraps of meat as far out as he could into the night. They hit the water with a series of splashes, which were instantly drowned out as the surface of the river erupted into a frenzy of thrashing scavengers. A startled commotion on deck joined the clamor, and swiftly as he could, Ratcatcher made for shore. The mud of the riverbank was cold under his feet, but no colder than the river water had been, and in seconds he'd scurried up onto the scrub grass that was the dominant feature of the landscape. Staying low, he zigzagged back and forth while heading as far from the river as he could. A line of trees up ahead, dimly visible in the starlight, seemed his best chance for shelter, and he made for them as best he could. He could feel the rough brambles and saw grass catch time and again at the sodden guard's uniform he'd taken in Sijan, and was shudderingly thankful that he'd decided against shucking it in the river. Had he done so, he'd be leaving a trail of scraps of flesh all the way back to the river.

Behind him, on the barge, noble sailors and rivermen from the city of Sijan were scurrying to find their nets and harpoons, for who were they to let a harvest like the one before them in the river to go waste? They landed a goodly number of fish and roasted them on shore in the morning. And when the cook's assistant gutted one particularly large specimen and found what he swore was a finger in the fish's stomach, he kept his mouth shut and simply made sure that he, personally, chose a different portion for his meal.

✦

It took an hour for Ratcatcher to reach the trees, which lay across a series of erosion gullies deeper than a man's height and filled at the bottom with soft, clinging mud. Finally, exhausted and bedeviled by gnats, he reached the line of trees, which turned out to be a series of lonely sycamores perched precariously on a slight rise in the terrain.

Gingerly, he tested his skeletal hand against the tree's rough bark. It appeared to be capable of supporting his weight, so with a minimum of fuss he scrambled up into the largest of the trees, startling a pair of jackdaws in the process. They flapped away noisily, pursued by an array of curses from Ratcatcher, then circled several times before settling, balefully, in the next tree over.

For his part, Ratcatcher ignored them, and wedged himself in at the junction of a pair of large branches. He'd heard wolves in the distance while he'd been fleeing the riverside, and suspected that being savaged by a pack of them would be far more inconvenient than being nipped at by ambitious catfish. Satisfied that he wouldn't fall, and weary beyond comprehension, he closed his eyes and fell into something that was not quite sleep, but would serve in its place for the moment.

❖

"You've taken our perch, and we're most distressed about that."

"Oh, yes, most distressed indeed."

"Can't let you get away with being that rude, you know."

"No sir, t'would set a most grievous precedent."

"Grievous and sad. Next thing you know every corpse for a hundred miles is going to want to sit here, and the neighbors are going to accuse us of being low-class."

"Low-class gluttons, I might add. Look at all the flesh on this one, ready to drip delectably off."

Slowly, Ratcatcher opened his eyes, and immediately regretted it. This, he decided, was a dream, and a particularly awful one at that.

Sitting in front of him were the two jackdaws he'd dislodged earlier, though how he knew they were the same escaped him. They stared at him with beady black eyes and chattered back and forth like an old married couple, each knowing what the other was going to say before it was spoken. They were perched on a branch the thickness of his arm, though he found himself unable to turn away and see what sort of tree it sprang from. Indeed, all he could really see were the jackdaws themselves. The rest of the scene was just hazily sketched in; enough to provide context, not enough to distract.

"In the name of the Malfeans and their children," he said wearily, "Would you please let me be?"

Both birds instantly turned their heads to him. "Ah, he's awake, is he?"

"That he is, at least here. Good thing that can't be said for his body, though. It needs its rest."

"That it does, what's left of it."

"Remind me to wring both of your necks and eat you raw in the morning," Ratcatcher said pleasantly, and tried to shut his eyes. A sharp peck on his cheek instantly scotched that idea.

"None of that, lad, not while we've a message for you."

"Indeed, it's rude once again. We've come all this way and

he threatens *and* ignores us. Wouldn't think he could do both, could you? Not at once."

"Takes talent, it does," the second jackdaw agreed, and both broke into a chorus of croaking hysterics.

Reluctantly, Ratcatcher opened his eyes again. He tried to bring his fingers to his cheek, to assess the damage the bird had done, but his body was curiously unresponsive. "Fine. You have a message for me. What is it?"

"What, don't you even want to know who it's from?"

Ratcatcher smiled. "I'd trusted you to enlighten me on that account, seeing as how you've done such a marvelous job of serving as messengers now."

"A touch, I do confess!"

"He's got us there, he has, he has."

"Indeed. Do you suppose we should riposte, or simply give the fellow what he wants?"

"Mmm-hmm, judging by the look in that gimlet eye, the latter seems wiser."

"It does, I concede it does," and once again, the rasping hilarity broke out.

Ratcatcher merely held his smile and thought murderous thoughts, many of them involving how many birds one could fit on a single spit. After a sufficient interlude, the jackdaws got some inkling of this, and settled down once again. "The message?" he prompted.

"Ah, that's the important bit. You're to wait here. Well, preferably in another perch, but roughly where you are."

"For another day," the second bird piped in. "Possibly two."

"Two would be best," the first jackdaw agreed. "Gives your company more time to get here."

"And that company is?" Ratcatcher asked sweetly.

"Someone who'll be very useful to you, according to Raiton. You *do* know who Raiton is, don't you? "

"If you don't, Raiton's going to be offended, no doubt. He's touchy that way."

"Except when he's being a she."

"Well, yes, there is that detail, but really, he's the king of tricksters and carrion birds. Who's going to argue with him?"

"The king or the queen. Wouldn't argue with her then, either. But in either case, he—or she—is sending you someone useful."

"Yes, very useful. You might say he'll carry you on the next stage of your journey."

"Raiton?" Ratcatcher furrowed his brow in confusion. That, at least, was left to him in this nightmare. "I don't serve the Hundred Gods and especially not that one. Why is the trickster sending me gifts, unasked for and unwanted?"

"You know, he told us you'd ask that," the second bird noted studiously. "He's a clever one, he is."

"I'm sure," Ratcatcher responded dryly. "But he's also got no love for me or those I serve. Why would he possibly want to help me out now?"

"Why, because he's a carrion bird, and you're carrion. Very important that you wait, he said. Extremely important. Otherwise you're going to end up in a wolf's belly."

"Several wolves' bellies, really."

"And possibly a lion's. Don't think there are bears this far out on the plain, though, so you're safe from that."

"Enough!" Both birds turned in unison to face him, momentarily silent. Ratcatcher took a deep breath, the product of habit, and glared at them. "I get the point. Raiton wants me to stay here. You've been tasked to tell me this, because apparently all of his coherent servants are on other errands, and I have to decide whether to trust the message. Fine. You tell Raiton that I will wait, and that if he keeps trust with me, I'll provide him with a trail of carrion the likes of which hasn't been seen since the Scarlet Empress called down the fires of heaven. If he's lying, I'll come for him, if it takes me a thousand more years to crawl back out of Hell to do so. Do you understand?"

"Oh, Raiton never lies," the first jackdaw said.

"Never," nodded the second. "But we'll tell him for you."

"That we will."

"Good." Ratcatcher closed his eyes once again. "And if either of you think of going for my eyes, I'd advise against it. The fish on the river were faster than you are, and I caught them."

"Not all of them," the first bird intoned hollowly, then both fluttered their wings and vanished into the haze.

"You'd think a corpse was safe from dreams," Ratcatcher asked of the void, and then let himself go once again.

Chapter Seventeen

"Wait." Idli held up his hand against the darkness and obediently, Wren halted. They'd traveled miles through the Labyrinth over the last several... days? Hours? Decades? Wren wasn't sure, but it had been a damned long time. Several times, Idli had told him to hush, or to wait, or to run like Ratcatcher's hounds were after him all over again, and each time he'd obeyed. They'd moved past caverns whose echoes told of immense size, and through burrows that were neck-deep in mud, but always Idli had proven correct, and Wren now trusted him, if not implicitly, then at least enough to listen.

"What is it?"

Idli's voice was grim. "Dead things. Hunting us, probably. Take a look."

Wren inched forward on his belly, careful not to brush up against Idli's form. Since the incident in the glass chamber, both had taken pains not to mention what had happened, but the priest found himself finding excuses to put more space between his guide and himself. He didn't ask what exactly Idli was, or what had happened to him, or indeed anything about Idli at all. He simply followed, and at a safe distance.

"There." Wren looked down. The tunnel they were in opened up onto a ledge running the length of a long corridor hewn out of what looked to be rusting iron. A dim, reddish light filled the room, apparently at levels that Idli could stand, but it made the entire corridor look as if it were made of clotting blood. At the far end of the room, the ledge was filled with a milling crowd of what looked to be shambling corpses, each armed with a crumbling mace or sword. Several were on their hands and knees, sniffing the broken iron or shambling toward the place where Wren and Idli lay hidden.

Wren inched back on his elbows. "What are our options? Can we go back?"

Idli, his figure silhouetted against the red light, shook his head. "No. That path was already closing when we took it. There's nothing behind us."

"Damn." Wren spat instinctively, then looked up. "So we'll have to go through them?"

"Not exactly. If we can drop off the ledge into the corridor below, we can get past them, hopefully without much of a fight. If we get bogged down, however, we're dead. They can keep throwing more bodies at us—quite literally, I assure you—until we are overwhelmed. You're not well enough trained to use the power you have, so speed is our only ally."

"Ah." Wren stood and stretched. "So it's over the ledge, then. How far down is it?"

Idli shrugged. "I don't know."

"Marvelous. Which way do we go when we hit the bottom?"

"Left, I think."

"You think?"

Idli shrugged again. "This is not, in case you were unaware, a precise science."

"Ah." Wren nodded. "Fortunately, I know something that is." And with that, he launched himself forward. Screeches of alarm came from the end of the corridor, but before any of the rotting corpses could so much as take a single step toward him, he was over the lip of the ledge and plummeting toward the base of the corridor below.

As he fell, Wren realized that he had made two miscalculations. The first was that he had no idea if in fact Idli was following him, which meant that there was every chance that he was on his own when he landed. The second was that he never bothered to see if the corridor below the ledge was filled with minions of the enemy as well.

Sadly, it was.

Chapter Eighteen

Dace had reached the courtyard at the center of the city, Yushuv a few steps behind, when the singing started. It was high and sweet and had no words, and came from a half-dozen points around the city's edge. Without even thinking about it, Dace knew who the singers might be.

"Fair Folk," Yushuv stated, rather than asked. Dace nodded.

"They're here. They knew about this place all along, and if I didn't know better, I'd say they led us here intentionally." He entered the circular courtyard surrounding the pyramid, walking now.

"So what do we do?" Dace noted with pride that the boy already had an arrow on the string and was scanning the deserted city for movement. "Can we escape?"

"I don't know. If you listen, you'll hear they're all around the city. There," he said, pointing, "and there, and there as well. They've got us surrounded. Now, they can't cover every entrance, but they can move from entrance to entrance faster than we can get from here to the wall. What we can do is hide. There are an awful lot of buildings in this city, and even the Fair Folk can't search every single one. Our best bet, I think, is to find a place to hide and wait for their search to sweep past, and then go."

"That makes sense," Yushuv agreed. "Where do we want to go?"

"Not here, I think. I don't know how good a faerie's eyes might be, but if the stories are true, they can see us out here from the edge of the crater. Let's get someplace with more cover."

"That might not be such a good idea after all," Yushuv said, pointing.

Dace turned and spat out a curse. Fair Folk horsemen

were clearly visible down the long avenue he and Yushuv had traveled, flanked by a herd of small, scuttling things, and now the entire city echoed with the hoofbeats of their passage. In the distance, the singing grew louder, echoed by the clamor of hunting horns blown from a dozen points within the city itself. "To the pyramid. They'll at least have to dismount to take us there!"

Yushuv ran, his footsteps light on the stone. Dace sprinted after him, cursing the weight of his pack and wondering how many Fair Folk he'd be able to take down before being killed himself.

The courtyard, he saw as they ran, had actually been a parade or staging ground, and most likely had been used for religious services as well. The pyramid's bulk was staggering; it was easily as high as the crater was deep, and the staircases carved into its sides to allow mere mortals to climb it contained an uncountable number of steps. From this vantage point, he could see that a number of tiny openings dotted the pyramid's higher levels. Presumably they were doorways to the edifice's interior, places where the enemy's advantage in numbers could be taken away from him. The chains, too, he now saw more clearly. They were iron, not stone, and went into the pyramid at its base. Each link was ten feet in height and perhaps twice that in length, and the few streaks of rust that showed merely emphasized the brute power it had taken to forge such a thing.

Ahead of him, Yushuv was already struggling with the steps, ones that had been designed for longer legs than his. *Longer legs than mine, too,* Dace added mentally as he reached the base of the staircase before him and began climbing. *The bastards who built this were too damn tall.*

The pyramid itself was built in a series of circular levels, each forty feet high. All were carved with what Dace recognized as astrological symbols and marks of binding, writ large on this titanic canvas. At each level, the staircases opened to a small landing marked with altars, stone benches and empty basins, and even as he hurried past, Dace noted the presence of what could only be grooves for catching the blood from living sacrifices.

Behind them, the Fair Folk horsemen had already reached

the edge of the parade grounds and begun urging their horses across it. Horses, though, was not quite an accurate term for all of the steeds the Fair Folk rode. Some were horses, true, but others had serpents in their manes, or goats' heads, or paws like a lion's. Others were scaled or feathered, and one looked like nothing so much as a giant bat, striding relentlessly forward on its ungainly wings. Around them surged a crowd of small, scaled things, built roughly like men, but tiny, with green pelts and clever, clawed hands.

The Fair Folk were nocking arrows now, Dace saw with a quick glance over his shoulder, and no doubt would let fly as soon as they reached the pyramid's base. In the distance, the singing was louder now, wordless yet somehow seductive, urging the fugitives to surrender themselves. By contrast, the brassy horn blasts within the city itself promised only sport for their hunters, and that as much as anything lent wings to Dace and Yushuv's heels.

"In!" Dace called when Yushuv reached the next platform, the first to feature a doorway to the pyramid's interior. "Go in now!"

Without bothering to respond, Yushuv darted into the entranceway. Dace followed a second later, pelting down the corridor past numerous small chambers, all now abandoned.

He caught up with Yushuv a second later for a very good reason: The boy had stopped.

They stood on the edge of a titanic circular shaft that sank down into the bowels of the earth, perhaps a hundred yards across. It was lit from beneath with a ghastly red glow and suffused with the stench of brimstone. Heat wafted up from it, and the four monstrous chains that had marked the outside of the temple ran down its sides into the untold depths below. Spiral staircases wound their way up alongside the shaft, providing access to the levels of the pyramid that still rested above them, and a dull clanging sound echoed throughout the massive chamber. There were, Dace noted thankfully, no stairs leading downwards.

"I think I know why the chains are here, Dace," Yushuv said thoughtfully.

"You're going to be explaining your theory to the Fair Folk in a minute if you don't hurry. Up those stairs! Move!" Dace had no doubts that even as the spoke and stared, the Fair Folk and their creatures were ascending the pyramid from all sides, hoping to catch them like rats in a trap.

"We have to go up!" Yushuv agreed, and again scampered faster than Dace could follow.

They'd ascended two staircases and made it halfway up the third when the first elf appeared in a doorway. She strode arrogantly into the chamber surrounding the pit, looking not at the marvel before him but rather for any traces of her prey. She was clad in white, but the red glow surging up the shaft made her appear as if she were garbed in rust. She had a bow strung across her back, and tossed a long knife negligently from hand to hand. Around her feet scuttled a trio of the misshapen beasts who'd accompanied the fey, and they chittered and whistled to each other with hateful glee.

"Yushuv?" Dace whispered, his real question unspoken.

"From this range? Easily." The boy knelt, nocked an arrow, and concentrated.

Perhaps it was the sudden flash of light from Yushuv's brow, perhaps some ancient sense native only to the fey, but an instant before the boy fired, she looked up, and her eyes met the archer's. She smiled, then, and mouthed an invitation of such sensuous depravity to the boy that Dace found himself blushing.

"Come to me," they both heard her whisper, in a voice that carried across the pit with ease. "Come to me and I will show you such pleasures that every man in the world will pay jade just to hear you tell of it." She smiled then, and brought her knife to her lips. She ran her tongue along the blade slowly, sensuously, and then tossed it into the depths. "Imagine."

Yushuv loosed the shaft from his bow. It took her just above the left breast and drove her back against the chamber wall. With questing fingers, she touched the arrow that protruded from her flesh, and dabbed lightly at her own blood. Then she smiled, as if benediction, and collapsed to the floor.

"She cost us time," Yushuv said, and kept running.

Two more Fair Folk were waiting for them on the next landing, whip-like swords out and no words of seduction on their lips. One engaged Dace, while the other dove past him and sought to skewer Yushuv.

The boy dove for the floor and rolled out of the way of the first blow, coming up with his dagger in his fist and an eye toward the distance between his back and the well behind him. The elf stalking him had already closed with him, and made a series of tentative jabs with his blade to test his defenses. Yushuv knocked each away with the dagger, and the elf smiled to see it.

"You'll not run so fast with your tendons cut like string," the elf said pleasantly, the contrast between the melodious sound of his voice and the ugly words he spoke almost stunning. Yushuv, for his part, said nothing, and contented himself with parrying each of the faerie's blows. Every pass forced him back, though, and the heat that rose up through the chamber was fierce at his back.

A dozen steps away, Dace wrestled with his daiklave to meet the serpent-quick thrusts of his opponent, who said nothing but pressed his attack with icy ferocity. He thrust high and Dace parried, but the faerie turned the parry into a sweeping cut at the soldier's gut. Dace gave ground, bringing the daiklave down in a move more suited to a woodchopper, but it forced the elf to spin away. He came to rest with his sword held low and in front of him, his eyes moving over Dace the way a snake's eyes moved over an unsuspecting mouse.

This is just buying them time for reinforcements, Dace thought, and in that instant, charged. The faerie's eyes widened infinitesimally, enough to let Dace know he'd caught his opponent off-guard. He brought his blade up to chest level, intent on letting Dace skewer himself as he advanced. Dace, however, had other ideas. At his third stride he let his feet slip out from under him, sliding underneath the elf's blow and bringing the daiklave around as he did so. The strike took the faerie at the knees, shearing through both legs and sending his torso tumbling in a welter of blood and severed limbs. The elf shrieked, which Dace found extremely gratifying, and then burbled to silence.

Out of the corner of his eye, Yushuv saw Dace's maneuver, and it nearly cost him. The elf's sword flicked past his guard and caught his cheek, leaving a stinging mark that he could feel was oozing blood. It startled him, and he fell over backwards as he tried to retreat further. His back hit the stone hard, knocking the wind out of him; his head lay over the edge of the pit.

"Afraid yet?" the elf inquired, and stepped forward. "You should be." He cut a circle in the air with his sword and stepped forward. "May your next incarnation prove more capable."

Yushuv brought the dagger up in front of him. "I won't beg," he said.

"I don't care," replied the elf. "As long as you end up d—" Suddenly, he sprawled forward, all his unearthly balance gone. One step, two steps, a third, and then he stumbled into the pit, screaming.

Behind him stood Dace, leaning on his daiklave and looking immensely pleased with himself. "Come on, get up, we need to keep climbing."

"What did you do to him?" Yushuv asked, scrambling to his feet.

"I hit him. Very hard. They're not very sturdy, you know."

Laughing, Yushuv ran for the stairs, while all around them the servants of the Fair Folk boiled into the room howling for blood.

Chapter Nineteen

Two days later, Raiton made good on his word.
Ratcatcher had spent the intervening time in the trees, carefully husbanding his strength and watching in dismay as the flesh began to fall from his bones in earnest. The fish had done more damage than he'd thought, tearing through his clothing and taking coin-sized hunks of meat from him in a hundred different places. These wounds now began to rot with a vengeance, and the pungent scent of decay wafted over him.

This proved something of a mixed blessing. Larger scavengers left him alone, but he now faced a two-pronged assault from air and land. Flies mobbed him on one hand, and ants and beetles plagued him on the other. His days and nights were mostly spent slapping, scratching, and using what powers he had to ward off the never-ending swarms. Adding to his displeasure was the omnipresence of the pair of jackdaws in the next tree over, who occasionally cawed to one another knowingly but otherwise kept their attention on Ratcatcher. They stayed, cleverly, well out of reach, and the one time Ratcatcher worked up the energy to leap from tree to tree in pursuit, they laughingly avoided him, often settling in the perch he'd just abandoned in the chase. Frustrated, angry and rapidly losing all the flesh on his left forearm, Ratcatcher had lowered himself to the ground with exaggerated dignity and reclaimed his original nest.

The jackdaws found it all very amusing, at least until a low bank of clouds rolled in from the west and disgorged a positive torrent. Ratcatcher, for his part, sheltered under the leaves and silently thanked the rain for the brief respite it provided from the insects.

On the evening of the second day, however, everything

changed. Two hours before sundown, the jackdaws began squawking furiously, rousing Ratcatcher from a half-doze. "What?" he demanded of them blearily. "Not more of your wisdom, I hope?"

In response, the birds hopped back and forth from one foot to another, clearly in a state of tremendous agitation. They clacked beaks once, twice and then a third time, and then flapped their wings. Within seconds, they'd left their perch of the last two days and glided over to where Ratcatcher sat, one landing on each of his knees. The one on the left preened itself, the one on the right simply stared at him.

"This must be another joke," he said, and looked from one to another. Neither moved. "You do realize what you're asking for, don't you?"

In response, they each let out a pitiful croak, one that mixed desperation with a hopeless plea for mercy.

"Ah," said Ratcatcher. "I understand. Raiton's got a sense of humor, he does." He reached out, grasping one bird in each hand. They made no move to avoid him, nor did they make another sound.

With infinite tenderness, he lifted the birds up and brought them close to his face. "I'm going to enjoy this, you know," he told them, and then squeezed. There was a gratifying set of matching snapping sounds, and a wet gush of blood. "I hope I don't have to eat you," Ratcatcher said to the tiny corpses, then looked down and cursed. A pair of wet, white spots on his much-abused garments told him that even in death, the birds had gotten the last laugh on him after all.

✦

It was perhaps a half an hour after he'd killed the jackdaws when Ratcatcher saw movement on the plain. His eyes told him it was a single man with some pack animals in tow, and his ears told him that the man was singing, badly. Both his sight and hearing, however, had begun deteriorating badly over the last day or so, and Ratcatcher was beginning to have serious doubts about the continued viability of this particular body. That morning he'd caught maggots crawling out of the hole the polearm had made in his chest, and the sight was not a reassuring one.

What his eyes could tell him, however, was that the man was apparently heading straight for the ridge where the sycamore trees sat, and that he was in no hurry to do so. Ratcatcher looked at the forked branch where he'd stashed the jackdaw corpses, then shifted himself into a crouch. If the traveler proved to be only a happy coincidence, Ratcatcher would be quite happy to kill him and take his animals in hopes of finding a more hospitable place to decompose. On the other hand, if the man were the one Raiton's message had spoken of, Ratcatcher wanted to be ready as well. Raiton's gifts, the tales said, tended to carry with them unexpected consequences.

It took nearly an hour for the man to reach the line of trees, singing all the while. He was tall, thin and emaciated, and he wore a knotted collection of gray robes that hid his true figure quite effectively. His hair was black and cut short, and he wore long sideburns that made him look even more equine than his heritage had. At his waist he'd belted a scimitar, one that had seen long use if the scores and dents on the scabbard were to be believed. The song he was singing was a dirge Ratcatcher recognized from his youth, the tale of a man left behind to guard his tribe's treasure even after all of the rest had been slain in battle. Oath-bound to tend the hoard, he could never leave the well-hidden cache and so he lamented the fact that his people's story would slowly die with him. Ratcatcher had always wondered where the song came from, if the story it related were true, but it was an old standard for the wandering singers he'd known in his youth, and one that he knew well.

Behind the man on a tether were a horse and two camels, each heavily laden with goods. The animals looked no better than their owner, and Ratcatcher could see their ribs clearly as they walked. They plodded forward relentlessly, too tired even to nip at the grass in their path as they walked.

Ten paces from the tree where Ratcatcher hid, the man stopped and looked up. Behind him, the pack animals shuffled to a stop as well.

"I was told you'd be here," he said, his gaze moving back

and forth. "I'm here to help."

Ratcatcher's response was to drop out of the tree, birds in hand. It was a decision he regretted instantly, as the impact with the ground caused twin daggers of pain to shoot up his legs. He stumbled, his intended threat reduced to a low howl of pain, and fell to his knees.

The stranger looked down at Ratcatcher critically, and scratched the bridge of his nose with one long, bony finger. "In bad shape, aren't you? Well, that's what I'm here for. Let me help you up, then I can start a fire and we can talk." He leaned forward, offering a hand. Hesitantly, Ratcatcher transferred both jackdaws to his threadbare left hand and reached out. The stranger gripped him, firmly but not tightly, and without any change of expression. He tugged lightly, and Ratcatcher rose to his feet.

"Thank you," the dead man said, feeling an odd tinge of embarrassment. "You should probably let me sit downwind."

The man shrugged. "Doesn't bother me none. Get some dry wood, if you can find it, and I'll dig us a fire pit." He stared at Ratcatcher speculatively. "I think your sinews can take that kind of work, but your meat can't."

He turned and started rummaging through the gear strapped to one of the camels. A minute later, a triumphant cry accompanied the emergence from the pile of a small shovel, with which he attacked the dirt under Ratcatcher's tree with grim determination.

Ratcatcher, for his part, had carefully set the dead birds down and wandered off in search of firewood. The previous day's rain had mostly run off, and he was able to find reasonably dry wood without too much effort. He noticed as he did so that the trees were now completely devoid of any birds, and in fact any life whatsoever. Even the ants that had bedeviled him were gone, presumably having vanished when the stranger arrived.

That, he decided, was curious. Then again, Raiton was involved in this, and that meant that all bets—even bets about how precisely this unprepossessing stranger was going to arrest the decay of his body—were off.

The stranger looked up when Ratcatcher returned and

nodded his approval. "Dump it by there," he said, and pointed to the side of the fire pit he'd dug and lined with stones. "Don't want to burn it all at once. That's a good way to make sure you have to go looking for more firewood in the middle of the night. The name's Faithful Hound, by the way. I probably should have said that earlier."

"Faithful Hound?" Ratcatcher dropped the wood where he stood. "Is this some kind of joke?"

"Yes, but not on you." So saying, the tall man tucked the shovel under his arm and retreated to the pack animals. With studied competence, he began offloading their burdens, much to the animals' obvious delight. "You don't have to help," he called back over his shoulder, "since the way you smell might frighten the animals, but I'd appreciate it if you'd build a stack of wood in the pit, and set up a spit to roast those two birds on. Thank you kindly. I'm going to need my strength for what comes next."

Shaking his head, Ratcatcher dropped gingerly to one knee in hopes of sparing his liquefying flesh, and began laboriously stacking some of the wood in the fire pit. When he finished, he drove a pair of forked twigs into the ground on either side of the dirt circle, and began plucking the birds.

"No need to do that." It was Faithful Hound again, with flint and tinder in his hands. "This'll work better with the feathers on. Got a spit?"

"Somewhere in the pile, no doubt." Ratcatcher hobbled to his feet and began poking through the broken branches. "Do you mind telling me what this is all about?"

"I'm here to help," Hound replied, plucking the two dead birds neatly and following. "Isn't that enough?"

"Frankly, no." Ratcatcher shook his head. "And don't think I'm quite so fragile that I can't beat an answer out of you."

"You probably don't want to do that, seeing as this body's going to be yours shortly," the man replied. "Hand me that branch, would you? The one at the far left."

"It's what?"

"It's a branch, and it's on the ground there. Never mind, save your strength." And with that, Faithful Hound leaned forward to grasp the sycamore branch he'd indicated.

Ratcatcher grabbed his shoulder and spun him around, leaving a wet handprint behind. "Don't play the fool with me. I want an explanation, and I want it now or you're going to have to worry about advanced decomposition as much as I am. Do you understand me?"

"Oh, perfectly," the man replied, unperturbed. "Though you've caused yourself a problem with that robe. That sort of stain never comes out, and it's going to smell sooner rather than later." He looked up at Ratcatcher's expression and nodded. "Right. Let's start at the beginning."

"Please." Ratcatcher's voice was heavy with sarcasm.

Faithful Hound carefully set the birds aside and sat down. "Some of the details aren't too important. Others won't mean anything to you. The short version is this: A long time ago, someone read in the stars that you'd come to this particular pass, and that you'd be in this particular place—all except the bits you left in the river—and that things could go one of two ways. Either you'd rot here and spend a good long while waiting for another body your soul could slip into to come along and die convenient-like in the vicinity, or someone could be trained up with the intention of being here in the right place at the right time for you to slip into. That's why you want to avoid hitting me, incidentally. You'll be feeling those bruises in a day or two, and once you're dead, the healing process pretty much stops."

Ratcatcher blinked. "Impossible."

Hound shrugged. "Maybe. But I'm here. You might as well take advantage of the fact." He jerked a thumb toward the pack animals. "I've been working as a trader out of one of the nearby shadowlands for a while. Everything you need to take my place is there. You'll want to go south and find a river crossing, then hook up with a Guild caravan. That's all I've been told to tell you. Personally, if I were you I'd be heading north in hopes of having this body last a little longer, but if I were you, this would be an awful short conversation and likely an uninformative one. But you're supposed to go with the Guild, and what happens with them is the key to finding that sword you're supposed to. I expect the caravan will stay on dry land, which should help you out a bit. There'll be plenty of places along the way to find new bodies, too, though how you handle introducing your new 'partner' is beyond me." He licked his lips nervously. "Me, I just get to die."

"Whose shadowland?"

"Beg pardon?"

Ratcatcher leaned forward, his ruined face a mask of concentration. "Whose shadowland did you dwell in? I'd like to know at least that much before agreeing to this… this whatever it is. And why the birds?"

Faithful Hound folded his arms across his chest. "Last question first. The birds are for eating. They're carrion eaters. Having them in my gut will be a sort of beacon to your soul once that body finally rots out. Which, I might add, looks like it will be very shortly, so we need to wrap this conversation up and get to the serious business of ritual. Find some dry grass and pull it, so we can use that for kindling."

"Not until you answer my other question." Ratcatcher was implacable.

"Whose do you think?"

Unsmiling, Ratcatcher replied, "The Prince of Shadows."

Faithful Hound shook his head. "Close, though. There are those out there to whom the prince owes his allegiance, or so I understand it. They don't share much with their vassals, if you know what I mean."

"Aha." Ratcatcher stood. "Suddenly, I'm more interested in rotting than in going through with this."

"Wait," Hound replied, and carefully spitted both birds, feathers and all. "Ah. Sorry, needed to do that quickly. Anyhow, I'm not quite sure I understand it all myself, but there it is. There's powers beyond the prince, as you no doubt know, and one of them's behind this. I'd give you a name, but it wouldn't mean anything to you, and speaking that sort of thing out loud tends to be unhealthy." He looked up at the sky and squinted. "Attracts all sorts of unhealthy spirits."

"Hmm." Ratcatcher took another step, then turned. "Speaking of unhealthy spirits, I was told that Raiton had sent you. What do you know about that?"

"Raiton?" Faithful Hound's face screwed up in concentration. "Nothing, I'd guess. My orders came from somewhere else. Hell, my name came from somewhere else. I don't know anything but what I've been told, and they told me to come here and do this. You'll find I'm not too well educated on other subjects."

"No, I suppose you wouldn't be." Ratcatcher took a moment to gaze at his hands. His left had already been stripped of almost all flesh, and the right was rapidly following. Most of the skin was already gone from his arms, and with each step he could feel bone grinding on bone. Soon there wouldn't be enough of him left to hold his skeleton together, a process the trip downriver had only exacerbated, and then what? Back to the Underworld, he guessed, to wait for another suitable body if he were lucky, or to suffer a considerably more unpleasant fate if he were not.

"I supposed I don't have any choice in all of this," he finally said. "Either I go through with whatever you have planned, or I crumble to dust."

"Well, the third option is that you beat me to death or some such, and then take this body for yours once that one finally goes to pieces. I don't think you want damaged goods, though, which is why we're going to do it this way."

"And this way is?"

Faithful Hound took a knife from his belt and began carving shavings off of one of the larger branches Ratcatcher had collected. "Once I get the fire going, I roast and eat these birds, then take a little something and lay down. If I get my chanting right, the process is going to speed up the process of getting you out of that body and into this one. Of course, I die in the process, but that's what I'm here for."

"Of course?" Ratcatcher was incredulous. "You're that willing to die?"

Hound shrugged. "Isn't that what you teach us? To embrace death? I feel honored that my death actually helps advance the great work. Should I feel any differently?"

Ratcatcher shook his head, gently. "No, no. It's just... rare to see that. You're a brave man."

"I'm not brave. I just believe, that's all." Hound finished creating shavings, squinted at the fire pit, and reached for his flint and tinder. After three attempts, the pile of shavings caught, and the first tongues of flame licked upwards through the stacked wood. "Now, would you do me the honor of getting a blanket for me to lay down on, and a skin of wine out of the baggage I took off the animals? I'll take care of tethering them as soon as this is ready."

"I still don't like any of this," Ratcatcher grumbled as he tottered off. "Raiton's mixed up in this somehow."

"Knowing who else is, I pity the bird," Hound called after him.

✦

"Aren't you worried about wolves?"

Ratcatcher sat in front of the fire, knees hugged to his chest. Faithful Hound sat opposite him, blowing on the toasted jackdaws to cool them and wincing at the scent of scorched feathers.

"Not really," he said. "The ritual's supposed to protect against anything like that. If a big wolf-spirit comes along, we've got troubles, but we'd have had those in any case." He looked up at the trees, swaying gently in the night breeze. "No need for anyone to go climbing tonight."

"That's good, at least." The light from the fire sketched in the hollows in the wreck of Ratcatcher's face. "I've been warned about wolves," he added vacantly.

"You've seen worse than wolves."

"That I have," Ratcatcher agreed. "Which is why it would be so embarrassing to end up in one's belly." He paused and shook his head, as if to clear an unpleasant memory. "How long is this going to take?"

Faithful Hound laughed. "Impatient all of a sudden, aren't you?"

"It's going to happen, so let it happen already," Ratcatcher growled.

"There is a certain logic to that, you know. Let me just... ah.

They're ready, or as ready as they're going to be. Wish us both luck, honored one."

Ratcatcher stared across the fire. "You know who we serve. We have no need of luck."

"There is that," Faithful Hound agreed, and then began chanting. The words were ones Ratcatcher vaguely recognized, echoes of things he'd heard in the Labyrinth or while pledging himself to the dead gods. Faithful Hound's chanting voice was deep and low, and now Ratcatcher could hear wolves howling far out on the plain, echoing the sounds coming from Hound's throat. The fire's crackling grew louder, and the dancing flames leaped higher. Tints of color that had no place in any normal flame appeared, flaring bright for an instant and then vanishing.

Ratcatcher watched, fascinated. Then, slowly, he reached forward with his ruined left hand and let the flames wash over the naked bones. He felt no pain, only a slight warmth, and was bemused to see that his fingers continued to burn when he pulled them from the fire. Faithful Hound's chanting was louder now, and with it came a throbbing, insistent pain behind his eyes. For an instant he thought that Faithful Hound had tricked him, and tried to rouse himself to anger, but the feeling quickly dissipated. How could he be angry, after all, when such beautiful flames danced in his hand? He could see streaks of blue there now, and dark green and a red so bright it could have been liquid blood. The pounding in his head grew more insistent, but somehow he understood that if he closed his eyes and lay down, the pain would go away. Dimly, he heard an unpleasant crunch of bone, and felt, rather than saw, Faithful Hound forcing himself to take a bite from one of the charred jackdaw corpses. *That's odd*, Ratcatcher thought, *his mouth is full and yet he's still chanting. I wonder how he does that.* Then, gently, he toppled over on his side, looking for all the world like a long-dead victim of plague.

Across the fire, Faithful Hound finished chewing the last bit of scorched bird and then lay himself down on his blanket for the last time. His mind was peaceful and his hands were folded across his chest. *And so I descend* were his last thoughts, before a tide of darkness rose up inside him and carried the spark of his soul away with it.

Three hours later, the fire had burned low. Strange colors still glowed among its ashes, but the flames no longer danced, and the light that played on the two still figures was dim and subdued. Ratcatcher's blazing hand had guttered out long since, after burning half of the way up his arm, and the only sound was the low crackle of the dying campfire.

Abruptly, the flapping of great, heavy wings broke the silence. A massive black bird, its eyes a luminous gold, descended from the night sky and landed next to Ratcatcher's crumpled body. Letting out a monstrous croak, it surveyed the scene. First it stared at Ratcatcher intently, prodding the corpse with its beak and stripping off tatters of exposed flesh, which it then proceeded to wolf down. An instant later it gave a satisfied bob of its head and waddled over to where Faithful Hound's body lay. Very lightly, the raiton pecked the middle of his forehead, and received no response. Again it bobbed its head, though the croaking that followed could almost be interpreted as laughter.

Slowly, it walked around Hound's body once, widdershins. Looking left and then looking right to make sure it was unobserved, it stealthily crept up to stand beside Faithful Hound's head. Then, with lightning quickness, it darted in and plucked out his right eye. The fire surged with fury, but then subsided as the raiton wolfed its treat down.

"Ah," it said when it had finally finished, in a voice that would not have sounded at all out of place coming from a man, "You half-guessed, little Ratcatcher. A pity for you that you didn't guess it all." It snorted then, saying "A wolf-spirit indeed," and plucked out the tall man's other eyeball. This one it simply punctured with its beak, letting the humors drain onto the ground.

"You'll see graves from that empty eye, and nothing more unless I let you," the bird hissed at the unmoving body. "Find the boy blind, will you? I don't think so. I don't think so at all."

And with that, Raiton spread his great wings once again and rose up into the night. Behind him, the fire coughed once and died, and once again the entire plain was dark.

Chapter Twenty

To say that Holok's appearance at the mouth of the waterfront alley caused consternation would be a vast and telling understatement. Contained within that alley were several of Port Calin's less savory citizens, none of whom expected to ever pass within a hundred yards of an Immaculate priest until they died, and even then it was even money their bodies would simply be dumped in the river. Occupying the space within this rough circle of bravos, cutthroats, slitpurses and ruffians was a dice game, one in which several of the aforementioned unsavory types were deeply involved.

It was a gesture demonstrating the depth of magnanimity which permeated Holok's heart that he did not call for the watch to shut the game down, and a further testament to that sterling quality that he didn't kill any of the three bravos who, convinced he was there to shut the game down, attacked him with knives. It was a further witness to his oratory skills, no doubt honed by countless sermons, that he managed to convince those members of the game who were not writhing on the ground in pain that he had no intention of shutting the game down or reporting it to the local gendarmes, but rather that his intention was to join the festivities. And who really can blame those gamesters for thinking, wrongly, that Holok's lifetime of study of the martial arts and theology would have left him no time to learn how to play craps. And if they'd made that logical supposition, they certainly would have agreed with the corollary that the monastic life would have left Holok no opportunities to learn about dice-switching.

Thus it was no surprise to Holok, at least, that he cleaned out all of his opponents, nor was it a shock to him to see them attempt to recover their moneys by means most underhanded, violent and despicable. Again, it rebounds greatly to Holok's credit that he did not kill a single one of them, though four would encounter great difficulty in walking for several weeks, two permanently lost the use of their right hands, and one was saved from ever having to consider the potential tribulations implicit in fathering children. As a further display of generosity, Holok left them their dice, which he had taken the time to remove the weights from, and a small prayer card which he suggested they study devoutly.

Not a one disagreed with the suggestion. Then again, not a one was conscious.

❖

"Don't like dice, do you?"

Holok's head jerked up as he entered the mapmaker's shop. "I beg your pardon?"

The proprietor, a short, plump woman with dark skin and fingers stained darker with ink, winked outrageously at him. "It's all right. About time someone taught those wretches a thing or two. They've been preying on travelers for months now, and not a damned thing done about it. Seems about right that it took a priest to show them the way of virtue and the wages of sin." She laughed, a motion which shook her whole body, not to mention her rough mop of black hair and her long beaded earrings, from top to bottom.

Holok nearly opened his mouth to explain that he had no problem whatsoever with games of chance, and had in fact taught a previous Mouth of Peace a dice cast that had increased her status among the kitchen staff of the Palace Sublime immeasurably, but instantly thought better of it. The shopkeeper clearly approved of what she thought was his one-man crusade against vice on the waterfronts. Allowing her to keep her illusions would no doubt be far less trouble than setting the record straight, and besides, she might be willing to offer a heroic crusader something of a discount.

"The ruffians needed to be dissuaded from what they were doing," he said with a noncommittal shrug, neglecting to mention that what they had been doing was attempting to perforate him thoroughly. "I was just in a position where I could do some dissuading."

"Well, the whole waterfront is just buzzing about it." She smiled, not unprettily, and laid down the tablet upon which she'd been scribbling. Her bookkeeping set aside for the moment, she then moved out from behind the massive wooden counter behind which she'd been standing. The front of the counter, Holok noted, showed clear evidence of at least one solid blow with a sword, and several other imperfections that looked suspiciously like ax-work.

"I do what seems appropriate, that's all," was what Holok said in response. *Five flavors of dung, this is not what I need!* was what he thought, however. His intention had been to raise the money from the dice game reasonably quietly, purchase what supplies he needed and then head out after a Guild caravan in search of who-knew-what. He most emphatically did not need to be hailed as the conquering hero of the dockside, with the inevitable and innumerable delays that would come along with it.

A possibility struck him, and he struck what he'd learned was his most impressive pose, in hopes that his spiritual authority would lend weight to his words. "In truth, discussing what I did makes me uncomfortable. For is it not written in the Immaculate Texts that 'The one who does good deeds in secret, so that his deeds are spoken of and not their doer, is one who walks most closely in the footsteps of the Dragon of Wood, He Who Hath Strewn Much Grass'?" *Please, please let that satisfy her,* he thought desperately.

"Is that so?" She smoothed her rather baggy black-and-green robes and looked vaguely disconcerted. "I don't remember that verse."

That's because you probably never got past the illustrated passage dealing with the thirty-seven appropriate positions for channeling dragon energy during lovemaking, you cow. Holok could feel a headache starting, the same headache that he alternately got dealing with new acolytes and Chejop Kejak, but didn't let it alter his expression of devout humility. "It's one of my favorites,

I assure you, and I have let it guide my steps for a great many years. A *great* many years," he added, with vaguely ominous emphasis.

"Oh. Oh!" Her mouth widened into a circle of surprise as she attached some self-conceived and no doubt ludicrous meaning to Holok's repetition. "If that's the case… in any case, my name is Daiash, and welcome to my establishment. What can I help you with?"

Holok looked around. Apart from the evidence of violence done to the front counter, the shop was neat and well-organized. The walls were lined with carefully labeled cubbyholes filled with scrolls, carved stone tablets and stoppered scroll cases. Mounted maps filled every other available inch of wall space. A barrel stuffed with damaged goods—water stains were prominent—sat in the center of the floor, near a potbellied stove whose neatly mended chimney ran up and out of the store. A flat worktable covered in inkwells, pens, straight edges and a slew of unidentifiable tools of the mapmaker's trade dominated the back of the shop, and the wood of the floor was well-worn from many visitors. Broad glass windows let in the late-morning sun, which made the shop almost uncomfortably warm, and the air was filled with the mixed scents of ink, burned paper, and incense.

He sniffed, once, and Daiash smiled wryly. "It helps keep them dry. It also makes me lose a considerable portion of the day to sneezing, but my comfort is secondary. The maps come first. Now, what are you looking for."

"I was going to say 'a map,' but I suspect you hear that joke too often."

"That I do," she agreed primly. "What country are you looking for a map of? I have everything from the great archipelagos of the west to the forest paths of the green men of the woods, all guaranteed to one hundred percent accuracy. Mind you, if they're not accurate you're never going to come back to complain to me about it, but I like to think I sell good merchandise."

Holok coughed. "I'm afraid I'm looking for something a bit more mundane than that. Specifically, I was hoping you'd have a map of caravan and trade routes east of here."

"Of course." She frowned, and her forehead furrowed. "Don't they have adequate maps at the temple for you, though? The scribes at the Shrine of Green Bronze do some *very* nice work."

"They do indeed, but the maps I was given were a bit too frail for me to travel with, you see, and since I'm due to depart on my circuit very shortly, I felt it was best to use some of my travel funds instead of overtaxing the monks in the scriptorium." He let his voice trail off regretfully, and paused to let the full import of what he'd said sink in.

"Ah. Of course. You're not only heroic, you're considerate." Daiash shook her head sadly as she walked over to the rack of cubbyholes and pulled a thin wooden tube down from a nook above her eye level. "This should serve. Guild routes are marked in green, independent traders' paths in brown, and hostels and taverns in red. I don't know exactly where your circuit is taking you, but this map should be good enough to get you on your way. You'll probably be able to get something a bit more..." she paused, and searched for the right word, "localized once you're closer to your destination, but I don't think any map you find out there will be as good as mine."

She ambled over to the counter, took out another wax tablet, and made a tick on it. "Normally the waterproof case would cost you more, but I'll include it as a small thanks for what you did this morning. If you don't mind, of course." Daiash added the last in a hurry, and blushed.

"'To refuse the sincere act of the generous heart is to sow the seeds of blight,'" Holok quoted. "I thank you."

"You *do* still owe me for the map, you know" the mapmaker retorted meekly, tapping her stylus against the countertop.

"I had not forgotten," Holok snorted. "*You* still need to tell me how much I owe. And, while you're at it, if you could recommend an honest shopkeeper who admires honest monks as much as you do, and sells bedding and travel supplies, I would pay for that information. You might even be so kind as to sketch the route on a piece of parchment for me, and I'd gladly pay for that as well."

"The temple isn't supplying you?" Suspicion began to creep its way across Daiash's face, moving slowly as it explored unfamiliar territory.

"I'm on a sponsored circuit," Holok replied gracefully. "One of the Imperial Houses wants to demonstrate its piety, and as such has kindly agreed to provide the financial wherewithal for my labors, so as not to tax the resources of the local abbeys."

"Which house?"

"I beg your pardon?"

"Which house is sponsoring you? I'm a V'neef by marriage, or at least I was, a long time ago." Daiash preened for a moment at the memory, and Holok bit down hard on his tongue to keep from bursting into laughter. The look on the mapmaker's face sobered him instantly. Clearly, this was something she took very seriously.

"I do not know," he said, and cursed himself for not having a better lie ready.

"You don't know?"

"The gift was anonymous."

"That's odd."

"Not at all." Holok drew himself up in righteous indignation. "Or have you forgotten the passage which I quoted earlier?"

"Of course not." Daiash flushed, and Holok knew he had won. She shoved the map at him across the counter. "Take it. A gift. Just in case House V'neef is your sponsor. I wouldn't want to take their money. It would defeat the purpose of them sponsoring you."

Holok felt a slight twinge of remorse at deceiving the shopkeeper, but not much of one. He'd done worse things for worse reasons, and been able to meditate afterwards with a pure heart and clear mind. Besides, if the boy he was chasing brought civilization down in flaming ruins, sweet innocent Daiash would have bigger troubles than the lost profits from a single map.

"Your generosity will bring you great rewards," he said, and bowed. Daiash gave an embarrassed little laugh and her plump face turned pink with pleasure at his words.

"You don't say," she tittered. "Now, about that other shop."

"If you please," Holok said, and mentally recited a calming meditation that doubled as a prayer for patience.

❖

It was another day before Holok could leave Port Calin and strike out due east. Part of the delay was in getting the directions for Daiash, who had an anecdote about every storefront and shopkeeper. Part of it was haggling with the second merchant, a withered old crone who regarded anyone Daiash liked with inordinate suspicion, and who fought over the price of each piece of equipment she sold Holok like she'd carried it in her womb for nine months.

Eventually, though, the negotiations had been completed and Holok had taken his fully laden pack out the door of the shop, only to run into friends of the ruffians he'd dealt with at the dice game. They wanted to remonstrate with Holok about his treatment of their friends, not to mention the ultimate disposition of their jade, and explaining to them with sufficient force that he wasn't interested in discussing the topic took some time. This, of course, meant that a crowd gathered, and Holok had to deal with the complications that came with that development.

Ultimately, by the time the crowd was dispersed it was too late in the day to being traveling, so Holok took a cheap, unfurnished room for the night and sat down with his map to plot his course. Following the string of trading posts seemed the best idea, at least to start, and as such he made a note of their names. Sweettree was the first, followed by Abundant Waters (neatly located in the middle of the savannah), and so on out to Reddust, the last of the major outposts before the trade route punched its way into sparsely populated, truly inhospitable terrain.

"Reddust," he said aloud. "Sounds like a little slice of the hells. Morning is soon enough to start walking there. Too soon, if you ask me."

And then, cautious man that he was, he put a chair against the door of his room and a bar across the window, and put certain protections against harm in place. For a moment he felt a twinge of embarrassment at the thoroughness of his precautions, but that, he reminded himself, was how he'd lasted fourteen centuries, when those who scoffed at him were dead.

Chapter Twenty-One

There were a dozen of the dead, lizard-like hobgoblins on the third level of the pyramid, with a clutch more in one of the doorways to the fourth and another six hacked to bits by Dace's daiklave on the fifth. The creatures fought like madmen or starving beasts, throwing themselves upon Dace and Yushuv in a whirlwind of fangs and claws. Some carried tiny, wickedly pointed blades, which they wielded with vicious precision. Others sought to bite and tear, and even the dying ones had clutched at Dace with the last of their strength, or hurled themselves under Yushuv's feet.

At every new floor the fleeing pair had been beset, and while they'd proved victorious in each encounter, they lost precious time. Every minute spent fighting allowed the rest of the Fair Folk to draw closer.

"Up the next set of stairs," Dace ordered, and Yushuv sprang to obey. Across the room, a grinning, green face appeared in a doorway. Yushuv stopped, spun, and loosed an arrow. There was a muffled thump as the face disappeared, and Yushuv turned to run again.

Dace was already ahead of him, taking the steps two at a time. "Hurry!" the older man called as Yushuv began the climb. *My legs are too short for this*, he thought in desperation. *What kind of things could have built this place?*

The sound of claws on stone told Yushuv that the Fair Folk had entered the chamber below. Ten steps up and climbing, he risked a look back and immediately wished he hadn't. A trio of Fair Folk archers were casually lining up their shots, forming a palisade in front of a tall elfin woman whose robes instantly proclaimed her to be a sorceress. A tide of the savage hobgoblins streamed past them, their claws and teeth shining hellishly in the reddened light.

From nowhere, an elfin warrior bounded onto the bottom step of the staircase Yushuv and Dace were climbing. Instinctively, the boy stopped to put an arrow into the pale figure, only to see it fade and vanish as the shaft passed through what should have been its throat.

"Illusion," Dace said from behind and above him. "Their best magic. Hurry, they're just trying to waste your arrows."

Yushuv nodded wordlessly and continued his ascent, but his eye kept on straying to the sorceress below. The archers protecting her had not yet fired. Why was that? What were they waiting for?

Suddenly, Yushuv had his answer. The sorceress pointed, and a blast of colorless light exploded from her fingertips. It struck the staircase the fugitives were climbing, and where the light touched it, the stone bubbled and dissolved. Eyes wide with terror, Yushuv scrambled for higher ground, but the magic outpaced him and the very steps boiled away under his feet. "Dace!" he screamed, even as he trod on empty air and began the long fall to the unforgiving floor below.

"I've got you." Dace turned and reached back across his body, his fingers closing on Yushuv's wrist like a steel vise. The boy cried out in pain, arrows tumbling out of his quiver as he dangled. Arrows rained around them, striking so hard that chips of stone flew from the walls and remaining stairs. Dace ignored them as best he could, one arm held up to shield his face, the other hanging onto Yushuv.

"Dace, hurry!" The boy's voice was shrill with terror

"I've got you, Yushuv. Don't worry." Dace shifted his feet and braced himself, the better to pull his charge to safety without yanking the boy's arm out of its socket. "Just one more second."

"The stairs! They're still crumbling!"

Dace looked down to see the stone underneath his boots melting away. With a curse, he flung himself backwards and up the steps, trusting in his grip and Yushuv's resiliency. The pack took most of the force of the impact, but Dace still grunted when he hit, his head cracking painfully against the stone. The boy hit him a second later, crying out briefly before having the wind knocked out of him.

"No time for that, boy," Dace growled, and scrambled backwards up the stairs. Half-dragging Yushuv with him, he turned and stumbled to his feet, the hiss of the dissolving stone growing ever louder in his ears.

They reached the next landing and Yushuv staggered to his feet, looking down. The stairway was almost completely gone, with only a few steps at the top and bottom remaining. Unless the Fair Folk could fly, there'd be no pursuit from that direction.

Unfortunately, he realized, there were still three other stairways, and even as they caught their breath, the first of the small, scaled hobgoblins emerged on the far side of the chamber. Yushuv whirled and dropped him with a single shot to the eye, but another took his place and then another, and suddenly an army of its snarling brethren was advancing toward them, eyes shining with hunger.

"Yushuv, arrows!" Dace barked out the command even as he dropped his pack to the floor and unlimbered his daiklave.

"I'm running out," the boy replied, but even as he did so the white light at his brow flared, and a rain of arrows began lancing out toward the charging beasts. They went down like grass before the scythe, but even as Dace coiled himself to leap forward into the mass of beasts, a searing pain cut across his back. He turned, and saw another ageless, sexless faerie noble, this one's face tinged with the colors of autumn leaves. It held a sword indolently in its left hand, one which dripped blood from where it had lashed across Dace's back.

"I'm afraid I'm going to have to keep you busy for a moment while our children play with yours," the creature said, flicking a shiveringly quick cut at Dace's arm. Dace countered it and brought the daiklave down in a brutal chop at the elfin warrior's head, but the creature pirouetted back and out of the way. "Ah, you *do* have some skill," it said. "That will make this more enjoyable." It then launched a series of feints at Dace's knee and wrist, each faster than the last, and Dace found himself parrying furiously. "You can even call on whatever powers you've been given if you want to make this last longer; I understand that some of your kind can fight competently if the Sun is running through your veins. I'm curious as to how fast you can strike. As fast as this?" Its sword moving faster than the eye could see, the faerie scored a hit on Dace's cheek. "Or this?" Another blur, and then another wound opened on his hand. "Really, I expected better."

"You'll get better," Dace growled, and tore open the floodgates of his power. Golden light erupted from his brow, crackling down his arms and encircling his head in a halo of lightning. He lifted the daiklave over his head and molten light poured from it, scattering on the ground like quicksilver.

The thing took a pair of involuntary steps back and brought a hand up to shade its eyes, its sword sagging from the guard position. "I never knew..." it whispered. "What *are* you?"

"An old enemy," Dace replied, and brought the daiklave down. The faerie raised its sword to meet it. There was a flash of light as the two blades met, then a sound like crystal shattering on a stone floor. The pieces of the elf's sword went spinning as it fell back, and with a vicious laugh Dace reversed his grip and pinned his opponent to the floor. The faerie gave one last kick and died, and Dace pulled his sword free to see if he was too late to help Yushuv.

◈

The bow was useless now, and Yushuv found himself fighting with dagger and desperation. He'd loosed as many arrows as he dared and cut down uncounted numbers of the miniscule, serpentine goblins. The stone floor was slick with their gore and buried under their corpses, but still they came. Most were no higher than his knee, but they were fast and fearless and clever, and they outnumbered him. No sooner had he impaled one on his dagger than another leapt up onto his quiver and started tearing at it while two more hacked viciously at his ankles. He kicked the two away and shook the corpse of the third off his blade as he tried to get at the one on his back, but it hissed malevolently and dodged his awkward blows. He tried again, and instantly felt a sharp pain the back of his neck where the beast had bitten him.

Instinctively, Yushuv dropped the dagger and tore the thing from his neck, but even as he did so he realized it was a mistake. The creature sank its fangs into his fingers, drawing blood and biting down to the bone. He flung the creature off into the pit, shrieking, but as he did so, another one of the twisted little monstrosities grabbed his dagger and plunged it into his boot.

Yushuv shouted in pain and kicked violently forward, yanking the dagger out of the creature's grasp. It chittered in glee, and Yushuv brought his now-bloodied fist down on top of it with a satisfying crunch. Collapsing, it gave a last, spasmodic kick, and then lay still.

Carefully, Yushuv leaned down and picked up the dagger. The remaining creatures—he estimated there were at least fifteen—watched him, warily. Then, with a cry, he threw himself into their midst. The dagger came down like a hard rain, and these decidedly Unfair Folk died.

❖

It was minutes later, at most, when Yushuv brought his blade up and saw that there was nothing left in front of him to kill. Panting, he looked around in amazement. Large piles of small corpses were arrayed in front of him, and his arm was coated in their blood up to the elbow. He was marked by a dozen bites and slashes, but none seemed deep. Even the one at the back of his neck had mostly stopped bleeding, as dried blood clotted his hair.

"Nice work," Dace said dryly as he strode forward. "Did you kill them all?"

Yushuv knelt down to pick up his bow, which he'd dropped when the beasts had swarmed him. "Almost. Three ran away." With nervous fingers he pulled an arrow from his abused quiver and brought it to the bow. "What now?" he asked, looking around for more enemies.

Dace pointed to the nearest stairs. "What happens is that I'll deal with the pursuit," he said. "You head up to the next level and wait for me there."

"All right." Yushuv stared at the carnage for a moment, then shuddered. "What are you going to do?"

"Wreak havoc," Dace replied, and started for the nearest staircase down.

◆

Yushuv was halfway up to what he guessed was the highest level inside the pyramid when he heard the first thundering crash. There was a shout and then another crash, the sound of what happens when metal meets stone and stone loses.

He's destroying the stairways, Yushuv thought. *I hope he does it in time.* His mind filled with images of Dace, his attention focused on the broken stonework before him, being swarmed by a million of the grinning serpent-men while he, Yushuv, ran away. Ashamed of himself, he pushed the notion aside and concentrated on taking the huge steps as best he could.

He reached the final landing in a matter of seconds and stopped, stunned at what he saw. The massive chains arched across the ceiling and met over the pit, where they were bound in what could only be a giant shackle. From there, they continued down into the depths of the earth, and Yushuv could see now that they were shaking. The room itself was decorated with frescoes, the only representative art Yushuv had seen in the city. The images told the tale of the race who had dwelt here once, of their history and triumphs, their customs and rituals and sorrows.

And standing astride the titanic lock, swinging a hammer taller than a man, stood the last inhabitant of the ancient city.

The creature stood nearly half again as tall as Dace was, its shape roughly that of a slender, noble man. Its skin, or more precisely its hide, was the dark green of old pine needles, and it gleamed. Scaly hands with claws the length of a man's finger were wrapped around the hammer's haft, and huge, unblinking yellow eyes surmounted the creature's skull. A small single horn rose up from its nose, and a frill of others ringed the back of its head. Its mouth was very wide and filled with sharp teeth, and the creature was singing in time with the blows it struck with the hammer.

It noticed Yushuv then, and hissed in curiosity. Its tongue flicked out to taste the air in the direction in which Yushuv stood, and it leaned on the hammer as it did so.

Carefully, Yushuv laid his bow on the ground and raised his hands, palms forward.

"Ah. You come at last. Do the accursed *slisstissir*, forgive me, do the thrice-be-damned Fair Folk follow you?" The creature's voice was a dry, disinterested rasp, and it drew out its sibilants with a flick of its long, forked tongue. "You have made me wait a long time for death."

"How did you know I was coming? What *are* you?"

"You, or one like you, were prophesied. There," it said, and pointed with its huge hammer at a section of fresco across the pit from where Yushuv stood. "It is a prophecy of endings. You are to bring the ancient enemy with you, and all will perish in fire." It brought the hammer down with a brutally loud clang, then turned to Yushuv, its expression unreadable. "It is about time you got here."

"I'm running from the Fair Folk, yes," Yushuv said, his eyes flicking around the room frantically. "My teacher and I have been fleeing them for days. Can you help us? Is there a way out of here?"

The creature nodded, but ignored his questions. "Days, yes. That is not so long. My people and I fought them for years." The creature cocked its head to one side and listened. "There are many of them, and their servants as well. Mockeries of my kind, they are. I kill them when I see them. Do you?"

"Yes, but more come with every one we kill." Carefully, Yushuv knelt and picked up his bow. His host made no motion to stop him.

"You kill the Fair Folk and their children. This is good. You are the one. You bring fire with you. You will help me loose what lies below. It is good to see you do not serve the Fair Folk. I have been waiting for a very long time for you to bring them back. "

"I will?" Confusion tinged Yushuv's voice. "You have?"

"Yes. So I could give them this!" And with that statement, the creature lifted his hammer in the air and brought it down on the lock. A hollow booming sound met his efforts.

"What are you trying to do?" Yushuv edged closer, convinced that this creature meant him, at least, no harm. Nervous glances over his shoulder showed him no sign of Dace.

"Loose the spirit," the creature responded. "Long ago, in the days of the first shamans, my people bound the beast of flame who dwelt in the lake of fire that once was here. While it slumbered, we built this city, and dwelt here until the Fair Folk came. They slew most of us and scattered the rest. That was centuries, as your kind reckons time, ago. I am Salastor. I am the last of my kind, and I have been waiting for this day."

"So we can help you make the Fair Folk burn?" Yushuv and Salastor both turned. Dace stood in the arch over yet another stairway, breathing hard. The light at his brow was dimmed, and he looked visibly tired. "Never mind me," he said, "I'm with the boy."

"Ah." Salastor nodded. "Yes. Fire is a gift I wish to give both the spirit and the *slisstissir.*"

"And you need to break that lock to do it." Yushuv's words were a statement, not a question. "Then what happens to you?"

"What do you expect will happen? I will die, in fire." Again, the creature raised its hammer and brought it down. The sound was deafening.

Yushuv walked over to one of the four entrances to the chamber that faced north and looked out. An arrow whizzed past him to shatter on the stone of the archway, and he ducked back in with alacrity. "Dace, they're coming up the stairs on the outside here," he said, unnecessarily. "Should we check the others?"

"Already doing so." Dace bounded over to the nearest arch, which opened to the east and nearly got himself spitted on a trio of arrows for his troubles.

"They're on this side, too," he noted, and ran for the doorway that faced south.

"Here, too," Yushuv called from the west. "More of them, I think."

Dace didn't even bother to peer out the last doorway. He merely waved his daiklave in front of the opening, and was rewarded with a metallic ringing as an arrow caught the blade dead center. "Damn. Made my hands sting," he said, and retreated toward the edge of the pit.

Yushuv was already there, worriedly counting the arrows in his tattered quiver. "What are we going to do? You can't seal the doors here or you'll bring the roof down on our heads. We can't hold them off at two doors. They'll just come in the other two." He paused and took a deep breath. "We're going to die, aren't we?"

Dace exhaled sharply. "Possibly. Then again, they may get tired first, or they might run out of their precious little goblin lizards. I doubt it, though. So, if we can't guard the doors and we can't get out, where do you suggest we go?"

Yushuv pointed. "There," he said. Dace nodded. "Of course. On the lock itself. Hard for them to get to, and we just might get our friend to help." He looked out at the south entrance, still deceptively empty. "Let's go, before more company arrives."

They ran to the nearest chain, Dace boosting Yushuv up and then climbing onto the massive steel links himself. "Salastor, we're coming over," he called out, even as he walked as fast as he dared along the chain's length to where the scaled and unblinking creature stood. Yushuv, as always, was ahead of him, scrambling along the links like he'd been born to it. Dace followed more slowly, the hot metal beneath his feet swaying slightly with every step. "Slow down, boy" he said with a hint of nervousness. "You're shaking the chain."

"I'm not," Yushuv replied defensively, even as he stepped onto the lock itself. "It's whatever the chain is holding. I think it's awake, now."

"Marvelous," said Dace, and picked up his pace. He lifted his foot for another step, but in that instant the earth itself groaned, and the chain suddenly shifted forward. Yushuv flung himself to the metal of the lock, but Salastor continued his labors. Again, he raised his hammer, and again it came down, and Yushuv saw that the metal that took the blow was barely dented.

"Salastor, how long have you been doing this?"

"Eight hundred years," was the measured response, followed by another swing. "It is… very good workmanship."

"Could you discuss that some other time?" Yushuv looked up to see Dace sprawled out on the chain, perilously close to sliding off. "I may need some help here."

"I'm coming," Yushuv answered, and rose to his feet. He took two steps, and then a whistling rain of arrows from all sides made him throw himself flat again. "Dace, they're here!"

"I know that. Arrrghh!" An arrow had taken Dace in the leg, just below the knee. Reflexively, he clutched at it and nearly lost his grip in the process. "Barbed head," he muttered against gritted teeth, and snapped the shaft off where it entered his flesh. The broken arrow he dropped into the shaft, and then he resumed crawling forward. Yushuv was up and firing, chanting the number of arrows he had left.

"Nine."

An arrow took a Fair Folk sorcerer in the eye, and the radiant globe of purple light he was conjuring exploded. Daggers of amethyst flew everywhere, and the servants of the Fair Folk fell like reeds before the storm.

"Eight."

With a thrum, another shaft flew through the air and burst into flame. The gouts of fire rained down on half a hundred of the tiny serpent-men. A stench of burned flesh rose up with the dense brown smoke, and the others of their kind set up a fearful wailing.

"Seven."

A sorceress calling up beasts of smoke from the air sagged forward, her hands leaving off their work to tug fruitlessly at the arrow that had suddenly pierced her belly. She gave a long, keening howl of distress, and collapsed, even as the creatures she had summoned set upon her.

"Six."

A servitor creature warrior who'd leapt up on the chain as agilely as a cat gave a burbling scream, then toppled sideways into the pit, spitted neatly through its tiny breastbone.

"Five."

Another firestorm rained down, even as the screams rose up.

"Four."

A faerie archer opened his mouth in a battle cry and an arrow smashed through the back of his throat.

"Three. Dace, hurry!"

A brace of goblins leapt from the edge of the pit toward the lock itself, mouths open as they screamed in fury. Yushuv's arrow punched through one and spun the other around, and they smashed into the side of the massive metal artifice before sliding off into the depths below.

"Make your arrows count, Yushuv!" Laboriously, Dace pulled himself along the chain, which was now thrashing like an angry snake. "Use what I've taught you!"

"I'm trying," Yushuv called back. "Two!"

He loosed the arrow and willed whatever power was still in him to follow it. It burst into flame mid-flight and caught another dozen of the servitors, washing them from the chain opposite Dace's with a rain of fire.

Without warning, a thunderclap echoed through the chamber. A sudden, scorching heat enveloped Dace for an instant, and then both he and the chain he clung to were swinging free, severed from the length that ran up the wall of the chamber and out a gap in the ceiling. Even know, those monstrous links were slithering away, and as Dace looked back in a panic he saw the same clear fire that had destroyed the steps eating away at the metal links. Desperately, he began scrambling up the chain, calling out for help as he did so.

Yushuv turned and saw the sorceress who'd severed the chain summoning another gout of power. "One," he whispered, and loosed.

She saw the arrow coming, and loosed her own blast at it. The arrow shone with a golden light as it flew, and its fire mingled with the Fair Folk sorcery. There was a sound like metal being torn, and then the arrow shivered into nothingness while the gout of magical fire skewed wildly to the right. It struck a second chain, and hungrily began eating into it. The sorceress laughed and raised her hands for another attempt.

"Yushuv! Stop her!" Dace called.

"I can't!" The boy stood there, his bow at his side. A single arrow jutted from the quiver, but he made no move to reach for it.,

"You have an arrow left. Use it!"

"You don't understand. I can't! I made a deal with a spirit. When I fire that arrow, he gets free, and he gets to come for me. I can't fight him!" Yushuv was near tears. Carefully, cautiously, the Fair Folk sorceress advanced. The lock itself was balanced precariously now, and Salastor looked around defiantly as he balanced on its tilted surface.

"I'll deal with the damned spirit, Yushuv. Fire!" Dace was clinging by one hand now, the chain whipping back and forth like a live thing. The other hand held his daiklave, which swung out below him like a rudder. Arrows rained past, clanging off the chain to all sides. He looked down and saw only the immeasurable depths of the pit, and resigned himself to the fact that he was most likely going to die.

However, he was not going to die, he decided, without taking more of the Fair Folk with him. "By all that's holy, Yushuv, shoot!"

His eyes wide and unseeing, Yushuv reached back into his quiver. A single arrow, painstakingly stitched into place, was all that remained. With a gentle tug, it came free. Yushuv set it to his bow, threw back his head, and *howled*.

Astonishingly, the Fair Folk stopped. Bows were lowered, spells abandoned half-cast. Charging warriors stopped in their tracks.

Yushuv's cry faded, a ragged, dying sound. The creak of Dace's chain echoed loudly in the silence. Then, one by one, the Fair Folk and their beasts began to laugh. Some pointed at Yushuv. Others clutched their sides; one abruptly sat down. The Fair Folk's laughter was high and clear, like their singing, and there was no joy in it. They laughed at Yushuv, at his pitiful attempts to resist them and the short chase he'd led them. They laughed at Dace's fear and Salastor's feeble efforts. They laughed at all before them that was not fey, and they laughed because they could without fear of jeopardizing their hunt. And with harsh, rasping sounds, their scuttling, predatory servants laughed with them

It is over, their laughter said. *We have won. Now it is just a question of how to play the endgame.*

Yushuv stared at them. He turned in a slow circle, looking out over the small army of fey who mocked him. White light flared from his brow and curled around his eyes, and still they laughed. Discreetly, Salastor edged his way to the spot were Dace dangled, reaching down with a clawed hand to lift him to safety, and still the laughter continued.

Yushuv, very deliberately, set his last arrow to his bow and drew it back. He sighted it at nothing, the strain of the moment telling in the trembling of his hands.

"You have one arrow," called out a voice from the crowd of Fair Folk. "One. There are a hundred of us in the city, and ten thousand of our servants. What good will it do you?" Slowly, the laughter died, drowning in a tide of voices murmuring *Surrender.*

"I would rather die," Yushuv said, and loosed his last arrow.

One arrow left Yushuv's bow amidst a blaze of white light. A hundred descended. Fair Folk died where they stood, or died fleeing. Archers fell next to swordsmen and sorceresses, and the hiss of descending arrows sounded like rain.

A long moment later, the rain stopped. The last arrow fell to the stone floor and rattled to a halt. A dozen Fair Folk looked around, counted their dead, and then numbered their foes. They were no longer laughing.

"I'm sorry, Dace," Yushuv said, and collapsed. Dace scooped the boy up with one hand and looked to Salastor. "Do you have any ideas?" Around them, the unmistakable crackle of chaos sorcery filled the air.

"Finish my work," the creature suggested. "Free the sleeper. At least we will not die alone."

Dace blinked, and then felt a grim smile crease his lips. "Why not?" he said. "But what you were trying won't work. I have a better idea. Here, take the boy."

Salastor nodded and cradled Yushuv gently in the crook of one serpentine arm, the hammer still in his other hand.

"Stand at the edge. When I give the word, jump." Dace raised his daiklave and swung it experimentally once. Power surged through him and lent strength to his arms. Face twisted in rage, he brought the massive blade down on the links of steel.

The first blow drew sparks, the second bit deep into the metal. Arrows flew, but he ignored them and hefted the sword for the final blow. "Now!" he shouted, and hewed at the damaged steel chain with all his might.

It snapped. Instantly, the massive lock tilted toward the abyss, the other chains slithering down into it with fearsome speed. Dace leapt for the side of the pit and barely made it, nearly impaling himself on the daiklave in the process. Salastor stood by him, providing a steadying hand as for an instant he tottered on the brink.

"What have you done?" One of the Fair Folk stepped forward with sword in hand, its beautiful face distorted by fury. "You've doomed us all!"

"Good," said Dace as he climbed to his feet. "I'll see you in one of the hells, I expect. Bring friends."

A low rumble started, deep in the depths of the pit. A blast of scorching heat followed on its heels, forcing all back from the edges of the shaft. Salastor sheltered Yushuv with his own body, but the wind drove them back even as the reddish glow inside the chamber brightened. Cracks split the stone floor, which surged and bucked like a horse with its first ride. Dace fell, as did the Fair Folk. Only Salastor remained standing, a rapturous look on his face.

"It is coming," he said. "Now we just wait to die."

❖

The lock was the first thing to emerge from the pit, spat forth with enough force to fling it fifty feet into the air before it crashed with an ear-splitting din. A titanic hand followed, grasping the lip of the pit, and then another one, and in seconds a massive, vaguely human figure had emerged from the ancient depths.

I AM ZAKHAS, AND I HAVE BEEN BOUND FOR TEN THOUSAND YEARS. I HAVE WAITED, AND I HAVE SLUMBERED. BUT I AM AWAKE NOW, it said, and the walls trembled.

WHO HAS FREED ME?

Before any could answer, the spirit—which Yushuv now saw resembled Salastor far more closely than it did a man—looked down and saw the remaining Fair Folk assembled before it. Their servants bowed down to the spirit, keening in terror, and the spirit roared its response.

YOU, it roared, and brought a fist down that scattered the Fair Folk like chaff. *I HAVE BEEN WAITING FOR YOU.* Its gaze swept the room, fixing on Yushuv and Dace. *AND YOU MUST BE THEIR PREY. WE SHALL SEE ABOUT THAT.*

It scooped Dace and Yushuv up in one hand, and used the other to sweep clear the floor of the chamber with fire and molten stone. Salastor fell to his knees in worship, keening his joy.

CHILD OF MY ANCIENT OPPRESSOR, WHAT AM I TO DO WITH YOU?

The Fair Folk were dead or scattered, and puddles of cooling lava marked the chamber floor. Salastor still knelt, but now he looked up to meet the spirit's gaze.

"My people bound you to make this place. I labored many years to free you," he said. "We owe each other nothing, and no one will remember either of us. Take the city, for it is rightfully yours, and many Fair Folk still walk its streets. Take my life, for I offer it as recompense for the years you spent bound."

THE BARGAIN IS STRUCK, the spirit announced. *DIE WELL.*

With painful dignity, Salastor rose to his feet and turned. The body of the spirit hovered over the well, and the serpent-man walked right to its edge. "I am ready," he said, and then hurled himself downward. There was the sound of one last chain breaking, and then the spirit shouted defiance and joy with a voice of thunder. Stones shook loose from the ceiling, smashing on the floor below. The entire city trembled, and cries of alarm rose up from the streets.

THIS CITY IS MINE, Zakhas announced, and burst through the roof of the pyramid. Stone splintered and fell away as the spirit rocketed skywards. It gazed out at what had long been its prison. *AND AS ITS KEEPER, I SENTENCE IT TO DESTRUCTION.* He reached out his long arms over the city, caressing a building here and a spire there. Where he touched, flame erupted and stone melted. The goblins in the streets fled frantically, only to be overwhelmed by the rivers of lava Zakhas called up from the ground itself. Buildings foundered and the air was split by the cries of Fair Folk and animals alike. Tortured stone split, and in the midst of it all, Zakhas reveled in his power.

I SHALL NOT BE BOUND AGAIN! THIS PLACE IS MINE, FOR NOW AND FOREVER. The spirit turned its monstrous head to Dace and Yushuv. *TELL THEM THIS,* it said. *TELL THEM WELL, AND MAKE SURE THEY HEED YOU. YOU DO NOT WISH, I THINK, TO SEE OTHER CITIES DIE.*

"We promise!" Yushuv called out, his voice swept away by wind and fire. "We'll tell them!"

"Whoever they are," Dace muttered, but even he could find little fault in making such a hasty promise to a spirit. Though Zakhas was clearly taking care to shield them from his heat, it was still painfully warm within his grip.

GOOD. The spirit flew higher, thunderclouds surging over his head. Lightning forked down, but no rain, and the carnival of destruction continued unabated. *GO NOW,* it said after a moment, *LEST I FORGET YOUR PRESENCE. I DO NOT WISH TO HARM THOSE WHO FREED ME.*

So saying, he set Yushuv and Dace down gently on the lip of the crater before whirling off in a blast of heat. They could see the waves of lava lapping at the pyramid before it sank out of sight, and everywhere buildings toppled to their doom. The avenues were completely submerged now, and fountains of molten rock flew high into the air.

"It's beautiful," Yushuv said. "It's a shame the city has to die, but this is beautiful."

Dace nodded. "And in an hour, we'll be the only things left alive who remember what this city looked like, or who lived there. That's precious, Yushuv. I can't tell you why, but it is.

Hold fast to that."

"I will," he said solemnly. Together, silently, they watched the city drown in liquid fire. At moments they could see Zakhas swooping hither and yon, and where its hands touched, stone glowed red-hot and flowed away.

When the last spire had fallen into the glowing lake that filled the crater from side to side, they turned and began picking their way into the forest. Yushuv's empty quiver dangled from his back, a wordless reminder of the cost of the battle they had just fought. They crested a low ridge and began to descend, and in an instant the lost city was gone from view. All that remained was the roar of the molten rock as it churned endlessly, and the faint smell of sulfur.

"We need to make you some more arrows," Dace said after a while, and Yushuv nodded. "That spirit of yours has a long way to go, but his kind runs fast and doesn't sleep."

"That seems right," Yushuv said carefully. "I don't know much about him except his name and what he looked like."

Dace sheathed his daiklave, which was getting caught on overhead branches, and pulled the shorter sword from his belt. Foliage blocked his way, and he hacked at it with weary determination. "So tell me what you do know."

"His name is Bonecrack, or at least that's what he told me." Yushuv ducked a branch that Dace had let go of, and which had swung back into their path. "It was shaped like a wolf, with red eyes and black fur. Bigger than any wolf I'd seen, though, and we used to have a lot of trouble with them back home."

"Hunh. It sounds almost like a Fair Folk hound gone feral. Definitely bad news. We'll want to be on our guard. The last thing we want is something like that sneaking up on us."

"Indeed," said a mellifluous voice directly in front of them. "That would be tragic."

Dace hacked through the curtain of green that lay before him, and nearly dropped his sword in astonishment. Standing in a small clearing was a faerie, wearing white and forest green and holding his hands in the air, palms out. "I have no weapons," he said, "though I do have a few horses just down the trail that you might find useful. Arrows I can supply as well. Ah, and before I say anything more, I should say this: I surrender."

The squirrel had no idea that it was a witness to great things. It merely thought, in its dim, squirrelish way, that it was being very industrious by searching for nuts in the trees along the creekside, long after the other squirrels had found their safe nests and gone to sleep. And so it scampered up the trunk of one tree and down another, growing increasingly disappointed by the stubborn refusal of the waterside willows to yield anything even vaguely delectable.

Overhead, thunder boomed. The squirrel stopped and sniffed the air, nervous eyes darting in all directions. There was no scent of rain that it could detect, and no clouds obscured the stars overhead. Confused, the squirrel put its head down and made the fearful dash to the next tree, perhaps a dozen feet away.

The sharp crack of wood made the squirrel freeze in mid-stride, halfway between the two trees. Vaguely, it was aware that this was possibly the worst place for it to be should a predator approach, but blind panic insisted that it stay stock-still, and like a good squirrel it listened.

More splintering sounds followed, mixed with a deep, angry growling. *Predator*, the squirrel's memory told it. *Wolf. Run!*

It ran.

Downstream, the sound of wood breaking rose to a deafening crescendo, then ceased abruptly, to be replaced by the noise of something big moving through the brush. Panicked, the squirrel leapt for the trunk of the nearest willow and scrambled up. It found a hiding place, then peered out around the trunk in hopes of seeing the author of the noise.

An instant later, its hopes were realized. A wolf trotted by, or something that looked like a wolf. Massive and shaggy, its black fur flecked with blood, it moved with an air of casual arrogance. Its muzzle dripped blood as well, and a foul stench of rot rolled off its hide.

The squirrel let out a tortured squeak and scurried higher

into the tree. The wolf-thing heard it and stopped. It turned, and the squirrel saw that it had only one eye. The other had been taken by a hunter's arrow.

In that instant, it saw the squirrel. Its gaze held the squirrel, and then it grinned, showing reddened fangs an inch long. "Run, little creature" it said, in a voice that was rusty from long disuse. "You can run. *He* cannot."

And then Bonecrack the wolf-spirit, a terror who had stalked the night since the beginning of Creation, lifted its head and howled.

The squirrel listened for a moment, frozen with fear, and then fled into the night. Laughing, Bonecrack followed.

Chapter Twenty-Two

Fighting ghosts was very different from fighting men, Eliezer Wren quickly decided. For one thing, the living felt pain, which made dealing with them much easier. A kick to the groin would double over any living man in breathless agony, a result that generally reduced their combat efficiency. On the other hand ghosts, even solid ones, had no such weakness. A solid blow to even the most sensitive area knocked them off balance at best, and did nothing at worst. And the problem with *that* was that when one landed a blow, one expected it to have an effect, and planned one's next move in accordance with the anticipated result.

Thus it was that Wren had leapt into the fray, opened with a devastating roundhouse kick to an enemy's head, turned to face a new opponent and promptly been staggered by a blow from the dead man he'd thought he'd dispatched.

Wren had dropped to one knee, just in time to catch a kick to the chin from the ghost in front of him and flop over backwards. *Where are the damned snakes when I need them?* he thought desperately, and rolled right to avoid a brutal foot stomp. Two revolutions brought him up against the shins of another enemy, a female ghost who wore the broken remains of ornate bronze armor. She let out a wordless shriek and stabbed down with a rusty diamond-shaped blade, causing Wren to fling himself to his feet in a hurry and plant a kick in the center of her chest. The ghost fell backwards, still howling, and let go of her sword. Wren grabbed in, made a face at its poor balance, and charged back into the fray.

Idli, he saw, was acquitting himself well. There was no grace or finesse to the guide's fighting style, just speed and unrelenting force. A dead man appeared in front of Idli and Idli struck him. More often than not, the dead man went down. If he didn't, Idli struck the shade again and again, until he collapsed under the sheer weight of the punishment. Most of the ones Idli struck, Wren noted, did not rise again. Apparently there were limits to the amount of abuse even ghosts could stand.

A man whose left arm hung by frayed strands of tendon swiped at Wren's face, who responded by diving under the blow to plant his sword in the thing's chest. It looked down and wriggled, and Wren realized he'd made another serious tactical error. The ghost looked at him and grinned, showing bloody stumps of teeth, and drew back its good arm for another strike.

Even as it did so, Wren brought his right leg up and planted his foot against the dead man's gut. He pushed, and the sword came free with a wet, sucking sound even as the ghost toppled over backwards.

"Dismember, don't impale!" Idli's voice could be heard clearly over the sounds of the fight, for the ghosts were mostly silent. Those few who did cry out did so wordlessly, screaming or grunting like animals in pain. Other than that, there was just the shuffle of feet on stone, the occasional clang of metal on ghostly metal, and the solid thump of flesh hammering flesh.

"I'd just about figured that out," Wren replied, and hacked down diagonally through the torso of another attacker. It sagged apart along the cut and collapsed to the floor in pieces. Wren pulled the sword free and made another sweeping cut. The ghostly bodies offered surprisingly little resistance to the sword blade, and Wren himself was astonished to see that he'd cut clear through two more opponents. A broken spear-shaft was thrust at his face, and with two blows he knocked the weapon free and then removed the hands of the figure wielding it. She ran forward to bludgeon him with the ragged stumps that remained, and almost casually Wren flicked her head from her shoulders. Even headless, the decomposing torso still advanced, so Wren sidestepped its charge and then shoved it, bodily, into the mass of ghosts behind him. Several went down in a tumble, and Wren continued cutting his way towards Idli.

"What the hell are we fighting?" he called out when the two were finally back to back.

"Lemures," Idli replied, dropping another one. "Mindless spirits of the dead. The siege engine fodder of the Labyrinth. The lords of this place count their wealth in the territory they control and the souls they oversee."

Wren hacked off an overextended arm and took a leg at the knee on his backswing. "So you're saying we're fighting loose change?"

Idli laughed. "I hadn't thought of it that way, but yes. They're just here to slow us down. The clamor of the fight will be heard soon enough, and then the real servants of the dark will arrive." He ducked under a blow, which clipped Wren on the back of the head. "Damn. Sorry."

"Watch it next time." More of the lemures had leapt down from the ledge above, wielding spears. A ring of clear space had developed around Wren and Idli as the ghosts finally seemed to learn that their current approach wasn't working. Spearheads jabbed in, slowly, but Wren was able to knock them aside with contemptuous ease. "They seem to have figured out that they're a delaying action. Any thoughts?"

Idli nodded, a maneuver Wren felt instead of saw. "You saw the ones from the ledge above jump down to join in the fight, yes?"

"Barely. What I wouldn't give for some more light."

Idli snorted. "I thought you priests were trained to fight blind."

"Yes, but that doesn't mean I have to like it. By the time you lead me out of here, I'm going to be blind as a cave fish."

"I'll settle for leading you out of this passage first. Then we'll worry about your good looks. Now, when I call three, jump up to the ledge."

Wren hazarded a look in that direction. "Jump up? That's quite a leap."

"You are chosen of the Sun, Eliezer Wren. You have it in you. Either that, or these dead things will have your guts out of you."

"If you say so," Wren muttered, and, without preamble, leapt straight up.

"Damn you, Wren, wait!" So saying, Idli launched himself

upwards as below, the dead men charged into the space where the two had been standing.

Wren landed on the ledge with a whoop. He'd expected to jump five, perhaps six feet straight up. Instead, his scalp had nearly brushed against the chamber's ceiling, and he'd come down as lightly as a cat. He peered over the ledge at the milling horde below, then turned to see Idli landing beside him.

"Why didn't you wait?" Idli was furious.

Wren shrugged. "No time like the present to get away from a mob of angry ghosts with spears. Besides, if it wasn't going to work, I wanted to know as soon as possible. Now, where do we go from here?"

Idli pointed. "There. The passage the ones up here had been guarding. Hurry."

Wren looked down again. "They can't get up here, can they?"

"No, but they have allies and masters who can. You think you're the only one in this maze who can jump? Move!"

Wren moved, the sword in his fist, into the dark.

✦

"Not to be impolite, but do you actually know where we're going?" Wren looked down a corridor that looked, in the unutterably dim light, to be precisely identical to the nine they'd just traversed.

"Where we are going, yes. Precisely how we are getting there? That's a more difficult question. The tunnels shift and move as if the Labyrinth itself were alive, and the wars between those who—I cannot say 'live,' so perhaps 'dwell' is the better term—dwell here mean that many once-safe avenues are now quite unsafe. Or would you prefer to stroll through a battleground where the soldiers make those things we just fought seem as normal as rain?"

"No, no, you're quite right. Forget I asked." Wren shook his head. Idli had been extremely touchy since the escape from the lemures. It couldn't have been because he'd leapt early, could it? He thought back. Idli had told him to prepare to jump on a given signal, he'd leapt, and below him the ghosts surged forward...

...*before* Idli would have given the word. But Idli had fought with him against the lemures, hadn't he? He'd struck down dead men by the handful.

"*Dismember, don't impale!*" The words floated out of the recent past. Dismember, yes, but Idli had used only his fists. The lemures he'd brutalized had fallen to the floor, but had they gotten back up again?

"Idli," he said, turning. "Before we go any further, I think we need to talk."

In response, Wren took a sledgehammer blow to the chin and then a gut punch that drove him to his knees. He brought up the sword, but a kick knocked it from his hands, spinning off into the dark. It clanged against the tunnel wall, and was lost.

"No, I'm afraid we don't." Another kick whistled past Wren's face, who threw himself backwards. "I get much more than a finger if I deliver all of you, you know. You're entirely too naive for this sort of thing, Wren. It's a miracle that anyone wants you at all."

Wren sprang to his feet, his fists in front of him. "I know how to hurt you, Idli. I'd rather not do it."

"Why not?" A flurry of fists came out of the dark, and Wren barely managed to parry each blow. "You owe me nothing except pain."

Wren tried a leg sweep and missed, then dodged a series of punches at his gut. "It attracts attention. I'd rather not do it if I didn't have to."

"You could just surrender." A kick caught Wren in the ribs, and he staggered back a couple of steps. Another kick flashed out of the darkness, but Wren was ready for it this time and caught Idli's foot above the ankle. Expertly, he twisted, and was rewarded with the sound of his opponent crashing to the tunnel floor. Idli's foot twisted out of his grasp, and rather than follow up his advantage, Wren turned and ran.

"There's no escape that way!" Idli called after him, but Wren didn't listen. Instead, he put his head down and channeled all his thought into his weary legs, willing them to propel him as fast as they could. His feet slapped against the warm stone of the tunnel, and in echo he could hear Idli's footsteps as well. His erstwhile guide was gaining on him, and while Wren didn't know precisely how far behind Idli was, it couldn't be far.

He'd been hoping to find a side tunnel to duck down, but none had appeared thus far. Once or twice he'd thought he'd seen one, but as he approached the apertures were revealed to be nothing more than illusions in stone.

Or perhaps Idli had found a way to close them. Wren shuddered at the thought and kept running. Light, he knew, would help, but he wasn't sure if he dared risk it, or even if he knew how. There was light living in him now, he was sure, but he didn't know how to call it forth or what else it might do, and to call on the power of the Sun in the depths of the Underworld might have unexpected, unpleasant consequences. If Idli caught him, perhaps he would try. Otherwise—

Light filled all of Wren's vision then, but no light that he wished for. His head struck stone as his body met the wall at the tunnel's end and came out on the short end of the encounter. Pain raced down every nerve as he fell back and collapsed on the tunnel floor, whimpering. He rolled over once and attempted to stand, but only made it to his knees before falling again.

Idli arrived a long moment later, his pace considerably slower than Wren's had been upon striking the wall.

"Well, well," the guide said, his voice full of mock concern. "Have we fallen down?"

Wren looked up and spat an obscenity, all the while wondering if his skull was broken or merely dented. Idli merely ran a condescending hand along the stubble on Wren's scalp, then roughly shoved him down. "You'll learn respect for the powers here soon enough. The great Eliezer Wren, avatar of the Unconquered Sun, runs into a stone wall and knocks himself senseless. How pathetic. I don't even see why the dead gods want you. Ah well. Mine is not to question why. It's just a pity I can't take my payment. I can, however, make sure that you are delivered in as timely a fashion as possible."

With a look of mild disdain on his horrific features, Idli clenched his fist. The floor beneath Wren vanished, and he plummeted into the abyss.

Chapter Twenty-Three

Unforgiven Blossom had ridden as far as Varsi, where she'd traded everything she'd taken from the bandits for river passage, good food and a healthy amount of jade. The men she'd killed had done surprisingly well for themselves, and the fruits of their unpleasant labors had proved quite profitable for her. She'd treated herself to a palanquin ride to the river, and thence boarded a ship heading north. Those who bore her rejoiced at the task, for an old woman was no heavy burden, and she paid better than the notoriously fat merchants who normally made use of their services.

The ship on which she booked passage was called the *Three Clear Moons*, and its captain was a short, stout man with a receding hairline and a mouth that was pursed in a permanent frown. He called himself Righteous Wolf, though behind his back the crew shared their beliefs that neither name was appropriate. He hauled passengers and cargo along the rivers of the east, going anywhere there was a profit to be made, and he asked no questions of those he did business with. This made him a popular man among the smugglers of the Threshold, who saw him as a reliable ally against the bully-boys of the Guild, and among the Deathlords, who were fond of a man who would take their servants on board without prejudice or disdain.

Unforgiven Blossom had asked her palanquin bearers to take her to a suitable vessel, and after a brief argument (one of the men carrying her had a brother who was a ship captain, whom the other bearers universally regarded as an idiot) they had taken her to the quayside where the *Three Clear Moons* sat. In exchange for additional jade, one of the bearers had negotiated her fee on her behalf with the captain, for Unforgiven Blossom did not like sullying her hands with such matters. Inevitably, those whom she bargained with took her for a feeble, doddering old woman who could easily be taken advantage of, and by the time she convinced them otherwise, either time or lives had been lost.

Her bearers carried her and her few belongings onto the vessel's deck, and she rewarded each with jade in accordance with their service, after having the leader of the men first pay for her passage. The one who had suggested taking her to his brother's ship she paid with coin taken from the men who had accosted her in the shadowland. It still bore their psychic stink, and Unforgiven Blossom wanted to be rid of it as quickly as possible. She was no Exalt and no sorceress, but she could read omens like few others, and she read death here. "Spend it quickly," she told the man, who blithely ignored her and walked down the gangplank counting his newfound riches.

One of the mates walked her to her rather cramped cabin on deck and did her the kindness of carrying her belongings as well. More luxurious (and thus, more expensive) cabins had been available below decks, away from prying eyes, but she preferred the fresh air and thus had instructed her agent to obtain lodging on the deck. And so, once the sailor had deposited her goods roughly on the cabin floor, he had departed, and Unforgiven Blossom sat and waited for the captain to make his appearance.

She did not have to wait long. Righteous Wolf blustered in perhaps half an hour later, still red-faced from shouting orders at the crew. He threw open the door after a cursory knock, bowed fractionally, and then addressed himself to his passenger.

"You'll want to know the rules of the journey, I expect," he began, but Unforgiven Blossom held up a thin hand to halt him.

"I am well aware of them," she said, "having traveled with you before. Though my circumstances then were a bit grander than they are now."

The captain's eyes widened visibly. "My lady," he said. "I did not recognize you. If I had known it was you on the litter—"

"You would have charged me even more, I know." She laughed, and laughed again at his discomfort at being caught. "It is no matter. I am here, and I wish for passage. It has been paid for, and your discretion has been paid for as well. Where are you bound?"

"Downriver, and then east to Mist Island. It's a long run. I'm transporting glass and gems from the far south with some of the stones being of—" he coughed, "—dubious provenance. Why are you traveling this way? You should have an honor guard, and palanquin bearers better than the riff-raff who escorted you on board. It is an honor to have you gracing my vessel again, and that, my lady, is the dragon's honest truth."

"You flatter me," she said, and gave him a bare hint of a smile. "But I have reasons for traveling as I do. My prince has less need for my services than once he did, and bid me travel for a bit. And so I find myself here, and led by happy accident to your vessel. I trust this bodes well for my immediate future, for you, dear captain, have always been quite the good luck charm."

"You do me too much credit," he mumbled, and bowed again. "If there's anything you need, just say the word. I'll have one of the sailors attend to it. Otherwise, you are welcome to stay on board to Mist Island and beyond." So saying, he backed out of the cabin and shut the door. An instant later, she could hear him bellowing at the sailors, who were, if available evidence was to believed, the laziest, weakest, feeblest-minded bunch of layabouts this side of the Imperial Palace, and whose best efforts might serve to keep them from sinking instantly the second they hit the deep channel. Unforgiven Blossom smiled at that, for she knew that Wolf's sailors were inevitably superb. The man demanded the best and got it, for the simple reason that he had enough run-ins with river pirates, unflagged Guild enforcers, Dragon-Blooded customs agents and water serpents to make sure that any incompetents either became competent or ended up floating face-down past the stern in short order.

Still smiling, she unpacked her baggage. A chest of drawers had been built into the cabin wall, something of a luxury, and she placed her clothing and much of her jade inside it. The dagger she kept inside her robes, while the powders, divination tools, inks and parchments she had bought in Varsi she kept in a pouch by the room's small bed. Her journey's destination was not yet clear, but the *Three Clear Moons*, she sensed, would take her closer to it.

There was a rap on her door, and she went to answer it.

Standing there was a young sailor with shaved head and black queue hanging down in back. He stood stock-still at attention when the door opened. Clearly Righteous Wolf had impressed upon this young man the importance of the guest in the deck cabin, and had thus terrified the sailor beyond comprehension.

"Ma'am," he said after a couple of false starts and throat clearings, "Righteous Wolf wishes you to know that we'll be casting off in about an hour, maybe two depending on the traffic from some barges up ahead. He also wishes you to know that he'd like you to dine with him, which is a rare privilege if I may say so." Message apparently complete, he stood there and saluted with comical stiffness.

"Thank you," she said, as gently as she could. "And please thank the captain for his consideration. I would be happy to dine with him." She reached into her pouch and pulled out a small jade square, which she attempted to press into the sailor's hand. He refused, but did not leave.

"Is there something else?" Unforgiven Blossom inquired.

"Yes, ma'am," the sailor said, blushing. "The captain also said that I'm to see to whatever, ah, needs you might have, and he emphasized that I'm to be at your service at any time unless I'm actively on duty."

It took a moment for Unforgiven Blossom to understand precisely what the sailor was saying, and then another moment while she struggled to contain her laughter.

"You may once again thank Righteous Wolf for his consideration on my behalf, but you do not need to worry. I have no intention of taking you, or anyone else, to my bed." The sailor slumped visibly with relief at that point, and Unforgiven Blossom felt a twinge of indignation. Surely, even aged as she appeared, she was not that hideous. "I may have other duties for you, however. You will no doubt find them less onerous. You may go."

"Yes, ma'am," the sailor said, and shut the door. His retreating footsteps across the deck were a touch faster than necessary, but all in all he had deported himself well, and Unforgiven Blossom made a note to herself to compliment the young man to Righteous Wolf at dinner tonight. Praise from her would result in praise from the captain, and that would make the nameless young sailor much easier to work with on the journey.

She was quite certain that his assistance would be required at some point on the trip downriver, and found herself hoping quietly that it wouldn't cost the earnest young man too dearly.

❖

There was now a picture pinned to the wall of Unforgiven Blossom's cabin, that of a bearded, bald man wearing rough priest's robes. It was done in black ink on yellow parchment, and the lines of the sketch were so precise that anyone save Unforgiven Blossom who viewed it would have assumed, wrongly, that it was the work of one of the masters of the Isle. The man's expression was captured perfectly, a mixture of nobility, pragmatism and brutality. His eyes focused on something distant, and his hands were clenched into fists.

Unforgiven Blossom had caused the sketch to draw itself on the first night of the voyage, after setting out the proper instruments of divination in the cabin and mixing some of her blood with the ink. The cut had been made in her wrist with the sharpened nib of the pen the ritual called for, and mixed with the ink and certain powders she'd bought in Varsi to create a thick, black mixture that, when invoked properly, could be induced to array itself on paper in the image of that which would be most significant in the near future. She had unrolled the parchment, invoked the aid of the appropriate spirits, and then spilled the black, tarry mixture onto the page. Within seconds, it had chased itself into thick, clear lines, lines that resolved themselves over the next three hours into the portrait that now stared at her from the wall.

"A priest," she said, wonderingly. "So far from home. A powerful one, too, or the ink would not have formed his image so quickly. I wonder if he knows Wren."

She rose from the bed, where she had been seated in contemplation of the image all morning, and strode out onto the deck. The sailors ignored her, which she took as a compliment, and she found herself at the prow, staring out over the river.

"This stretch is kind of dull, ma'am."

She turned, and saw the young sailor Righteous Wolf had sent to her on the first day. He was still spear-shaft straight in his posture, but she'd seen him at work enough to know that he was supremely competent aboard the vessel. The captain, it seemed, really did want her to have the best.

"What makes you say that? And what, while I have you here, is your name?"

The sailor stared straight ahead. "Nothing but flatland and straight steering here. Nothing even worth calling rapids, and all the land on either side of the river's either grassland or farm. Dull. There isn't even a place for pirates to hide. The tributaries are all too shallow."

"Ah." Unforgiven Blossom rested her elbows on the rail. "I thank you. And my second question?"

"Jade Waters, ma'am."

"Interesting." She turned, and fixed her gaze on him. He met her eyes for an instant, and then turned to look at the passing banks again. "Do you intend to have a ship of your own someday, Jade Waters?"

He shook his head, and his queue danced as he did so. "Right now I'm just happy to be sailing on this one."

"And learning, and planning how you might someday put it to use." She leaned over and patted his hand conspiratorially. "Your secret is safe with me."

And with that, he laughed, and Unforgiven Blossom knew that she had his trust.

Looking embarrassed, he drew his hand away, though not as abruptly as he might have an hour before. "If I can ask, ma'am, how do you and the captain know each other? He doesn't act like this with any other passengers."

She sighed then. "That, of all questions, is the wrong one to ask. Suffice to say that your captain gave me passage once on a matter of great importance to the prince whom I served, and that he was richly rewarded for it." She paused, and looked out over the river. "I was more beautiful then."

"I'm sorry," Jade Waters said softly, and to Unforgiven Blossom's surprise the young man actually sounded as if he meant it.

"Don't be," she replied, and hugged herself as if against a chill wind. "It was a long time ago, at least as I see things, and there is no pain there." He nodded, clearly not comprehending, and Unforgiven Blossom felt no need to enlighten him.

Abruptly, she turned. "I need to retire and meditate," she said. "But later in the afternoon, I may have need of you. There are some questions about my route that you can perhaps help me to answer. Bring a map of the rivers, if you would be so kind, and perhaps I can teach you something." Jade Waters blushed again, and Unforgiven Blossom gave a delighted peal of laughter. "No, not that, silly boy. Something you might find more useful than knowledge of how to please a woman, as impossible as that sounds."

And with that, she glided regally back to her cabin, leaving a confused, embarrassed and slightly disturbed Jade Waters in her wake, to absorb the jeers and laughter of the rest of the crew.

❖

The map, it had transpired, had provided some very interesting answers. She'd told Jade Waters to watch and to make no sound as she bathed it in several oils, then set it aflame. It consumed itself in seconds and then crumbled to the cabin floor, forming a tiny bas-relief version of itself out of ash, perfect in every detail.

"That's astonishing," the sailor breathed, leaning in for a closer look. "Are those moving?"

"Hush. Your voice could blow it away, and then where would we be?" she admonished him, and held her breath as she gazed over the tableau. Pieces of it were moving, shreds of ash flowing like rivers and riding over the miniature landscape like birds. Moving slowly, she backed away until she'd reached what she considered to be a safe distance.

"Quickly, bring me the portrait from the wall," she ordered, and Jade Waters hastened to obey. Pressing the portrait, only slightly crumpled, into Unforgiven Blossom's hand, he waited for the next miracle.

Thanking him by means of a curt nod, she dipped the edge of the portrait into the flame from the oil lamp that hung near the door. The flames licked up the edge of the parchment, then ate into it greedily as she brought it over the ashes of the map.

"What are you doing?" Jade Waters whispered.

"The ashes from the portrait will tell me where the man it portrays is going. This is a form of divination not often practiced, and with good reason. Too much talking ruins it almost every time." Jade Waters caught the rebuke and bit his lip, and Unforgiven Blossom returned to the task of watching the fall of ash.

The portrait burned more cleanly than the map did, and the ashes that fell from it were white, not gray. They traced a line from the Isle to Port Calin, and then off to the east until the portrait itself was consumed and the trail ended at a point just north of the great river that they would soon be traveling.

"There," she breathed. "Where the ash ends. Where is that?"

The sailor's brow furrowed in concentration. "That's the middle of nowhere, ma'am. But if I had to make a guess, I'd say that's pointing to Reddust."

"Reddust." She leaned back. "And what is in Reddust?"

"Dust, and a trading post, and not much more," he retorted. "Do you want me to get one of the navigators in here? Perhaps he could tell you more."

"No, no, I trust your word," she said distractedly, and waved her hand over the remnants of the map. They scattered, and predictably, Jade Waters sneezed. "Tell no one of what you saw here tonight. The captain understands, but some of the sailors might not, and I would hate to have to explain to them what transpired. They might think it," and she paused to smile devilishly, "sorcery. Good night, Jade Waters. I thank you for your assistance."

"You're welcome, ma'am," he said, and practically bolted the cabin. The door slammed behind him, and Unforgiven Blossom rose serenely to fasten the latch.

She leaned heavily on the door for a moment, and pondered what she had seen. "A priest from the Isle and a trading post too far east to be important and too far west to have anything worth trading for. Why does fate love the obscure?"

The night did not answer, nor did she expect it to. Suddenly feeling the weight of all of her assumed years, Unforgiven Blossom blew out the lamp and took her weary self to bed.

❖

They put in due south of Reddust a fortnight later with much swearing from the river pilot, who vowed that it was the worst damn anchorage she'd ever seen, and that they'd never get out of the mud. Righteous Wolf had ignored her, lowering the dinghy that contained Unforgiven Blossom, her belongings and the attentive Jade Waters to the river below.

"Are you sure you want to leave here?" the sailor asked as he steered the craft toward shore. "Reddust is days walk north of here for a young man, and…" His voice trailed off.

"You are very sweet," she said, "and your concern is appreciated. But the map told me that it must be here. One does not argue with these things, unless one wishes to pay a very high price. And I am certain I can walk these bones to Reddust. I walked them to Varsi, after all."

In response, Jade Waters put his head down and rowed. A moment later, a soft bump indicated that the keel had struck bottom, the prow resting on the shore. The sailor leaped out into the water with a convincing splash, then waded onto the bank and pulled the dinghy up higher. Through it all, Unforgiven Blossom sat as immobile as a statue, watching the scene as distantly as if it had all been a play staged for her benefit.

"Here," Jade Waters said, and extended his hand. She took it, and stepped off onto the low grass of the shoreline. Once certain she was on dry land, he reached into the boat and fetched her small satchel of belongings, as well as the supplies Righteous Wolf had provided. This she took from him with grave thanks. He turned to go, and she called out, "Wait."

He stopped. "Ma'am?"

"Take this." She reached into the pouch and drew forth a small charm carved from a bead of amber, dangling from a thin leather cord. "You may find this useful someday. It will help hide you from unwanted eyes." She smiled. "Your captain has one as well. They both come from the tomb of a man who is far better off dead, and whose ghost I tormented for five days and nights to learn where he kept his treasure. Do not tell your captain that you know any of this." She leaned forward then, and kissed him on the cheek. He bowed, deeply, and then devoted himself to pushing the dinghy back into the water. Within seconds, it had slid off the bank and Jade Waters was splashing alongside it, the charm securely looped around his neck.

She watched him go. When the rowboat had vanished around the side of the *Three Clear Moons*, she turned her back on the river and began picking her way north over the countryside to where the promised rendezvous at Reddust awaited.

Chapter Twenty-Four

The caravan found Faithful Hound wandering an odd dozen miles from the river, blind and leading his pack animals in a path that could only be called erratic. His face was covered in blood, and his eyes had been torn ungently from their sockets.

"Bird did it," said the physicker who traveled with the caravan, after she'd made a cursory examination. "See here? Claws tore the cloth on his chest. Whatever found him was huge. I just don't know how it could have gotten both eyes without doing more damage to him elsewhere, though."

She'd taken moist cloths, then, and cleaned the wounds. Salves were applied, and bandages, and rough men and women who tended the caravan's animals took competent charge of the beasts who'd followed on Hound's tether. The caravan mistress, eminently practical, ordered more guards to take bows, and that any large birds that flew near the caravan were to be shot down, plucked and roasted. "Eyes," she reasoned, "cost money."

The price of the assistance rendered Faithful Hound was assessed, and his trade goods docked an equivalent amount. Faithful Hound was known and liked among the caravan folk, but stopping for him had cost time, and time was money, and had their positions somehow been reversed, Faithful Hound would no doubt have charged the members of the caravan as well. Such was the life of trader in the Scavenger Land, or indeed anywhere the Guild traveled.

Carefully, Faithful Hound's body was loaded into a wagon and strapped down to a board, so that he might travel in a bit more comfort while he recovered and the physicker tended to him. His fevered ravings about rats, princes, and small boys clad in the raiment of the Sun were, of course, ignored.

Ratcatcher awoke, blind and bound, and immediately started swearing.

"You're awake? Good." The physicker, whose name was Clever Tiger but whose appearance would have been better served by Timid Mouse, leaned back over her shoulder and greeted him. "You've had a rough patch of days, Hound. It's been three since we found you, and there are times when, if you hadn't still been moving, I'd have given you up for dead." She flicked the reins and the team of horses hauling the wagon swiftly came to a halt. "Let me have a look at you now to see if those bandages can come off."

"No!" Ratcatcher. "I mean, please, no. Where am I?" He rolled his head from side to side. "Why can't I see?"

"Easy," the healer laughed. "All right, I'll just untie you. And to answer your questions, you're on a wagon in the Caravan of Nine Effervescent Wonders, under the stern direction of caravan mistress Revolving Mirrors. Outriders found you and your animals—don't worry, they and your goods are safe—three days ago. You were wounded and delirious, and you had the good grace to collapse by the time the main caravan arrived. You've been riding in my wagon ever since so I could keep an eye on you and make sure you didn't become buzzard bait all over again. As for why you can't see, well, that's a different matter. Hold still."

Ratcatcher held still and, with greater difficulty, held his tongue. He could feel rope sliding across his chest, wrists and ankles, and then it was gone. Slowly, gingerly, he sat up. "Thank you," he said, not trusting himself to say more. Something about the healer's prattling and incessant good cheer got on his nerves, but for now, she was the sum total of the protection he had from the outside world, and he needed to learn more before he decided on a course of action.

"Think nothing of it. Now, as for your eyes, well, that's the bad news. Something got at them. I was hoping you could tell me what it was."

"My eyes? Again?" The words slipped out before Ratcatcher could think, and he instantly regretted them. His hands went to the bandages on his face and tore them free. "What happened?"

"No! Leave the bandages be!" The healer tried to stop him, and reflexively he slapped her aside. She fell, heavily, against the cloth side of the wagon even as he stripped the bloody cloth away.

"What's going on in here?" A man's voice called out suspiciously. Ratcatcher jerked his head to the right, toward the source of the sound. A faint shape was there, dark gray against the black.

"Nothing, nothing at all," he could hear Clever Tiger say. "I just slipped while removing his bandages, Ragged Fox. He was a little surprised by the news I had for him, that's all. Everything is fine." Her voice was surprisingly soothing.

"Well, all right," the man she'd called Ragged Fox said. "Call me if you need anything."

"Of course," the healer replied, and turned back to Ratcatcher. "Don't make me lie for you again," she hissed. "Ragged Fox is very protective, and if he thought you'd hurt me, you'd have a whole new set of injuries to deal with."

Ratcatcher opened his mouth to retort that Ragged Fox would be torn to rags if he tried anything, then remembered his situation and covered for himself with a cough instead. "I'm sorry," he said as humbly as he could manage. "Just a bit of a shock, as you said."

"Think nothing of it. Just don't do it again." He could hear her clambering forward, and again, a maddeningly vague shape appeared in his field of vision. "I got a fast look at you while you were taking the bandages off, and I think you're as healed as you're going to get. No damage to the sockets, thank goodness. You'll be able to add a glass eye when we stop for the night, assuming we've got any in stock. You will want to cover the gaps, though. They look nasty, and that won't help you with women." She giggled, then, and Ratcatcher shuddered. From her voice, the physicker was at least in her mid-30s, and women of that age who giggled tended to be overprotective spinsters. He sniffed, once, and was gratified that he didn't detect the telltale odor of cat urine. Well, perhaps there was hope for her yet.

"I don't have much use for women, and less now," he answered in what he hoped was a credible imitation of Faithful Hound's patois. "'Sides, having them showing might make for better leverage in a trade. Never know when a man's going to be staring at something ugly instead of all his pretty money."

The healer laughed again, a sound blessedly removed from her earlier tittering. "Same old Faithful Hound. Nothing to you but the deal." She paused and clucked to the horses, urging them to move again. "I always thought that was a pity."

Dumbfounded, Ratcatcher lay back down and tried very hard to think about anything else, anything at all.

❖

Over the next few days, a sort of routine grew up around his travel in the wagon. She fed him broth, which he discreetly spat out later, and asked him if he remembered anything about the attack which had cost him his eyes. He responded truthfully to that, and told her that he couldn't remember a damned thing about the attack itself.

He did remember waking up and feeling the sticky blood on his face, and cursing Raiton to a hundred hells and back. The fire was out and a wet pile of moldering flesh across the fire pit was all that remained of his old body.

He'd wiped his hands in the ashes and then untied the animals, which followed with a reasonable degree of docility. Anywhere, he decided, was better than where he was, and so he struck in a direction that the evening heat of the sun on his face told him was west. He'd walked for days, always pursued by cawing raitons which he'd done his best to ignore. Water he found by stumbling into low creeks, and pasture for the animals came when they stopped and would go no further, and he could hear the sound of chewing.

He'd gone a little mad then, Ratcatcher suspected. He'd heard the prince's voice telling him where to go, and he'd obeyed, because obeying his prince was something he was used to doing, regardless of whether doing so made any sense or not. He'd felt something like a knife to the gut, but when he'd dropped the tether rope he'd felt nothing there, just a vague sense that something powerful had been unsheathed to the south and east. He heard sobbing, too, a woman's voice that echoed back and forth and rang out with pain. And there had been scents—burning flesh, brimstone, hot blood and horse dung.

The latter, at least, he felt he could account for rationally. The rest he simply gave himself up to as visions, and he followed the phantom voices in his head for eight days. On the ninth, he'd collapsed, and he had no further memory until awakening in the healer's wagon. For that, he was profoundly thankful.

For his part, he asked Clever Tiger about the caravan ("run with a firm hand, and always profitable"), their route ("already across the River of Tears and heading east on the circle route") and their next destination ("a trading post in the middle of nowhere, called Reddust"). He also learned a great deal of caravan gossip, including the rumor that the caravan mistress took only other women as lovers, though Clever Tiger had not been approached herself, she confided with a giggle. There was a great deal that was said about Ragged Fox, whom she imagined as some sort of suitor, and about the exploits of the roughnecks who served as caravan guards. One was apparently a disgraced Immaculate monk, and Ratcatcher had perked up at that, though it quickly became obvious from the description the healer gave that the man looked as much like Wren as a holly berry looked like a ruby.

Revolving Mirrors had stopped by after a few days to pay her respects, and to offer a bargain: Faithful Hound would continue to travel with them, and his goods would be included with the caravan's at each stop. In exchange, the caravan got a ridiculously high percentage of any profits and goods he acquired. Ratcatcher haggled back and forth, in large part because doing so was expected, but in the end agreed to a cut for the caravan that pleased the caravan mistress to no end.

Meanwhile, the gray shapes in his vision grew clearer every day, though surreptitiously Ratcatcher had probed his empty eye sockets with his fingers to make sure that this dead body was not the seat of remarkable powers of regeneration. Soon he could make out the difference between Clever Tiger and the always-pursuant Ragged Fox, though their faces as yet were blurred, and their forms seemed oddly decrepit. This development he kept to himself, and instead made an effort to keep his new body as pristine as possible. Avoiding extended submersion—and the attendant scavengers that went with doing so—seemed to be the key to maintaining a dead body longer, though Ratcatcher was worried that the damage to his eyes would spread rot sooner rather than later.

And so he was, if not trusted, then at least an accepted member of the caravan when its lead elements pulled into the Reddust trading post. He could hear animals being unhitched from wagons and led to water, and could even vaguely see the packs and crates being unloaded in preparation for seeing whatever trade might be available in this forsaken piece of terrain.

Clever Tiger had described Reddust to him as a tavern with a stables and a brothel attached, and joked that the teamsters didn't know the difference. They were the real reason the caravan stopped here, she confided. They liked the place, and there were generally enough locals who came by when they got word from the outriders of the caravan's presence that there was something of a market. None were here yet, apparently, but come the morrow they would be, and then Revolving Mirrors would open up shop. In the meantime, the teamsters and the caravan guards were taking their leisure at the tavern itself, something which Clever Tiger, with a disdainful sniff, informed him that she wouldn't recommend he do.

Besides, she told him, one of the outriders had reported seeing a priest headed this way, and the guards tended to be a little rough with that lot. It was best for all concerned, she decided, if the blind man stayed right where he was. That way he wouldn't get hurt.

Ratcatcher shook his head with annoyance, but he knew better than to argue. Besides, he told himself, the priest might be able to discern what he was, and that would cause more problems than he was currently equipped to solve. As much as he hated to admit it, the healer was right.

"So tell me more about Ragged Fox," he said, and hoped his voice was eager enough. From the enthusiasm with which she launched into her next story, it was.

Chapter Twenty-Five

Wren awoke to surprisingly little discomfort, which is to say that he may have been bound hand and foot with thongs of leather, but he was neither in danger of immediate torture nor in possession of any more lacerations, broken bones and other ailments that a man in his position might reasonably expect. Struggling against his bonds, he found that they were tight, but not uncomfortably so, and that they were unlikely to succumb to his struggles at any point in the near future.

Having determined that escape was unlikely, Wren turned his attention to his surroundings. He lay, stripped stark naked, on what looked to be the sort of slab used to prepare bodies for burial, though he suspected that precious few funerary slabs had blood grooves like the ones he felt beneath him. Iron rings had been set into the obsidian of the table at each of the four corners, and it was to these that the thongs binding him had been knotted. The chamber in which he was held had a high, vaulted ceiling of some sort of gray stone, and from where he lay he could see several other slabs akin to the one he was bound upon. They looked to be perhaps five feet off the floor, far higher than necessary if they were used for strictly human purposes.

The room itself was square, the walls made from the same gray stone as the ceiling. Torches in rusted sconces gave off a flickering, melancholy light, and illuminated the scene just enough for Wren to see that each wall had a tall, narrow door set in it. The way the firelight played across the doors led him to suspect that they were made from iron, a suspicion reinforced by the scent of blood and rust in the air. The door to his right was unadorned, as was the one at his feet. The one to Wren's left, however, was guarded by a monstrous statue.

The carving was at least seven feet tall and roughly human

in shape, though slender and angular far beyond the point of attractiveness. Its eyes were large and it showed no visible sign of either sex, though if he had been forced to guess Wren would have wagered it depicted a female. In its hands was a stone spear at least as tall as it was, and it had been sculpted with some form of light armor. There were six fingers on the hands that gripped the massive spear, and the expression on the statue's face was one of intense concentration.

"Marvelous. This is simply marvelous." Wren expected his voice to echo, and was mildly surprised when it did not. Instead, the sound was simply swallowed up by the space around him, giving him the unnerving impression that the walls had devoured his words. He opened his mouth to speak again, if for no other reason than to dispel the disturbing impression, but then held his tongue.

Faintly, above the muted crackle of the torches, he could hear the breathing of something monstrous. The breaths were slow and steady, like those of a contented sleeper, but the very timbre of the sounds suggested that whatever lay dozing nearby was of gigantic stature.

Wren closed his eyes and listened. The sound, such as it was, stirred around the whole chamber, but seemed to originate from a point behind the door which the statue guarded. He listened intently for another moment and shook his head. There could be no doubt. Something huge and awful lay slumbering beyond that door, though with the way sound traveled in the Labyrinth, it might be next door or a thousand leagues away. The two, he decided after a moment, were not mutually incompatible.

"This," he said quietly to himself, "is perhaps not where I wished to find myself."

"Silence."

The voice that rang out through the chamber was rough, giving the impression that its owner was unaccustomed to speech. It was accented in a style that had rarely been heard since the days before the Empire, one which Wren recognized only because it was echoed in some of Kejak's more florid pronouncements. The voice was slow and cold and deep, and reminded Wren of stone wearing away under the weight of ages.

The single word hung there in the chamber, then faded. For an instance, there was rough silence, marked only by the sounds of fire and sleep. Wren sighed and slowly opened his eyes. "I was wondering when you were going to begin speaking. What's your name, anyway? If I'm going to be trapped with only a talking statue for company, we might as well be on friendly terms."

"I have no name." The statue took a stride forward, slow and awkward, and then slammed its spear-haft against the ground. A thunderous booming sound rang out, and the torch flames danced away from the figure as if in fear. "It is not necessary that I have one."

"But everything has a name," Wren protested. "Bees, trees, women, pieces of animate statuayyyeeaaarrgggh!" The last died as Wren's voice was yanked into a cry of pain. The statue had lifted its spear and pointed it at the slab, and of their own accord Wren's bonds tightened. After a few seconds of agony, the creature lowered its weapon and the leather thongs relaxed.

"I have no name," it said, "and I will not be questioned."

"Right," Wren gasped. "Absolutely. It makes perfect sense. You have no name. I'll simply refer to you with pronouns. Will that do?" Again the statue raised its weapon, and again Wren cried out. He could feel his tendons on the verge of snapping, sense that his shoulders were about to pop out of their sockets, and still the agony continued.

A full minute later, the spear was lowered once again. "This is not a place for levity," the statue intoned solemnly. "You are here to learn."

"Learn?" Wren coughed, weakly. "Learn what?"

In response, the statue strode across the room, fine dust trailing behind with every step. "You will learn pain," it said, and brought the shaft of its spear down across Wren's naked belly like a staff. This time, Wren did not cry out, though the strike left a red welt across his gut.

"You will learn obedience." Another strike, this time across the chest. "And you will learn submission." After a second's deliberation, the statue turned its spear and gave Wren a wicked jab in the groin with its haft. This time, the monk could not resist crying out in pain, and a grim smile crossed the statue's cold lips.

"This is why you were brought here, for you are deemed worthy to submit and judged capable of obeying. Were you not, your soul would have long since fed the things that dwell in the uttermost depths. But you have been deemed worthy, and thus I will guard you until such time as another comes. I will teach you what you must know, and then you will come before the slumbering dead gods in all their majesty. They will know you, and you will submit to them so that you might labor for their greater glory." Abruptly, the statue paused. "What is your name?"

"Wren. Eliezer Wren." He said it weakly, his chest and belly on fire with pain.

"Wren." The statue frowned. "An odd name. Do not grow attached to it. Soon, you will not need it any more."

With that, the statue turned and lurched back to its guard position, its stone eyes ever vigilant.

Wren, for his part, closed his eyes and softly wept.

✦

Wren was no stranger to silence. His training in the Guild had taught him the value of letting the other man speak and not speaking himself, and as a test once he'd gone an entire fortnight without saying a word. His time in the Temple had brought weeks of wordless meditation, as he knelt with a hundred other Initiates and silently contemplated the Immaculate Texts. And endless hours in the field had taught him the wisdom of saying nothing and moving less, as he waited in ambush or hid from enemies who would have been alerted by the slightest sound.

Here, though, silence was something new. It was the coin of his suffering, and the key to an end to his pain. In the wake of his first encounter with the statue, he had simply shouted his defiance, and received a dispassionate wealth of beatings as a result. It had been necessary to him at that time, however, to howl his resistance to the stone figure's orders, and to call out his name again and again. "You have become tiresome," it told him once before smashing his hand with the butt of its spear, but it did no more than that, and from that odd incident Wren drew hope.

Thus it was that he and the golem engaged in a contest of wills. It became clear to Wren after a day's worth of beatings that the statue actively wished him to speak, so that it might find reasons to punish him. It became equally clear that it was only permitted to exercise its wrath against him if he transgressed certain codes, the details of which had never been made clear to him. But experimentation, at the cost of more buffets to his sore ribs and more time spent with his bonds straining at his sinews, showed him some of those limits: speaking, meditation, and not spending enough time in contemplation of the statue's magnificence.

Saying his own name, it seemed, brought the worst punishments. Asking questions also incurred the stone figure's wrath, though not as severely. Speaking to himself generally brought milder punishments still, and no matter how brutal the statue's attentions were, it never struck his face.

And most interesting of all was the effect on the stone figure of Wren's silence. When he finally chose to hold his tongue, it seemed at first to gratify his captor, which stood at its post with an expression that bordered on a smile. As the minutes of silence stretched to hours, and the hours to days, however, the golem's patience grew thin. It longed to punish Wren, it seemed, and was not prepared for the possibility that the captive might have learned the lesson of silence without absorbing it.

Finally, the statue strode over to where Wren lay. "Speak," it commanded.

Wren said nothing.

"Speak!" The spear haft came down and halted an inch above Wren's eyes. "You mock me with your silence."

A hundred retorts died in Wren's throat. Instead, he stared up into the golem's unblinking stone eyes and kept his expression calm.

"You do not accept silence as your rightful lot. You mock it! You mock me!" Again the spear came down, and Wren could feel it touch, just barely, against the skin of his throat.

Suppressing a shudder, Wren screwed his eyes shut, and the golem roared with rage.

"I was charged to punish you until you learned the lessons the dead gods wish to teach you, Eliezer Wren, and I will not fail in that duty. You were to have learned the value of submission and the rewards for doing so. You were to learn the value of imposed silence, and the joy of the privilege of speaking when granted permission to do so. You were to have held your spirit up to me so that I could test its mettle and break it, and reshape you so that you might serve." This time the spear came down for real, slamming into his ribs hard enough to crack one. "You have chosen silence. You have not accepted it." The spear haft crashed against his belly with a sickening, wet sound. "This is how you pit your will against mine? It is foolishness. I will make you cry out, and then I will drive your soul to a place where you will beg me to cut out your tongue." Another blow, this one on the groin. Wren stiffened in pain, but said nothing. "Do you understand?" The spear haft caught his throat. "Answer me!"

Slowly, painfully, Wren turned his head. His gaze met the golem's, and the stone man flinched.

You will not teach me, Wren's eyes said. *You will not silence me. You are nothing, a tool, a machine, a toady. You have failed, and you will be punished, and the punishment waiting for you is worse than anything you can do to me. Try to teach me, stone man. Try, and fail again.* Somehow, he knew, the golem understood.

"You can learn how to die!" the statue said and raised its spear. The point gleamed dully in the light. "Speak, damn you, or I'll hear your heart's blood flowing from your mouth!"

Wren found himself biting the inside of his lip. The urge to scream defiance was strong, the one to struggle even stronger, but he resisted. If he were to die here, he'd do so on his own terms. He saw the spear come down, and tensed in anticipation.

The golem exploded. Gray dust showered Wren as his ears rang from the impact of the sound. In seconds, there was nothing left of the stone creature or its spear. They were gone, reduced to powder.

"What in the name of—"

"Do not say that name here." A cloaked and hooded figure

glided into Wren's view, its face and hands hidden inside its robes. Its voice was cold, not in the way the golem's had been, but rather as if it had once been warm and had all humanity stripped from it. "I thought that display might loosen your tongue."

"You destroyed..." Wren found himself unable to compose sentences, so great was the shock.

"Yes, when it overstepped its authority. It thought it was teaching you a lesson in silence. We were teaching you a lesson in power. You learned the appropriate lesson." The figure's gnarled and claw-like hand emerged from its sleeve and traced the lines left by the golem's spear. Where its fingers touched, the pain vanished.

When it had finished, it drew forth from its belt a hooked knife with a black and pitted blade. "Hold still," it warned, and Wren cheerfully obeyed.

Four swift strokes cut Wren's bonds, and he immediately began trying to rub some feeling back into his ankles. "Who are you?" he said. "And what do you want from me?"

"There is no time for that," the figure replied. "Garb has been brought for you." It gestured, and Wren saw other figures clad in similar fashion leaving a pile of fabric on one of the other tables. "Prepare yourself. Tonight, you have an audience with a god, and then every question you have ever asked will be answered."

Chapter Twenty-Six

Pelesh the Exchequer was, if truth be told, worried. The Prince of Shadows had grown ever more irritable of late, and Pelesh had become increasingly convinced that the prince might decide to begin including the members of his staff in his nightly amusements, which ranged from the simply debauched to the debauched, terrifying and lethal.

Primarily, Pelesh was worried that the prince would include Pelesh, but a strong second was his concern for the prince's well-being. This was not an entirely altruistic fear; if the prince descended into madness or worse, there was no shortage of those who would be happy to eliminate him, raze the citadel to the ground and put the staff to the sword. With the prince's most powerful servants either dispatched on errands or destroyed (*Alas, poor lovely Shamblemerry*, he thought briefly) and news of the prince's bizarre behavior spreading, Pelesh had grown increasingly aware of the possibility of that scenario, and increasingly determined to forestall it.

Thus it was that he'd decided, in his own, diffident way, to suggest to the prince a course of action that would, Pelesh hoped, reenergize him and allow him to shake off the doldrums in which he was mired. He'd pondered the plan, examined it from every cautious angle, and could find no flaw. Surely it would catch the prince's fancy, fire his imagination and restore him to his dynamic former self. Brimming with pride, he'd actually gone so far as to set it to paper, a monumental act of impetuousness unmatched by anything he'd done since the ill-advised attempt to poison Ratcatcher.

Then the summons to dine alone with the prince had arrived, and all of Pelesh's bravado had drained out of him like rain in a gutter. He'd set the parchment that recorded his plan to a candle, only to think better of it last minute and blow the creeping flames out. The singed parchment he'd hidden among his records and then, arrayed in his best finery, he'd crept downstairs to dine with his prince.

The dinner was, of course, marvelous. Dinners here always were. The prince was a man who permitted himself few luxuries, but a fine table was one of them. He'd raised the issue of the prince's expenditures for wine, exotic spices and rare fruits before, and the prince had simply noted that the money was his to spend, not Pelesh's. Since that time, Pelesh had simply found other areas in which to scrimp, and enjoyed when he could the benefits of the prince's culinary largesse.

Tonight the meal was a roasted goose, seasoned with a sauce made from the hideously expensive blood oranges that traders sometimes brought back from Chiaroscuro. On rare occasions the peeled orange rinds would reveal diamonds and other shining gems, or so the stories went. Pelesh had long since decided that the story was a cover made up by some smuggler who'd decided that fruit peels would make a clever means of concealment for his cargo, but regardless, the fruits cost as much as they would have if they had been made from finest crystal.

Served along with the goose was piping hot bread smeared with honeyed butter, and fine, long-grained rice mixed with a delicate blend of herbs. The wine was excellent, but the prince's wine always was, and Pelesh was briefly sorry for his self-imposed rule of one glass and no more.

It was not entirely unheard of for the prince to ask Pelesh to dine; not common, certainly, but not unheard of. It was, however, rare for the prince to go so far as to speak to Pelesh during those meals. Usually, the prince's mere presence was assumed to be enough.

"I understand," the prince began precisely as Pelesh put the first morsel of goose into his mouth, "that you are worried about me. I find that very touching, Pelesh. Very touching indeed." Tonight the prince was garbed in one of the more ornate costumes that Pelesh had seen, a black doublet with flared sleeves and red-and-gray piping, matching hose and black silk slippers. His nails had been lacquered black, all save the last one on each hand, which was red. A thin band of iron sat on his brow, resting just above the mark which proclaimed his power and his loyalty to the dead gods, and a long silver earring that bore a tear-drop shaped ruby hung from his left earlobe.

Pelesh felt distinctly underdressed.

"It's my duty, my prince," the exchequer replied around a mouthful of goose. "You are my liege, and it's my duty to see to your well-being, financial and otherwise." He laid his chopsticks down and took a hasty swig of wine. *Too hasty*, he realized; the wine was strong and went straight to his head.

"It has been more than other servants of mine have shown, and I am touched." The prince neatly skewered a piece of goose on one of his long, red-painted fingernails, and popped it into his mouth. "Such devotion should not go unnoticed."

"My liege?" Pelesh asked with a sinking feeling. More often than not, getting noticed by the prince was a very poor thing indeed.

"No, no, nothing like that." The prince made an airy gesture, spattering drops of goose grease everywhere. "You look so comical when you think I'm going to have you tortured. I wonder what you're up to that gives you such a guilty conscience."

Pelesh's heart nearly leapt out of his chest in fear, and the prince laughed. "That's of no moment now, though," he added, and took a sip of wine. "So tell me of this cunning plan you have devised to rouse me."

"I would not call it cunning, my prince," Pelesh replied cautiously. "I'm not even quite certain I know what you're talking about."

"Please, Pelesh, don't play games. They bore me." The prince snapped his fingers, and one of the liveried servants shambled into the room clutching the flame-marked parchment the Exchequer had so recently attempted to destroy. The prince took it and tapped it thoughtfully against the table while the servant retreated, and raised a quizzical eyebrow.

"Now, are you going to tell me what this says, or will you make me attempt once again to decipher your handwriting?"

Pelesh sighed. "I will tell you, my liege. I was thinking—above my station, I know—that things began to go awry the last time you rode out, in search of Talat's Howe. You've remained here ever since, and in that time you've lost Sandheart, you've lost Shamblemerry, you've lost your prisoner and Unforgiven Blossom and even Ratcatcher. I do not think staying here is good for you, my liege. Not now. I'm no seer, but I do see this: You should close the circle. Ride forth once again. Reaffirm your strength. Make your enemies fear you and your allies glad of their allegiance." He paused, embarrassed by his own passion. "You might even go to that temple where Ratcatcher found the boy and take it for your own. Surely another act of desecration will win you more favor… below."

The prince leaned forward. "Pelesh, I believe that is the longest speech I have ever heard you make. Your eloquence astonishes me." Pelesh stammered half a thanks but the prince waved him off. "No, no. You have given me something to think on." He rose abruptly, and turned to leave.

"Enjoy the goose," he said. "And when you are finished, make ready to travel with me."

❖

This chamber, Shamblemerry decided, was new. It was vast, with an arched ceiling and symbols of the hated sun roughly carved onto every pillar. Ghost-lights flickered and flared across its length as she stood at its entrance, wondering. Piles of skeletons lined the walls, caught in their death agonies. Broken weapons were everywhere, and in the center of the room was what looked to be a small stone hut. The door was bound, she could see, with iron bands, and the ghost-lights shone quickly and often around it. Eager to see what it held, she stepped forward into the chamber.

The ghost of a soldier, a man clad in breastplate, helm and armored skirt, materialized before her. "This place is not for you," it said. "Find another path."

Shamblemerry laughed and spat. The wad of spittle passed through the ghost's face, much to its discomfort, and Shamblemerry laughed again. "Do you think you can stop me, little ghost? I've put your kind to the whip in the Labyrinth a hundred times."

"You are not in the Labyrinth," the ghost replied calmly, and more soldiers faded into view. All wore the same armor, emblazoned with the sigil of a long-forgotten legion. "And you have no whip here."

"I still have more than enough power to deal with you, you arrogant shadow." Still, she took a step back. A chill behind her told her that the ghosts were there, too. She was surrounded.

"No harm will come to you if you leave this chamber now," the ghost said, and pressed forward. Its companions did likewise, and Shamblemerry found herself hemmed in. She looked frantically left, then right, and everywhere saw the same remorseless expression.

"Liar," she whispered. "You'll not let me go, not after I've seen this. What are you hiding?"

"Something you'll never see," it answered, and placed its hand on her brow. It was cold, colder than even the catacombs, and Shamblemerry screamed. She could feel the very life draining out of her, could see the ghost in front of her becoming more solid and shining more brightly.

In a panic she tore away and turned. More ghosts, so solid they seemed real, barred her way, but she burst through them and hurled herself down the tunnel. A chill wind told her that the ghosts were following. Their keening rose up and echoed through the corridor, a hunting song which she was suddenly sure they'd sung many times over the centuries.

She was the hunted one now, and they would not rest until they had taken her. The thought lent wings to her feet and fanned her sparks of anger into flame. How dare these pitiful dead men lay hands on her, when she served the lords of the Labyrinth? It went against all reason. They had betrayed the Abyss, the most profound treason imaginable.

They would pay, she decided. They would pay, and she would exact the price. She would make these hunters the hunted and strike them down, and then she would rip the door of that mausoleum from its hinges and take what it hid for herself.

And then, maybe then, she'd venture up the stairs to see if Holok was still waiting.

✦

Kejak read the daily dispatches and frowned. There had been some sort of disturbance in Sijan about which the Sijanese were being particularly closemouthed. His agents reported that something had gotten loose in one of the lower embalming chambers and killed a few guards, but Kejak suspected there was more than that to the affair. A few guards were hardly worth the efforts the Sijanese were putting into stonewalling. Elsewhere, the news was equally disquieting. There was some kind of a revolt in the Varang states, one being put down with the assistance of some imperial military advisors, and that meant disruption of trade from that quarter of the Threshold. The rebels were preying on trade caravans to support their activities, and the great houses were growing very irritated. The Lintha pirates of the western seas were especially active, and there were panicked reports from some peasants in a western district that one of the Lintha vessels had been seen off the Isle. This Kejak firmly disbelieved, but rumors like that tended to take on a life of their own unless firmly quashed, and the last thing the Empire needed right now was for the dung-footed farmers to be jumping at shadows.

He sighed, and consigned all of the dispatches save one to the brazier, where they caught instantly and curled into fragrant smoke. The last he saved and re-read, his mouth quirking in a smile. It was nothing, really, a minor report from Port Calin of a crusading monk who was supposedly waging a one-man war against corruption on the city's docks. The local temples, meanwhile, were tearing their non-existent hair out over who the mystery monk might be, as they had long since abandoned any such efforts and no itinerant matching the descriptions given by eyewitnesses had presented himself of late.

The descriptions were, ultimately, the interesting and amusing portion of the tale. While the stories would have one believe that the monk in question was nine feet tall and breathed fire, certain details remained the same in every instance: tattered robe, beard, and a gruff demeanor with little patience for questions. Ballads of the Monk of Humble Anger, as this mystery fellow was being called, had already begun circulating, and bands of citizens upholding his supposed ideals had taken to patrolling the docks themselves.

"You always produce the most interesting stories, Holok," Kejak said, and read it again.

Chapter Twenty-Seven

A procession of robed and hooded figures led Eliezer Wren down into the tomb of a god, and closed the great marble door once he had entered. Outside the tomb, they whispered among themselves over how greatly this new guest had been honored, and how he was clearly favored above all of them, and why they would count themselves lucky for centuries hence to have been present for this most august occasion. Then one by one, they drifted back to their other duties and labors, but more than one cast an envious eye on the titanic stone door carved with the sigil of twin serpents devouring the sun and moon, and wondered what transpired within.

✦

The door slammed shut behind Wren with a sound like a mountain committing suicide, echoing throughout the chamber he'd entered. The room was lit by a single brazier by the entrance, which gave off a soft orange light that somehow penetrated every corner of the room. The brazier also gave off a pungent, musky scent, one that made Wren slightly dizzy. He moved a few steps further into the room and the smell abated, allowing him to concentrate.

The place was a temple, he realized instantly. The walls were marked with half-carved columnar structures, and rows of stone benches for worshippers stretched from where Wren stood to an open space at the far end of the chamber. Wide pathways between the pews led to the front, where seven steps led up to a titanic altar.

And upon that altar slept a god.

The figure was vast, so huge that Wren wondered how the stone of the altar could support its weight. What he could see of its frame was roughly human, in the same way that a child's first attempt at woodcarving is roughly executed. Its skin was the color of deep, dirty water and its nails had grown and curled to tortured, horrid lengths. Some turned back upon themselves and pierced the flesh of hands that were taller than he was, and for an instant Wren imagined being swept up by that monstrous grip, to be held and forced to stare into the eyes of something which no mortal should ever be able to gaze upon and live.

SERVE ME, AND I WILL SPARE YOU THAT.

Wren looked around, startled. No voice had spoken, and yet he had heard the words as clearly as he heard the thudding of his heart. He looked up at the figure on the altar and slowly, almost unwillingly strode closer. "You can hear my thoughts?" he said, as much a statement as a question.

I CAN, AND THROUGH ME, MY BRETHREN. There was a rumbling sound, and one of the thing's fingers twitched, barely. *I SLEEP. WE ALL SLEEP. BUT WE ARE NOT IDLE WHILE WE SLUMBER.*

Wren digested that tidbit for a moment. He'd been taught by Kejak that the dead gods slept in the Labyrinth, and that they did so eternally. There had been no mention, he was quite sure, of sleeping dead gods who were still able to think, converse and act.

AH, KEJAK. Wren got a sense of a satisfied chuckle, and felt a sudden chill. *HE HAS TRAINED YOU WELL. NOT WELL ENOUGH TO HIDE YOU FROM THE ACCURSED SUN, HOWEVER, AND NOT WELL ENOUGH TO PROTECT YOU FROM ME. WOULD YOU LIKE TO KNOW THE LIES CHEJOP KEJAK TAUGHT YOU? I CAN SHOW YOU TRUTH.*

"Does Kejak work for you? Is that his secret?"

Again, there came a sense of titanic laughter. *HIS ENEMIES ARE MY ENEMIES, THOUGH HE HAS VERY GOOD REASONS FOR WHAT HE DOES. ASK HIM. HE WILL TELL YOU.*

Wren sat down. The stone was pleasantly cool, and he settled into a lotus position, The discussion, he sensed, would not be a short one.

"What do you mean by that? Kejak doesn't tell anyone anything."

IF YOU KNOW HIS SECRETS, HE WILL SPEAK. AFTER ALL THESE YEARS, THE GUILT STILL GNAWS AT HIM. HE WILL TELL YOU THAT THE AUGURIES SHOWED HIM THAT UNLESS HE STIRRED UP THE POGROM AGAINST THE CELESTIAL EXALTED, ALL OF CREATION WOULD BE SWALLOWED BY MY MAW. HE WILL TELL YOU THAT HE HAD NO CHOICE, AND THAT HE BITTERLY REGRETS WHAT HE HAS DONE. AND HE WILL NEGLECT TO MENTION ONE THING: IN THE PURGE OF THE CELESTIAL EXALTED, CHEJOP KEJAK FORGOT TO PURGE HIMSELF.

"Interesting." Wren stroked his chin, where the beginnings of a beard were making themselves known. "So what does that mean? You're going to triumph in the end, and that I'd do better to be with you than against you?"

YES.

"Why me?"

BECAUSE YOU ARE HERE.

Wren shifted, and strove to keep his mind as blank as possible. *Let my words speak for me,* he told himself. "Is that all?"

A HAPPY COINCIDENCE. There was a sense of a cosmic shrug. YOU ANGERED THE PRINCE. THE PRINCE'S ANGER CAME TO MY—TO OUR ATTENTION. YOU EXALTED WHILE IN THE PRINCE'S DOMAIN, AND AT A LATE AGE. ALL OF THESE THINGS BESPEAK AN ODD DESTINY, ONE WHICH IT IS IN MY INTEREST TO CHANGE.

"Because if you don't change it, your triumph isn't quite as inevitable? Is that it?"

THE VICTORY OF THE ABYSS IS INEVITABLE. IT IS SIMPLY A QUESTION OF WHEN. SUBVERTING YOUR DESTINY MERELY SPEEDS THE PROCESS. I GROW WEARY OF SLUMBER, AND WOULD ONCE MORE AWAKEN.

Wren stood and paced in a wide circle, silent for a long time. The situation, he realized, was far beyond anything for which he had been prepared. Debate in the temple with the other acolytes was one thing. Debate with a god, even a dead one, was entirely another. The sheer force of the thing's words shattered his concentration, filling him with the urge to prostrate himself and worship.

THERE ARE WORSE GODS TO WORSHIP. THE FALSE DRAGONS, FOR INSTANCE.

"I would seem to have been removed from their purview, thank you," Wren said, and pointed significantly to the mark on his brow. "I only deal with deities who speak to me directly these days."

THE UNCONQUERED SUN WILL NOT SPEAK TO YOU HERE. YOUR HEART IS NOT HIS, IN ANY CASE.

"That remains to be seen."

YOU WILL BE WAITING A VERY LONG TIME TO HEAR HIS VOICE, I PROMISE YOU, AND THE FALSE DRAGONS CANNOT SPEAK TO YOU AT ALL. HEARKEN UNTO ME. THE UNCONQUERED SUN HAS GIVEN YOU NOTHING. WHAT POWER HAS THE SUN SHOWN YOU? WHAT GIFTS HAVE YOU BEEN BESTOWED? YOU HAVE BEEN SEDUCED AND ABANDONED. I OFFER YOU POWER. I OFFER YOU KNOWLEDGE. I OFFER YOU DOMINION OVER THOSE WHO WOULD HAVE HUNTED YOU.

Wren's mind filled with images, scenes of himself working dark magics and sitting in judgment on a chained row of Immaculate monks. He saw Shotan Fong's grave desecrated, the fat man's corpse burned and his ashes fed to others in the Guild who'd tormented Wren as a youth. He saw himself humbling Kejak himself, and forcing the old man to kiss his feet and beg for a swift and merciful death.

ALL OF THIS I CAN GIVE TO YOU, ELIEZER WREN. ALL OF THESE THINGS WILL I GRANT UNTO YOU IF YOU SURRENDER YOURSELF UNTO ME.

"Why?" The question, Wren felt, was an important one. If the dead gods were so potent, why did they need him, and why did they feel compelled to bribe him so extravagantly? Not, he reflected, that the images he'd been shown were such a great enticement. He had no wish to so much as think about Shotan Fong, let alone exhume him, and besides, Guild custom generally called for exposing the bodies of the dead for scavengers. Knowing it was impossible made the fantasy instantly less appealing, and said much about those doing the temptation.

A POWERFUL SERVANT IS AN EFFECTIVE SERVANT. A POWERFUL, WELL-TRAINED SERVANT IS VERY EFFECTIVE INDEED. IT COSTS ME LITTLE TO AWAKEN AND FOCUS THE POWER IN YOU, AND IN RETURN YOU CAN DO MUCH FOR ME AND MY BRETHREN.

"I suppose that makes sense," Wren said noncommittally.

YOU STILL THINK THIS IS SOME SORT OF TRICKERY, I SEE. PERHAPS I CAN ALLAY YOUR DOUBTS. There was a long pause, and then the voice added, THIS WILL MOST LIKELY HURT A GREAT DEAL.

Wren had no time to make a witty response, or even to formulate one. What felt like lightning detonating inside his skull made it impossible for him to speak, impossible for him to think, impossible for him to stand. He collapsed, convulsing, while a series of images etched themselves indelibly upon his memory. Each showed him how he could draw power from the very air around him, channel it through himself, and use it to do marvelous, terrible things. Each traced the path of the power through him, leaving him twitching like a broken-backed dog. Lightning danced from his fingertips and flares of golden light shone from his brow. He screamed, once, a sound that would have gratified the now-destroyed golem to hear, and then lay still.

THERE.

An eternity later, Wren's eyes opened. "What..." he croaked. "What happened?"

YOU HAVE BEEN GIVEN A GIFT.

"A... gift?"

YEARS OF TRAINING, YOURS IN AN INSTANT. THE POWERS OF THE ZENITH CASTE ARE YOURS, PRIEST. THINGS YOU WOULD NEVER HAVE LEARNED ON YOUR OWN, AND THINGS THAT WOULD HAVE TAKEN YOU

A HUNDRED YEARS. CONSIDER IT A SMALL TOKEN OF WHAT CAN BE DONE FOR YOU, IF YOU PLEDGE SERVICE.

"I see." Wren sat up, groggily, and rubbed his head. "And if I pledge service, what do I give up? What happens then?"

YOUR NAME. YOUR SELF. THESE I SHALL TAKE FROM YOU, AND GIVE YOU IN RETURN FAR GREATER GIFTS. THIS IS YOUR TRUE PATH, WREN. YOU ARE NO PRIEST, NOT OF THE DRAGONS AND NOT OF THE UNCONQUERED SUN. YOU ARE A WARRIOR AND AN ASSASSIN. THE WELL-LAID TRAP PLEASES YOU, AS DOES THE DEATH OF A FOOLISH ENEMY. YOU HAVE KILLED MORE THAN YOU NEEDED TO, WREN, AND YOU KNOW THIS. YOU KNOW THAT YOU HAVE TAKEN PLEASURE IN THE DEATHS OF OTHERS.

"That's not true."

ISN'T IT? WHY SET THE TRAP IN THE TOMB, THEN? YOU DIDN'T KNOW WHO FOLLOWED YOU. THE FACT THAT IT CAUGHT SOMEONE YOU THOUGHT OF AS AN ENEMY WAS MERELY A HAPPY ACCIDENT. DEATH FOLLOWS YOU, ELIEZER WREN. MAKE IT YOUR HOUND, NOT YOUR PURSUER.

"You're wrong about me." Wren turned away from the altar, hunched over as if he were in a high wind. The force of the dead god's words staggered him, sending doubts racing through his mind. Why *had* he planted those traps? They had cost him valuable time, after all, but he remembered grinning like a fool at the surprise his pursuers were likely to receive….

"No."

YOU DO NOT KNOW WHAT YOU REFUSE.

"I am not what you say I am. You do not know me."

I KNOW YOU BETTER THAN YOU IMAGINE. I HAVE READ EVERY PAGE OF YOUR MIND, WREN. I KNOW THE LUSTS YOU HIDE FOR THE WOMEN AT THE TEMPLE, AND THE WAY THE THOUGHT OF COMBAT ENFLAMES YOU. I KNOW YOUR HATRED FOR KEJAK AND YOUR FEAR. I KNOW THE ANIMAL AT THE HEART OF YOU, WREN, AND I WOULD EXALT IT. JOIN ME.

"No." The power of the god's words drove him to his knees. Tears streamed down his cheeks. Every syllable, every sound had the ring of truth, battering at the image he'd built of himself. He was Eliezer Wren, the man who could escape anything. He was Kejak's faithful hand, striking quickly and wisely. He was a monk who strove to be a better one, and a warrior who strove to be less of one.

YOU ARE A KILLER.

"I am not."

YOU ARE. YOU HAVE KILLED FOR SHOTAN FONG, FOR CHEJOP KEJAK AND FOR THE UNCONQUERED SUN. KILL FOR ME INSTEAD, AND REVEL IN IT. FOR I AM MALHAVOSH, FATHER OF SNAKES AND LORD OF MURDER, AND I CLAIM YOU FOR MY OWN.

"I belong to no one." Wren's cry of defiance was barely a whisper, and he dug his nails into his palms so that the pain could anchor him to himself.

YOU BELONG TO THE UNCONQUERED SUN, AND BEFORE THAT TO MERE MEN. I GIVE YOU A CHOICE OF MASTERS.

"I have no master!"

YOU ARE A SLAVE. BECOME A WILLING ONE, AND YOU WILL BE REWARDED.

He fell forward, and slowly, laboriously, began clawing his way toward the door through which he'd entered. "No."

YOU OWE NOTHING TO ANYONE IN THE WORLD OF THE LIVING. ABANDON IT.

He crept forward. "No."

WHOM DO YOU CALL FRIEND? KEJAK HAS DISMISSED YOU AS A LOST PAWN IN HIS GREAT GAME. THE GUILD CURSES YOUR MEMORY, AND THE TEMPLE HAS FORGOTTEN YOU. WHO WOULD MOURN YOU, ELIEZER WREN? WHO WOULD CARE?

A tear rolled down Wren's cheek and splashed against the floor. He watched it in fascination. It puddled on the stone, quivering, until another tear fell and scattered it.

Water...

YOU ARE HERE NOW, WREN. THERE IS NOWHERE ELSE FOR YOU. FORGET THE PAST.

Wren lifted his head. Was that a faint hint of worry he'd heard in the god's voice? He clawed his way to his knees and tried to remember why water would matter.

Water, and a promise...

WREN, LOOK AT ME. BEHOLD YOUR GOD.

Water, and a promise made to a friend... a spirit who had sheltered him once...

"Rhadanthos," he whispered. "I owe a debt to Rhadanthos."

THE GOD OF A TRICKLE? YOU OWE HIM NOTHING!

"I owe him my life, freely given. As long as I am in his debt, I cannot give myself to you." He spat and staggered forward once more, his back to the altar. "Not that I want to, you fraud."

YOU ARE MINE.

"I renounce your gift. Take it back and kill me, but I am not yours!"

IT CANNOT BE TAKEN BACK. IT IS PART OF YOU, AND THUS I AM A PART OF YOU AS WELL.

Wren stood. "Then I'll cut you out," he howled, and clawed at his chest. Light shone from his brow, and his nails sank deep into his flesh. "Take it back, you dead thing." He spun, blood spraying everywhere. A few drops landed in the brazier which smoked ominously.

Where the blood touched, it shone with the sun's light and stone crumbled.

WHAT ARE YOU DOING? THIS PLACE IS SACRED.

"To what? To whom? I'll see it in ashes!"

Gathering himself, Wren leapt straight up. Behind him, the doors burst open and a half-dozen of the hooded shapes he'd seen before charged in. Their hands clutched hooked knives with serrated blades, and they flowed with inhuman speed toward where Wren had stood.

Wren, however, was in the air, a nimbus of light around him. He could see the temple spread out before him, the recumbent form of the dead god and the weaving rows of the benches.

Only now did he understand that they were a sigil, that the very way in which the room had been arranged was a sink for power. No more, he vowed. No more.

He hung in the air for an impossibly long moment, his bloody palms pressed against the chamber's ceiling, then began to fall. Again, he tore at himself and again the blood scattered, the stone melting away under its very touch. A few drops struck the advancing figures, who fell to the ground, writhing in agony.

YOU CANNOT DO THIS.

"I just did." Wren smiled raggedly, and walked up the seven steps to the altar. Overhead, jagged cracks appeared in the temple's ceiling, and chunks of stone began raining down. "And what's more, I'm going to do it again." He spread his arms wide and, bleeding from a dozen wounds, embraced the stone before him.

EVEN IF YOU ESCAPE, ELIEZER WREN, YOU TAKE ME WITH YOU. YOU WILL ALWAYS BE MINE.

"Never!" cried Wren, and let the sound of the temple's collapse drown out the dead god's screaming.

Chapter Twenty-Eight

The thing that Holok liked best about being on the road was the tea. Spending time with Kejak on the Isle meant nothing but the finest teas, leaves delicately crushed by trained slaves and steeped in boiling water for precisely the right amount of time, then served in translucently delicate porcelain cups painted with liquid gold and crushed gems. It was served with a great deal of pomp and ceremony, and sipped daintily amidst much knowing nodding of heads and discussions of exactly which leaves had gone into it and in what proportion. One was expected to discuss this at great length, and to have an extensive knowledge of why, say, Nellens tea plantations in the south were inferior to those in the northwest.

Holok, for his part, thought this was a load of bollocks, and sincerely believed that ninety percent of the tea served on the Isle tasted like camel piss. Wisely, he'd refrained from voicing this opinion on the Isle more than once. Kejak, for his part, had found it "amusingly rustic" and as a joke, had ordered a slave to bring him some boiled pine needles.

Holok had accepted the proffered cup without comment, swallowed the contents in a single gulp, and gravely pronounced it excellent. That had ended that particular discussion, and Holok had never raised the matter again.

But he much preferred the sort of tea one got in hostels and taverns, strong teas brewed for too long in overworked kitchens. A good black tea that would make a functionary at the Palace Sublime choke was just the thing Holok preferred to start his day with, and a green tea cut with whatever shrubbery the merchant had passed en route just made the priest smile.

And that was why he found himself grinning hugely before a large bowl of tea in a rough trader's hostel called Reddust, sixteen days out along the caravan track from his last port of call. The tea itself was green, more or less, and the steam that came up from the bowl gave strong evidence that nettles had played a prominent role in its ancestry. Holok didn't care. It smelled strong enough to make a mule's tail curl, and that was all that mattered.

The hostel itself was designed for tradesmen and their teamsters, all roughhewn wood furniture around a central fire pit. The bar was more polished, and better attended than the tables scattered around the room. Most of the illumination came from the fire pit itself or from torches in sconces on the walls, resulting in dim, uncertain light even more obscured by thick, pungent smoke. At the back of the hostel was a door leading to a long row of tiny sleeping quarters, each graced with a single straw-stuffed mattress housing innumerable bedbugs. The stables lay beyond that, unfortunately upwind, and every time someone walked into or out of the place, the scent of unwashed horse and camel wafted in.

The customers were a rough lot, a suspicious mix of travelers, animal tenders and caravan guards. Holok had noted a fistful of tents and wagons out front when he'd arrived, alone and on foot. He'd given the encampment a wide berth, making certain not to meet the eyes of the robed and turbaned men who sat watchfully near the tents. They were Guildsmen, or more accurately the Guild's bullyboys, and they had no love for priests of the Immaculate Order. Sensing their eyes on him, he kept his head bowed and made for the hostel itself. There was no way, he knew, that they could miss seeing him for what he was, but the less provocation he offered, the better.

Inside, however, there were no obvious Guildsmen, and for that Holok gave a sigh of relief. The other travelers still gave him a wide berth—he had a table by the fire all to himself—but better distance than insults or hurled cutlery. The latter grew more likely the further one went out into the hinterlands. The Immaculates were seen as an extension of the Realm out here, and while Holok knew that in the main that impression was correct, he still felt it was rude to take that sort of thing out on individual priests. After all, most of them had been four generations shy of conception when the Order had tied itself to the Scarlet Empress's political program, and really had no idea what was going on behind the scenes.

Of course, behind the scenes was where he'd dwelt, at least until recently, and where Kejak still lurked. He sipped his tea and chuckled. In a sense, that almost made it appropriate for him to take some fashion of abuse, though propriety was not high on Holok's list of concerns right now.

Behind him, he heard the serving girl say, "Rice," tonelessly, and then a heavy bowl thumped on the table in front of him. Long brown rice spilled over the edges onto the tabletop, and a dirty pair of chopsticks clattered next to it as the girl practically threw them down.

"Thank you," he said softly, without turning. "The tea is excellent." A bark of laughter generally echoed throughout the room was his only reply, so he bent his head to his rice and picked up a couple of grains between his fingers. It was, as he expected, cold and undercooked. Then again, caravan hostels were not where one went to find fine cuisine. Summoning a modicum of enthusiasm, he picked up the chopsticks, wiped them carefully on his sleeve, and began eating.

It wasn't until Holok was halfway through the bowl that he realized that everyone in the tavern was watching him expectantly. He looked up from the bowl, his eyebrows raised quizzically, and looked around the room. Most of the faces he saw looked away when his eyes met theirs; few had the courage to stare back even for a second. The serving girl was nowhere to be seen. Only an old woman in the corner locked gazes with him. She seemed more amused than defiant, as if she were sharing a joke with him, and the dust on her black travel robes showed that she'd been walking for a very long time.

An unlikely suspect, Holok decided, and looked back across the room. Here and there he could see Guild caravan guards mixed in, and wondered when they'd arrived. No matter, really; he was sure they'd come in to see him collapse in his tea, and then to kick his corpse. It was almost a pity he had to spoil their fun.

"Who," he said softly, just over the crackling of the fire,

"paid the serving girl to try to poison me?" He pushed his chair back from the table slowly, but did not stand. "I'm just curious, mind you. I'm not interested in vengeance. Although I would like more rice."

Silence met his query. The old woman in the corner coughed, once. No one else stirred. Holok felt a sudden wave of annoyance. "Oh, come on," he said. "Someone here wants me dead, and he's not willing to admit it? All of you against one lone monk, and one who hasn't finished his supper? Surely I can't beat all of you."

"How'd you survive the poison?" The speaker was one of the Guild caravan guards, standing now with his hand on his knife. "It's supposed to kill in seconds."

Holok nodded slightly and stood, stretching. His back popped loudly, once. "It is poisoned, isn't it? For a moment I thought they just had a poor dishwasher back in the kitchen. What did you use? Something that kills everyone who tastes it, I trust? The trick, of course, is getting the victim to do just that, isn't it?" He held up the chopsticks he'd been eating with, then made a complicated pass with his fingers. Suddenly, he held two pair of dingy chopsticks, the second covered in an oily sheen. "Hmm. I wonder who put this on my chopsticks. Good thing I switched them for my own, don't you think? I do hope whatever this might be isn't a contact poison, however. If that's the case, my robe is doomed."

A murmur of dismay rose up from a dozen throats. Around him, Holok could see and hear the signs of a large number of men working themselves up for a fight. There were perhaps twenty in the hostel, of various ages and conditions, and it was clear that none of them wanted to throw the first punch. Silently, he calculated the odds. Bad, but not impossible, and in a crowded room their numbers wouldn't be an advantage.

He sighed, and half the room flinched. Two or three, he saw, actually jumped, and that got his blood flowing just a touch faster. *Admit it to yourself,* he said silently, *you've been itching for a fight since you left the Isle. Why not here and now?*

"It's a shameful lack of discipline," he said, and realized he'd said it aloud. Suddenly, he grinned. No doubt someone here thought he was talking to them.

"A lack of discipline?" It was the caravan guard again, of course. He was broad-shouldered and short-legged, wearing a long rough tunic belted at the waist and high leather boots. Bearded and mustached, with his long hair tied in two greasy braids, he looked like nothing so much as an escaped circus bear, one that was angrily seeking its former keeper. He pushed forward through the crowd, dagger out. Holok let him approach.

"I suppose it won't help if I say that I wasn't talking to you? No? I didn't think so." Holok could sense the tension in the room building, felt his nerves crackle with excitement. It would be very soon. The caravan guard would have to attack him or back down, and if he backed down he'd lose his men forever. So he'd attack, because there really was nothing else he could do.

The fact that he'd almost certainly end up broken in nine different but very precise places as a result was, however, still Holok's little secret.

"I don't like you, priest," the man said, and from his tone it was clear that he was used to having this sort of pronouncement taken for deep and subtle wit. "I don't like you at all."

"I'm sorry to hear that," Holok said mildly. "Would you like some rice?"

In response, the man spat into Holok's tea. Then, deliberately, he looked up and stepped as close to the monk as he dared. "No, priest, I don't want any rice. But you know what I do want?"

Holok frowned and looked down. He was perhaps six inches taller than the caravan guard, and the man's attempt to intimidate him was frankly ludicrous. It was all he could do to keep from laughing. "You want the money you paid the serving girl to poison me back?"

The man opened his mouth, closed it, and opened it again. He looked as if he'd just stepped on a rake, tines up. Holok felt laughter coming again, and this time couldn't restrain it. "Oh, Dragons!" His guffaw boomed out over the table. "You mean to tell me that you were actually going to say that? My dear, dear man, you really must work on your threats. They're too funny!"

Out of the corner of his eye, Holok checked the man's reaction. If skin color were any indication, the laughter had hit the mark; the man's face was the color of uncooked meat, and he was trembling with rage. Mentally, Holok began ticking off the seconds before humiliation turned to berserk fury, and waited.

At three, the caravan guard leaped, dagger poised. Holok ducked underneath the clumsy swing, then spun and gave the man a push on the rump. He stumbled into the crowd of his supporters, blade still out, and there was a sudden sharp shriek, abruptly cut off. "Get the priest!" someone shouted, and Holok smiled. As much as he loved quiet meditation on the Dragons' mysteries, this aspect of the Order definitely had its appeal. Then the wall of surging humanity closed on him, and there was no more time to think.

A chair came sailing towards his head and he sidestepped. It crashed to the floor and broke into pieces, tripping another assailant as she charged. Holok whirled and two of the chopsticks he'd been holding flew forward to bury themselves in the throats of a pair of burly caravan guards, men who looked liked the ringleader's disliked brothers.

"Did I mention that I keep my chopsticks sharp for a reason?" he shouted over the din, and then dodged a series of blows from a man carrying a short dagger in each fist. As he charged, Holok grabbed the man's left wrist and jammed the dagger deep into the tabletop. As expected, the man dropped his other weapon to concentrate on prying loose his stuck dagger, which gave Holok enough time to flip his still-steaming bowl of tea into the man's face. The unfortunate let out a yell, let go of the knife, and sagged towards the floor.

Holok kicked him twice in the back of the head on the way down as a safety precaution, then ducked under another wild swing from a woman holding what could only be a leather sock filled with sand. It whistled past again, and he jabbed upward to puncture it with one of the two chopsticks he still held as it passed. With a soft hiss, sand began leaking out. The woman wielding it developed a look of dismayed surprise and half-halted her swing, which gave Holok all the time he needed to reach inside her guard and apply an open-fist punch to her throat. She fell backwards into the fire, gurgling, and the leaking bag of sand fell from her fingers.

Before it hit the ground, Holok kicked the bag, and it flew straight into the face of yet another onrushing traveler. With an unpleasant wet sound, he sat down abruptly, bleeding from what had once been his nose. He wobbled there for a moment until Holok took pity and hit him again, an elbow to the side of the head as he reached for the heavy earthenware bowl of rice with his other hand.

"Seconds, anyone?" he called out, and hurled the bowl into a knot of onrushing attackers. They scattered, and he took the opportunity to leap up onto the table. A trio of knives slammed into the wood near his feet and he jumped up, coming down on a pair of wrists too frail to support his weight. A pair of perfectly synchronized snaps cut through the din of the brawl, followed rapidly by a pair of shrieks.

The third man swinging at his ankles made another strike, and Holok leaped effortlessly again. The knife flashed where his feet had been a second before, slicing first through the air and then through the arms Holok had just neatly broken. Even as the man stammered out an apology, Holok came down on one of his wrists as well as the other one he'd already broken.

A new round of howls went up, and Holok permitted himself a moment's satisfaction. He dropped to a crouch and spun in place on the foot planted on the third man's wrist, striking each of the heads around the table with a deftly placed elbow as he did so. They collapsed in sequence, the first one still hanging from the table he'd been pinned to by his friend's knife.

Grinning hugely, he looked up in time to see the initial instigator charging at him, dagger red with blood. Without thinking, Holok flipped both poisoned chopsticks at the man, who cooperated by going down with a horrified gurgle.

"Damnation. Should have saved one of those," he muttered to himself. He hopped down from the table, the breeze from his robes brushing away the sand from the bag he'd punctured earlier. His latest assailant wasn't so lucky, as her feet slid out from under her as she leapt forward and tried to land in a fighting stance. Her eyes met Holok's for a moment, wide with panic. He shook his head at her, said "Sand's such a nuisance, isn't it?" then lifted his left foot and stomped down, once.

There was a rigid crunch, and then Holok moved on to a new opponent.

To his left, a pair of caravan guards had flipped over a table and were kneeling behind it, slings whirling. The distinctive whir of the sling bullets in midair warned Holok, and he turned in time to feel the breeze from both as they whirred past his head. He dropped into a split, his right leg kicking a stone into the rim of the fire pit. It hit the pile of blazing brands and flipped a shower of sparks up into the air, one that neatly descended on the reloading slingers. They quickly dropped their weapons in a fevered attempt to brush out the flames that were threatening to envelop them, and this gave Holok all the time he needed to rise to his feet and punch each man, quite deliberately. They went down with amazing rapidity, stinking of cooked meat.

"Look out!" A woman's voice came from behind him, sharp with alarm. Rather than turn to see who called to him, he hurled himself over the table. A chair leg came crashing down where his head had been an instant before, held in a massive, meaty fist. The man the fist was attached to was huge, and the chair leg looked positively dainty in his grip. Shaven-headed and tattooed, he smiled to show teeth that had been filed to sharp points. "Table's not going to hide you, priest," he growled through a snaggletoothed smile.

"It won't have to," came the woman's voice again, and an expression of puzzlement suddenly appeared on the giant's ugly face.

"That's... not... fair," he suddenly gasped, and fell forward. He landed heavily on the table Holok hid behind, which with a groan collapsed under his weight. A single, slender metal spike stuck out of the back of his neck. Behind him, silhouetted by the fire, stood the old woman in black.

"Very impressive," she said. "And you relied only on your skills, not your other talents. I should applaud."

Holok half-rose from his crouch. "You should check to see if anyone else still feels like fighting first." One of the slingers moaned, and Holok kicked him, hard. "It's hard to fight when you're clapping, though it is possible."

The woman shrugged. "The rest are dead or fled. I saw to that.

Most, however, were your handiwork. You fight exceptionally well, even for a monk."

"I'm an exceptional monk," he said sourly, and stood. Pieces of his tea bowl crunched underfoot. He looked around the tavern, but it was deserted apart from him, the old woman, and the dead or unconscious bravos who'd piled into the fray. "Who are you?"

"Someone who would like to travel with you," she replied primly.

"Is that so?" He slogged through the debris to where she stood. She really was tiny, he thought, as he loomed over her. *Made of sterner stuff than the brigand who started this mess, though.* "Why in Creation would I want to take you with me? You don't even know where I'm going."

"Neither do you," she noted, and smiled serenely. "And you want to take me with you because of this." She reached inside her robes and, after a moment's incongruous fumbling, drew forth a gleaming dagger.

Holok's jaw dropped. "That's not gold, is it?" he whispered, half to himself.

"You are quite observant. Would you like to learn where and how I obtained this?"

The priest rolled his eyes. "No, I have no curiosity whatsoever about how you came up with a piece of orichalcum that size in this late day and age. Of *course* I want to know, woman."

"Excellent." She tucked the dagger away inside her robes once again, and surveyed the destruction. "We should probably start walking before the bodies start to smell, and at some point during our travels, I will tell you."

Holok scratched his beard, which for over ten centuries had been a sure-fire signal of distress. "In this heat, that might not be too long. Though I'm more worried about the possibility that these unfortunates had friends than I am about our delicate noses." He ducked behind the bar, gathered up a trio of water skins and some food, which he stuffed into his pouch, then headed for the door. At the last minute, he looked back over his shoulder. "What should I call you, anyway? I should know if we're going to be traveling together, at least for a little while."

"You may call me Unforgiven Blossom," she said, and followed.

Chapter Twenty-Nine

Wren came up out of the dark as if all the hounds of a particularly unpleasant hell were on his tail which, upon reflection, he suspected was only a slight exaggeration. The Labyrinth was not technically one of the hells, nor had he seen anything particularly hound-like in his travels, but he had no intention of staying in the Labyrinth long enough for anyone to note the discrepancy.

The collapse of the dead god's tomb had been an exercise in pure terror. Pieces of ceiling the size of townhouses had come pinwheeling down, splintering upon impact and filling the air with shards of razor-sharp stone. One of the first impacts had crushed the brazier near the entrance and plunged the vast chamber into darkness, and from that point on the tomb had been a deadly cauldron of sound and whirring shreds of debris. The only light came from the sparks made by stone striking stone, and Wren had dodged the flying shrapnel and falling debris as best he could by listening for the tell-tale whines and rumbles.

He'd been mostly successful, surprisingly so. One long cut ran down the length of his arm, and he'd been picking needle-like stone fragments out of a gash in his left leg for days, but other than that he'd escaped unscathed. The tears he'd made in his own chest had proved to be startlingly shallow, and Wren wondered where all of the blood had come from. He'd been certain he was shedding his heart's blood on the floor, and to find that so little had done so much was a trifle disturbing.

That led him to thinking about the Father of Murders, whose resting place he'd seen buried under a small mountain of rubble. Wren had no doubts that the thing on the slab had suffered no real harm from the collapse, but it was reassuring to see countless tons of rock piled over it, in any case.

The pile of stone had also provided him with his exit, allowing him to climb through the gap in the ceiling and into a broad, flat corridor paved with millions of green mosaic tiles. The ceramic was hot, but the walls of the corridor glowed with a soft light, and to his left the passage led unmistakably upward.

He'd heard wailing from behind him as he half-staggered, half-ran along his new path. Mourners for the dead god, Wren supposed, and wondered what sort of observance would be held for something already dead. Nothing he'd care to see, he'd quickly realized, and pushed his pace as much as he dared.

They'd followed him, of course. The more vengeful and the more adept of the dead god's followers had found his trail easily enough and loped after him, intent on extracting vengeance. He'd dispatched them all, though, with a single-minded ferocity that left Wren wondering how much of his tempter's assessment of his true self had been accurate. The pale gold light that enfolded him during these battles had done half of his work for him, striking down weaker foes and wounding stronger ones, and his determination and skill had done the rest. Nothing was going to hold him in this soul-devouring place any longer, not serpents or ghosts or the commands of the dead gods themselves. Eliezer Wren wanted to go home.

And now, up ahead was the light, or at least a square trapdoor in the ceiling that had daylight spilling through around its edges. A thin stone ring was set in the door's exact center, and by stretching to his utmost Wren found he could reach it. His fingers closed around the smooth stone and for the first time in he knew not how long, he smelled flowers.

"Forget-me-nots," he said, and laughed. "It only makes sense, doesn't it?" The scent of flowers made him wonder, however, how long he had been down in the dark. He'd have a hell of a time explaining his absence to Kejak, if he were so inclined to return to the Isle to see how the ancient Sidereal dealt with an operative who'd been touched by the sun's reawakened power. Putting those worries aside for the moment, Wren tugged with all his might on the stone ring. It didn't budge. He tried again, and a thin shower of dust drifted down, but nothing more.

"This is just cruel," he mumbled, as he glanced backward to see if he was still alone in the corridor. He was, for which he gave a quick prayer of thanks before trying his strength once again. Once again, he made no progress.

A brief surge of panic threatened to overwhelm him, but Wren forced it down, willing himself to focus on the problem at hand.

The problem itself, it seemed, was simple. It was a door, and a door which showed light coming through around it. That meant light on the other side, and presumably a way to open the door. There was a ring on this side, which would suggest to a logical man that the appropriate response was to tug down. However, this was the Labyrinth, and nothing was logical. Besides, Wren noted, the appearance of the slab suggested that it was heavy indeed, and the pattern of the light around the stone indicated that there was no angle at which it could be tugged that would allow it to swing down.

That left two possibilities. One was that the trapdoor was simply a showpiece, a trick to offer fugitives like himself some hope before dashing them down into despair. This would be in keeping with the general theme of the Labyrinth as he'd viewed it thus far, and would not surprise him one bit.

Or, he thought, *there could be another option.*

Gently, he pushed. The stone rose as if it weighed nothing at all, and Wren stared up into the light.

"I will, almost inevitably, be damned," he said, and looked around himself one last time. There was no one. Apart from the sterile corridor, there was nothing.

"Unconquered Sun, protect your servants from themselves," he prayed, and then leapt up into the breach.

The corridor went dark behind him, and the stone trapdoor thudded back into place.

❖

The good news, Wren decided, was that he was once again breathing. There was air here, stale cold air but air nonetheless. He was back in the world he knew, the world he'd grown up in and labored in most of his life, the world that he now knew was fragile beyond belief. A slow, chill draft reassured him that he was in no danger of suffocating, either, though the occasional whiff of carrion stench he caught made him wonder where exactly that breeze came from.

The bad news, unfortunately, was that the promise of light and fragrant blooming flowers had been as bald-faced a lie as any the Labyrinth had ever perpetrated.

He was in a stone-walled room, and not a particularly large one, either. The room was made smaller by the presence of yet another mortuary slab in the center of its rectangular space, and the irregularly arranged skeletons huddled in the corners. There was no light, and no carving on either the stone walls or the slab to give the slightest hint of where he was. The surface of the slab was covered with a coarse powder, which he assumed was the remains of its original inhabitant, and as a result he tried to avoid moving too quickly lest he stir up a breeze and get a noseful of corpse dust.

His probing fingers found a door, one which seemed a great deal more solid than the one he'd pushed aside to clamber up into the chamber. For a moment he considered trying to find his way back down, but he dismissed the notion instantly. For one thing, even slow death and starvation here was likely to be better than what was waiting for him in the halls of the dead gods, and for another, the trapdoor had vanished so thoroughly as to make Wren wonder if it had ever actually existed.

Tapping the stone of the walls yielded precisely the result Wren anticipated, which was to say, nothing. Whoever had built this room—*this mausoleum*, he corrected himself—had done so with the intention of having it endure through this cycle of the world and possibly the next.

"At least I'm not buried," he said aloud, and marveled slightly at how quickly the sound was deadened. "The draft tells me that much. Now if only I could get some light."

You have light within you. I would see it swallowed by darkness.

The memory of the dead god's voice startled Wren, and then made him smile. If he wanted light, he could have light. Idli had learned that, and the Father of Murders—he still didn't dare say its proper name—had taught him how to control it.

"Light indeed," he said, and spread his hands. Gold light flared out from his palms and brow, and the tomb was suddenly lit with a radiance as brilliant as the sun's. The gray stone was washed almost white by the radiance, and he could see now the intricate pattern of painted sigils that encircled the walls well above the height of his head. He could also see a flash of reflection from something higher in the tomb, and lifted his eyes to see what it could possibly be. A lantern, he suspected, or perhaps gilt on the ceiling.

Instead, it was a sword.

It hung there, suspended by nothing and impossibly huge. Gleaming in the golden light, it somehow seemed even more golden itself, and it chimed faintly in the light. It was as long as a man was tall, with a slight curve to its blade and a double fistful of rubies set in its hilt and guard.

Wren swallowed a most profane and unworthy exclamation and gazed at it. If he hadn't wanted the light, he realized, he never would have seen its reflection. And if he hadn't seen its reflection, he never would have looked up. And had he not looked up...

"You would not have seen the sword."

Instinctively, Wren leapt up onto the slab and reached out for the sword. It fit in his hand, warm to the touch and so well balanced that a lame child could wield it. Clouds of dust swirled around his feet as he realized an instant too late he was desecrating a tomb, but that was a secondary concern at the moment.

"Who are you? Show yourself."

"Not while your anima still shines. It is destruction for me and my kind."

"Aha." Wren backed to the edge of the slab and brought the massive blade down in front of him. "You're another undead, are you? I've dealt enough with your kind of late, and I'm in no mood to trade riddles or be led by the nose. What do you want?"

"To let you out." The voice was measured and calm; a bit calmer, Wren realized, than he was himself. "I serve the sword, and the Unconquered Sun, and I would be most upset if you starved to death inside that tomb."

Before he could answer, Wren heard stone grinding on stone, and the rasp of metal sliding across ancient rust. "As proof of good faith, however, I will release you before you dim the light, and thus risk destruction for myself and all those who serve here with me. The decision is, of course, up to you."

The door started to swing open, and Wren could see out into what appeared to be a large stone chamber beyond. He caught a faint glimpse of more skeletons, broken weapons, smoothly carved stone. Faint, piteous screams touched at the edge of his hearing. The door swung open wider.

"Damn you," said Wren, and swallowed the light back into himself. The chamber plunged into darkness, and Wren leapt down from the slab to see who, or what, had just rescued him.

◆

She saw the light first. So long had she been in the tunnels that her eyes were now adjusted to the dark, and the faintest scrap of glow—be it from fungus or a sliver of daylight through a hair's-breadth fissure—was as bright as the glow of a torch to her.

And there, up ahead, was a flash of golden light.

She knew where she was, of course; near the damnable chamber the more damnable ghosts had driven her away from. She'd been fighting a running battle in the tunnels with them for days, forced to retreat by some, wreaking havoc on others, and always she'd kept trying to circle back here to see what they'd been so intent on keeping her from. Some of her powers, she found, remained to her, and these were effective enough against the ghosts that she could hold her own.

Furthermore, she'd found that they didn't stray far from the chamber. Clearly, guarding what it held was more important than punishing her, and so she'd been able to lurk around the perimeter of their domain, retreating to safety whenever she felt it prudent.

But now there was light, bright light, and the ghosts were nowhere to be seen. This, Shamblemerry decided, was her chance. Moving silently, she advanced toward what looked to be the golden glow of the sun.

✦

The ghosts materialized as soon as he stepped forth from the tomb, which Wren had half anticipated. Clad in the armor of long-gone armies, they looked the part of eternal sentries, right down to the uniformly dour expressions that both the men and the women wore.

"So you've been guarding the tomb since it was created, or more accurately, what it held, and I'm the first person in all this time to actually place my hands on the sword?"

"The daiklave," the ghost who seemed to speak for the rest corrected. "And that is largely the truth. Others have walked these catacombs, many in recent months. Priests, soldiers, children, fortune-seekers, servants of the Abyss. Many have passed this way, but few have even found this chamber."

"Children?" Wren pursed his lips. "I wonder..."

"Wonder what?"

"I heard tell of a child who found a dagger much like this sword. It passed out his hands and into the possession of some very unpleasant people. Does this strike you as familiar?" Wren squatted down on his haunches while the ghosts conferred. While this lot of ghosts was a lot more responsive than most, they still were handicapped in conversation quite a bit by the fact that they were dead. It made, he'd found, for a bit of hesitation on the uptake.

"It would seem likely," said the ghost Wren found himself thinking of as the captain of this merry band. "And that is indeed unpleasant news. What do you know of the dagger?"

"That it's heavy, for one thing," Wren retorted. "I had it for a while. Your boy apparently sold it to a Guild stringer, who sold it to a Guild caravan master named Shotan Fong. Fong had contacts with the wrong sorts of people, people who also wanted me, so he used word of the dagger to lure me out to his caravan, where his client had laid an ambush. I got away briefly with the blade, but Ratcatcher," he paused and noted the stir amongst the ghosts at the name, "caught me. He took the dagger, hauled me off to a place I'd rather not think about, and handed the dagger over to his master, the Prince of Shadows. I take it you're familiar with at least some of these players?"

The ghost nodded. "Ratcatcher spoke to some of the other ghosts who dwell here. He has the stink of the Void on his soul and blood on his hands. When he left this place, death followed him."

"So there's a way out?" Wren looked up eagerly. For an instant, he thought he saw a flash of movement in the corridor beyond, but it didn't repeat itself, and he put it down to the vagaries of talking with mostly translucent ghosts.

"There is. We will show you. First, though, you must understand the nature of the blade you carry. You must also pledge to retrieve the dagger if you can. It cannot remain in the Prince of Shadows' hands."

"That seems like a good idea," he said neutrally. "I've been a prisoner in his dungeons once, and have no love for the man. Getting the dagger away from him might be difficult, however. He seems rather attached to it."

"You will not be alone in this," the ghost reassured him. "The sword is not for you. It is for the boy. You are simply its keeper until he is ready."

"Marvelous. I get to be the practice dummy for history." Wren turned away in disgust. "You mean to tell me that my grand and glorious destiny as an Exalt, one who roused the dead gods themselves out of their beds, is to serve as fetch-and-carry man for a boy who's already fumbled away his *first* magical weapon? By the Dr—by the Sun, can't you find someone else to be your yeddim?"

"Rest assured, your labors will be quite sufficient. So, at least, I have been told."

"Told? By whom?"

The ghost spread his hands in a gesture of benediction. "By the Unconquered Sun, of course."

"By the Unconquered Sun." Wren stood and leaned on the sword as best he could. "Of course."

And then Shamblemerry came screaming out of the dark, and there was no more time for talk.

Chapter Thirty

It was just before sunset when Dace finally decided that it was safe to stop. There had been no sign of pursuit, but still they had followed a punishing pace since before dawn. There had been a brief stop to water the horses late in the morning and another halt for lunch a few hours later, but otherwise Dace had urged them relentlessly onward. The terrain had grown steadily rougher as the day had progressed, and signs of any habitation were rare. The horses had picked their way steadily along trails that had clearly been made by animals, and which men had done little or nothing to improve.

Through all of this the prisoner maintained a stoic silence. Bound and slung over the pack horse, he said nothing and made no attempts to escape. Yushuv could feel the man's cold eyes upon him, however, and when he turned to meet them he was met with a sardonic grin. Dace, too, seemed to feel the pressure of the elf's stare, as he was more irritable than usual, and often made efforts to keep Yushuv's steed between his own and the prisoner's.

Finally, they'd crested a slope that was thickly wooded with pine and juniper, and Dace had decided that they'd traveled far enough. In the valley below they could hear rushing water, and with the last of the day's light as their guide, they picked their way down to the creek side. Halfway down, Dace dismounted and gestured to Yushuv to be silent. Then, he vanished into the underbrush, his footsteps mere whispers on the carpet of pine needles.

"He needn't worry."

Yushuv turned. The prisoner was speaking, his voice high and musical and his tone condescending.

"Needn't worry about what?"

"About whatever's waiting down there, or isn't, or might be. This is all a sham on his part so he can convince himself he's being suitably cautious with you. He's not, but that's another matter entirely." Even slung over a horse's back, the man looked graceful, as if it were the most natural thing in the world for him to be carried like a sack of meal, and that any observers were clumsy oafs for daring to ride in a different fashion.

Yushuv shrugged, and turned to stare down into the rapidly darkening forest. "I'd rather be safe," he said. "I'm glad Dace takes the time to make sure that there's a good place to stop."

"And what is he afraid might be down there, that could tax the powers of two mighty Exalted? A bear? An angry turtle? An army of Immaculate priests, hidden in the trees against the off chance that you'd wander this way? No, there's nothing down there that could worry the likes of you."

Yushuv could feel the contempt in the man's words, the same contempt he might once have felt for one of his playmates who refused to dare the catacombs without a light. "There are worse things than bears out there," he retorted. "Spirits, for one."

"Ah, yes." Suddenly the prisoner's voice took on a tone of delighted glee. "That's right. You must have met Bonecrack. We sent him looking for you, you know. We've been hunting you for a while."

"You sent him?" Yushuv whirled. "How did you—"

"Stop talking to it, Yushuv." Dace emerged from the wood, his head bared and his expression weary. "His kind always lies. Their words are traps and their stories fetters."

"And our poetry far better than yours, oh bald and wise one." Yushuv could not restrain a snort of laughter at that, and Dace shot him a warning look.

"We're going down into the valley," he announced. "There's a nice, flat sandy area by the creek side, and the wood cover's dense enough that I think we can risk a fire. We'll see if we can catch dinner—the stream looks good for fish. Then you and I, Yushuv, can figure out what to do with our friend here."

"Slit my throat?" the prisoner suggested hopefully. Dace ignored him, took the reins of his horse and led them deeper into the valley.

The patch of sand by the creek side was exactly that, a wash of land that the trees had not yet bothered to take root in. As Dace dealt with the horses, Yushuv dug a small fire pit and carried stones from the water's edge to rim it.

Wood, thankfully, was plentiful, and he did not have to go far into the forest before returning with an armload of fallen branches. Two more trips brought enough wood to last the night, and before long a small fire blazed merrily under Yushuv's watchful eye.

When the horses were tended to, Dace sat the prisoner up against a tree at the edge of the sandy area and made sure his feet were bound together with strips of twisted cloth. The man's hands he left bound, perhaps a bit tighter than absolutely necessary. "Don't even think of running off," he said, "And don't talk to the boy anymore. Do we understand each other?"

"I understand you," was the reply. "You'll never understand me."

Dace nodded, then lashed out with his foot and struck the faerie in the ribs. It grunted in pain, and Dace smiled grimly. "You'll understand that much, I think," he said, and walked toward the waterside, where Yushuv had already begun the process of catching them dinner.

❖

Yushuv had just finished throwing the fish bones from dinner into the water when Dace finally turned to the prisoner again. "So," he said lazily, "What are we going to do with you?"

"Very little, I expect." The faerie had barely moved since Dace had set him down. "I'm not supposed to talk to the boy, and I've no interest in talking to you."

"But I'm very interested in talking to you," Dace rumbled. "Are you hungry?"

"Not for mortal food, no. Water might sustain me better, if you haven't fouled it beyond recognition." Dace made no move to fetch any, and instead started removing his boots. Yushuv took a tentative step toward the creek, then glanced querulously at Dace for approval.

"You can fetch it water if you want, Yushuv, but don't talk to it. It'll get into your dreams if you do." Dace kept his eyes firmly on his boots, frowning as he took a knife and worked mud from the seam between the leather and sole. "For that matter, don't let it touch you, either. No sense giving it any more chances than the ones it'll make for itself."

Yushuv looked from Dace to the prisoner and then back again, and shook his head before half-sprinting for the sand of the creek side.

"Now look what you've done. You've confused the boy, Dace." The elf's voice held cold amusement. "He'll probably fetch me wine instead of water."

Dace continued working on his boots, frowning. "You can talk your throat raw, you ancient thing, and you'll get nowhere with me. I'm wise to your ways."

The faerie shook his head. "You're not wise to us, Dace. Your lady love is, and she gave you some lessons you only half understand. But, and I'm simply making a guess here, I'm thinking that you do not wish to appear less than the master of any situation in front of your pupil, and so rather than risk seeming—how shall I put it?—ignorant, you'll bully him and bully me. Am I right? You don't have to answer, you know. I'll take silence for assent."

"You'll take a minute face-down in the fire if you don't shut up," Dace said, a touch too mildly. "Here's your water. I hope you choke on it."

The faerie turned to see Yushuv trudging up from the waterside, a cupped leaf full of water in his hands.

"Here," the boy said. He stopped perhaps a yard from the prisoner and extended his hands gingerly. "Drink."

"I can't very well drink with my hands tied and the water over there," the elf said reasonably. "You'll have to come closer."

"Dace?" Yushuv half-turned, looking for guidance.

"Do you remember what I told you about making your own choices?" Dace glanced once at Yushuv, then looked away. "You need to decide for yourself right now what you're going to do. It's your destiny, boy. Choose it."

Yushuv shook his head. "This happens every time someone

asks me for a drink of water, you know." He knelt down, and held the makeshift cup to the Fair Folk's lips. "Drink it all. You're not getting more."

"You're too kind," the elf replied, and then raised his head so that he might drink. A few sips was all it took before he was satisfied, and he shook his head when offered more. "Take it away, Yushuv. You've slaked my thirst and proved my point." Confused, the boy stood and stepped back, the leaf unfolding in his grasp. It slipped from his fingers and fell to the sandy ground amidst the last few drops of water. "I'll tell you a secret, though, as payment for your labors. Your soul used to be a woman's. It's one of the reasons you make Dace so uncomfortable."

Yushuv took another step back and frowned. "My soul's my own. I don't care what it used to be. You're lying anyway."

"You may be the only one who doesn't care about your soul's provenance, Yushuv."

"Don't speak my name." Yushuv felt something taking shape behind him, even as a dim glow filled the hollow. "My name is not for the likes of you to give voice to. You've no power over me."

The elf's eyes widened slightly. "Impressive. And I only have the power over you that you give me. Which, I might add, is considerable."

"I don't understand you," Yushuv said, and walked off with deliberate steps to a position on the far side of the fire. He stood there, glowering, and stared at the prisoner. Unconcernedly, the prisoner stared back. Yushuv broke away from that immortal gaze, and stared at the dirt. As he did, the glow faded, and for a moment all was silence.

The elf smiled, until a handful of dirt caught him in the face. He spat, and looked up to see Dace grinning like a schoolboy. "Proud of yourself? I don't see why. All you've done is make a boy wonder why he got you some water. He's got a wild power in him, he does, and you just might set it off, to your sorrow. You'd do better to keep your mouth closed, unless you want to answer my questions instead."

"Answer your questions?" The prisoner laughed. "Why in Creation would I want to do that?"

"Mmm, I don't know." Dace sat back on his haunches. "To save yourself some pain? I could hurt you, you know. I could hurt you very much."

"I am a lord of magics ancient and terrible, and I hold chaos in the palm of my hand. If I speak to you, it is because I wish you to know that which I have to say. If I decide that it pleases me to hold my tongue, then no power you are capable of summoning can make me speak. Do we understand each other?" The Fair Folk lord's tone was bored, as if he were speaking to particularly dull schoolchildren about the matter, and doing so for the third time.

Dace looked up from the fire, his expression skeptical. "I suspect that if I really thought about it, I could find something that could convince you to talk." His eyes on the prisoner's, he took the knife he'd used on his boots and held the blade in the flames. With theatrical flair he turned it this way and then that, so that the reflected light from the blaze played across the Fair Folk's face. The look he saw there was one of utter disdain.

"As I said, child of the sun, there is nothing you can do to me. Sear my flesh? Do so if it pleases you. My flesh is nothing to me, a passing fancy so that I might walk to and fro in your world. Destroy it and you release me. After all," he added with a cold smile, "it is only flesh." He drew his hands, still bound together at the wrist, across his face.

Yushuv gasped. Where the prisoner's mouth had been was now smooth, seamless skin. His eyes remained, though, their gaze mocking and direct. Dace cursed and dropped his dagger in the fire, then cursed again as he burned himself retrieving it. With another pass of his hands across his face, and the faerie's mouth reappeared, open now in laughter. Dace growled another oath under his breath and turned to face the fire. The set of his shoulders gave mute evidence that he was pointedly ignoring the prisoner.

"So what do you want to tell us, then?" Yushuv walked over to where the man sat, propped up against a tree trunk. The ancient, mocking gaze fell on him now, and Yushuv realized with a start that "man" was not the right term for the thing that smiled up at him. It had donned the shape of a man, much as a man might ask a tailor to garb him in the fashion of a man he'd seen in the street, but this monstrosity was no more human than was a branch or a stone. It looked up at him, and Yushuv could see the terrible hunger that resided behind its eyes. Involuntarily, he took a step back, and the thing grinned at him. Obscurely, Yushuv knew that he had just failed some sort of test, and he could feel his cheeks burning in shame. To cover his embarrassment, he squatted down where he stood, his back to the fire.

"Don't ask me what I want to tell you, child." All traces of amusement had left the prisoner's voice now, and his tone was flat and low. "You know what I am. The things I want to tell you can't be told in words formed by any mortal's lips, and the songs of chaos I'd sing you can't be sung here. But I can tell you that which it is useful for you to know, and which serves the purposes of the so-called Fair Folk. Do you wish to kill me now? You might be happier if you did so." Without waiting for an answer, he shifted his weight and tilted his head back, baring his throat. Even in the firelight, his skin was very pale, and as smooth as stone.

Involuntarily, Yushuv felt his hand going for his knife. The figure before him was beautiful, but every second he laid eyes on it made his guts knot in fear. It was too perfect, too cunningly sculpted to the idea of what a form based on man's should be. Looking at the prisoner Yushuv found himself hating his tangled hair and his scarred hands. He hated his small stature and his sharp features, which he knew could never be as beautiful, as perfect as the ones he saw before him. To see one of the Fair Folk, he realized, was to see a mirror in which all of one's imperfections were exposed, mercilessly. The only way to end this would be to kill the prisoner, and even then, Yushuv knew that the memory of the face before him would haunt his memory. Then, suddenly, the feeling passed. The faerie lowered his head, one eyebrow raised quizzically, and nodded.

Shuddering, Yushuv took his hand away from his knife. "How did you do that?" he demanded. "Why did you do that to me?"

The prisoner shrugged. "I can, and I wanted to. I need

no other reason. Now, have you decided to listen, or have I frightened you sufficiently?"

"I'll listen." Yushuv dropped to the ground and sat cross-legged. "Tell me what you want me to know."

The faerie's lips curled in a thin smile. "So curious. What a fascinating flaw. It will destroy you eventually, you know." Yushuv refused to rise to the bait and said nothing, waiting. "Ah. Curious and clever. Much better."

"You're not telling me anything I haven't already heard from Dace." Behind Yushuv, the fire crackled, and a trail of sweet smoke drifted up into the night.

"Then your Dace is a cleverer man than I gave him credit for being, though I doubt he and I say what we do for the same reason. Listen well, little man. Now is the time when old souls will come home to the world and not like what they see. Their time will be a time of blood and fire and steel, and their wars will fill the very seas with the stinking corpses of the dead.

"You are the harbinger of that time, boy. Or you will be, if you survive. That is why we hunt you. Not to kill you, at least not just to kill you. If we kill you, then we wait. Your soul will make the great circuit again, and time is nothing to us. But if we hunt you and you survive, then your power grows. Every battle makes you stronger. Every trial tempers your steel. And one day, yours will be the power to plunge the world into chaos. That is when we will come for you, child, and that is when we will come for your sad little world. You will open the gate for us, as sure as death, and every choice you make will lead you closer to the day when you break the seals that bind the outer chaos. You will do so for the best of reasons, of course. You will of course have excellent justification for killing your world—but you will do it anyway, and we will be waiting."

"You're lying," Yushuv whispered. "That can't be true."

The elf laughed. "It isn't true. Not yet, anyway, my pretty little imbecile. But it might be. Or it might not. And in the meantime, what I have just told you will haunt your sleep every night. You will wonder if I have lied to you. You will wonder if, should my tale be true, you should let Dace cut out your heart lest you bring the entire world to ruin. You will doubt every step you take and every breath you draw, and in the end it will help you not at all, save to give you the most delicious nightmares imaginable. Most mortals never dream about killing a world, you know."

A shadow fell across the prisoner's face. Both he and Yushuv looked up, startled. It was Dace, and his naked daiklave was in his fist.

The faerie smiled blandly up at him "Oh, you wish to listen, too?"

"No, actually, I don't." Then Dace's sword arm came down, swifter than the eye could see, and the air was filled with a spray of thin, cold Fair Folk blood.

Chapter Thirty-One

Ragged Fox stuck his head into the wagon with what Ratcatcher could now identify as an expression of puzzlement. "Something odd's happening at the tavern," he announced, and then hung there, as if he expected his pronouncement to shake the heavens or provoke some kind of suitably dramatic response.

Instead, Clever Tiger said, "Oh? Really. We were just talking about you," and went back to reorganizing her herb pouches. Ratcatcher bit his lip to keep from sniggering, and instead did his best to look properly interested.

"No, really, I mean it." Ragged Fox's face settled into a stubborn pout, and mentally Ratcatcher rolled his eyes. Approximately once per day the man settled on some perfectly explicable occurrence or other as evidence of a sinister plot, and either ran himself ragged chasing it or spent hours explaining his theories to a rapt Clever Tiger. The rest of the caravan community, Ratcatcher had quickly learned, regarded Ragged Fox as something of a mascot, and occasionally took to leaving suitably enigmatic items around for him to find.

Now, however, he was fresh on the tail of something new, and he was aquiver with excitement. Ratcatcher decided it was hopeless, and bowed to the inevitable. "Oh?"

Ragged Fox took the bait and ran with it. "Well, I was going over to the tavern to get a drink and maybe some supper—they've got the cookfires going in the camp but the stew here is always fantastic—and I heard these noises coming from inside."

"Noises?" It was best, Ratcatcher knew, to simply provide catchphrases and let Ragged Fox get around to the actual content in his own time. Any attempts at actual conversation would only go nowhere.

Ragged Fox nodded solemnly, nearly lost his balance, and then nodded again. "Noises. Loud ones."

"What sort of noises?" Clever Tiger was interested now, looking away from her dried plants. "Not another bar brawl, is it? I hate those. It's always bruises and broken ribs from those. I do wish Reddust would learn to use lighter furniture. It would be so much easier on their customers."

"Well, they were brawl noises, mostly. Loud ones. With a bit of screaming, now that I think about it. I just waited outside for the noises to stop, because I didn't want to walk in and get a mug in the face."

"And well you didn't," Clever Tiger said primly. "I remember how long it took to stop the bleeding the last time you walked into one of those. It was very brave of you to tell them to stop, but you should have known they wouldn't listen."

"Well, er, yes, " Ragged Fox looked around frantically, trying to regain his equilibrium. For a long instant, Ratcatcher pitied the man. "In any case, I waited for the noises to stop. But instead of some of our people coming out, it was someone else!"

"Someone… else?" Despite himself, Ratcatcher felt himself growing interested. Anyone who could lay out a passel of Guild drovers and muscle was bound to be impressive in the extreme. "What did they look like?"

"Actually, that was the strange thing. There were two of them."

"Only two?" Clever Tiger was incredulous. "That's impossible."

Ragged Fox shrugged. "Unless they'd left friends in the tavern, there were only two. But that wasn't the strangest part." He emphasized "strangest," trying to sound mysterious but only succeeding in coming across as befuddled.

"Well, what *was* the strangest part, or do you wish to drag this out all night?" Ratcatcher spoke sharply, and he could sense Clever Tiger's shocked eyes upon him. To the hells with her, he thought. They could use Ragged Fox's storytelling technique for a new torment in the Labyrinth, and the Deathlords would be amazed.

"The strangest thing," Ragged Fox replied petulantly, "was

that one of them was an old woman, and the other was a bald, middle-aged priest."

Ratcatcher clambered forward. "An old woman, you say?" He resisted the urge to clamp his hands around the man's throat and squeeze answers out of him, but only barely. "What did she look like?"

"She was, well, old. Short. Very delicate hands. White dust on her robes, which was odd, because all the dust around here is red, in case you hadn't guessed. Wore black, and used a perfume I could smell halfway across the compound. Had gray hair done up in a bun in back of her head."

The dead man interrupted him. "Held in place with a metal pin?"

Ragged Fox nodded. "Yes. How did you know?"

"A lucky guess," he muttered. "What else?"

A shrug was all he got. "I didn't see them well. It was getting dark, and they were moving fast off into the scrublands."

"And the people in the tavern, Fox. What about them?" Clever Tiger's voice was suddenly strident. "Was anyone hurt?"

Ragged Fox visibly deflated. "I don't know," he said. "I didn't go in. I thought it was more important to come here and tell you."

"Tell us what? That you don't know anything? Oh, sometimes you are so useless!" Clever Tiger flounced around the interior of the wagon, hastily gathering her supplies. "Go back to the main building and see if anyone's hurt. I'll be along in a minute." She turned, her hands busy stuffing pots of salve into a leather pouch. "Faithful Hound, you stay here. I'll be back as soon as I can."

"Of course," said Ratcatcher, who obediently waited at least a full minute after she'd taken off at a dead run before slipping out of the wagon himself. He looked left and right as best he could, and then trotted off into the desert. The lingering scent of a rare perfume guided him on his way.

That, and the almost tangible heat of his hatred for Unforgiven Blossom.

In the lee of a small rise marked by a single, sad tree, Holok stopped. The mysterious woman who called herself Unforgiven Blossom marched right past him and kept going. "Hey!" he called. "I'm stopped here."

"And I am not," she replied, and marched on.

Cursing, Holok ran to catch up with her, and seized her arm with reasonable gentleness. She stopped, turned and looked at him. "I would remove that if I were you," she said.

"And I would stop walking for a moment if I were you," the priest said in return. Nonetheless, he let her arm drop, and in return, she stood still.

"Why the halt?" she asked, raising her eyes to the crest of the rise they'd just passed over. "We may be pursued, and we have only been walking for a few hours."

"I don't much care if we're pursued, to be honest. That little fracas was just a warm-up, as far as I'm concerned. For another thing, I've been taking care to cover our trail. They've got a lot of land to cover and not much to go on." He sniffed. "Are you wearing perfume?"

"I carry some with me." She reached inside her robes and brought forth a delicate stoppered bottle of black glass. "It must have spilled. You have my apologies if the scent displeases."

Holok waved the apology off. "No matter. I don't think they'll be hunting us by smell. I didn't hear any dogs when I passed the caravan. "

"So why did you wish to stop?" Unforgiven Blossom tucked the perfume back away and folded her hands before her breast. "The scenery is not, I think, that inspiring."

"No, but the company does inspire some questions. I trust you're the one who gave that idiot in the hostel the poison?"

"I did not give it to him. I sold it for a pittance, after telling him suitable tales of your debauchery including children, his sister and a goat." She paused and thought for a moment. "I also bought him a drink, which was rather strong. That might have made the process easier."

"I suspect so, yes." Holok nodded owlishly. "The poison seemed a bit sophisticated for a Guild bully to be carrying, not to mention expensive. You picked it up in Chiaroscuro?"

"Varsi."

"Ah. Of course. Tambledane's establishment?"

"She does sell the finest. I'm surprised you're acquainted with it."

Holok made a face. "Don't be. I'm not, as you might have surmised, your typical Immaculate. So you goaded the man into trying to kill me so that he'd start a fight that you knew I'd win, but which would give you a chance to ingratiate yourself to me by 'saving' me, thus convincing me to let you travel with me. Am I right so far?"

The one-time astrologer nodded. "In all of the particulars, yes. I expected you to be able to win the fight handily. I am pleased to see that my confidence was not mistaken." She put her fingers to her lips in a gesture of mock surprise. "Of course, I was stunned to see a Sidereal adept fighting in so… mundane a style."

"The idea was to have no one there realize I was a Sidereal, obviously," Holok grumbled. "I'd think that, at least, would be obvious. By the by, how did you discover me? A good answer might prevent me from having to kill you later. I'm fond of my privacy, you see."

"It took approximately nine nights' worth of divination, tied to several other rites and one extremely costly sacrifice to a stag spirit during my journey here, to uncover who and what you were. Have no fear, it's not something that's likely to be repeated any time soon. Now, shall I tell you the rest of my story and spare you the need to be clever, or shall we indulge our wits to the detriment of our purposes?"

Holok made an exaggerated bow. "Please, milady."

Unforgiven Blossom responded with a form-perfect curtsey. "As you wish. I have been seeking your company for several weeks now, since an augury told me to seek you. The most logical reason for me to do so is the dagger I now possess, which was stolen from the Prince of Shadows and before that, from an Immaculate priest."

"A priest named Eliezer Wren?"

Her eyes widened infinitesimally in surprise, but that was the only evidence of Unforgiven Blossom's shock. "Yes. You know him?"

"We share an employer," Holok said wryly. "Where is he, if I may ask? Still in the prince's dungeons?"

"If only he were. He escaped, unfortunately."

"Unfortunately?"

"Unfortunately. There is but one route of escape from the prince's dungeons, and it leads down."

"Oh. A pity. He was a talented man." Holok digested the tidbit of news for a moment, and then found himself fighting the urge to grin. Kejak, he realized, was going to be very disappointed by all of this.

"In any case, certain events to which Wren's presence was central caused me to leave the prince's service, and to take the dagger which you saw with me."

"The prince's service." Holok's voice was flat. "Not the best recommendation for a traveling companion."

"And do not forget that I tried to have you poisoned as well."

Holok grinned humorlessly. "Yes, well, I was going to let that one slide. But you seem so charmingly open about the whole affair."

"Honesty is one of my virtues."

"I could not possibly count them all, nor will I insult you by trying. The dagger is orichalcum, isn't it?

"Yes, it is. Do you want it?"

"Possibly." The priest frowned. "I'd rather know what it means."

"It means?"

"Things like this always have trouble swirling along behind them, usually for all parties involved. I'd like to know what particular flavor of trouble this one will bring and how best to deal with it."

"I think part of the answer might have arrived. Look." Calmly, Unforgiven Blossom pointed to the top of the rise. Holok followed her gaze. Standing there was a man dressed in gray leggings and a brown tunic, his eyes nothing more than bloody sockets.

"He smells odd," she added. "That, I have found, is generally not a good sign."

✦

The chase had been surprisingly short, and for that Ratcatcher was thankful. Unforgiven Blossom and her companion were moving carefully, not quickly, and that would have served to throw any mortal pursuers off the track. *It's a pity*, he thought, *that instead they are being pursued by me.*

It had been perhaps five hours since he left the caravan when he first heard the voices. They came from the other side of a low ridge before him, perhaps the only element of interest in the terrain as far as the eye could see. A lone tree stood at its crest; scrub acacia, perhaps. Ratcatcher knew only that in his altered vision it was ugly, and looked to be impossible to climb. Down below, he heard the voices, and of those two voices, he knew one.

It was at that moment that he realized just how much he had always hated Unforgiven Blossom. Her clipped, arrogant phrasing, her elegant disdain, the ease with which she had swept into the prince's favor—all of these inspired a deep core of volcanic hatred in him, one that had always seethed but never made its presence known until now. She'd always delighted in making a fool of him; why else would she have harbored Wren right under his nose? It had been the grandest humiliation of all.

Well, now it was time to make a fool of her, a dead fool, and then to sink back down to the Underworld to torment her more there. This was why he'd been brought back, he was sure of it. Vengeance. Simply contemplating the thought warmed him.

Filled with renewed purpose, he crested the rise.

✦

"He doesn't smell odd. He smells dead. That's rotting meat." Holok took a wary step forward. "Might he be an old friend of yours?"

"I do not recognize him," Unforgiven Blossom replied, and took an equally wary step back. "That means little, though. Some of the walking dead change their shells on a regular basis, so long as there are fresh corpses about." She paused, inhaled, and wrinkled her nose. "This one, it would seem, is not fresh."

"No, it would appear not," Holok agreed, then called up to the figure descending the ridge. "Hoy there!"

Ratcatcher paused. The man, what he could see of him, was almost radiant with light. Bald, bearded and burly, he seemed as rooted in the landscape as the tree was. Behind him was Unforgiven Blossom, shrunken and frail in the gray landscape.

That tidbit overwhelmed any other consideration, and he continued his march down the ridge. Unforgiven Blossom was only paces away. Surely, there was nothing to discuss.

Holok moved to a point between the oddly shambling man and the woman who was clearly his target. "I said to stop," he added, and settled into a fighting stance.

An inch in front of Holok's nose, Ratcatcher stopped. Holok breathed in, and nearly gagged. The scent of rotting meat was hidden by herbs, but it was there, and it was clearly growing stronger.

"I want the woman," the dead man said. "She owes me a life."

"Unforgiven Blossom?" Holok called over his shoulder. "Do you know him?"

She shook her head, then realized that Holok could not see her. "No."

Ratcatcher snickered. "She's lying, you know. She knows me. I just look different from when she killed me. You'd think the eyes would be a dead giveaway, though. She *likes* eyes."

Unforgiven Blossom took down her hood and pulled the metal pin from her hair. It cascaded down, a gray river, and she frowned. "Ratcatcher?"

"You *do* know him," Holok said, exasperated. The dead man was pressing forward, and Holok had a vague urge to step back rather than let this thing touch him. Instead, he stood his ground.

"I did. He served the Prince of Shadows, poorly. He also captured and tormented your friend, Eliezer Wren. And yes, I did kill him, an act for which I should have received hosannas of praise, and instead received nothing."

"Wren?" The dead man leaned in, so close he could have kissed Holok had he wanted. "You know Eliezer Wren?"

"After a fashion," Holok admitted.

"Ah," said Ratcatcher, and leaned forward to bite.

Holok brought his arm up to catch Ratcatcher underneath the chin, simultaneously falling back and away from the attack. The blow spun the dead man around, buying Holok enough time to hit the ground on his side and bounce up, just in time to meet the charging revenant.

Holok brought his hands up, but Ratcatcher went low and hit the priest in the knees with his shoulder. Both went down in a pile, tumbling down the last few feet of the slope in a tangle of blows.

Ratcatcher came out on top, one hand digging into the flesh of Holok's throat while the other came down again and again with superhuman strength. Holok fended them off as best he could, taking blow after blow on his arm while trying vainly to dislodge the hand from his windpipe.

A kick in the ribs caught Ratcatcher mid-punch, and he stopped and turned. Unforgiven Blossom stood there, defiant, the long needle in her hand. "I killed you once," she said. "It would be a pleasure to do so again."

"You can't hurt me any more," Ratcatcher replied with a leer. "I'm dead now, remember? But that gives me certain advantages." He raised his fist for another blow, but Holok had brought his legs up to his belly and thrust forward with them, tearing Ratcatcher's grip and sending him tumbling back.

Holok surged to his feet. Upslope, Ratcatcher did the same. They stared at each other, warily, with Unforgiven Blossom's glance switching back and forth between the two.

"I can destroy you, you know," Holok said, very softly. "I've fought many of your kind. They've all gone screaming back to hell. I'm still here."

"You don't understand," Ratcatcher replied, sliding forward

a step. "She has to die. That will make the prince take me back. I've died in his service. I've lost my eyes twice for him, and once she took them. *You don't know what I've gone through because of her.*"

"Her?" Holok snorted. "She's ancient. Tiny. How could she do anything to you?"

"You don't know her," Ratcatcher warned, and pounced.

This time Holok was ready. He brought up his fists, blue flame trailing behind them, and caught Ratcatcher squarely in the midriff. The revenant screamed, then tumbled to the ground. Flames licked at him, but he seemed not to notice. He charged again, this time catching Holok's first blow and pulling him off balance. He struck the monk across the back as he went past and sent him sprawling.

Holok fell, sand and dust in his eyes. He rolled and stood, and saw Ratcatcher menacing Unforgiven Blossom. She held the long steel pin out before her like a dagger, and as he watched, put it right through Ratcatcher's palm. This didn't seem to bother the dead man greatly, however, as his other hand struck her in the belly, and she folded. He brought his hands down on the back of her head, and she collapsed to the ground.

"Now," he said and dropped down on all fours to whisper to her. "Vengeance. I should take your eyes first, bitch, but I don't have time. You're going to meet death, Unforgiven Blossom. It's about time."

With a shout, Holok flung himself at Ratcatcher. The revenant turned, hands instinctively out for protection, and Holok barely missed losing an eye to Unforgiven Blossom's needle. The impact knocked Ratcatcher to the side and over, away from the woman, but he rolled to his feet in one smooth motion. "Two against one? No fair. Then again, where she's concerned, it's never fair." He advanced on Holok, though, not Unforgiven Blossom, and rained down punches and kicks with lightning speed. Holok for his part dodged the blows, parrying only when he needed to, then leapt straight up and landed a pair of kicks to Ratcatcher's chin. His head snapped back, and even as Holok landed he unleashed a devastating series of blows against the dead man's midriff.

Ratcatcher grinned. He clenched his fists, the pin piercing him through again, and black flame surrounded his hands. "I've brought a little taste of the Labyrinth with me for you, Unforgiven Blossom," he said. "I can't wait to caress you with this." And with that, he struck an open-palmed blow towards Holok's face. The monk ducked and caught the revenant's wrist, but the dead man's strength was astonishing. Within seconds, he'd torn free, and pressed his hand into Holok's face.

The monk screamed in agony, a sound he had not uttered in eight hundred years. He struggled, but the black flame burned away his very strength, and feeding on him, it burned very hot indeed. His hands scrabbled at Ratcatcher's wrist, but to no avail.

"It will burn out your life," Ratcatcher said. "Quickly, in your case. And it won't even leave too many scars. Especially, I think, if I do this."

Slowly, deliberately, he clasped his other hand to Holok's face, and pressed. "You have such a lovely scream," he whispered. "What a shame so few people get to hear it."

Then, once again, Unforgiven Blossom was there, a golden dagger in her fist. "Is this what you really want, Ratcatcher?" she asked. "I return it to you, and gladly."

Ratcatcher turned, surprised, and she brought the dagger down, hilt first. It caught Ratcatcher on the back of his head, and caved in the back of his rotting skull. He sagged, and the second stroke crushed the bridge of his nose, and crushed bone and cartilage. Her third stroke caved in an eye socket, her fourth a cheekbone. The flame in his hands flickered, went pale, and went out. Ratcatcher thrashed about like a fish in a net, pulling his hands away from Holok's face and preparing to run, but the burly priest was having none of it. Blinded by the flames, he wrapped his arms around Ratcatcher's midsection and squeezed, oblivious to Ratcatcher's violent thrashing in his arms. Tighter and tighter he held it until suddenly, there was a short, sharp crack, and the pile of bones that held Ratcatcher's body was still.

With relief, he dropped it. It twitched, nothing more.

"Thank you," he said to the heavens, and then again to Unforgiven Blossom, and then he collapsed.

The burns that marked Holok's face had faded to rough marks in the shape of Ratcatcher's hands, and he could ignore those. They still felt like they were burning, but no more was his heart's strength being drained from him through those monstrous, hideous flaming hands. Once more he touched his face, so as to reassure himself that he was truly no longer alight. *A healer should probably look at those*, he thought when the pain intensified. *Assuming, of course, I can find a healer in this forsaken waste.*

And in the meantime, there were tasks to accomplish.

"What are you going to do with that?" Unforgiven Blossom asked. She stood next to Holok but not too close, pointing to the bloody and battered pile of flesh that, until further notice, was Ratcatcher.

"I'm going to make sure he doesn't go anywhere," Holok replied, and slung the dead man over his shoulder.

Up the rise he trudged, making his way to where the tree stood. Its branches were many but slender, and it bore only a thin crown of foliage. Still, it would do for his current purposes, Holok felt. It would do nicely.

Ratcatcher was still unconscious, or worse, when Holok slung him into the tree. His left hand caught nicely in a fork between branches; the right one less so.

"No need to worry," Holok mumbled to himself, and took the offending hand in his fist. With just the barest show of concentration, he crushed it, and wedged the broken extremity into another, smaller fork in the tree. Busily, he smashed Ratcatcher's legs and folded them through the snaky branches, weaving the dead man into the fabric of the tree itself.

"You are cruel," Unforgiven Blossom observed.

Holok looked up from threading a broken leg through a particularly tricky troika of branches and frowned. "No, I'm realistic," he said. "I can't afford to be cruel, not and keep the vows I've made. But something like this bag of bones—" and with his free hand he pointed to Ratcatcher "—is outside the bounds of all of that. There is alive, and there is dead, and anything else is an abomination."

"And what about the dying?" she asked.

"Still one or the other, as far as I know." He wedged the cadaver's foot into a hole in the trunk that he sincerely hoped was inhabited by stinging ants, and looked at his handiwork.

Ratcatcher, astonishingly, was still alive. He stirred, moaning, and Holok smiled. "You'll be staying right there, I think. That should keep you a good, long while." He turned to Unforgiven Blossom. "Shall we?"

"Where do you wish to go now?"

"I don't know," he replied. "I suspect we'd better finish the discussion we started before he arrived."

She nodded, and walked off. He followed, and behind them, the first great black carrion birds settled into Ratcatcher's tree.

Chapter Thirty-Two

The ghosts scattered like ninepins as Shamblemerry howled into the room. She'd seen the light go out, and had used the darkness as a chance to creep closer and listen. The man who spoke, the man with the sword, had escaped from the prince's dungeons? Impossible! And yet here he was, talking calmly of the feat as if it were nothing.

And the sword, dead gods below, the sword! If she could take that back to the prince, she'd be richly rewarded, placed forever over that sniveling creature, Ratcatcher. Retrieving his prisoner as well, that would earn her all the more praise. She had no doubts that somehow this man's escape was Ratcatcher's fault, and the ache to bring him back in chains and cast him before Ratcatcher's feet was almost palpable.

You'll be mine, she thought. *All of you, sword and all.* And with that, she'd pounced.

The man she faced was good, she realized instantly. He'd spun effortlessly out of the way of her first blow, nearly slicing her in two with the daiklave as he did so. She dropped underneath his swing and launched a kick at his ankles, but he leapt up out of the way and her strike landed on empty air.

The daiklave swept down in a vicious diagonal cut, and Shamblemerry threw herself into a backwards flip to get out of the way. She landed near one of the piles of bones, a rusted halberd near her feet. With a wicked grin, she hooked one toe under the shaft and lifted it into the air. Catching it, she brought it up in time to parry another blow from her enemy, while all around her, the ghosts milled about in confusion.

"Who in the hells is this?" the man roared as he parried a series of thrusts. "Are they waiting for me everywhere I go? By the Sun, all I want is a little peace and a little light!"

So saying, the man hacked at the shadowy figure before him savagely. Shamblemerry saw her chance and, reversing her weapon, caught him in the gut with the haft. He let out a whoosh and took a step backward, and she reversed the halberd again in a strike that caught him on the scalp—a glancing blow. Shamblemerry heard a curse and swung again, grinning. She could hear the crackle of dark flame behind the halberd's blade as she thrust and parried with it, and exulted in it. *This* was what she had needed to restore herself. *This* had brought her back to herself.

Another pass brought her to a rough *corps-à-corps*, and for an instant she stared into the face of her opponent. His scalp wound was bleeding profusely, covering his brow in a mask of blood, and he seemed to be having difficulty seeing. His hair was short and matted with blood, and his robes looked vaguely like those the man who'd wounded her so badly before had worn.

Another priest, she realized with a thrill of excitement, *no doubt a servant of the old man*. Oh, this was turning out to be better than she had imagined. "Can you do something?" the man called out, and Shamblemerry realized he was talking to the ghosts. Before they could answer him, she'd dropped one hand off the halberd and landed a savage punch to the priest's stomach.

He broke the *corps-à-corps* and jumped back as far as he could, skidding a bit on a fragment of bone as he landed.

"We shall try," came the voice of the ghost who'd sicced the hunt on her before, and then they swarmed her. She lashed out with the halberd, a whirlwind of still-sharp bronze surrounding her. Thin, unearthly shrieks told her that while her blade might not be cutting her foes, the fire it bore certainly was. "Come get me, you dead fools!" she called out, and laughed.

The priest, she saw, was trying to staunch the flow of blood from his scalp. Good. He was out of the fight for the moment, and when she'd finished with the ghosts she'd then turn her attention to finishing him.

"Sunchild, we need you!" It was the ghost's voice again, tinged with desperation. "Her power has grown!"

"I can't fight her in the dark," the priest retorted, but nonetheless charged back into the fray, swinging high as Shamblemerry ducked under his blow. "And I can't summon the light without destroying you."

"The safety of the sword is more important. Do what you must!"

He didn't answer, instead pressing his attack with a windmill of swift cuts. Shamblemerry went on the defensive, parrying each blow and seeking an opening to riposte, but the priest's offensive was relentless. Pressed back against the skeletons along the wall, she began kicking bones and rotted armor into the air. He swatted each out of the air with the daiklave, but the distraction was enough; as he neatly bisected a flying skull, Shamblemerry's blade scored a cut just under his left knee. His leg collapsed from under him, and he dropped to one knee.

"Not the best stance for a sword like that," Shamblemerry said, and then the tide turned and it was her raining blows down on him.

◆

This has to end.

Mosom V'tayn, once a captain in the Legion of the Ascending Phoenix and soldier in the great war against the Anathema, and since his death, a devoted servant of the Unconquered Sun, watched the one-sided duel between the priest and the shadow-eaten monstrosity, and knew fear. The Exalt was losing, his blood spilling on the floor from a myriad of cuts. His enemy was toying with him now, drawing out his agony. He fought well, but his leg had turned traitor on him, and without the ability to move he was as good as dead.

At least, he was as good as dead in the dark.

Leave. Now. All of you. Mosom silently commanded his fellows, the soldiers who'd served under him in life and now continued that service in death.

But we must help him! came the expected response from one of the lieutenants. He'd been young and callow when he'd died, and he was young and callow still, and Mosom felt a sudden surge of pride in his soldiers. Even now, they would not desert a comrade.

He can help himself better without us, and he will not do so as long as we are here. Leave! I shall remain to tell him that he must do what he must do. He paused for a moment, and then added, *You have all made me very proud.*

The other ghosts left them, swirling away into the dark until only Mosom remained. He gave one last look to the tomb, the chamber that had been his home for so many centuries, and then uttered the words he so dreaded.

"The others are gone," he said. "Call the light!"

◆

Wren heard the ghost only faintly, over the blood pounding in his ears. He'd been cut on the scalp, the leg, the arm, and a half-dozen times across his chest. He was weak and sore, and blood and sweat kept on pouring into his eyes. The woman he was fighting probed at him again, and he flicked away her attack with the daiklave, but he was growing weaker and she knew it. It was only a matter of time.

Unless he had some light. His opponent seemed quite well adapted to the dark. No doubt she'd been here some time, and her eyes were well suited for the current conditions.

Call the light, the ghost had said. The sword was more important. Eliezer Wren didn't know about that, but at this point, he was no longer in a position to argue.

"Light," he said, and summoned the power from inside himself. "Light!"

◆

Mosom stared at the priest. Light erupted from his face and his scarred hands, whipping around him like flame, like a live thing. It was a warm light, golden in color but shading from almost white to deep amber in places. It caressed the priest, he saw, brushing against his wounds with a tenderness like a lover's touch, and then it flared outward.

Next to him, the woman was on her knees and sobbing. Her halberd lay on the floor, forgotten, and her hands covered her eyes. He could see rivulets of blood seeping between her fingers, and wondered briefly what *she* had seen in that first instant. "No, no, no, please no…" was all she could say, and he almost felt a feather-touch of pity for her. Surely the light had not been merciful to her. Not as merciful as it had been to him, at least. He could feel it taking him to pieces, slowly and painlessly, and he knew that this was a gift from the Unconquered Sun.

Slowly, agonizingly, the priest stood. He leaned heavily on the daiklave for support, and looked at his foe with all the compassion of a butcher confronted with a particularly plump and docile steer.

"Who sent you?" he said without expression. "What is your name? Whom do you serve? Or does it even matter anymore?" He bowed his head in disgust. "I know enough about you to know you have to die. I swear, the Unconquered Sun is turning me into his hatchet man, just like Kejak did. When this is all over, I want to have a few words with the light."

Shamblemerry whimpered once, and then Wren struck and she didn't whimper any more. Mechanically, he hewed her body again and again, severing limbs and cutting great gashes in her torso. With each blow he let out a scream of pure rage, the light around him flaring so bright that he could hardly be looked at.

Finally, when all that could be seen on the floor was a bloody, horrid wreck, Wren turned. "She's dead now," he said, unnecessarily. "I don't think she'll trouble you anymore, and the sword is safe. I'll find the boy. I'll take the sword to him. I'll tear out the Prince of Shadows' heart with my bare hands if I have to. But when this ends, no more. I want to be a monk again. Tell the Unconquered Sun that, will you? I think you're going to see him very soon."

But Mosom V'tayn heard only the first few words. The light had already reached out for him, and willingly, he'd gone into its embrace. It felt warm for an instant, and loving for an eternity, and then he felt nothing at all.

Wren found the stairs up to the temple some hours later. No ghosts showed him the way, but none hindered him, either, and eventually he stumbled upon the method of just following the breeze. It worked well enough.

The daiklave he strapped across the back of his now-tattered robes with strips torn from some of the more severely damaged garments. With luck, he thought, there'd be water in the temple above, and monks who would hopefully not see the mark on his brow before he could make good his escape.

He would, he suspected, be less gentle with those who stood in his way in the future. If the Father of Snakes had given him the knowledge of how to use his powers, who was he to refrain from doing so? He had a task now, or more accurately, several. The debt to Rhadanthos must be paid, and paid in full. The dagger must be retrieved, and the sword brought to the boy, whoever and wherever he might be.

And then, Wren decided, he was going to get some rest. He looked at the spiral staircase before him, and put his foot on the first step. It was time for him to see the sun again.

Chapter Thirty-Three

It had been three days since Dace had killed the Fair Folk prisoner, and there had been little conversation between Yushuv and his mentor in that time. They rode, camped, hunted and slept in near-total silence. Occasionally Dace would point out an interesting feature of the forest they were passing through and Yushuv would grunt in acknowledgement, or Yushuv would warn Dace of some loose footing and receive a terse "I know" in reply, but few other words passed between them. Nights, when they stopped to make camp and prepare their meals, were silent battles of wills, as Yushuv stared accusingly over the campfire at Dace, who didn't bother to meet the boy's eyes.

Now they stood at the banks of a broad, nameless stream, the horses munching contentedly on the grass and reeds that grew there in abundance. Dace's leg was still stiff, but the bandage he'd tied beneath his armor showed no blood, and he moved at a reasonable approximation of his normal speed. The smaller sword he'd tucked in among the packs on one of the horses they'd taken from the fey, and he wore his daiklave slung across his back, loose in its scabbard.

Yushuv, for his part, looked more ragged than ever. Sleep had been hard to come by since the battle at the lost city, and when he did manage to slumber, his dreams had been filled with visions of Bonecrack's toothy maw. *I'm coming, boy,* the spirit had said in his dreams. *Run while you can. It won't take me long.* More than once he'd woken up, screaming, to see Dace staring at him from across the fire with an inexplicable expression on his face.

The inevitable return of the wolf-spirit was Yushuv's primary concern. Every crack of a branch, every fall of an acorn into dead leaves made him sit bolt upright. He'd laboriously stitched up his quiver and filled it with arrows. The dead elf had been as good as his word, and there had been a bundle of barbed-headed shafts strapped to one of the mounts. Dace had examined them and declared them to be of passable quality, but Yushuv was a bit more impressed.

It was late afternoon, and the wind had turned cold. The sky was a deeper blue than it had any right to be, and Dace worriedly scanned the skyline for evidence that a storm was brewing. He found none, but that didn't reassure him. He knelt and pulled a blade of grass up between his fingers, hoping to find an oracle there. Instead, sap stained his fingers green, and he flung the stem to the ground.

"Why are we here?" Yushuv's voice was flat and clipped, the question as much an accusation as anything else.

"Because," Dace said wearily, "we need to get *there*." He pointed to the bank across the swollen stream, which housed a luxurious grove of willows.

Yushuv crossed his arms across his chest and peered out across the water. "Why? Why don't we just go downstream? There's nothing special over there."

Dace turned, the effort of reining in his temper showing on his face "We need to cross here, boy, because if I'm reading the stars right our rendezvous point is about a day's ride due west of here on the other side of this creek. This is supposed to be a ford, but either I've been told wrong or we're badly astray, and neither situation is designed to make me happy." He cocked his head and glared. "Do you have any other questions?"

"Yes." Yushuv sat, slipped off his sandals, and dangled his feet in the water. "You said we're going to a rendezvous. Who are we meeting?"

"Help. If you're being chased by a spirit as powerful as this thing you've talked about is supposed to be, we'll need all the help we can get, especially from someone who knows spirits. Her name is Lilith, she's visited the camp a few times while you were sleeping or off in the woods, and she should be able to help you." *Even*, Dace added to himself, *if she scares the hell out of the boy. Perhaps especially if she does.*

"Why didn't you tell me about this?"

"You didn't ask."

"What if I don't want to go?"

"Then you'll probably get eaten. Anything else?"

"Why did you kill the faerie?"

Dace exhaled explosively. That had been it all along, of course. The damned elf. He'd let the pointy-eared bastard goad him too far, and he'd lost his temper. In retrospect, it was probably what the Fair Folk had wanted in the first place, to drive a wedge between Yushuv and Dace. Now he was irritated with the boy, and the boy didn't trust him, and it was going to make them easier prey for whatever it was that hunted them through the woods.

Sighing, he squatted down by the water's edge and tossed a pebble in. It skipped once, twice, a third time before sinking beneath the surface. "If I told you that it was for your own good, you wouldn't believe me, would you?" Yushuv shook his head to indicate the negative, and Dace gave a grim little smile. "Of course not. I didn't think so.

"Look, Yushuv, I regret the way I did what I did, but not what I did. The thing I killed back there wasn't human, not even a little bit. It didn't like you except in the way you like trout roasted on a flat stone, and it didn't mean you well. Anything it told you was a lie, with just enough truth salted on top of it to make it seem like sense. The longer he stayed with us, the more poison he'd have poured in your ears. Another week and he'd have you thinking he was a wide-eyed innocent and I was a bloodthirsty kidnapper."

"And you're not?"

"No, I'm a dispassionate killer. There's a difference. Yushuv, I am a warrior. A general. I've led men on the field and in the arena, and I don't do well with word games and tricks. That's Fair Folk stuff—illusions and lies and half-truths and fantasies. I'm just good at two things: killing my enemy, and keeping my people alive."

He stared out at the water, ignoring the uncomfortable sense that something on the opposite bank might be staring back. "I'm a terrible teacher for you, Yushuv. I'm no good with children, never have been. I only know how to command grown men who'll take my orders like they came from Heaven itself and not ask why. I don't know why I was made to fetch you and teach you, except maybe Lilith knew something I didn't and wanted me there to protect you. I'm no good at answering questions and I'm no good at fighting duels with words. All I know is that I'm supposed to keep you safe, and every minute that thing was alive and with us I could feel him eating away at you. I don't know what fate's got in store for you, Yushuv. I assume it's great things. But I do know that elf," he practically spat the word, "was trying to make you doubt yourself. Make you unsure of everything you're going to do. You can't afford that. The things you're facing already are fast and deadly and cruel, and if you hesitate for one second you're going to be dead. So forget everything it said to you. Forget it all. Just follow your gut, Yushuv, and do what you think is right. All I'm here to do is train you so that when you do decide to act, you do it as fast and as well as possible."

Yushuv turned to look at him, his gaze an accusation. "That's not really an explanation, you know. Why did you kill him?"

Dace shrugged. "You're right. It's not. In the end, I killed him because he got me mad. Some of that was because he was threatening you, and the rest was because he'd told me that he was going to threaten you and dared me to do something about it. I suppose I shouldn't have killed him like that, though. It made him look better than he was."

"It still doesn't make sense, though. Why would he have let us capture him unless he really wanted to help? Why the supplies? Why put himself in a place where he might get killed?" Yushuv's questions were filled with terrified urgency, his expression pleading.

Dace chose his words carefully. "Why do you put honey out to catch flies? It costs you something; honey isn't cheap. It costs the flies more, though. Don't confuse what you want to be true for what is true. Smiles hide knives often enough to make a man nervous. Think. If he'd simply wanted to hurt you, he either would have shot you in the woods or charged, and then one of us would have killed him. This way he got close enough to you to do real damage."

Yushuv's frown showed he still wasn't satisfied. "If he wanted to hurt me, though, then he should have put an arrow in both of us. We didn't know he was there until he said something."

"I think, Yushuv, he wanted you hurt more than he wanted you dead." And with that, they both lapsed into silence for a while.

❖

It was Yushuv who stood first, shaking the water from his feet and slipping his sandals back on. "We should get moving," he said, and looked out across the water. "It will be dark soon, and we want to get across by then, I think."

Dace rumbled to his feet and looked up at the sky. "Well, we're not going to ford here, that's for certain. That water looks deep and fast, and I, for one, don't float. Downstream it's likely to get wider but slower; upstream might offer better luck. Tomorrow, though. We've got a good campsite here and forage for the horses, and we've been pushing hard for the last few days. We can take it easy for one night, I think. Why don't you see if you can catch something for dinner. I'll start the fire."

Yushuv nodded, more eagerly than he had in days. "All right." He walked over to the horses, who seemed completely oblivious to anything save the grass in front of them, and began rummaging through his pack for the excellent, thin line the Fair Folk had provided. "And Dace?"

The older man turned, a half-step away from the forest. "Yes?"

"I won't say I'm sorry. But I think I understand. "

Dace grunted something that might have been "You're welcome," and vanished into the wood. "Got to get firewood," he called back, much more clearly, and then was gone.

Alone for the first time in days and wishing he weren't, Yushuv turned his attention to the rushing waters and the possibility of fish therein.

✦

"We're being watched," Dace said as he poked their small fire with a stick. Overhead, the sky was dark, a thin sliver of moon doing little to banish the gloom.

"I know," Yushuv said, his bow in his lap. His quiver was nearby, and casually he shrugged himself into it. "I can see eyes shining in the woods behind you. Wolves, I think. Real ones."

Dace stretched exaggeratedly and yawned. "That's good. They'll probably be smart enough to stay away from the fire." Still yawning, he stood and walked over to Yushuv's side of the fire, closer to the water's edge. "You hear that? Shoo! We're ready for you!" He picked up a brand from the fire and waved it threateningly.

"The eyes aren't moving, Dace," Yushuv said quietly. "Should we be worried?"

Frowning, Dace looked at the semicircle of glowing green eyes. "There's eight or so pair, it looks like. A respectable pack. No threat to us unless we both fall asleep, though."

In response, Yushuv slipped an arrow onto his bowstring. It was of Fair Folk make, and bespoke a grace and craftsmanship that contrasted sharply with Yushuv's handcrafted and roughly used bow. The feathers of its fletching were black, and the arrowhead was hammered glass. "Think this will do for a wolf?" he asked, and looked up.

"Doubtless," Dace snorted, and waved the brand again. "I wonder what they're waiting for."

A howl rose, off in the dark. Another wolf took it up, closer, and then another closer still. More and more howls answered, and all the while, the number of glowing eyes grew.

"I think there's more than eight," Yushuv said mildly, and rose to his feet just as the wolves burst from the forest.

✦

Yushuv dropped three of the beasts before they were fully in the clearing, and Dace's flung brand caught another between the eyes. It crumpled, whimpering, but its packmates came on, and Dace reached for his sword.

The horses screamed in terror, and Yushuv spared them a look. Wolves were among them, nipping at their legs, and it was only a matter of seconds before they would be hamstrung and hauled down. They struck out with their hooves, but the wolves were persistent, and had numbers on their side.

"Back to the fire!" Dace ordered, his daiklave clearing him a wide path. Yushuv blinked, put another arrow into a wolf's throat and leapt over a second one to land before the fire. The wolves were coming out of the forest now like a gray river, and for every one he or Dace dropped, another emerged with a snarl to take its place. A huge, dark-furred one with a gray muzzle leapt for Yushuv's face and he caught it on the side of the head with his bow. It fell, whining, and Yushuv kicked it out of the way. Others were already circling at the edge of the firelight, uncanny intelligence in their shining eyes. Even as Yushuv watched, two smaller wolves took the downed one's hind legs in their jaws and dragged it out of the fray.

"Dace? These aren't ordinary wolves."

His response was a grunt and a warm, wet shower of blood on his arm as Dace cut another attacker down. "So I'd noticed. We could be here all night."

"We could be here longer than that," Yushuv retorted, and fired again. A yelp of pain rewarded his efforts, and he reached for another arrow. The horses' panicked whinnies were growing more insistent, though, and the cascade of howls had not let up. *Every wolf in the forest must be here,* Yushuv thought, *and we can't hold them off all night like this.*

Still aiming, he willed the power inside him to rise up, the dancing motes to flee their orbits and lend him their strength. The mark on his brow flared to life, and in that instant, the wolves cringed.

Can it be? he thought. *They're afraid of it!*

Silently, he willed more power into the corona of energy around him. The fire grew pale by comparison, and spokes of white light radiated out to pierce the night. Behind him, he could sense Dace was doing the same thing, the light emerging from him in serpentine coils even as the daiklave went up and down with brutal efficiency.

A wolf at the back of the pack turned and ran, whining. Others took a step back, or bowed their heads submissively. Several lay down, their tails thumping the earth frantically.

"Go," Yushuv commanded, and stepped forward. Much his surprise, three more wolves did. The howling was gone now, replaced by plaintive whimpers, and all around them the forest was alive with the sound of wolves fleeing. "Go!"

The last of the wolves wavered for a moment, then broke. Yapping defiance, they retreated, leaving their dead behind.

Yushuv watched them go, leaning on his bow. They ran swiftly, easily, and once they broke, they seemed utterly disinclined to resume their assault.

"Hunh." Dace moved next to Yushuv, daiklave still out. "I wonder what got into them."

"I don't know," Yushuv said truthfully. "Maybe we're trespassing."

"More likely that wolf-spirit chasing you put them up to it." Dace looked around warily, his eyes on the woods. "I would expect he's around here somewhere."

"A good assumption."

The voice that had haunted Yushuv's dreams came from the river, and he turned and fired in a heartbeat. The arrow skipped along the surface of the water and vanished into the dark, and Bonecrack rose up from the stream, laughing.

"Is that what you've been talking about, Yushuv?" Dace asked, holding his blade before him. "When you make enemies, you don't fool around, do you?" The wolf, he saw, was huge, as tall as a man at the shoulder, if he were judging the water's depth correctly. Its broad, shaggy muzzle was flat, and blood leaked from its mouth. Where the reddish drops struck the water, it boiled and steamed. One eye gleamed red, the other was marred by the broken shaft of a rough arrow. Its fur was straight and black, unbroken by any other color. It put one huge paw on the bank and then another, and grinned in most un-wolflike fashion.

"I have come for what's mine," it said. "Time to keep your end of the bargain, boy."

Dace stepped in front of Yushuv. "Nothing here is yours, spirit. The boy's mine to protect. You want him, you'll have to come through me."

"Unnecessary, but perhaps enjoyable." The spirit yawned, showing rows of sharp yellow teeth and a tongue marred by a bloody, festering wound. The wound, Dace noted, didn't seem to bother it much. "And don't think the trick that frightened off my children will scare me. I've eaten the hearts of your kind before, Exalt. Step aside, give me the boy, and you'll live to see dawn."

"Brave words from someone a child's already beaten," Dace retorted. "Think you can get past me to take him?"

Bonecrack's response was to hurl itself out of the water in a thunderous shower of spray, fangs snapping. Dace made a broad cut at the spirit's muzzle, but one huge paw slapped the sword aside. Even as Dace spun to recover, the wolf-spirit lowered its head and rammed his chest, knocking him backwards and to the ground. The daiklave went flying, and Bonecrack pounced, landing on Dace's chest and pinning his arms to the ground. It leaned its huge head close to his face and growled, low in its throat. Spittle and blood spilled from its muzzle and onto Dace's face, stinging his eyes and filling his mouth with a foul, bitter taste.

"So much for the mighty defender of the light. If I kill you, do you think anyone will notice? I've been offered great things for the boy. Your death might bring in an extra trinket."

"Step away from him." Both Bonecrack and Dace turned to see Yushuv standing, bowstring pulled and arrow pointed at the spirit's good eye. "It's me you want, not him. I swear, I'll blind you."

"And what if you do, boy? I have your scent, and I'll find you. Or let's say you kill me. Every spirit in Creation will know you broke a bargain, and there's a price to be paid for that sort of thing." Bonecrack gave a low, lupine chuckle. "And who knows? If you shoot me, I just might take it out on your poor friend here."

"I'm warning you, Bonecrack. I've learned things since we last met." The arrow and his voice were both steady.

"I'm sure you have." The spirit's tone was bored, unimpressed. "So have I. I've learned what it's like to have beetles trying to pluck my tongue out for carrion, and to endure a winter pinned to the cold earth. I don't think you've learned as much." Abruptly, it swatted the side of Dace's head with its paw, and Dace's head snapped back. "You're boring me, and your friend is worthless. Put down the bow and kneel, or I'll strip the flesh from your bones an hour before I kill you. It's your soul I want, anyway, and I can make taking that hurt a great deal more." He gave Dace's head another blow for good measure, then rose up and strode toward Yushuv.

The boy fired. Effortlessly, the spirit knocked the arrow out of the air. "You don't have the bond of a bargain on me this time, boy. Your arrows will do nothing."

Yushuv's power flared, and he drew again. The arrow flew straight and true, and again the spirit batted it aside. "You waste your energy. Save it, so that your soul will taste sweeter."

Sweating, Yushuv shot again. Arrow after arrow blazed out of his bow in rapid succession, a storm of glass points faster than the eye could see. The air was filled with them, blurring sight and drowning out the sound of the rushing stream.

Every single one ended up broken on the ground.

Stunned, Yushuv reached back into his quiver. It was empty. His fingers closed on air. He dropped the bow and reached for the dagger at his belt, but it seemed pitifully small and inadequate in his grip.

"You're owed to me, boy," the spirit growled. "You can't hurt me. You made the deal yourself, and running won't help either, not that there's far for you to run." It was close now, smelling of rot and wet fur and death. The stink of its breath made Yushuv want to gag, and the nearness of its fangs made him want to flee. He did neither.

"Whatever the Fair Folk are offering you for my soul, I'll match it," he said, staring into Bonecrack's eye. His hand itched with the irrational urge to pluck the broken arrow from the creature's other eye, but he resisted. Now was not the time....

"They're offering me things you can't imagine, boy. Raw chaos. Glamour to weave into dreams. Sweet, plump children. Nothing you can match, I assure you. A clever try, though. What did you think to offer?"

"I know where the tomb of a dead Exalt is," Yushuv said, gritting his teeth against the stench that wafted from the spirit's mouth. " Surely that's worth more than a few fat babies."

"Tempting, but not enough." The gigantic wolf's head pulled back a bit, though, and appeared to be considering. "Bargains can be renegotiated, after all, if both parties are willing. What else would you give me?"

Yushuv took a deep breath. "My service for a year and a day."

"Yushuv, no!" Dace had reached his knees and was crawling toward the daiklave. A disinterested kick from Bonecrack sent him sprawling again.

The spirit's face split in a most predatory grin. "Interesting. An Exalt as my slave for a year and a day. What would I do with you? And what terms would you place upon this service?"

"You'd send me to buy slaves to feed you, of course, and to take what you desired so that you would come to no more harm. You'd have me tend your eye and your paw and your tongue, and use what I've learned to heal you. And you'd have me lead you to treasures. In return, I'd simply ask that I never be asked to do anything that would shame a true servant of the Unconquered Sun, and that you help me take vengeance on the one who killed my father." He bowed and closed his eyes. "Is that satisfactory?"

Bonecrack cocked his huge head for a moment, as if considering the bargain, then yawned. "No. I don't think so. I know better than to bargain with you, boy. No doubt you'd say that service to a spirit was demeaning to a true servant of the Most Radiant Coward, and you'd try to shoot me all over again. No, better that I devour you now, I think, and explain to the Fair Folk that there was an unfortunate accident. It was a good attempt, though. A most excellent try."

Yushuv stabbed forward with the dagger, but Bonecrack was faster and took Yushuv's hand in its mouth up to the wrist.

it big down, hard, and Yushuv dropped the dagger in pain. The spirit let go then, and even as Yushuv pulled his savaged wrist free, Bonecrack spat the dagger onto the grass.

"Have any more toys?" it inquired. "If not, your time is over." It opened its mouth wide, Yushuv's blood and its own mixing to film over its teeth, and advanced. Yushuv looked behind him and saw nowhere to run. To the right were woods, to the left, the water.

If only Shooth were here, he thought, and threw himself into the stream.

Bonecrack gave a howl of fury and coiled itself to leap after him. "You won't escape that easily!" it roared, and sprang off the beach. Landing in the water with a titanic splash, it knifed after Yushuv, whose own efforts seemed feeble in comparison.

Looking over his shoulder, Yushuv saw Bonecrack surging through the water after him. The spirit's mouth was open, its fangs gleaming in the firelight, and spray rose up behind him. He could see Dace staggering to his feet on the riverbank, but Dace was too far away to help him now. Turning, he saw that the far side of the stream was too far away for him to reach before Bonecrack caught him. He heard the spirit's gurgling laugh rise up behind him, and knew that Bonecrack understood that as well. There was no escape for him.

Unless...

He filled his lungs with air and dove, trusting to luck that the water was deep here. It was. Smooth stones and mud lined the bottom, but it was deep enough. Faintly he could hear Bonecrack roaring defiance, but he ignored the sound and instead put one hand on the token that his father had been given, so long ago, by Raiton. Then, with a sudden burst of strength, he snapped the thong on which it hung, and called out as best he could.

"Shooth!" The rush of bubbled drowned his voice, but he hoped, somehow, the water spirit could hear him. "Do you remember me? I need you! I need your help!"

There was no answer, and a surge of water pressure told him that Bonecrack had submerged as well. His lungs began to ache, and a red haze rimmed his vision. He kicked forward, to put a little more distance between himself and Bonecrack, and tried again.

"Shooth! My father was a friend to spirits. Here's the proof! Teach me to be one as well. I'll learn, I swear. Just help me!"

And then Yushuv felt Bonecrack's teeth close on his ankle, and he knew he was lost. He closed his eyes and ceased struggling. The fire in his chest was all-consuming now, and he felt his grip on the fetish weakening. He let it drift from his fingers. *Perhaps someone would find it*, he thought hazily. *Perhaps it would bring someone else luck....*

Then the world exploded into a mix of spray and firelight, and he went tumbling into the darkness.

✦

"The sword. Where's the damn sword?" Dace looked around as frantically as his battered head would permit for his daiklave. He found it resting halfway in the fire, and his first attempt to retrieve it had ended when he'd scorched his hand. He could hear splashing out in the water, but by the time he'd turned to face it, both Yushuv and his pursuer had vanished. The water's surface was deceptively calm, marred only by a few bubbles.

"No." Dace threw himself into the water, holding the daiklave high above his head. "Damnit, no!" Angered beyond further words, he raised the sword and brought it down, hewing the waters as if they were his enemy.

And the waters responded. A column of dark water burst from the stream, flinging Dace back into the shallows. Wrapped in its embrace was Bonecrack, snarling and snapping furiously, his claws tearing at his formless foe.

"You will go," the amorphous shape demanded, and Dace realized with a shock that it was Shooth. "You will leave Shooth's friend be!"

Bonecrack's answer was a hate-filled howl. He tore himself out of Shooth's grasp and leapt for shore, but the water spirit rose up before him and wrapped him in a hundred shining arms. Spray flew like blood, and for every limb of Shooth's that Bonecrack snapped at, another rose from the stream's surface.

"Mine!" the wolf-spirit bellowed. "The boy is mine!" With shock, Dace saw that Shooth was actually weakening; Bonecrack's spittle ate away at his enemy like acid, and steam boiled off from his surface as he suffered.

"You thought you'd keep me from my prey? Fool! I've pissed in your father's headwaters." Bonecrack was on the offensive now, and all of Shooth's energies were devoted to defending itself. No longer did it seek to crush Bonecrack. Rather, it stumbled back, and Bonecrack pursued.

"The boy's bound to me. By acting for him, you're bound to me, too." He snapped his jaws, and Shooth reeled in pain, retreating into the shallows. "I think I'll take your soul, then the boy's, and I'll let him watch you die so he knows that he's damned you, as well. Then I'll have you both.

"You won't have either," Dace said, forcing every drop of Essence he had into his daiklave and sliding it through the back of Bonecrack's neck. "I don't know what you're made of, but this should hurt you plenty."

The wolf-spirit gurgled horribly and tried to turn its head, but this only tore open the wounds the sword had made wider. In pain it thrashed about, impaled, while Dace struggled to cling to the sword. It rolled, seeking to dislodge him against the streambed, but Dace held fast, the image of Shooth's pain burned into his mind.

Finally, with a superhuman effort, the spirit tore free, its half-severed head hanging at an odd angle and its blood pouring down. Dace's daiklave tumbled into the water at its side and vanished. "Find yourself a better sword," Bonecrack said, in a voice thick with blood and contempt. "Be ready to use it. You'll see me again." And with that it threw back its head and howled, a thick, wet sound that shook leaves from the trees and stirred the stream to white froth.

"You talk too much," Dace said, and stepped forward.

"So do you." Smiling horribly, Bonecrack slid into the river and vanished under the water. A trail of steam, quickly fading, on the surface was the only proof it had ever been there.

With Shooth's help, he found Yushuv on the bank, perhaps two hundred yards downstream. The boy was fine, though his quiver had gone missing. Instead, he was clutching at a charm on a doubly knotted leather thong around his neck, and after a moment Dace decided not to ask about. There would be plenty of time for that later, he hoped.

The water spirit, for its part, was weakened, and would not talk of why it had appeared. "Good-bye, Dace," it had said. "Good-bye for a hundred years," and then vanished into the stream. Dace had followed it out into the water and nearly stumbled across the daiklave. He fished it from its resting place, and saw to his disgust that Bonecrack's blood had seared the blade. *Perhaps I can find a smith to repair it*, he thought. *Or perhaps I'll just keep it this way as a reminder.*

In the morning, he decided, they'd head upstream and look for a ford, moving as fast as they could. Lilith would be waiting somewhere up ahead, and perhaps she could make better sense of this than he could. But that would be in the morning. Tonight, he had a boy, who for once seemed very small and very young, to tend to, and Dace, one-time scourge of the Threshold, took that responsibility very seriously indeed.

The epic concludes in book three.

About the Author

Richard Dansky is a twenty-plus-year veteran of the video game industry. He has written for games including The Division, Splinter Cell: Blacklist, Outland, and many more. GHOST OF A MARRIAGE is Richard's eighth novel. He has also published a short-fiction collection titled SNOWBIRD GOTHIC. Richard has numerous tabletop roleplaying game credits, and was the developer on the critically acclaimed WRAITH: THE OBLIVION 20th Anniversary Edition. He lives in North Carolina with his cat and an ever-changing roster of books and single malt scotches.

Curious about other Crossroad Press books?
Stop by our site:
http://www.crossroadpress.com
We offer quality writing
in digital, audio, and print formats.